PACIFIC PREP BOOK THREE
R.A. SMYTH

Beyond Vengeance
Brutal Lies Copyright © 2021 R.A. Smyth

All rights reserved. No part of this book may be reproduced, or stored in a retrieval system, or transmitted in any form or by any means, electronic, mechanical, photocopying, recording, or otherwise, without express written permission of the publisher.
The characters and events portrayed in this book are fictitious. Any similarity to real persons, living or dead, is coincidental and not intended by the author.
ISBN: 9798486675713

Cover & Interior Design by Nikki Epperson. All Rights Reserved.
Editing by Lunar Rose Editing Services.
Formatting by Rachel Smyth.

I know better. I know better than to be complacent.
Finding my family was supposed to be a dream come true, but it's only brought more questions, more secrets and forced family responsibilities. Surprisingly, Hawk is by my side while dealing with the utter ridiculousness our parents keep pushing on me. I'm learning how to have a brother and I think we might actually like each other?
Mason, West, and Beck have been my saving grace, patient and kind. Still distant, Cam and I are trying to navigate a way to be around each other.
But just when I start to feel like I have a life worth living with my guys and my new friends, my deepest fear comes back to haunt me.
He knows. He knows the truth and where to find me.

My walls are coming down and I'm learning to love, but my past may ruin it all.

PACIFIC PREP PLAYLIST

Sober – Letdown
Astronaut in the Ocean – Our Last Night
Nightmare – Set it Off
I am Here – P!NK
Legends are Made – Sam Tinnesz
My Name Is... – Once Monsters
I Miss the Misery – Halestorm
The Rain Just Follows Me – Hawthorne Heights
Better Days – Dermot Kennedy
Karma – Letdown
Are You Listening – Wake Me
The Verdict – Dear Agony
Open Road – North of Nine
...And many more

Play Now

TRIGGER WARNINGS

This book is a dark, contemporary, new adult reverse harem romance, meaning the FMC will end up with 3+ males.

Before you go any further, I must state, this is the darkest book in the series so far, so *please* take head of the following trigger warnings—sexual assault, graphic physical and psychological abuse, reference to STDs in the form of jokes.

The book also ends on a killer cliffhanger. I am not responsible for any broken phones or kindles, however I do offer a support thread in my facebook readers group—Rachel's Rebel Rehab—if you need somewhere to rant or yell. You will also be able to find some amazing bonus scenes under the files section, to help tie you over until book 4 releases in December.

The series consists of 4 books and will ultimately have an HEA.

PROLOGUE

Lawrence

Very sneaky, Dove. Very sneaky, indeed.

You've proven to be much more of a challenge than I expected. I wouldn't say I like having to chase after you, but I've worked too hard to let you slip through my fingers now. It was fate, the way things worked out. I was only keeping you nearby for insurance; instead, I became infatuated with you. Watching you grow older, with your blonde hair and petite features so strikingly similar to your mother's, I knew I had to have you. With you, I could finally have everything I always coveted, and this time no one would take you away from me.

The compound was the perfect place to hide you. *I'm* the one who runs all the day-to-day operations. None of them spend any time there. They prefer to hide in their offices and fancy houses—pretending the torture and pain required to make cold, unquestioning soldiers isn't happening—but I live off watching those children become what I want them to be.

WHEN YOU WERE YOUNGER, YOUR EYES USED TO SHINE WITH SUCH fierceness. You took every punishment I inflicted on you like a champ, and it only seemed to make you stronger, more defiant.

Well, I couldn't have that. I needed you broken and pliable, so I could build you into who you were always supposed to be. I gave your mother too much freedom, and she left me. For *him*. I wasn't about to let that happen again. I had everything planned. I was going to do things right with you. Make sure you could never leave me.

Having your little friend killed was your breaking point. I should have had it done years ago, but better late than never. Watching the light go out in your eyes was the greatest thing I have ever witnessed. You have no idea how fucking hard I was when I showed up for my monthly visit, and you were barely a shell of your former self. I'd have fucked you then and there, but it wasn't the right time. You needed more training, and I could wait.

I was patient. I was *nice*. I brought you gifts and complimented you. I was willing to wait until you were old enough to ultimately mine. While I waited, I dedicated years to training you, to mold you into my perfect wife.

And you thank me by running away mere months before all of my plans were due to come to fruition.

I thought I had you all worked out. That I'd broken you down, but you've been deceiving me all this time. Pretending to be what I wanted you to be, all the while planning your escape. What you don't realize, however, is that I'm not letting you go.

You might have done an excellent job of masking the defiance in your eyes, but I now know you've been planning too. I wonder what kind of friends you've made at that school, how they've been able to protect you against not one but two of my men. Whoever they are, they won't be enough to save you from me. They'll pay for their transgressions…and you'll pay for yours.

CHAPTER 1

Hadley

"Hawk, dear, is that you?" a female voice calls out from deeper in the house as I follow Hawk into the mansion and close the door behind me, ignoring my racing heart and sweaty palms.

Hawk's already walking into the posh-looking seating area, not bothering to check if I'm behind him.

"What is this all about? You know we're b—"

Hawk's mother—*my* mother—stops when she sees me loitering awkwardly in the foyer. She's dressed in a black flared pantsuit, dolled up to the nines as her high heels echo on the tiled floor.

"Oh. You brought a...girl home," she states blandly, her face pinched which tells me exactly what she thinks of me. There's no recognition in her eyes, and I'm not sure if she remembers me from the party last month.

Her gaze drops to take in my thrift store jeans and worn top, her face scrunching up in disgust. She doesn't even have the common decency to hide her dislike of me.

"Yeah, Mom, this is Hadley. Is Dad around? We need to talk," Hawk says, diverting his mom's attention.

"Yes, yes, you said as much on the phone." His mother waves her hand, dismissing his words. "I don't understand what this is all about."

"Well, when Dad gets here, I'll tell you," Hawk responds, getting irritated.

"I'm here, I'm here," an older gentleman calls out as he comes down the stairs, buttoning a suit jacket, seeming like he's about to head out for the evening.

Reaching the foyer, he all but ignores me as he strides over to his wife, kissing her on the cheek. Seeing them standing side by side, I realize they *are* on their way out for the evening. There's no way they would be so dressed up for their son's visit.

Staring at them standing together, I recall the few details I know about them that I have written in my notebook—*the* notebook. Maria and Barton Davenport. Married for thirty-one years. The two of them, along with Wilbert Warren, Lawrence Rutherford, and Frank Hayes, attended Pacific Prep together. However, I couldn't find any information on whether or not she was one of his girls of the month, or whatever they called it back then. The first mention of them being a couple that I could find was whenever they were at college together.

"What's this all about?" Hawk's father asks him.

Noticing me *still* standing awkwardly by the door, his father gives me a once-over, his blank expression giving no indication of his initial thoughts about me.

"Who's this?" he asks, turning to look at his son.

"This is Hadley," Hawk repeats. "Let's just sit down, and I'll explain everything."

With his lips pinched in displeasure, Barton escorts his wife to a couch. When I hesitate to follow, Hawk pins me with a stare, jerking his head for me to move. Reluctantly ungluing my feet from the floor, I follow Hawk, and the two of us sit opposite...our parents? *God, that sounds weird.*

Hawk sits back on the uncomfortable couch, his legs spread wide, looking far too at ease considering the awkward as fuck conversation we're about to have. Meanwhile, my back is as straight as an arrow while I perch on the edge of the seat, ready to flee at any moment.

His father's eyes dart between us, lines marring his forehead as he frowns at us. "I think I know what this is about." There's a serious ring to his voice, and he shakes his head, frowning at Hawk in disappointment.

My eyebrows climb up my forehead as my gaze jumps from him to Hawk, confused. *How can he possibly know what's going on?*

Barton sighs disappointedly. "I thought I taught you better, son. We want to *avoid* scandals like this." With pursed lips, he side-eyes his wife. "Maria, you have Dr. Mitchell's number, don't you?"

His mother gasps, her hand coming up to cover her lips. I am beyond confused at this point. I honestly have no idea what they're talking about.

"Oh my." She stares pointedly at my stomach before answering her husband, "Yes. Yes, I do. I'll phone him right away. He can take care of the, eh, problem."

What the fuck is going on right now? What has a doctor got to do with any of this?

"How far along are you?" Her tone has a sharp edge as she sears me with an unimpressed look.

"I don't—"

"Jesus, Mom," Hawk exclaims, outraged, having caught on to what his parents are talking about. "She's not fucking pregnant."

My eyes must be the size of saucers as I gape at the three of them, unable to string a sentence together. Hawk's face is scrunched up, and he looks like the idea makes him physically ill.

That makes two of us.

"Well, if you haven't knocked her up, what is this all about?" his father demands.

"Fucking hell," Hawk growls, leaning forward in his seat as he runs his hand through his short blond hair. "She's my fucking sister."

Well, that's not exactly how I saw them finding out about their long-lost daughter.

Silence reigns supreme as his parents first gape at Hawk before their attentions focus on me, making my skin itch as I tug on the hem of my shirt, looking everywhere but at them.

"What are you talking about?" his mother snaps, eyeing me critically.

Hawk rubs at his eyes before he answers her. "Hadley enrolled at Pac this year. Since the first day, there was something about her I couldn't put my finger on. With her blonde hair and eyes the same unusual color as mine, I felt like I knew her."

I guess we're skipping over the whole part where we hated each other.

"I couldn't put my finger on it," Hawk continues, "so I did a DNA test."

He pulls pages out of the back pocket of his jeans—the same reports West received from the DNA labs. I hadn't even realized he'd brought them with him tonight. "They came back positive."

His parents stare dumbfounded at the pages when Hawk sets them on the coffee table, neither reaching out to lift them. Instead, they glance at the reports from a safe distance as though they are a bomb about to go off. *I guess that's not far from the truth.*

"What...I don't—" His mother's voice trails off as she continues to gape at the ominous pieces of paper. "There must be some sort of mistake."

Ouch.

Hawk sighs, pinning his parents with a 'cut the crap' look.

"I found the stuff in the safe in your bedroom," he states bluntly, letting them know he's not buying their splutters of denial. I can only assume he's talking about the birth certificate and photos he showed me.

His father's gaze turns to steel as he scowls at Hawk. "You know you're not supposed to be in our room," he barks out.

Seriously? That's the main concern right now? Talk about fucking priorities.

Hawk silently meets his father's gaze, although I'm too focused on Maria, who hasn't stopped staring at me. I can't decipher the look on her face. A mixture of confusion and doubt, possibly.

She casts her eyes over me with a critical look. I look exactly the same as when I walked through the door, and I didn't meet her high standards then, so I doubt she will find anything about me that she likes now.

"I really don't think that's the issue," Hawk grinds out between gritted teeth, his thoughts on a similar wavelength to my own. "How come you never told me I had a sister, let alone a twin?"

His father—fuck, *our* father—hasn't looked at me once since Hawk spilled the beans. It's as though he's concentrating on pretending I'm not there.

"What's to tell?" Maria shrugs, sounding a tad defensive. "One day, she was here and the next, she was gone. We looked for her everywhere, but when no one could find her, we had to accept that she was gone for good. After all these years, we assumed she was dead."

She says it with such indifference. If I were more emotional, her detachment would have left me feeling like she had just ripped my heart out and stomped all over it. The child who used to cry for her long-lost family would have been sobbing on the floor by now, but thankfully, I learned to harden my heart. I've carefully wrapped it in barbed wire, placing it behind a sharp fence where no one can get to it.

Hawk's thigh presses against mine in a silent act of comfort, yet he needn't bother. Other than a twinge of tightness in my chest at her cruel, heartless words, I feel nothing. The white-picket-fence childhood, with smiling parents who hugged and adored me, was only a fantasy. Something I dreamt about in the dark of night to keep the demons away. I've known for a long time that it would never be my reality.

I haven't sussed out my father yet, but my mother is clearly a conniving bitch, only giving a damn about her own self-preservation. I call fucking bullshit at her words, though. The child of a wealthy family just disappears, and no one asks any questions? There's no investigation? I've already done my research. I *know* the police were never contacted. No report was ever filed, and no official search was ever conducted.

Whatever is going on here—and there sure as fuck is something strange going on—she and her husband are up to their necks in it. They fucking know a lot more about what happened to me than they are willing to share.

Barton looks at his watch, the lines around his eyes and mouth tightening. "Look, we have to go," he says, glancing up at Hawk. "I'll make an appointment for the, uh, girl"—he can't even say my name—"to meet with our doctor this week. I want him to do another DNA test. We can talk again when we get the results back."

Without waiting for a response, he stands, holding a hand out to help his wife get to her feet. With a final nod at Hawk—still fucking ignoring me—he escorts his wife from the room.

"Come on," Hawk practically growls once we're alone. Not waiting for a response from me, he gets to his feet and strides toward the door. I scurry after him, because I sure as fuck don't want to be left alone in this house with either of them.

"Well, I'm so glad you talked me into doing that," I gripe once I've closed the front door behind me, earning an unimpressed glare from Hawk as he strides over to the car. Following him, I climb into the passenger seat. We sit silently, staring out the front windshield at the extravagant house. Lights shine out from the foyer and front room, lighting up the circular gravel drive and manicured shrubs lining the garden.

"They know more than they're letting on," Hawk grits out.

Starting the ignition, he puts the car in drive and we head away from the house.

Hawk's hands repeatedly flex around the steering wheel, and I can feel the tension radiating off him on my side of the car as the gates out of the private residence slide open. He guns the car down the dark lane that winds its way along the cliff toward the school.

I wait him out, staring unseeingly at the night sky out the passenger side window as he stews for a long while.

"I can't fucking believe them," he eventually spits out, jolting me out of my inner thoughts as I turn to look at him. "He couldn't even look at you, and my mom was a complete bitch." He shakes his head, scowling out the front windscreen at the dark road ahead. "I don't even recognize them anymore. I can't work out if they've always been this cold and selfish and I just never saw it, or if I've been deluding myself this whole time."

"I'm sorry."

Hawk whips his head around to look at me, his brows furrowed.

"What are *you* apologizing for?"

I shrug. "It must suck realizing your parents aren't who you thought they were." I mean, they're supposed to be your role models, right? The people you turn to for help and advice. I can't imagine asking either of the people I met tonight for anything.

"Well, yeah, but you're the one who had to grow up without parents." He doesn't say it in a nasty way, more like he can't understand why I would feel sorry for him when, in his opinion, I got dealt a worse hand.

"Maybe so, but you can't miss what you never had," I tell him easily, being honest. Sure, I've always wondered who they were and what happened. Except after having met them tonight, I'm honestly glad they weren't in my life. They can't disappoint me or let me down, because they've never been there or shown me a different side of themselves.

I message Beck on our way back to campus, telling him to meet us at the guys' apartment. Once we are all together, Hawk relays the whole—relatively uneventful—evening. All of them are angry at our parents' blasé attitude, but none seem surprised. The one thing we're all in agreement on is that they know more than they're letting on.

On Tuesday, Hawk drives me to some fancy private clinic where a doctor swabs the inside of my cheek and takes some blood. We're in and out in less than half an hour, and it all feels so anticlimactic, considering the outcome will change everything.

I still have so many reservations, and having now met my parents, I'm even more hesitant to dive further into this world. Do the answers to my questions about my past truly matter this much? What will it change? Nothing. Ultimately, it doesn't matter how I ended up in the life I have. I'm here, surviving and doing the best I can.

Nevertheless, the second Hawk told them the truth about it, the choice to back out of this hair-brained plan was eradicated. Sure, I could still run. There's no denying the thought crosses my mind several times a day. However, every time I picture myself somewhere else, living a life without Emilia or the guys, or even Hawk—*I know, I can't believe I'm even thinking it*—I get this strange tightness in my chest, and I realize it's not as simple as running away. There's some sort of connection between the guys and me. I don't know how to explain it, but it's pulling us all together. It's a force that would be impossible to fight, and frankly, I don't want to. I'm sick of fighting. Fighting for my life, fighting for freedom, fighting to be happy. I just want to live. To enjoy the easy moments with Beck, soak up the strength I get from Mason, and bathe in West's calmness. I don't know what will happen with Cam, but I need to help him find his light again. I need to see his easy, carefree smile and assure myself I haven't completely broken him.

So no, while running might seem like the easy solution, it's not the answer.

After we leave the clinic, I spend the next few days on tenterhooks, waiting for the phone call that will upend my life. I already know what the test results are going to be. Even so, it's the final confirmation the Davenports need before anything more happens—although I have no idea what comes next. Somehow, I doubt we will dive straight into family dinners and vacationing together on the holidays.

"Do you want to talk about what happened with your parents?" Beck asks during our Thursday session. We're lying on the sofa, which has become our usual position during this hour every week.

"Not particularly," I grumble.

He wraps his tattooed arm around me and I lean against his chest.

"What was it like when you met your dad for the first time?" I ask.

"Well, I was just a kid when I first met him—after my mom and I moved out of Black Creek—but I knew as soon as I laid eyes on him that he would never be any sort of father figure. Not that he hung around long enough to even try and get to know me.

"Most of the kids I grew up with didn't have fathers. If they weren't in prison or dead, they were neck-deep in gang life. That was always their priority over their own kids, so I never felt like I was missing out on much.

"When he showed up last year, it became painfully obvious he saw me as a pawn. Someone he could manipulate into doing his bidding. Which is precisely what happened. After growing up in Black Creek and all the lowlifes I met there, I thought I'd be able to handle whatever he wanted in return. I stupidly figured whatever he would ask of me would be worth it." He sighs dejectedly. "But things have gotten so fucked up."

Yeah, he can say that again.

"What does he want from you?"

There's a moment of heavy silence.

"I'm not sure yet." His voice sounds tense, tighter than it did a moment ago.

I glance up at him through my eyelashes, noticing the deep frown on his face, and the moss-green of his eyes seems duller than they did when I first walked in. It's possible that not knowing what's going to be asked of him has him on edge. Why wouldn't it when he knows what he does—but if that's the case, why do I feel like he's lying?

"Maybe he's just using you so he can threaten West's life," I suggest. I've been trying to think about it, to determine what use Beck could be to the company. Honestly, being used as a tool to threaten the rest of them is the best-case scenario, but I'm concerned they will want to use the skills he's learned through his degree, analyzing people and figuring out what makes them tick. If that's the case, our parents might want to involve him with the new recruits, somehow. I know Beck is tough, and he's seen and done some fucked-up things in his youth, but I don't know how well he—or the others—would handle knowing their parents don't just offer mercenaries for hire. In actuality, they train them, more or less from birth, ensuring that each child grows into a formidable machine. Some of these kids become so removed from their humanity that they barely even see their targets as human beings.

"Yeah, maybe." The hopeless tone of his voice has unease churning in my stomach, only intensifying the feeling that there's something he's not telling me. Worry for him courses through me. If Beck was forced to devise new and creative ways to dehumanize those kids, or differentiate the weak from the strong, I don't think he could live with himself.

He coughs, clearing his throat before changing the topic. "How have things been going with you and Hawk?"

As much as I want to know what he's hiding, I welcome the change in conversation. I trust Beck enough to know he'll tell me when he's ready.

"Okay, I think." I shrug. "He doesn't seem to hate me, which I guess is a win. Things are still awkward, though. Neither of us knows how to be around one another without biting each other's heads off."

He chuckles softly. "It'll get easier with time. At least he seems to be trying."

"Yeah, he's still a dick most of the time, in any case. Especially when he doesn't get his way. I really don't understand how West put together that we were related. I'm nowhere near as infuriating as him."

Another rumble of laughter vibrates through his chest.

"Did you get things sorted with all of them after Valentine's Day?"

"Yeah, I think so. Well, West and Mason explained that none of them had anything to do with Bianca's stunt. And now that I've had time to think about it, Cam has been so busy beating himself up, I don't see that he would do something to hurt or upset me. It was stupid of me to believe Bianca at all. I was just…"

"After everything you've been through with them, it's understandable that you weren't sure what to believe. The main thing is that you worked everything out."

"We did, yet I still don't like how much trust to put in them. We're blindly going along with this plan of theirs. What if it blows up in our faces, or they turn on me?"

"Unfortunately, they know more about their parents than we do, so I don't see that we have any other choice but to listen to their advice for now," Beck says, voicing my own thoughts. "I don't believe you have anything to worry about, anyway. Hawk's been different with you recently. As for the other guys, well, the way they look at you…I don't know how the whole school hasn't caught on to it."

"On to what?" I question, confused. All four Princes have always watched me closely, but they're perpetually attuned to their surroundings, constantly observing everything happening around them.

"Their feelings for you."

He says it like it's obvious. Something I should already know. I mean, I know Mason and West like me, but I wouldn't say there is anything obvious about the way they look at me. As for Cam… well, I can't deny the way my body flushes when I feel his eyes on me or how my heart rate picks up when he's nearby. Regardless of my body's physical reaction, we're just friends. After everything the two of us have been through, I don't see how we could ever be anything more.

"Don't talk crap," I grumble, pushing up onto my elbow so I can scowl down at him.

"I'm not," he insists with a small laugh, as though he can't understand how I don't see what he sees. "I realized it the first day I saw them with you, when you had your panic attack. Sure, they were freaking out, but they were genuinely concerned for you. Mason wouldn't even leave until I reassured him you'd be okay."

Well, if my sappy little heart doesn't go all gooey at hearing that.

"And Cam is determined to do whatever it takes to make it up to you. The steadfastness in his eyes that night they found us in the clearing was more than obvious."

"That doesn't mean he has feelings for me," I argue.

"Maybe not," he reasons. "Although the fact he said he was done with the tradition and was using Bianca to taunt you is."

I'm not sure what to make of his words as I mull them over. "None of that means they're trustworthy, however."

"It doesn't," he agrees readily. "But they did help us get rid of a dead body, so maybe they deserve the benefit of the doubt."

Hmmm, maybe.

CHAPTER 2

Cam

"YOU NEED TO STAY HERE WHILE WE'RE GONE," HAWK orders in his usual no-nonsense tone. You'd think he would have worked out by now that that's not the way to handle Hadley. The second the words are out of his mouth, her back straightens and she frowns at him.

"Now I know you didn't just *order* me to do something," she snaps, defiance glowing in her eyes.

She's so fucking sexy when she's spitting fire and ready for a fight. I'm used to people cowering and bending to our every whim, but Hadley doesn't take any of our shit. She's never given a damn about our power or influence.

I agreed to be friends with her—so my dick definitely shouldn't be getting hard as I watch her stand up to Hawk—but *fuck me.* Friends? I haven't got the first fucking clue how to be friends with a girl, and there's no way Hadley and I can just be friends. Not with how my dick strains to get to her every time we're in the same room.

I'VE NEVER BEEN SO ATTUNED TO SOMEONE'S PRESENCE BEFORE. MY whole body comes alive when she's nearby. My skin heats and my cock swells, not understanding that this girl is off-limits. Despite my body's reaction to her, my brain isn't on the same page. I don't know how to behave around her. The easy banter we used to have is no longer there; instead, we're left making awkward conversation, neither of us sure how to respond. It's fucking exhausting.

"I'm not a fucking idiot," Hadley seethes, drawing me back to her argument with Hawk. "I'm not about to go wandering around in the forest after what happened, but I'm perfectly safe in *my* room."

Hawk got a phone call earlier today from his dad. Apparently, all of our parents are demanding a meeting with us. Our guess is Hadley's DNA results are in, and they want to discuss what that means for them and our ruling over the school.

The five of us were chilling in the apartment; Hadley was playing a video game with Mason while I watched them—well, *her*—and West was fiddling around on his laptop, before Hawk had to open his big mouth and start this argument. He looks ready to strangle her as he gives her a look that has most other students pissing themselves, ready to do just about anything to get him to stop staring at them like that.

Jesus, are siblings supposed to be so aggressive toward one another? The only difference between them since finding out they're twins is that Hawk's dickishness no longer comes from a place of hate, yet they still snipe at one another like they want to tear each other's heads off.

"Your room is on the ground floor," Hawk argues. "Anyone could break in."

Hadley throws her hands up in exasperation. "I'm pretty sure killers can climb stairs," she snarks. Her comeback has Mason not-so-subtly swiping his hand over his mouth, hiding his chuckle behind his large palm. The girl has an answer for everything.

"You could invite Beck over. Then you'll both be here for when we get back," I suggest, earning a glare from West.

Both siblings turn to look at me. Hadley has a thoughtful look on her face before a cunning smile graces it.

"That works," she agrees far too easily, and Hawk gives her a suspicious look, most likely trying to work out her angle.

She's probably thinking about fucking Beck on Hawk's bed just to piss him off. *Damn, why does that thought have my dick twitching?*

***

THAT EVENING, WE ARE PICKED UP IN A CHAUFFEUR-DRIVEN CAR AND taken into the city to the modern office building which houses our parents' company. Our families own various properties throughout California, but the base of their operation is here. This building is the powerhouse of Nocturnal Enterprises.

An hour later, we exit the vehicle and make our way into the building, pushing open the glass door into the vast, mostly empty foyer. At forty stories, the high-rise is tall and sleek, comprised entirely of glass that reflects the setting sun, causing a glare that burns my eyes.

Besides the security guard manning the door—who doesn't even bat an eyelash as we walk past him—and a couple of women seated at a reception desk, the ground floor is otherwise empty as we stride toward the bank of elevators. No one stops us or says anything. Everyone here knows who we are, even though we rarely visit.

None of us say anything—you never know who could be listening—and all too soon, the doors are opening onto the thirty-seventh floor. Our parents own the entire building, renting out all but the top three floors. Everything from the thirty-seventh floor up is all Nocturnal Enterprises. How much of that is actually Nocturnal Mercenaries? I'm not sure.

"Welcome, boys," the receptionist greets, a seductive purr to her words. She's got curvy hips and is lasciviously licking her lips as her eyes bounce between the four of us, her pupils dilated with desire. Any other visit and I'd be all over that, but my dick doesn't even stir. Frustratingly, only one fiery blonde gets any sort of response out of me anymore, even though I'm not supposed to think about her like that.

It's not for lack of trying. No matter how many times I tell myself I can't go near Hadley and that I've fucked things up so badly I should be grateful she's even talking to me, my dick still doesn't get the message. Neither does my heart, based on the way it picks up speed whenever she's around. It's making it impossible to be near her, yet, I can't stop gravitating her way. I guess I'm a glutton for punishment.

The receptionist escorts us toward a large boardroom. "Can I get any of you a drink? Your parents should be here momentarily."

"No, we're fine," Hawk responds succinctly, barely sparing her a glance as we filter into the room.

Nodding, she turns to leave, but not before casting one last longing look over each of us.

"Well, let me know if you need anything." Her voice drops to a husk as she says 'anything,' and she trails her finger down my arm before she steps out of the room, leaving us alone.

Scowling, I uselessly wipe down my arm as though her touch might have left cooties or some shit. Mason snorts, shaking his head at my antics as he follows Hawk toward the table.

The four of us take our seats along one side of the long glass table, looking out the floor-to-ceiling windows that offer a spectacular view of the city skyline. We're only left waiting a minute before our parents filter in—Maria and Barton Davenport, Theresa and Frank Hayes, Wilbert Warren, and last but not least, Daddy Dearest. West's mom is off god only knows where, pretending she doesn't have a son or a cheating sleazeball of a husband, and, well, I never really knew my mom. She was nothing more than an egg donor.

I can barely look my dad in the eye as he struts into the room, not a care in the fucking world, and it takes everything in me not to throw myself across the table and murder the fucker right here. I've already been given a stern warning by Hawk not to do something stupid. We need the element of surprise if we stand any chance of taking him down. He doesn't know it, but he's a dead man walking, even if I have to kill him myself. He's never been a father to me. There's no love lost between us, and even if there was, nothing could negate his actions. What he's done to Hadley is beyond fucked up, and he clearly knows where she's been all these years.

From what Hawk said, their parents know something too, but we can't be sure if they were in on whatever the hell went down, or if they're just covering up the reason for her disappearance. Regardless, all six of our parents are suspicious as fuck.

I can't tear my eyes away from my father as all of them sit down on the opposite side of the large boardroom table. He looks so normal. Yeah, he's got a suffocating air of arrogance around him, but he doesn't look like someone who would be involved in the kidnapping and grooming of a little girl. Shouldn't he give off some sort of sicko signal?

"We need to discuss this new development with Elizabeth," Hawk's dad states, his words slicing through my thoughts. It sounds so weird to hear her being called Elizabeth, and I turn the name over in my head. *Yeah, I can't imagine calling her that.* It was Hadley I called out when I was dick-deep inside of her. Hadley is what she will always be to me.

"I take it you got the DNA results back?" Hawk asks.

"We did. She is who you thought she was."

Obviously. Who the fuck else was she going to be? We had our own DNA results, but of course, that wasn't good enough for any of them.

"What happened to her? Where has she been all this time?" Hawk demands, staring pointedly at his father.

"We're looking into that."

That doesn't help in bringing me any sort of comfort.

"What does that mean? How did she even go missing in the

first place?" Anger, as per usual, gets the better of Hawk as he practically snarls out the words, and his father's eyes narrow, not appreciating his son's tone.

"Watch it," Barton growls in a warning.

Everyone else is observing us closely, their faces void of any emotion. I can't keep myself from repeatedly glancing toward my father, trying to pick up on any little tell that he was involved in any of this. I mean, he *has* to be, right?

"As your mother told you the other day, she just disappeared."

"How?" Hawk is walking a dangerous line with his tone, not that I can blame him. We're all anxious for answers, him and Hadley most of all.

"We were having a party, and the two of you were up in your room. The nanny had put you to bed and claimed she didn't hear anything all night. The next morning when she went to get you, Elizabeth was gone." He casually shrugs his shoulders like that discovery wasn't life-altering for him or his family. "We questioned everyone who attended the party, but no one had seen or heard anything suspicious. When we couldn't find any leads, we had to accept that she was gone."

That was it? They asked a few fucking questions, and then they just gave up on her? What the fuck is wrong with these people?

It takes everything in me to hold my tongue. Out of the corner of my eye, I can see Mason's body coiled tight, just as furious as I am about the bullshit coming out of Barton's mouth.

"And you didn't think to go to the police?" Hawk argues.

"You know we couldn't have done that. Not with the line of work we're in," West's dad pipes up dismissively.

Right. Can't have the authorities finding out about your little mercenary business. Much more important than finding your missing daughter. *The whole fucking lot of them are nut jobs.*

"We hired a PI at the time," Barton states, as if that's some compromise for not going to the cops. "However he never uncovered any leads."

It's clear Hadley meant nothing to them. She wasn't worth

investing the time or resources into tracking down, and they noticeably don't give a shit where she's been living or what she's been through the last fifteen-odd years.

"The more pressing concern is what we do now that she's shown up," Maria Davenport speaks up, not sounding the slightest bit relieved to have her daughter back. If anything, she makes it sound like this new development—the return of her fucking daughter—is an inconvenience.

"What do you mean?" I question, struggling to keep the sharpness out of my tone.

"We need you to keep an eye on her and find out what you can about her."

"We've already looked into her past," Hawk informs them. "She's just a foster kid who got a scholarship here. Pac is one of the most prestigious schools in the country, so it's not much of a stretch that she would end up there."

"It's good to see you taking some initiative, son," Barton says, a proud gleam in his eyes. "Lawrence has already confirmed the same, but nonetheless, we can't be too careful. Especially now."

Well, that's not suspicious as fuck that my dad confirmed her background. And what the hell does he mean by 'especially now'?

"Alright, we'll stay close to her," Hawk agrees, sounding reluctant. It's all for show. If anything, this works in our favor.

"We've also been hearing from disgruntled parents that you boys refused to pick a girl last month," Mason's dad takes over, looking furious as he brings up the topic. "What the hell is going on there?" he demands, his sharp tone enough to have Mason sitting straighter in his chair.

That man has fucked his son up good. Mason does his best to hide it, but there's no denying his dad has done one hell of a number on him.

"When we found out about Ha...Elizabeth, we decided it was time for a change in traditions," Hawk explains easily, as though it's no big deal.

"Did you now?" There's a warning growl in Frank's voice. "Don't you think you should have discussed this with us?"

Hawk's jaw tightens. "I thought you wanted us to prove to you we could control the school."

"What Frank is trying to say," Barton interrupts, "is that we don't understand your decision to do away with a tradition that's been effective for generations."

"The senior girls were getting too big-headed about it. They've formed a club and everything, and it's only serving to make them harder to control. I figured changing things up and having Elizabeth take over control of the girls would be a good way to test if she's cut out to be a Davenport."

Our parents are silent as they think over Hawk's proposal.

"It's an interesting idea," Barton speaks up. "Nevertheless, let's stick with the tradition for now. We'll see how Elizabeth handles coming out as a Davenport, and then go from there."

"Elizabeth should also be included in the tradition," Maria chimes in. "It will be good to see how she handles the vultures. She's pretty enough. We could get some useful contracts out of her."

What the fuck? Does this woman only see her daughter as a bargaining chip?

Tension seeps into the air, none of us keen on the idea of Hadley being involved in the tradition. Casting a subtle glance toward my father, his eyes are narrowed and jaw clenched. Nope, he's not a fan of that idea, either. I wonder what he'd think if he knew three of us have fucked her—four, if you count Beck, which I'm assuming we can. Not that I'd tell him any of that. He's controlling enough to do something reckless if he ever finds out. Something that would only put Hadley in greater danger.

"Yes, a good idea," Barton agrees, neither of them giving two shits about the fact they're essentially pimping out their daughter to the senior boys. To what end? The whole point of the tradition is so the next generation of male heirs can prove to their parents they are capable of running a multimillion-dollar conglomerate one day. Sure, families from all over the country enroll their children in Pac Prep in the hopes that they can make friends—or more —with us and gain their families a foot in the door when it comes to doing business with our parents. But what do our parents truly gain from it all? They have their pick of companies to do business with. Is it all a control thing? A way for them to seem more important than they are?

None of us can protest or say anything about involving Hadley in the tradition without raising any red flags that might have our parents realizing we care more about her than we're letting on. Instead, we're all forced to nod and agree with their asinine idea.

How the fuck this is going to work is beyond me. I might not be dating Hadley or anything, but she still consumes my every thought. The idea of sticking my dick in any other chick is seriously unappealing. Despite the fact it's been fucking ages since I had sex, my cock doesn't even stir at the thought of having a sure-thing lay. All it wants—all *I* want—is Hadley, and the idea of watching some douche from school with his arm draped over her, acting like she's his, pisses me the fuck off.

"Right, now that we've sorted that out, let's move on to Easter break. The four of you will be spending the break at the company, shadowing each of us and learning the ropes. You'll also be expected to attend our "Annual Open Day" later in the year so you can all get an understanding of the quality of recruits we have. Then, when you graduate, you'll start taking on some of the more minor responsibilities."

"What about Beck?" West asks in a tight voice. "What's his job?"

"Don't worry about him." Wilbert waves off his question. "He's already doing his job."

Huh. We didn't know that. What the hell is he doing for them? Maybe it's time we had a little chat with him, especially if he's keeping secrets. We've let him in because he's West's brother, not to mention he's dating Hadley. And he *appeared* genuinely shocked and horrified at Christmas when he found out what our parents did, but what the fuck do we actually know about him? Typically, West would have researched the fuck out of someone new in our lives. However, he's completely buried his head in the sand when it comes to his brother, choosing to pretend he doesn't exist. Well, he's done with that shit now. If his brother is involved in stuff with our parents, we need to know whose side he's on. And if it's not ours, he needs to go.

Having seemingly discussed everything they needed to, our parents get to their feet.

"Oh, one more thing," Barton begins. "We will be announcing Elizabeth's return home tonight. We expect you all to be there. Let her know."

Without waiting for a response, the six of them filter out, and once we're alone, the four of us share a knowing glance.

"Not here," Hawk states in a quiet order, when I open my mouth to speak. Nodding, we exit the boardroom silently, none of us saying a word as we leave the building and get into the car to head back to campus.

"Not it!" I rush out, throwing my arms in the air the second we're all standing back on campus, watching the car drive away. "I'm not telling her." No fucking way do I want to be the one to tell her that not only do West and Mason have to continue picking a girl each month, but she has to pick a guy too.

"Not it," West and Mason echo quickly, making Hawk scowl at all of us.

"I'm not fucking telling her," he insists. "She'll tear my balls off. At least she has a vested interest in you keeping yours."

"Sorry, dude." I shrug. "You lost."

He presses his lips together, mumbling something about 'not it' being a stupid fucking way to decide anything as he stomps toward the dorms. I'd laugh, but I'm reasonably certain he's walking into his own funeral.

CHAPTER 3

Hadley

"Wʜᴀᴛ ᴛʜᴇ ʜᴇʟʟ, Hᴀᴅʟᴇʏ?!" Hᴀᴡᴋ ʙᴀʀᴋs ᴏᴜᴛ. *Oʜ ɢʀᴇᴀᴛ, ʜᴇ found me.* Now he can yell at me in person instead of via text.

He and the others got back several hours ago, and I got a string of pissed-off messages when he discovered I wasn't in his apartment where he *ordered* me to stay. *Yeah, that shit was never going to fly.*

"Calm your tits, big guy." His eyes narrow to deathly slits, and I have to swallow my laughter. "I've been here the whole time. See"—I wave my hand over myself—"totally fine."

Such a fucking temperamental bastard. All I did was come to the library, where I've been surrounded by students. It's not like I decided to go for a walk alone in the forest. Even if I decided to do that, I can handle myself. Although, I guess he doesn't know that, so fair enough. I have every right to be pissed off, though. I didn't fucking escape Lawrence and everything else just so he, or anyone, could boss me around. Hell no. There's no fucking way.

When he continues to frown at me, I change the topic. "What happened at the meeting?"

Sighing, he lets go of some of his anger, sitting beside me so we can whisper quietly without worrying about nosy students nearby overhearing us.

"Not much. We have to spend Easter break with them, learning the ropes." He scrunches his nose up, not fond of that idea.

"That sucks," I empathize. "But it could be a good opportunity to get some dirt on them or find something we can use to help bring them down."

Hawk's eyes roam over my face for a second before he responds, "Is that what we're going to do? Destroy them?"

The way I see it, there are only two options. "Well, do you want to work for them, knowing the truth of what they do?"

"Hell no." He stares at me with wide eyes like I'm insane.

I shrug my shoulders. "Then we have to take them down."

After a second, he chuckles, shaking his head like he can't believe what he's hearing. "You make it sound so simple when it's going to be anything but. Not only do they have the financial means and know-how to evade discovery all these years, but they have a fucking army at their beck and call."

He's right. It's a Herculean task if ever there was one. Nevertheless, escaping the compound seemed impossible too, and I achieved that all by myself. So why can't the six of us accomplish this?

Dropping the topic, for now, he leans back in his chair, running his hand through his hair as he watches me closely.

"Our parents are throwing a party tonight," he blurts out.

"Okay." I shrug, not caring about some meaningless party filled with rich assholes who all think they're god's gift to humanity, focusing my attention back on my homework. "Have fun with that."

The guys may have had a face-to-face meeting today with the parents, but no one has reached out to *me* since I took the DNA test. Although Hawk hasn't mentioned it yet—it looks like he's getting the mundane news out of the way first. I'm assuming the results were discussed today, but jeez, is it asking too much to pick up the phone and let me know too? Apparently so. I guess they've been too busy planning a party to bother with little old me.

Despite my complaining, I'm more than happy for them to leave me alone. I just don't like decisions being made about me behind my back, and I'm sure that's what happened this afternoon.

"We're all invited. You too." The bottom of my stomach drops as I tear my eyes away from the homework I was working on, giving Hawk my full attention.

"I'm what? Why?"

"The DNA results are back."

What the fuck...That doesn't explain anything.

Seeing my utter confusion, he continues, "This is how things are done in our world."

Nope, he's still not making any sense.

He taps a finger against the wooden table, leaning in toward me. "You best put on your finest jewelry, 'cause tonight you're coming out as a Davenport." Hawk's words send an ominous chill down my spine. "Welcome to the family, Elizabeth."

WEST HAD YET ANOTHER DRESS DELIVERED FOR ME TO WEAR TONIGHT. The fact that my wardrobe mainly consists of fancy, overpriced dresses does not sit well with me. I'm a jeans and t-shirt girl. All this expensive shit is just not me. I want to open my wardrobe and see clothes that I *want* to wear, something that is me.

Regardless, the dress he bought is beautiful. It's a deep, midnight blue, with a high jewel neckline—West once again ensuring my scars aren't on display for every asshole to gawk at. It falls to the floor at the back, with the front lifting so it finishes mid-thigh. Diamonds are sewn into the fabric on either side of my waist, looking like twinkling stars against the dark material when the light hits them.

Emilia again does my hair and makeup, her constant chatter helping to ease the nausea that keeps rolling through my stomach, as sweat coats my forehead and makes my palms slick.

"You need to calm down, girl," she admonishes, seeing how fucking stressed out I am. She moves to stand in front of me, pinning me in place with her serious expression. "You've stood tall against Bianca and her bitches, and the Princes all year. You've got this."

It's a decent pep talk, and I give her a weak smile in thanks, but dealing with Bianca and the guys was nothing compared to what I'm going to face tonight.

I'm not ready. I don't want this.

Why the fuck did I let those shitheads talk me into this?

I lift my hand, fiddling with the necklace West got me for my birthday, closing my eyes as I try to draw some semblance of calm from it.

My heart rate starts to settle, the churning in my stomach slowing, but a knock on the door breaks me out of my reverie, and I scowl as I stomp toward it in my heels.

Yanking the door open, I glower at Hawk, pissed off that he interrupted the zen I had going, not to mention the fact he talked me into this stupid, half-cocked idea. Really, I'm just happy to cling to my anger rather than sit in the sickening anxiety I've been struggling through since he informed me about tonight.

Ignoring the dark glare I'm giving him, he roams his eyes over my dress and matching heels.

"It'll do, I guess," he laments, looking unimpressed with my ensemble. I bark out a half-hysterical laugh, finding some reassurance in his dickish behavior. I just hope Emilia didn't hear him. She'll have a bitch fit that her hours of primping weren't acknowledged.

A small smile lifts one side of his lip, and I think it's the first time I've ever seen him do it. Not that you could really call it that. It's so small, barely more than a twitch, and he quickly wipes it off his face.

"Where are the others?" I ask, peering past him, half expecting to find the rest of the guys standing in the hall behind him. One is rarely far from the others.

"They're already on the way there. It's better if they arrive separately."

Right. Can't let any of our parents know how close we've all gotten in the last few months. *God, things are getting so complicated.*

Emilia chooses that moment to come bouncing over. "Doesn't she look amazing? She'll have no issues fitting in with you pompous pricks."

Hawk's eyebrows climb up his forehead, and he stares slack-jawed at Emilia as another—more genuine—laugh bursts out of me. I don't think he's ever heard her talk so condescendingly about the Princes, or the upper class in general. I love that she's no longer afraid to be herself around them. I don't know if she thinks she has immunity against their tyrannical ways because of who I am now, or because I'm basically dating two of them. Whatever the reason, I wouldn't hesitate to cut a bitch—even if that bitch is Hawk—if they tried to put her in her place.

"Have fun tonight, kids," she chuckles, turning toward me with a giant smile on her face that's totally out of place, considering the tension in the air and the nerves still somersaulting in my stomach. "Remember, you're a badass bitch, and the Davenports can go fuck themselves if they don't see how great you are." Still, with that blinding smile in place, she glances at Hawk before tacking on in a sickly-sweet voice, "No offense, Hawk."

Hawk continues to stare at her quizzically, likely trying to work out what the fuck is happening right now, as I bite my lip to stifle my laugh. Kissing me on the cheek, Emilia skips past him and down the hall to her room.

"Is there something wrong with her?" he asks, eventually finding his words.

"No, you asshole." I shove him in the shoulder as I close the door behind me, the two of us making our way down the hall.

"Then she must have a death wish."

I yank on the sleeve of his jacket, bringing him to a stop.

"If you do anything to her, I will become your worst living nightmare," I threaten in a deadly tone. "You think getting throat-punched was bad? Touch her, and I'll slice open your stomach and use your intestines as a noose to hang you with."

"Fucking hell, Hadley." He rolls his eyes like I'm being melo-dramatic, unfazed by my grave threat. "I'm not going to do anything to her. I'm just not used to anyone being so uncaring if they piss me off."

"I don't care if I piss you off."

"Yeah, and you're the first person to be so cavalier with their life."

Eh. What's life, if not odd moments of peace between staring death in the face and giving it a big, old fuck you.

Stepping outside the dorms, the light breeze blows my hair back out of my face as we walk along the path. "You realize they all just bitch about you behind your backs, right?"

Hawk's eyes narrow, and he gives a lethal glare to some random student walking in the opposite direction, making them whimper as they pick up their pace, practically running to get away from him.

"They better not be," he snarls, making me roll my eyes. We reach the car, both of us hopping in and leaving the school behind as we drive toward the Davenports' mansion.

By the time we arrive, the party is in full swing. People are milling about everywhere, drinking expensive champagne and pretending to give a shit as they listen to each other droll on about their pathetic little lives.

I recognize many of the kids from school as they gather in groups and traipse around with their parents. It looks like just about everyone the Davenports know or have ever spoken to has been invited, and nerves do a jig in my stomach as Hawk and I make our way across the foyer.

We're barely across the hall when I feel eyes boring into me, and I turn my head to find Lawrence's menacing gaze watching me intently. He looks more haggard than the last time I saw him, in the headmaster's office. *Good. It serves him fucking right.*

The last time I was in the same room as him, I was on my knees, having reverted back into the scared child I used to be as he shoved his dick in my mouth. Straightening my spine as my eyes meet his, I stare defiantly back at him and refuse to let him make me cower this time.

It's easy when there are other people around and I know he can't do anything to me, but when he had me cornered alone in that office, it was just like every other time I've been around him. I felt scared and helpless, frozen in terror. It doesn't matter that I'm a big, badass assassin bitch. When he's around, I'm nothing more than a frightened kid, willing to do anything to avoid his punishments.

Nonetheless, I've made a stand against him now. I've moved my chess piece, and while I may not have him in checkmate yet, based on the daggers he's throwing my way, I've certainly made the game more difficult for him to win. I smirk before dismissing him, something that I know will piss him off. *The arrogant asswad always did love it when all my attention was focused on him.*

Walking beside Hawk through the crowd, I spot the guys interspersed throughout the room, stuck in various conversations. West catches sight of me from across the room as I walk by, throwing me a dirty smirk before responding to whoever he's talking to.

Beck is standing nearby, and his eyes trail me across the crowded room as he absently nods his head at whatever the person he's engaged in conversation with says, his intense gaze heating my skin. The lighting in the room emphasizes just how tired he looks, the bags under his eyes worryingly dark. I'm becoming increasingly concerned about him. The light in his eyes isn't as bright as when I first met him, and it doesn't look like he's sleeping much, if at all.

"We should find our parents," Hawk murmurs in my ear, steering my focus back to the room. His eyes dart around the crowd as he searches for them, so he misses the way my face scrunches at his words. *Our parents.* I'm never going to get used to that.

Giving Beck a soft smile, I tear my eyes away from him as Hawk and I continue pushing our way through the partygoers. Hawk is stopped several times by men who shake his hand and look keen to engage him in conversation before he politely blows them off, and all the women do is eye him up like a piece of meat, quickly dismissing me. Currently, I'm a nobody to them. I can't do anything that would benefit them, so in their eyes, I'm not worthy of their precious time.

Spotting our parents—*cringe*—we make our way toward them. Maria Davenport notices us first, her shoulders sagging in relief as she waves us over, scowling at Hawk.

"There you are," she chastises. "It's about time you showed up." Barely sparing us a glance, she gains her husband's attention. "Barton, they're here. Let's get this started."

Get what started?

Before I can ask, Barton excuses himself from his conversation with some random old dude and nods his head at his wife, taking off toward the front of the room as Maria follows dutifully behind him.

Hawk tugs on my arm, indicating that we're to follow, and my legs become heavier with every step I take, until it feels like I'm trudging through marshland.

My hand squeezes Hawk's upper arm, my fingernails digging into his suit jacket. My grip is so tight I'm sure it must be painful, but he doesn't shrug me off, his face impassive as we reach the front of the room.

Barton coughs loudly, tapping the side of his glass with a butterknife—*where the hell did he get that from?*—until the rest of the room quiets down, conversations coming to a halt as everyone turns to look at him. At us.

"Thank you all for coming tonight," he begins when he's gotten everyone's attention. "We've gathered you all here to share some special news."

It would be impossible to tell from his blank expression—creepily similar to Hawk's—whether or not the 'special news' of the return of his long-lost daughter is good or bad. *Does he even give a shit that I'm alive and well?* He hasn't spared me a glance, never mind a kind word, so I've no idea.

"Fifteen years ago, our family was struck by a terrible tragedy," he says, pausing dramatically as a few people whisper and gasp in surprise. "Not many people know that when Hawk was born, Maria also gave birth to a baby girl. She was stolen from us, and although we have dedicated extensive resources in the hopes of finding her, we feared the worst."

What the fuck is this shit he's spouting?

I glance at Hawk out of the corner of my eye, giving him a 'what the fuck' look, which he returns with a roll of his eyes, clearly used to his parents spinning stories to suit their own agenda.

"Now, however, we are over the moon to have finally found her. Tonight, I'd like to introduce you to our daughter, Elizabeth Davenport."

They make it sound like *they* were the ones to find *me*, not the other way around. I don't, for one second, believe they've put any time or money into searching for me. I've been right under their fucking noses all these years, trapped inside the confines of their own goddamn organization.

Lawrence made sure to hide me away on the rare occasion the other benefactors—which I now know are our parents—came to the compound, but even so. Surely, I should have been easy enough to find?

My father holds out his arm, pointing me out to the gathered crowd, and suddenly all eyes are on me as whispers break out around the room. My cheeks stain red under their scrutiny, and I self-consciously press my shoulder against Hawk's, as if he can somehow hide me from these money-hungry gawkers eyeing me up as if I'm a weak link in the Davenport stronghold that they could manipulate their way through.

Men step forward to shake hands with Barton, congratulating him like he fucking achieved something.

"Come." Maria's sharp tone snaps my attention in her direction, where she's got a forced smile on her face. It's painfully fake, only further emphasizing this is all a sham and that there's no real happy family reunion in my future. "There are people we need to introduce you to."

As she strides forward, her eyes focused on whatever rich dickhead she feels the need to force on me, Hawk moves to follow after her, obviously more used to blindly obeying her orders at these things.

"Hawk, dear, you're not needed. Why don't you go mingle with the other guests."

Hawk's lips flatten, the only tell that he's not happy with that order, although he reluctantly nods his head before pinning me with a look. Basically, telling me with his eyes to behave.

What does he think I'm going to do? Cause a scene? I would never! It's just not in my nature to do such a thing.

I watch him disappear into the crowd before reluctantly chasing after Maria, nerves fluttering in my chest. She drags me around the party, introducing me to people whose names I immediately forget, but I've noticed a trend by the fifth introduction. All of the couples I've met have entitled-looking fuckers as sons, all of whom seem to be in and around my age.

As we walk away from yet another couple whose names I don't care to remember, I blurt out, "I have to go to the bathroom." I've had enough of being paraded around like I'm a new piece of art they've acquired. I can feel a headache forming behind my eyes, and I'm so beyond done with all the fake happy family bullshit for one night. If I have to hear this bitch tell one more person how fucking happy she is to have her daughter back home, even though she hasn't talked directly to me all night, except to order me around, I'm going to lose my ever-loving shit.

Her face tightens in disapproval, like I'm being rude, but what does she expect me to do? If I have to pee, I have to pee.

"Fine," she relents. "But hurry back. There's a lot of other people you have to meet tonight."

Yeah, that shit ain't happening.

Turning my back on her, I shove through the crowd, feeling everyone gawking at me as I go. I don't even know where the fuck I'm going; I just know I need to get out of here.

CHAPTER 4

Hadley

Mason must catch sight of the murderous look on my face as I push through the gawking crowd, desperate to get away from them all before I snap and do something I'll regret. Like a fucking white knight, he comes striding toward me. "Follow me," he murmurs quietly before taking off again, leaving me confused as I trail after him.

He walks purposefully through several rooms filled with guests, his stony expression enough to deter anyone who appears as though they're about to approach him, until we reach a door that leads outside. Once we're alone, he slows down, waiting for me to catch up.

"You looked like you needed a break."

"Yeah, you could say that. I don't know what I expected, but this was not it. I'm pretty sure my mother was just trying to pimp me out."

"Oh yeah." He chuckles, like it's no big deal. "I guarantee you she was."

My face scrunches. Having him confirm my suspicions only makes me feel worse. Nothing about tonight was designed to reunite us as a family or get to know me. It was all a publicity stunt, so they could turn my arrival into something they could use to elevate themselves.

"Where are we going?" I ask, changing the subject before I can get myself even more worked up about the whole thing. I'm not even sure if I'm hurt, disappointed, or just pissed-off. A mixture of all three, probably.

"The pool house. It's where we go when we need a break from everything in there," he explains, gesturing toward the party we left behind.

Circling the side of the house, we skirt around a large pool before coming upon the pool house. The door is unlocked, and we let ourselves in. Mason flicks on a lamp that provides a dim glow, showing a large room with a wide-screen TV, several sofas and chairs, and a small kitchenette.

The place is empty, and Mason pulls me toward the nearest sofa, dropping onto it and dragging me onto his lap.

"Don't let them get to you. It's the same with all of our families. Everything is about presentation. It's all a show for other people. None of them give a fuck about us beyond what they can use us for."

"What is it they want?"

"Dutiful children who will continue their legacy and marry into the right families, thereby boosting their status and financial earnings," he cites off, as though someone has repeatedly explained to him his purpose in life.

His eyes meet mine, the trapped look in them flooring me. "They'll do anything to ensure they get what they want. Remember that."

I watch him closely, noticing the shadows clinging to him in much the same way they did when I saw him with his father at Hawk's birthday party. Something about being in that man's presence brings Mason's darkness to the surface, and seeing him so depressed doesn't sit well with me. He's always quiet and subdued, his features carefully kept blank when he's around others, but the world is missing out on a whole other side to Mason Hayes. Despite whatever abuse he's experienced in the past, he's got a big heart and a wickedly dry sense of humor.

Wanting to help quiet his demons, I run my fingers through his dark hair, brushing the strands back from his face. "It was your parents, right?" I don't need to elaborate any more than that. His eyes are shrouded in misery as his hold tightens around me.

"Yeah, Little Warrior." His words are a soft sigh filled with sadness.

I lean against his chest, breathing him in and hoping my presence can lift some of his emotional baggage. "Parents aren't supposed to treat their kids that way." It baffles me how people can do that to their own flesh and blood. How can anyone be so callous? I would make sure my kids knew they were loved and cherished every moment of every day. I'd go to the ends of the earth to protect them and personally castrate anyone who so much as thought about causing them harm.

"No, they aren't, but who's going to stop them?"

His dejected tone has anger burning in my gut. How dare his parents try to destroy this giant marshmallow of a man.

Vengeance has flowed through my veins for so long now. It's an integral part of who I am. For years, my goal has been to get back at the people who have wronged me, the people that killed the only friend I had growing up. Mason's parents, as are all of ours, have since been added to that list, but seeing how much they tried to beat down their son and turn him into what *they* wanted, has me fighting the urge to track them down and eviscerate them.

We sit in silence for a moment, each of us lost in our own thoughts.

"I used to pretend I had a family out there," I tell him, my words barely audible. "Parents who wanted me, who missed me, whose lives had been completely upturned in their search to find me. I used to picture how it would all unfold if we were reunited. It definitely wasn't anything like the reality is turning out to be."

Mason's eyes roam over my face, and I wish I knew what he was thinking when he looks at me so intently, as if he's trying to read everything there is to know about me.

"Where were you all these years? We know you weren't in foster care. West checked into the fake background you gave the school, and he couldn't find anything about you. It's like you didn't exist until you showed up at Pac."

"I didn't." At least, that's how it feels. My life didn't begin until I got my fake ID and escaped the compound. "I was trapped in my own personal hell, and I didn't know how to escape it. I didn't think I could. Only when I learned about Cam did I feel like I had the power to fight back against Lawrence. Against all of them."

Finding out about Cam changed everything. I was falling down a dark hole of accepting my bleak fate, unable to see any way out of my cemented future. Before that day, I knew nothing about Lawrence. Not his name, who he was, or what he had to do with the mercenary organization I had somehow become a part of. Knowing that little thing about him gave me the strength to stop accepting the shitty hand I'd been dealt in life. All of a sudden, I didn't feel so helpless. It wasn't much to work with, but it was more than I'd known before, and I was desperate to find out everything I could about Cam and his family.

His eyes eat me up as they slowly climb up my slim frame. He always gets a carnal look in his eyes when he sees me dressed up in whatever outfit he brought—usually some sort of form-fitting dress that highlights my newly developed curves and pushes up my perky breasts.

"Perfect," he breathes. "You can always wear clothes like this when you come to live with me. Won't that be nice?"

"Yes, Sir."

I've learned by now that there's no point in arguing with him. It's best if I grin and bear his visits, nodding and agreeing with whatever he says.

As he tucks my hair behind my shoulder, his cell phone goes off in his pocket, making him frown. The call rings out before starting up again, and he tugs harshly on a strand of my hair as agitation gets the better of him.

Huffing out a breath, he digs his hand into his pocket, retrieving his phone and moving to the corner of the room, getting as far away from me as possible so he can gain some modicum of privacy before answering the call.

"Yes," he hisses, the blatant rage more than obvious.

Great, I'm going to be the one that pays for this intrusion with brand-new bruises on my body.

I slowly edge toward him, intent on overhearing his conversation.

"Now isn't a good time…Yes, I understand my son has been acting out."

My eyebrows lift in surprise. He has a son? He's been coming to see me my whole life, and I know absolutely nothing about him. I don't even know his fucking name. He's always insisted on me calling him 'Sir,' and he's never divulged anything about who he is. I stupidly assumed he didn't have any family. But a son? That could be useful to know. A possible weakness I could use against him.

I've been trained to identify people's weak spots and to poke and prod at them until they become gaping holes. The problem is, Sir has never given me anything to work with…until now.

"Fine," he snarls, after whoever is on the other end of the line has droned on for several moments regarding whatever new issue there is with his son. "I'll speak to Cam. No, I don't think a meeting with the headmaster is necessary."

Now I have a name. It's not much, but it's a hell of a lot more than I had this morning.

Another moment passes where he fumes at whatever the person on the other end is saying. He repeatedly glances my way, as though expecting me to disappear or jump him—I fucking wish I could, but fear freezes me in place every time I so much as think about taking him on.

"Listen here," he growls, furious at whatever is being said to him. Based on his tone alone, I know I'm in for a rough afternoon of slaps and degrading comments as he takes his anger out on me, but right now, I don't care. I'll take anything he throws at me if it means I can finally learn something I could use against him. "You seem to have forgotten who you're talking to. My family is one of the founding families of Pacific Prep. My son can do whatever the hell he wants. He answers to me, and me alone. If you have a problem with that, I'm sure Mr. Phister will happily help you find an alternative place of employment."

He hangs up the phone before whoever is on the other end can respond, spinning in his overpriced loafers to face me. His nostrils flare as he grits his teeth, anger consuming him. I hate when he's like this. He's truly terrifying. Completely demonic looking.

"What are you doing just standing there?" he snarls, startling me into action.

"S...Sorry." I lick my lips nervously as I fumble with my hands, frantically trying to stop them from trembling. "C...Can I get you anything?" I ask. "Perhaps a drink?"

Normally, if I'm not training, I'm in my room. Except, on visitation days, I'm brought here to this room with a bed in the corner, a small living area, and a kitchenette. I have no idea how to cook—not that Sir seems to mind. He loves it when I offer to make him a drink. I don't understand why, but right now I'd do pretty much anything to tamper down the rage inside of him and ease the onslaught of abuse I know is coming my way.

I've barely gotten the words out before he's striding toward me, quickly closing the distance between us until his chest is pushing up against mine. His hand wraps around my hair and he yanks it back, so my neck is bent at an awkward angle.

"Do you think a drink is going to solve my problems?" He's so close, spittle hits my cheek as he yells at me.

His eyes drop down my body, hovering over my heaving chest. With how he's stretched my neck, my back is arched, pushing my boobs out in an inviting gesture.

He growls as he grits his teeth, the grip on my hair tightening to the point of pain, and I bite the inside of my cheek to hold in my whimper.

"There's only one thing that would make this better, and your worthless ass can't give it to me until everything's in place."

Tugging on my hair, he throws me across the room, and I go crashing to the ground, not understanding what he's talking about. Honestly, the intent behind his words is crystal clear, and whatever the reason he may be holding back, I don't give a fuck, so long as it keeps him away from me.

THAT CONVERSATION CHANGED EVERYTHING. CAM HAS NO IDEA, BUT he saved my life that day. I don't know what he did to instigate that phone call, but regardless of what happens between us, I'll be forever grateful to him.

"Hey, where did you go just now?" Mason asks. I hadn't realized how closely he was watching me. His eyes are filled with concern, and I quickly shake away the thoughts of the past. Lawrence is still an ever-present threat, but I have so much more to fight for now. I'm no longer trapped and, more importantly, I'm no longer alone.

I press my lips to his in what I intend to be a chaste kiss, a thank you for being here. I don't know how temporary what I have with him and West is, but for the time being, I'm glad to have the two of them in my corner.

He responds immediately, his hand resting on the back of my neck and holding me to him as he deepens the kiss, both of us getting lost in the taste of one another.

As heat spirals in my lower belly, I shift in his lap, hiking up my dress as I straddle him.

Now, this is a much better way to spend the night.

His hands slide up my thighs, and he groans as I grind against his growing erection. Trailing my hands over his shirt until I reach his belt buckle, I deftly undo it and lower his zipper, reaching into his boxers. I wrap my hand around his thick girth, testing the weight of him in my palm. I need to feel him inside me...now. I sit up on my knees, hovering above him as he pushes my panties to the side, and I don't waste any time lowering myself onto him, my head falling back as he easily slides inside, filling me to the brim.

We're both breathing heavily as he fully seats himself, and I look deep into his eyes, the connection between us stronger than ever as the air crackles around us. My pussy clenches with desperate need and he grunts in pleasure as I rock shallowly against him.

The squeaking of the pool house door has me freezing as I tear my gaze away from Mason's blissed-out expression to find West standing in the doorway, his pupils dilated at finding us fucking.

"Don't mind me," he purrs huskily, moving to lean against the wall, obviously intending to watch us. *Fuck, why does the thought of that make my pussy spasm?* Mason groans again as I practically strangle his dick, and his hands move to grip my hips, holding me still as he thrusts into me, setting a faster pace. I moan, my eyes drifting shut as he hits that perfect spot deep inside me.

I don't even hear *him* approaching, but in the next second, I feel a tug on my hair as my head is pulled backward and my eyes snap open, staring up into West's lust-hazed green ones.

"Don't close your eyes," he growls, his rough voice coated with sinful promises, only making me wetter.

He releases his hold on my hair, moving to undo the zip at the back of my dress until he can push it down my arms, exposing my breasts. The fabric of the dress made it impossible to wear a bra with it, and my nipples peak as the cool air hits them.

Mason leans forward to suck one into his mouth as West's hand once again entangles itself in my hair, pulling until my head is bent back and I'm looking up at him. The angle has me pushing my tit further into Mason's mouth, my back arching. Mason's dick slides impossibly deeper as my lips part, and a wanton moan escapes me.

I keep my eyes glued to West as Mason picks up his pace,

rapidly sending me toward the edge as he palms a tit in one hand while sucking and biting on the other.

My face is flushed as Mason thrusts frantically, every pant a breathy moan. I'm so lost in my pleasure that I don't hear the door opening and someone new arriving to the party.

West obviously hears it, though, as his eyes snap up to see who entered. Mason doesn't stop his relentless pounding, and I try to turn my head to look at the newcomer, but West's grip tightens, keeping me in place for a second before he uses his firm hold to turn my head. I see Cam standing slack-jawed in the doorway, seeming both unsure and turned-on.

My eyes drop to his crotch, taking in the noticeable bulge, and *fuck me*. Even though we agreed to just be friends, the way he's looking at me, and the dirty thoughts I'm having about him joining in, are anything but friendly.

My pussy spasms as I picture him closing the distance and slamming his lips against mine—oh, how I've missed the taste of him—and Mason groans.

"Fuck, baby, I'm gonna blow if you keep doing that."

Cam stares transfixed at the three of us, frozen in the doorway.

"Well, are you in or out?" West barks impatiently.

Cam's eyes widen in surprise, not having expected the invitation, his gaze bouncing between all three of us—not that Mason is paying him any attention as he licks along the column of my neck, rolling my nipple between his fingers as I buck against him. Between his magical dick, hot mouth, and talented fingers; plus West's controlling nature, and feeling Cam's eyes on me, I'm about to combust.

"I..."

Even though I know what his answer will be, I'm still wracked with disappointment as he shakes his head.

He doesn't get a chance to turn me down with words since Hawk chooses that moment to storm into the pool house next— *great, now it's really a fucking party*—his eyes widening to the size of saucers at what he sees.

"What the fuck?" he roars, slamming his hand over his eyes and quickly turning around. "Someone tell me I didn't see what I think I saw," he growls furiously.

I try to climb off Mason's lap, but West is still holding tight to my hair, and as I attempt to move, Mason's hands grip my hips, cementing me in place so he can continue slamming into me, unfazed by Hawk's presence.

"Get out if you don't want to see it." His words come out in an angry tone. However the breathless quality as he maintains his relentless pace, not sparing Hawk a second glance, shows where all of his focus is right now.

Mason circles his hips, causing him to grind against my clit, and my eyes fall closed as I bite my lip to hold back a moan. Fairly certain Hawk won't appreciate that.

Hawk's voice is nothing but background noise as he rants before stomping out, and when I crack open an eyelid, both he and Cam are gone.

West directs my head so I'm looking up at him standing behind me.

"Forget about him," he says softly, referring to Cam, before he seals his lips to mine in an all-consuming kiss.

Mason's fingers move to rub my clit, and that light touch is the final straw as I come apart on his dick, crying out my release while staring into West's lustful gaze. I feel Mason swell within me after another couple of thrusts, his seed hitting my inner walls.

"So beautiful," West murmurs, his lips brushing over mine.

Knowing it won't be long before someone other than one of the guys comes searching for us, we quickly clean up and redress, reluctantly heading back to the party.

West and Mason disappear into the crowd, leaving me alone as I do a loop around the room, smiling politely at people before hurrying off through the crowd in a vain attempt to avoid getting dragged into any unwanted conversations.

I can't find my mother, which suits me perfectly fine, though I do catch sight of Lawrence at the far end of the room. His eyes are trailing my every move like laser beams, making my skin itch with the intensity of his gaze.

Shivering, I move as far away from him as possible, ensuring enough people are between us that he can't see me as I head to the bar, ordering a coke with ice. I sit and watch the party going on around me, picking out each of the guys, all of whom are stuck in various conversations appearing as bored as I feel. As I sip on my drink, I can feel everyone's lingering stares on me, hear the whispers behind their hands as they speculate about where I've been all these years.

I'm only halfway through my drink when I cannot take it any longer. Staying in one place is the worst thing I can do. It's better if I'm constantly circulating through the crowd. At least that way, I won't feel the eyes on me as much.

Getting to my feet, I push through the gawking herd, already needing another break from all this bullshit. Just when I think things couldn't get any worse, Bianca steps up to me, an ugly scowl on her face. "Don't think just because your surname happens to be Davenport that you're no longer trash," she sneers. "Someone like you isn't worthy of such a name."

"And you are?" I laugh coldly.

She frowns. "You don't deserve it," she whines, like the entitled bitch she is. "I've been doing everything the Princes want for *years*, and you just waltz in here and get handed everything I've worked for? It's not fair!"

I'm surprised she doesn't stamp her feet like a two-year-old having a fucking tantrum.

"*Life* isn't fair," I snap, getting irritated. She thinks just because she bent over and swallowed their dicks when demanded that she *deserves* to be given one of their surnames?

I tilt my head slightly, thinking. "You're a self-centered bitch, and I think it's past time someone reminded you of your place." An evil smile plays at the corner of my lips as I step in close to her, my heels putting us at eye-to-eye level. "I've wanted to slap that pretentious fucking look off your face since the first day we met,"

I tell her quietly enough so that no one nearby can overhear us. Her eyes widen. *Is she seriously surprised at my admission?* "And now I have the immunity to do it." She gulps, and I'm sure her face has paled, not that you can see it under her layers of makeup. "I may be trash, but I'm trash that can do whatever the fuck she wants," I say sweetly, a broad grin on my face that I'm sure looks maniacal.

Oh yeah. I think I might have found a silver lining to this whole Davenport name bullshit.

It's later that night, and I'm contemplating the appeal of alcohol—God knows you need something to drown out the boring as fuck conversations—when I recognize West's father as he comes hobbling toward me, his pudgy belly straining the buttons of his shirt. His cheeks are ruddy from too much alcohol and sweat clings to his temples.

"Elizabeth, it's so great to meet you. I'm Wilbert, Westley's father." His words make me think he doesn't remember meeting me before. Of course, I was only his son's whore that night, so why would he?

"You're quite a beautiful young lady, aren't you?" I don't miss the way his gaze heats as it lingers on my tits. *What is with all these rich assholes being sleazy perverts?*

He licks his lips with no zero shame, and subtly adjusts himself in his pants. *Fucking gross.* It takes everything in me not to wrinkle my nose in disgust, not that his gaze ever ventures further north than my chest, as he continues with his conversation.

"The day you disappeared was a somber day indeed," he goes on, nodding his head in agreement with himself. "We were all distraught."

Yes, it sure seems that way.

"What happened?" I ask, deciding I may as well try and get some information out of him. I'm hoping the alcohol I can smell on his breath might loosen his lips enough to let slip something that could be of use.

"Oh, I couldn't say." Wrinkles form across his forehead as his eyebrows draw together and he frowns. "It was a long time ago."

"Of course," I agree readily. "But it must have come as a shock that someone could get onto your well-secured property here and steal one of your own children."

His eyes bulge. "Oh yes, we were all very shocked." He looks like a bobblehead as he nods vigorously. "Took us all quite by surprise." He lifts a handkerchief out of his pocket, dabbing at the sweat along his hairline.

"And you never found out who did it?"

"Oh, well, you know how it is. The trail ran cold and all that."

Yes, I'm sure the trail did run cold when you didn't put any resources into following it.

"You truly are quite stunning," he repeats, his gaze once again falling back to my tits. It's not like they're even pushed up or falling out of my dress. There isn't an inch of skin on display, yet he can't stop fucking gaping at them like he's never seen boobs before in his life.

I notice Beck in the crowd and silently beg him with my eyes to come save me from his father. Because he's a fucking godsend, he switches directions, coming toward me.

"Ah, this is my other son," West's father explains, spotting him. "He's actually a counselor at your school."

"Nice to meet you." Acting as though we're complete strangers, Beck's tone is nothing but polite as he holds his hand out for me to shake.

"Likewise." I smile innocently up at him as I slip my palm into his, and his hand squeezes mine, holding it for a second longer than is socially appropriate before letting it go.

Mr. Warren flicks his gaze between us. "Maybe you two know each other?"

"I don't think so," I respond, giving Beck a once-over as though I'm trying to work out if I recognize him from around campus, when in reality, I'm picturing stripping him out of that suit.

"I think I'd remember someone like you." The seductive undertones in Beck's baritone voice have goosebumps pebbling on my skin. Heat flares in his eyes, and he runs his hand slowly down the length of his tie, drawing my attention to it. My panties grow damp as I remember how, the last time he wore it, he stuffed it in my mouth to silence my cries while he hammered into my dripping wet pussy.

His pupils seem to dilate, a dirty smirk flitting along his lips as similar dirty thoughts likely dance through his head.

His father chuckles, clapping his son on the shoulder, not noticing the dark scowl Beck fires his way.

"She's a pretty piece, isn't she?" he expresses to Beck, like I'm some sort of fucking possession and not a human being standing right here listening to him. Utterly unaware of the ticking of my jaw or the clenching of Beck's fists, the arrogant dickwad keeps talking. "Beck here only recently came into the fold himself. I didn't even know I had another son until last year." The idiot chuckles, lying through his teeth. "But he's been a great addition to our family and has been instrumental in increasing the efficiency of our business."

My eyebrows rise in a silent question as I sear Beck with my probing gaze. *What the fuck does his father mean by that?*

"Is that so?" Beck's lips pinch and his father rattles on, oblivious to the silent conversation going on between us.

"Oh, yes. He's been very helpful, but my apologies. It's rude to talk business at a party." He laughs.

I give him a tight smile.

"If you'll excuse me, I should be finding my parents," I tell him politely—look at me acting like a fucking Davenport—not waiting for an answer before taking off, storming out of the hall as questions swirl around my head.

I fucking knew Beck was keeping secrets!

Knowing what I do about our parents' company, whatever

they have Beck doing is bad. Seriously. Fucking. Bad. The fact that his dad singled him out instead of saying he *and West* have been helping only confirms my suspicions that Beck has been more involved than the other guys.

Storming outside, I can hear Beck's heavy footsteps smacking against the ground as he chases after me. When he catches up to me, his large palm wraps around my forearm, and he uses his grip on my arm to drag me toward his parked car, his free hand yanking open the passenger door with more force than necessary.

"Get in," he snarls between gritted teeth, pushing me forward and giving me no choice. Doesn't he know I want fucking answers from him? He doesn't need to drag me. *Stupid fucking testosterone-fueled male.*

My ass has barely hit the nylon seat before he slams my door shut, stomping around to the driver's side and climbing in. His car is nothing like Hawk's. It's old and rusted, with the dash scored, the seats worn, and the odd tear here and there. The engine sputters for a second before starting, and Beck takes off, the two of us sitting in silence as we drive to god knows where. All I know is that it's not back toward the school.

"What do they have you doing?" I demand when I can no longer keep my questions to myself, regarding him out of the corner of my eye.

His hand on the steering wheel tightens while he irritably runs his other one over the coarse hairs of his short stubble. His jaw is clenched and the stubborn asshole shakes his head, refusing to answer me.

"Fine," I seethe, throwing my hands in the air in exasperation. "How about I guess, and you just let me know when I get it right."

There's only one reason I can think of why his dad sought him out and dragged him into all this bullshit, and the thought makes my blood boil. My vision blurs red as the urge to demand Beck turn this car around so I can go back and slice his father open from sternum to groin rides me hard.

I sigh, yet again knowing I will have to give up more of myself by talking about this. Talking about Lawrence was one thing. What he did…that was something that was done *to* me. Other than making me look like a victim—something I seriously hate thinking of myself as—it was unlikely to negatively affect how Beck, or anyone else, would look at me. But this…*this* is who I am. Once Beck knows this, it will change everything. He'll never look at me the same, and who could blame him?

I keep my gaze fixed firmly on the inky blackness out the window. It seems fitting that we're shrouded in darkness as I spill my secrets for the first time. Akin to splitting open my skin and showing him how black my blood runs, he's about to get a glimpse of how demoralized I really am.

"They have you psychoanalyzing the kids, right? Helping to pick recruits and turn them into mindless soldiers." My voice is hollow, my heart cracking as I accept how deeply Beck has been dragged into all of this. My chest constricts as I think about what fresh hell the new kids these sickos find have to go through. Isn't what they're doing bad enough? Why do they need to find new and inventive ways to strip the soul from these innocent children too?

Another moment of silence, this one fraught with tension, the weight of our topic of conversation suffocating.

Beck pulls over to the side of the road, slowing the car to a stop, and the two of us stare out the windshield, seeing nothing in the darkness. We're in the middle of nowhere, surrounded by woodland and fields.

Eventually, he turns to look at me, letting his eyes roam over what he can see of my face before he asks, "How do you know about that?" His deflated, pained tone makes me suspect he already has an idea of the answer. As I turn to meet his gaze, I can see the pleading in his eyes, begging me to refute it.

Dropping the last of my barriers so he can see into every dark crevice I keep carefully hidden, I stare back at him, revealing to him every little bit of my suffering. I show him every strip of humanity they took from me every time they tore my skin open and tried to break me. I allow him to see how much every death affected me, even if I was murdering people just as corrupt and devious as our parents. I let him see how much it killed me to stand back and watch while they punished and tortured other children, some of whom were no older than five or six.

When he's seen all he can bear to see, he tears his gaze from mine, staring unseeingly out the windshield as he shakes his head in denial.

"Don't," he pleads.

But I've come this far.

I *have* to say it.

"Because I was one of those kids." It's barely more than a whisper, but in the silent car, the words are akin to a gunshot, confirming his worst fears.

CHAPTER 5

Beck

BECAUSE I WAS ONE OF THOSE KIDS.

Those words echo around in my brain, giving me a headache that beats a steady drum against my skull.

I have so many questions.

How did she end up there? Why? How did I not notice or put it together?

Everything suddenly made so much sense as soon as she uttered the words. The scars, her closed-off behavior, her insane fighting skills, and how she so easily killed that mercenary. After the blitz attack at Christmas, I *know* how well-trained they are. They're fucking machines. The five of us were struggling to fight off two of them, so I didn't much like my odds in a one-on-one battle.

Yet I thought she got fucking lucky getting the better of one of them? I snort just thinking about it. There was nothing lucky about it.

THE TRUTH OF HER WORDS SITS HEAVY IN THE AIR BETWEEN US, strangling any sort of conversation. I don't even know what the fuck to say to that. I'm professionally fucking trained to deal with people who have been through fucked-up shit, but this is next level. It's not like there was a class that taught me the appropriate way to respond when the girl I'm falling in love with tells me she's a trained mercenary.

Thankfully, I'm saved from having to think of a reply when Hadley keeps talking. Focusing on her, her eyes are cloudy and her face is withdrawn as the memories hold her hostage.

"Lawrence didn't want me to learn to fight like the other kids, but the guys in charge of us didn't share his opinions. When he wasn't around, I was thrown in the ring and treated to the same grueling training as everyone else. They would work us until our legs couldn't hold us up and we were puking our guts out. Anyone who couldn't hack it was made an example of."

Her expression darkens, and there's so much sorrow in her eyes that I don't know how she doesn't drown in it.

"They were never short of cruel and inventive ways to torture us. Beatings, food and sleep deprivation, preying on our fears."

She shudders, withdrawing further into herself. I want to reach across the short distance between us and drag her into my lap, but I sense she wouldn't respond well to that. It's clear she was seriously deprived of gentle touch growing up, and wherever she is in her memories right now, I fear any physical contact would only trigger her further.

"The normal fears any kid would have. They would lock me in the dark, alone, for what felt like days. I hated it." Her voice breaks and tears start to leak out of her eyes. "It was their punishment of choice, especially when we were getting close to another visit from Lawrence. He didn't like when they touched me, although he was always in agreement with their methods to keep me in line in his absence, so long as the scars didn't show." She snarls out the last sentence, anger burning away the despair in her features as her hands form tight fists.

"After Meena died, I stopped fighting. I was never getting out of there, so what was the point? I became what all of them wanted. A soldier. A fighter. A doll." A caustic, unhinged laugh breaks free, and she shakes her head. "The funny thing is I became an asset to them. One of the best fighters they had. Rather than putting all my energy into fighting them, I became one of them. But I couldn't switch off my humanity the same way the others did.

"Every death stuck with me—even if it was deserved. We were hired by bad people to torture and kill other bad people." Sighing, she shakes her head again. "I didn't want to. Every time I did, I could feel a part of myself revolting, screaming at me to stop. But I was too far gone. Too lost inside myself to do anything except blindly follow their commands."

She lapses into silence, and when it doesn't look like she's going to tell me any more, I ask softly, "What happened?"

Lifting her gaze, she looks at me through watery eyes. "Cam did. Lawrence had been talking more and more about me coming to live with him. I'd shut down years ago. I was a mere shell of myself, yet I knew whatever he had planned for my future would destroy the last thread of who I am. I...I would have done anything to avoid that."

I don't like the way she's talking, and it only makes me more furious at Lawrence for the pain he's inflicted. As though stealing her from her home—because there's no way he wasn't involved— and hiding her in his own company, away from the rest of society, guaranteeing she was isolated and alone wasn't enough. He had also to destroy any hope she could have for a future by ensuring she would forever remain chained to him.

I can feel my blood boiling as it pounds through my veins, demanding vengeance. Every single one of those sick fucks is going to pay for what Hadley has had to endure. I'll rip their fucking heads off myself.

As the adrenaline pumps through my body, anger swelling like a tsunami within me, I throw open the car door, barely getting my seatbelt unclipped before I launch myself from the vehicle. The cool night air does nothing to calm the raging inferno as I walk away from the car, wishing the darkness would just suck me up and expunge my brain of the last fifteen minutes. Knowing what Lawrence had put her through was bad enough, but this...*I* don't even know how to handle this.

I faintly register the car door opening somewhere behind me and before I've given more than a passing thought to the action, I'm striding back toward the car. Hadley is perched on the hood appearing like an angel of darkness in her long dark gown that stands out in such contrast against her alabaster skin as she watches me approach, her face unreadable.

I open my mouth to say something—what I was going to say, I haven't the faintest clue—but Hadley beats me to it.

She peers up at me with vulnerability shimmering in her eyes. Nonetheless, she juts out her chin, righting her armor, and preparing for battle. Although I have no idea what war she thinks she has with me.

"If this changes things between us, I understand."

Her words grind me to a halt as I stare at her in confusion. When I don't say anything, she swallows—the only tell showing she's nervous—and continues speaking.

"I'd get it if, you know, you didn't want to be together now. Knowing what you know. It's a lot to take in, and well, you didn't know what you were signing on for when we agreed to try this dating thing. So, yeah, I, uh, would understand...I guess."

She's rambling, and it would be cute—laughable, really—if it wasn't for the heaviness of her honesty sitting like a lead balloon in the air between us. Unable to go another second without feeling her in my arms, I reach out and wrap my hand around her wrist to tug her toward me.

I sink my other hand into her soft, luscious curls, crushing my lips against hers and swallowing her gasp of surprise as I drown in the taste of her.

She thinks this could change things between us? She's so

fucking wrong. It only makes me want her more. Not only is her strength awe-inspiring, but I want to be the one to show her what love is. I want to be the one to hold her when she has a nightmare, to bring a smile to her face on rainy days, to bask in the light that is Hadley Parker when she laughs. Most importantly, I want to be at her side when she gets the justice she deserves. I'll ride into battle with her, bleed every fucker out, and when we're done, we'll burn that motherfucking compound to the ground.

Her small hands fist my shirt, pulling me impossibly closer as our tongues clash like weapons, our kiss ferocious and hungry. I could never get enough of this. Of her.

Pulling back just enough to break the kiss but also so I can still feel her breathless pants against my lips, I stare into her turbulent gray-blue eyes. They're chaotic, churning with so much emotion, and her pupils are dilated as she stares back at me. I'm seeing all of her for the first time—every little part. She's got nothing left to hide. For me, she has peeled back all the layers she usually keeps carefully hidden, revealing all the grim parts of herself that she never allows anyone to see.

I stare deep into her eyes, feeling as though I'm seeing into her very soul. "I love you. There's nothing you could say or do to make me change my mind."

Her eyes widen in surprise, her features softening even though she looks unsure, like she doesn't believe what I'm saying. I get the impression she's never heard those three words before, and why would she? She didn't have anyone to tell her, to *show* her what love was.

After a moment's hesitation, she tightens her hold on my shirt, yanking me toward her, her lips closing over mine. Her kiss is scorching and my body comes alive, acknowledging her touch. It's heated and desperate, but it's also a promise. As my tongue slides over hers, I can taste everything she feels but doesn't know how to put into words.

"I'm not sure I know what love is," she whispers softly, making my heart ache for her. "I've never experienced it before. I don't know what it feels like…but if there were ever someone I thought I could fall in love with, it would be you."

Cupping her cheeks in my hands, I kiss her harshly, taking as much from this moment as possible and burning it into my memory. Our time is running out. We'll have to head back to campus soon, and the second I tell her so, she'll re-erect her walls. I want to remember every second of this moment, when I had all of her.

Eventually ending the kiss, I rest my forehead against hers, committing to memory how fiercely beautiful she looks at this moment, before I murmur, "We should probably get back to campus."

Agreeing, the two of us head back to the car. As I open the door, I can hear my phone vibrating in its holder in the center console, and it goes off again as I start the engine. Sighing, I already suspect who is blowing up my phone as I lift it out. Yup, as expected, it's Hawk, wondering where we are. I fire off a quick reply, letting him know I'm taking Hadley back to campus. As soon as it's sent, a notification pops up saying it's been read, and dots appear at the bottom of the screen. *Great. He has more to say already.*

Hawk: *Drop her off at her door and meet us at our apartment.*

Such a demanding asshole. I can understand why he grates on Hadley's nerves. She would deny it if asked, but as much as his bossy attitude annoys her, I think she secretly likes the fact that he cares enough to boss her around.

"Everything okay?"

"Yeah, fine. The guys are just checking in, wondering where you disappeared off to."

Ignoring Hawk's demand, I throw my phone back in its holder

as Hadley rolls her eyes. Starting the engine, I laugh, and the two of us head back to campus.

We're halfway down the road when she says, "You never answered my question." Her detached tone tells me she's carefully tucked her heart away again and re-erected her walls, just like I knew she would.

I let out a long exhale. I'd been hoping to avoid discussing it, but I should have known she wouldn't let it slide.

"They have me going through profiles and telling them which kids I think could be molded into what they want and which ones won't hack it."

I glance briefly at Hadley, finding her jaw clenched tightly. Her leg bounces in irritation.

"How do you even know that?" she asks, a curious ring to her voice.

"I don't, really. For some of the older kids, I can look at their history. If the police have brought them in for fighting or assault or anything like that, but for the most part, it's just looking at how shitty their upbringing has been and trying to work out if that's enough to help them survive what our parents are going to do to them."

The way I say it, with no emotion in my voice, makes it sound so clinical. Over the last few months, I've managed to remove myself from the reality of what I'm doing. I've learned to set aside the wrongness of what's being asked of me when my father hands me those profiles every week and tells me to pick the best ones. The first few times, the guilt nearly ate me alive. I barely ate or slept for weeks. I *had* to learn to live with the fucked-up decisions I was being forced to make. It wasn't only my life that relied on it but West's too. He might not trust me—hell, he doesn't even know me—but where I come from, family matters. Whether it's the family you're born into or the one you make for yourself, it *means* something. A fuckton more than whatever 'family' means to the rich assholes here; they don't give a shit about anyone but themselves.

"They want me to go to the compound and start assessing them face to face," I say bleakly, noticing how Hadley tenses beside me. "I have to go. They'll hurt West if I don't."

I spare her a quick glance, and she nods her head sharply, understanding why I have to go, but I don't miss her tight expression as I return my gaze to the dark road in front of us. In fairness, we don't know for sure that they would hurt West. Maybe it's all a bluff, and they wouldn't really hurt one of their own kids. But is it a risk worth taking, testing them to see what they do? Hell no.

Driving onto campus, I park my car in the staff parking lot and walk Hadley to her dorm. Very few people are around. Most of them are probably still at that pointless party, and anyone left on campus has better things to do than lurking outside the dorms on a Saturday night.

"Lock your door when you get in."

She gives me a placating smile that's full of attitude. *Yeah, yeah, I know she can take care of herself. Doesn't mean I'm not going to worry, though.* Rolling my eyes, I gently push her back, nudging her toward the building.

"Get in there, you pest."

She chuckles, waving at me over her shoulder before disappearing behind the door.

When she's out of sight, I take off toward the guys' dorms, climb the stairs to the fourth floor, and knock on the door.

With a perpetual scowl gracing his face, Hawk answers. "You should have told one of us you were leaving," he snarks before I even enter their apartment. Seriously, what is so permanently lodged up his ass that he can't even give me a fucking hello before ripping into me?

"It wasn't exactly planned," I drawl dismissively as I walk past him into their open-plan living and kitchen area and spot the other three musketeers sprawled out across the sofas.

"What happened?" Hawk demands, gaining the attention of the others as their eyes pin me in place.

"Nothing. Our father was killing her with boredom," I

respond calmly, looking at West. His features tighten, but I ignore him, turning back to glare at Hawk. "What the hell were your parents thinking, throwing her into that party tonight?

"I think the better question is, what are *you* doing *for* our parents?" West snaps from behind me, making me spin to face him.

"What are you talking about?"

"We had a meeting with our parents today, and they so kindly informed us that you were already working for them. So what the hell have you been doing that you didn't think to tell us about?"

I grit my teeth. "I can't tell you."

West scoffs. "Of course not. That's not suspicious as fuck. How do we even know you're on our side? You could be a mole, reporting back everything we say and do."

"Seriously?" After all the shit I've had to do the last few months—shit that has slowly eaten away at my soul—all in order to keep his ungrateful ass alive, and he accuses me of this?

Before I know it, I've closed the distance between us. Wrapping my hand around the front of his shirt, he glowers back defiantly as I hiss at him, "Everything I've done has been to protect you. You have no fucking idea what I've had to do to keep you safe. To keep *you* alive."

Hesitation and confusion flicker across his face, but they're gone in an instant.

"I never asked you to do that," he bites back, infuriating me further.

"Why would you do that?" Mason asks, interrupting the stare-off between my brother and I.

"Because where I come from, family means something." I take a step back from West but keep my gaze on his. "You can be pissed at me all you want, but we *are* family, and that means something to me.

"What do you even know about family?" West sneers, even though there's a curious lilt to his voice, which is the only reason I don't fucking punch him.

"I lost the closest thing I've ever had to a sister and, not long after, my brothers. I've been mourning their loss every day for years, so don't tell me I don't know anything about family." The words are nothing more than a furious snarl, and I'm practically shouting by the time I'm done.

It shouldn't be this fucking difficult. After feeling alone for so long, I just wanted the opportunity to get to know West, to maybe find somewhere I belong. Since we have the same blood running through our veins, I wondered if he felt as lost and confused in this world as I do, but it's obvious he doesn't. Unlike me, he's managed to hold on to the family he built around him, and he's made it painfully clear he's not looking to add to it—not in the form of a brother, anyway.

Yet, the thought to cut and run, and leave him to stew in this fucked-up shit, never once crossed my mind. Maybe it's because I know I'd be leaving Hadley too, or perhaps it's the urge to protect West, no matter how big of an asshole he might be to me. He might not want me as a brother, but in my heart, he's always been mine. So regardless of whether or not he wants me here, I'm fucking staying.

The sound of the front door banging open has all of us turning to face the intruder, everyone on alert and ready to jump into action.

My eyes widen as I take in all nearly six feet of Hadley standing in the doorway, glowering at Hawk and the guys. She's changed out of her dress into a pair of short shorts and a loose t-shirt. Her hair is piled up on top of her head, with loose strands already falling out of it. She shouldn't look intimidating, but with the dark look on her face and the glint in her eye that is intended to deter anyone who so much as thinks of crossing her, she's pretty fucking scary looking. *Why do I find that such a fucking turn-on?*

Her abrupt and unexpected appearance breaks the tension in the air and, thankfully, stops any of these dickheads from asking me any more personal questions.

"What the—" Cam murmurs, gaping at her with hearts in his eyes. *Pathetic sap.* I give him a week before he realizes he can never just be friends with her and makes his move.

"What are you doing here?" Hawk barks.

"I saw Beck coming this way, and I know what you four idiots are like, always sticking together and ganging up on everyone. I figured if you were at least going to give him a hard time for not telling you we left, the least I could do is be here so he has someone on his side."

"We weren't—" Mason begins, earning a raised eyebrow from Hadley.

"How did you even get in here?" Hawk demands, ignoring her little speech. I have to say though, it feels kinda good that she came to back me up. Not that I give a shit what these assholes have to say, but still, it's been a long time since I had anyone in my corner.

She shrugs, giving him a quizzical look. "Who doesn't know how to pick a lock these days?"

Hawk grumbles under his breath, something about normal people not knowing how to do half the shit she can, except he's got no idea just how far from *normal* Hadley truly is. She's exceptional.

Rolling her eyes, she slams the door shut behind her, stalking across the space toward us with all the attitude in the world.

"Well, I guess since we're all here, we, uh, have some news," Hawk declares, looking reluctant to broach whatever he needs to discuss as he moves the conversation on to a new topic—*thank fuck*. He's rubbing the back of his neck and looking anywhere else but at Hadley. His behavior is making me nervous. *What the fuck could he have to tell us?*

Glancing at the other three, they look equally uncomfortable.

I feel Hadley's arm lightly brush against mine in a silent act of reassurance, likely having also picked up on the sudden tension in the room.

"Our parents want us to continue with the girl of the month

tradition," Hawk blurts out quickly, similar to ripping off a Band-aid.

Hadley opens her mouth to protest, only Hawk speaks again before she can say anything.

"And they've insisted you take part as well."

Eh, what now? There's no way Hadley's about to publicly date some rich pompous fucker with a permanent hard-on. Hell no. Based on the various looks of disgust and anger on the other guys' faces, they agree.

There's a moment of silence while everyone waits with bated breaths—like the calm before the storm. You know shit's about to hit the fan, but you can't do anything but wait for it to come.

"What?" The word is a sharp bark, but her voice sounds slightly higher than usual. "You'll have to repeat that. I'm certain I heard you wrong 'cause there is *no fucking way* I'm going to stand up and pick one of those sorry sacks of shit to fake date."

She looks wholly revolted by the idea as she uses her fingers to make air quotes.

"We don't like the idea either," Mason assuages. "However they've already threatened West's life if we don't do as they say."

"Yeah, but that's for the business, right?" Hadley's eyes jump between the four of them. "They wouldn't kill him just because you refuse to date some girl at school."

The guys all look at one another, a silent communication occurring between them that Hadley nor I are privy to.

"Honestly, we don't know." Hawk sighs, running his hand through his short blond hair in irritation, mussing it up.

"I've been thinking about it," West musses, his brows furrowed in thought. "And I don't think they would. I'm their only bargaining chip. If they offed me, there wouldn't be anyone else to threaten all of you with."

"Maybe so, but that sounds like too big a risk to take." As much as I don't want Hadley having to act like a piece of arm candy to some rich prick or see her upset at having to watch the guys do the same, I equally don't want West to end up hurt or dead just because they decide to push the boundaries of what they can and cannot get away with.

"It's your decision, man," Mason says to West. "It's your life that's at stake. We'll all do whatever you want."

Hawk and Hadley both nod their heads in agreement, the movement strangely synced and oddly similar in a freaky twin way.

West's gaze focuses on Hadley, the two of them sharing some sort of moment before he reaches his hand out for her to take. Slipping her hand into his, he tugs her toward him so she's standing right in front of him.

"Fuck them," he states confidently, his eyes never leaving Hadley's face. "Let's run the school our way."

It takes a second, her eyes jumping back and forth between his, as though she's checking if he's sure about his decision. She must see the resolve in his eyes as a bright grin splits her face. His decision to go against our parents worries me. I have no idea what they might do in retaliation, but I can understand that none of them can continue doing our parents' bidding with this stupid tradition. Especially if Hadley is now going to be involved.

Wrapping her arms around his neck, she gives him a quick kiss before he spins her around in his arms, her back flush to his chest and his hands resting possessively on her hip and abdomen.

"Alright then," Hawk agrees. "Fuck them."

CHAPTER 6

Hadley

"No." I shake my head, adamant I'm not letting Hawk browbeat me into doing what he wants. "I am not sitting at your table."

Hawk glowers at me, like I'm deliberately being difficult. "You have to."

"I don't *have* to do anything," I bite back.

"We have to present a united front. If everyone sees that we have accepted you into the fold, they will treat you with the same fear and respect they treat us."

"I don't care what any of those rich assholes have to say about me."

Hawk throws his hands up in exasperation. "You have no idea what it's going to be like. You're basically living every girl's fantasy right now, and the guys will be all over you, hoping you might be their meal ticket."

I scrunch my nose, but Hawk's words don't scare me.

"I can handle myself. I did kill a mercenary, after all," I snark with a devilish grin, making him roll his eyes.

"Yeah, by accident."

The smirk drops off my face, quickly replaced with a fierce glower as my hands clench into fists, and I hold back the urge to show him exactly what I'm capable of. It was no fucking accident—just like the other mercenary I killed.

"Have you forgotten I beat your ass without much effort?" My voice is sickly sweet, and I top it off with a deadly grin, making him scowl. Well, tough shit. It's something I'll happily hold over his head and taunt him with when he's being an asshole, which is pretty much all the time.

"It's the *Princes'* table," I argue. "Meaning it's only for boys. Obviously, no previous daughters of the founding families have been forced to sit there."

"That's because no daughters have ever come to Pac," he retorts.

"What?" I gape, surprised. "Why? Where do they go?"

"Some finishing school for girls." He shrugs. "Mason could tell you. His sister is at one."

"His what?" My head is spinning with all this new information. "Mason has a sister?"

"Yeah. She's a couple of years younger than us. I haven't seen her since we were kids. I'm pretty sure Mason's only seen her a handful of times."

"Doesn't she come home for the holidays?"

"Maybe for a bit over the summer."

What the hell? I have so many questions, yet it's clear from Hawk's vague responses that he's not going to be able to give me any actual answers.

"Are you going to be picking a girl this month?" I ask, moving on to a different topic. I know we discussed this last night, but there's really no reason for him—or Cam technically, but my stomach churns violently when I think about that—to not pick someone, and at least keep their parents happy. However, if he thinks I'm about to sit at that table and watch him make out with some tramp while I try to eat my breakfast, he's got another thing coming. It was nauseating enough having to witness it from across the hall.

"What do you mean?"

"I know Mason and West agreed not to pick girls anymore, but that doesn't mean you can't pick someone."

"None of us will be picking girls." He must see the surprise on my face as he explains, "We stand together. If one of us decides something, we all go along with it."

"I thought that just applied to bullying," I snide.

Yeah, I'm still a little pissy over that.

I don't understand that level of loyalty. Of just blindly following someone else's orders because you have such a tight bond with them. It makes no sense to me. I think it's beyond stupid how easily the others fell in line with Hawk just because he didn't like me. What the fuck was all of that about anyway?

He rolls his eyes. "It applies to everything. That's what loyalty is."

"Loyalty is all of you being total dicks because *you* decided for no reason you didn't like me?"

I can feel my blood heating at the reminders of what assholes they all were—Hawk refusing to give me a bottle of water, the others not standing up to him or telling him what an asshat he was being, the stupid fucking video he and Cam emailed to everyone, the *grapefruit*.

"It's having one another's backs," he retorts. "It's understanding that, no matter what, someone will always be on your side—even if you're wrong. It's knowing that you're not alone. When you grow up not being able to trust anyone, knowing you have three people who will support you in anything you decide… it makes life bearable."

A heavy silence falls between us, threaded with tension, although underneath it, there's a slither of similarity. We both grew up not being able to trust the people around us. Not knowing who we could rely on and who would only use us for their own gain. The difference is that Hawk never had to survive on his own.

"I wouldn't know." There's a heaviness in my voice as I wonder how different things might have been. "I didn't have anyone I could trust."

The anger bleeds out of his face, the tight lines smoothing until he's looking at me softly. What appears like regret flashes across his eyes, but it disappears so quickly I'm left wondering if I imagined it. It's most likely that I only saw what I wanted to see.

He sighs as he steps toward me, closing the distance between us. "I know I was an ass to you." *Understatement of the year.* "But things are different now."

"Because I'm your sister," I say, spelling it out. The thing is, I don't want things to be different just because I'm related to him. Maybe it's stupid, but I want him to actually *like* me. To *want* to be friends with me. I don't want him to just put up with me because we share the same DNA and the guys have forced him into it.

"I guess you're kinda growing on me," he grumbles with a small, barely there smile lifting one side of his lips. "Like unwanted mold."

I snort, breaking the tension between the two of us before his expression sobers once again.

"I'm serious, though. I'm sorry you've had to go through life alone, but that's not the case anymore. Whatever happens between you and the guys, I'll still be here for you."

Well, fuck me, this grumpy brother of mine might just have a heart, after all.

"So," I begin hesitantly, gnawing on my bottom lip. It's early evening, and I'm curled up on Emilia's bed with her. She's been nagging me all day to catch her up on the events at the party last night. Having just spilled all the very unexciting details, I'm now trying to broach the subject of me sitting at the Princes' table.

Yup, the fucking asshole suckered me into eating with them. The other three shitheads agreed with Hawk—of course—and I was totally outnumbered, with no actual argument for why I didn't want to sit at their table. Other than that, I just didn't want to.

Emilia looks at me impatiently with a quirked eyebrow.

"Ihavetostarteatingattheprincestable," I blurt out, the words all running into one another in my haste.

Her eyes widen as she tries to comprehend what I just said. "You, what?"

Grimacing, I repeat myself, "I have to start eating at the Princes' table for breakfast."

"Yeah, I figured you would," she remarks sadly before plastering on a smile.

"I'm sorry." I reach for her hand, giving it a squeeze. "I'd much rather sit with you than up there being gawked at."

Her smile turns genuine. "I know you would, except no girl in their right mind would turn down eating breakfast with all that hotness."

I can't help but laugh. She does have a point.

"Besides, we can eat lunch together on the days I'm not busy, right?"

"Definitely," I promise.

"And I'll still have Michael in the mornings."

"Crap. Michael. I should probably explain all of this to him before he finds out tomorrow, right?" My eyes widen as realization dawns. "He probably already knows. Most of the school was there last night."

Emilia shrugs. "He might not. The scholarship kids rarely listen to the school's gossip. It's up to you, in any case. You could tell him when we see him later."

We're meeting Michael tonight for our standard weekly movie night. Usually, we do it on Friday or Saturday, only things have been a little hectic the last few days, and I had to push it back. I guess tonight is as good a night as any to tell him.

Several hours later, the three of us are sprawled out in the movie theater with our popcorn while Emilia hums and haws over which movie she wants to watch. I don't know why it's such a big decision. She can always pick the other movie next time it's her night to decide—or, more likely, she'll sucker me into picking it on my night.

On the plus side, it gives me the perfect opportunity to broach the whole Davenport subject with Michael. Emilia is the only other person I've told, and I'm a nervous wreck as I try to find the words to tell him. It's strange because I didn't feel this way when I told Emilia. Sure, I was nervous, mainly because I didn't want to lose her again. However, with Michael, it feels different. I'm not sure why, though.

"Uh, Michael. Can we talk for a sec?"

He looks up from where he was typing on his phone beside me, and I notice Emilia giving me an encouraging smile from his other side before focusing back on her movie choices, trying to give us some semblance of privacy. We discussed it earlier, and she offered to sit out tonight if I wanted time to talk to Michael alone, but I feel more confident with her here. I worry I would have chickened out otherwise.

"Sure, what's up?"

Biting on my lower lip, I swallow around the lump in my throat before continuing, "So, some stuff is going to come out tomorrow about me, and I wanted you to hear it from me first."

"Okay," he says hesitantly, drawing out the word as he looks at me with wary confusion.

"Uh…" I fiddle with a strand of my hair, glancing away from him. "This is kind of difficult to say, and I only found out a few weeks ago, so I get it. I struggled to wrap my head around it too. Honestly, I'm still coming to terms with it all—"

"Hadley." His tone is sharp but soft, halting my rambling as he places a hand on mine. "Just spit it out."

"I'm a Davenport."

His eyes widen before his brows furrow, confusion evident in his brown irises.

"What?"

"I'm a Davenport," I repeat. "Hawk's my brother."

"I don't...How?"

I explain the craziness of the last few weeks to him, skipping over a lot of the details and leaving out anything that would raise red flags to the fact I'm dating two of the Princes—he definitely doesn't need to know that yet.

"Wow, that's insane," he mutters when I'm finished, still trying to wrap his head around everything I've told him.

"Yeah, you can say that again." I chuckle awkwardly.

"Is that why they've been nicer lately?" His brows furrow. "But they've been acting differently toward you all semester. How long have you all known?"

"Oh, well, the guys knew before they told me," I blurt. I don't know why I lie. I guess I don't want him to know I've known for two months and I'm only telling him now. We are supposed to be friends, after all, but there's no other explanation for the guys' behavior.

"And they had some making up to do after the shit they pulled last semester," Emilia tacks on helpfully.

Michael nods like that all makes sense, lapsing into silence as he mulls it all over.

"Okay, *The Princess Diaries*, it is," Emilia proclaims excitedly, having finally made her decision. I groan internally. *Great, another rom-com.*

THE DINING HALL FALLS INTO A DEATHLY HUSH AS WE WALK IN THE next morning. Eyes follow us as we stride toward the Princes' table—can it still be called that now? Pretty much every asshole in here was at the party, and whispers have been running rampant all weekend, so even the other scholarship kids probably know who I am by now.

Reaching the table, I stand beside Hawk, with Mason on my left, Cam on the other side of him, and West at the far end of the table.

"I'm sure you've all heard by now," Hawk begins, his voice booming across the otherwise silent room as everyone clings to his every word. "Hadley is my long-lost sister, Elizabeth."

Just one more fucking thing I can't get used to. Apparently, the change of name is non-negotiable. The school has already updated its system, and everything now says 'Elizabeth Davenport'. I was even offered the top floor of the girls' dorm to do with as I please —an offer I quickly refused, to the shock of the admin woman who couldn't seem to understand why I would want to keep my room on the same floor as the scholarship girls.

"That means she's one of us. No one is to mess with her." He looks pointedly at Bianca, who is glaring daggers in my direction, steam practically pouring out of her ears as she vibrates with silent fury. I guess she's feeling more confident today, surrounded by her friends and peers. "Or they will deal with us."

Jeez, he makes it seem like I couldn't handle any of these pampered pricks myself, and I have to hold back an eye roll at his words. I swear, I roll my eyes so much at the shit that comes out of his mouth, they are going to stick to the back of my head one day soon.

I'm so not done with Bianca, though. After the abuse she has hurled my way all year, not to mention the shit she pulled at the Valentine's Day dance, making me doubt Hawk and the guys, she is in for some serious hurt this semester. The fact I'm practically invincible now has a smirk curling at the corners of my lips as I smile darkly at her, causing her eyes to widen a fraction. *That's right, bitch. You better sleep with one eye open 'cause I'm coming for you.*

"What about the girl of the month tradition?" someone calls out.

"Yeah, is she going to get to choose a guy?"

Whispers break out at that suggestion, and I have to force my facial expression to remain neutral, not giving away how unappealing that idea sounds. There isn't one sniveling idiot in this hellhole I'd willingly put up with for a whole month.

"No," Mason growls, glowering in the direction of whoever spoke up. Based on the guys' pissed-off expressions the other night, they didn't like the thought of me being included in their stupid tradition any more than I did. Still, we haven't had a chance to actually discuss it—it kind of seemed redundant since we've decided to fuck the whole tradition. However, Mason's sexy growling tone makes it obvious how much he hates the idea, and I press my lips together to restrain my smirk at his possessive nature. *What can I say, his jealousy makes me feel all sorts of sappy, girly feelings.*

"There will be no more girl of the month tradition," Hawk continues, speaking over the top of them and sparking an uproar of disagreement amongst the girls in the hall.

"Why?" someone shouts.

"This is ridiculous. You can't just ignore tradition," an angry voice calls out, and several others nod their heads in agreement before Hawk raises his hands.

"The decision is final," he barks, glowering at the crowd with steely eyes, daring anyone to question him. "Things are going to change around here." Whispers break out around the room as students share unsure looks with one another. "Everyone seems to have forgotten *we* are in charge. *We* are the Princes, and what we say is law."

As the warning bell goes off to tell everyone to hurry their asses up and get to class, his penetrating gaze roams around the hall, his cold expression enough to silence any other complaints.

"Get to class," Mason barks in a threatening tone that has everyone jumping into action.

The hall is a chaos of noise, students gossiping and

complaining to one another, speculating about the turn of events as they get up from their tables and head to class.

"Well, that was fun. So glad you talked me into all of this," I grumble sarcastically, my attitude earning me an eye roll from Hawk, which I promptly ignore, focusing on Cam and Mason. "English?"

"You two go on. I'll catch up." Mason winks at me, and I can't tell if he's trying to give Cam and me some time alone or if he genuinely has something he needs to do before class. There's no denying that things have been tense between Cam and me lately. There's still none of his old flirty banter and easy conversation—which I miss terribly. Instead, everything feels stifled and awkward, but at least he's no longer avoiding me, so I guess there's that.

"Alright, we'll catch you later." Cam grabs his bag, and with a final wave at the others, we head out of the dining hall.

As we make our way to class, everything is a complete one-eighty to how it was last week. Girls I don't even recognize greet me by name—the wrong name, of course—and guys blatantly check me out, giving me flirtatious smirks as I walk past.

"What the hell?" I whisper to Cam. "What is happening right now?"

He snorts, shaking his head. "Welcome to the top of the food chain. Now everyone wants to be your best friend, or date you."

I scrunch my nose up. "No thanks."

"Hey, Elizabeth," some guy calls out as I reach the classroom door, giving me a typical dude chin-lift greeting as he walks past.

"Who the fuck is that?" I ask Cam, confused.

"One of the many leeches that will crawl out of the woodwork and attempt to stick themselves to you."

"Gross. Make them stop," I groan, taking my usual seat and lifting out my notebook and tablet. I'm already not liking all of this extra attention.

Cam laughs at me, but I'm being serious.

"No can do," he unhelpfully sing-songs as he sits beside me, taking far too much pleasure from my pain. "It's all part and parcel of being a Davenport. May as well get used to it, *Elizabeth*."

"Don't call me that," I snarl, my sharp tone making him raise his eyebrows.

"It's only a name."

"My name is Hadley." I seethe out the words so it's perfectly fucking clear for him. "Regardless of what other name these idiots call me, *that* is my name. It's the name *I* chose. Hadley is who I am. Not Elizabeth, or anything else. Had-ley." I spell it out for him loud and clear while he looks at me in bewilderment.

He doesn't get it, and why would he. He's never had to live his life as someone he never wanted to be. I grew up being D. A fucking letter. The same as everyone at the compound. I don't know if the D was for Davenport, or D for Dove, or if it was just the next letter in the alphabet when I walked through the door. It doesn't even matter what it stands for because D is my past.

D is the scared kid who cried herself to sleep every night. D is the assassin who had to kill people to ensure her own survival. D is *not* who I am anymore. And I'm sure as fuck not Elizabeth, either. After having so many rights withheld from me, the least I fucking deserve is to pick my own goddamn name. I picked Hadley. I *am* Hadley. The rest of these assholes can call me whatever the fuck they want, but Cam and the others, *will* call me by my goddamn name.

He raises both of his hands in surrender. "Okay. Sorry. I was only teasing. Hadley suits you much better, anyway."

When he looks at me like I'm crazy, I realize I probably went a little overboard. He was only joking, after all. Blame it on the stress of the last few days and the complexity I'm developing from carrying around so many different identities. After everything this morning at breakfast, and all the unwanted attention I've been getting, his little joke just sent me over the edge.

The rest of the day is the same. I swear more people have tried to engage me in conversation today than have spoken to me since

I arrived at Pac Prep. By the time lunch rolls around, I'm fucking exhausted.

I'm not paying any attention as I order food at the kiosk and take a seat at my usual table. The Princes' table is always free, but I'm more than happy to only sit there when I have to. I've had enough people staring at me today; I don't need them all gawking at me while I shovel food in my mouth.

I drop my bag on the chair beside me, sagging back in my seat and closing my eyes, needing a moment to myself. They've only been closed for a few seconds when the sound of someone sitting down opposite me has me huffing out a breath. Assuming it's Hawk, I open my eyes to scowl at him, yet I'm taken by surprise to find another weirdo I don't know slouching in a chair at *my* table with a cocky smirk on his face, acting like he fucking belongs here.

"Who the fuck are you?" I snap.

Yup, I've totally lost any control I had over my composure. Can't I just eat a fucking sandwich in peace?!

His eyes widen at my sharp tone, but my closed-off expression and unmistakable fuck-off vibes aren't enough to get him to take a hike.

"You should come to the party with me this weekend, baby." The guy leers at me in such a way that he's obviously thinking about all the dirty things he'd do to me at the party—evidently, he has a death wish.

I pretend like I'm giving his offer some consideration, letting my eyes roam over his face before dropping down to take in his broad chest and muscular biceps. He's attractive, but the stench of arrogance coming off of him is suffocating. I know Mason, West, and Cam all have that same air about them, but somehow it comes across as sexy and domineering. On this guy, it just makes him seem like a pretentious dickwad.

I scrunch my face, letting him know I'm unimpressed by what I see and internally preening when his features tighten and his jaw ticks.

"No, I don't think so. Finishing the night unsatisfied is not my idea of a fun Friday night."

His body tenses and he leans forward in his seat, losing his calm, cool façade as his hand clenches into a fist. Rising out of his chair until he looms over the table in an attempt to cower me, he growls out in a menacing tone, "What did you just say?"

Unfazed, I lean back in my chair. *The poor guy must have a hearing problem. Maybe I need to speak louder.*

"I said," I begin in a much louder tone, attracting the interest of students from nearby tables, "even in your dreams, your teeny-weeny peen couldn't get a girl off."

Students at the tables around us snicker behind their hands as they watch us. The guy's face reddens with anger, and he looks like he's about to launch himself across the table when a large hand slams down on his shoulder, anchoring him in place.

"What's going on here?" Mason demands, his usual impassive expression in place as his eyes dart between the two of us. The only hint that he's angry is the dangerous gravelly tone of his voice as he spears the nameless dude with a cold enough stare to have his heart stuttering to a stop.

"This guy was trying to get me to go to the party with him this weekend and didn't seem to like my answer." I shrug innocently.

"You were being a bitch," the guy protests.

He winces as Mason's grip on his shoulder tightens to the point of pain, the move a muted demand for the asshole to watch his tone.

"You were being an arrogant asshat," I argue back. "Next time, try getting to know a girl for five seconds first. And for god's sake, fucking ask her instead of acting like a cocky shithead."

"Fuck off, Joshua, and don't talk to her again," Mason snaps, shoving the guy away from the table.

Stumbling over his feet, he glowers at us before stalking off, not daring to face off against a Prince.

"Why are you always pissing people off?" Mason huffs, sitting down in the now vacant chair opposite me.

"Me? He's the one that came over here and was bothering me. Besides, if you'd had the day I've had, you'd snap at some fucker too."

He grins. "I might have something that will cheer you up." I perk up at his words, curious as to what it could be. It would have to be something pretty fucking spectacular to get me out of my crappy mood.

"What is it?"

He leans forward in his seat so no one around us can overhear him. "There's a fight night tomorrow. I thought you might like to come."

Excitement thrums through me. *Hell yes! Beating the shit out of some assholes is exactly what I need.*

"You can't fight, though," he tacks on, pouring cold water over the happy light beginning to spark inside me at the thought of slamming my fist into some idiot's face.

"That's not any fun." I pout.

"Babe." He chuckles. "There's no way any of the guys here would fight you after last time. And we can't let you fight us in front of them."

I tap my finger against my chin as an idea comes to mind.

"What if we had our own fight night afterward?"

I see the second he misinterprets my words, lust flaring in his eyes as they dilate. "You want me to pin you beneath me and fuck your brains out, Little Warrior?" he growls in a sexy as fuck husk that has my panties growing damp.

"I'm not going to say no to that." A coy smile plays on my lips as I lean in toward him, crossing my legs in such a way that my foot deliberately runs up his calf under the table. "But that's not quite what I was thinking. The six of us could have our own exclusive fight club after everyone else has fucked off. That way, no one can witness you get your asses kicked by a girl." I smirk, shrugging a shoulder innocently like it's no skin off my teeth if he says no. He's not going to say no, however.

His eyes sparkle in exhilaration, more than ready to rise to the challenge I've just laid down. "The six of us?"

"Beck too. He usually comes to watch the fights. I'm pretty sure he could even give you a run for your money," I jibe.

"Ha, I'd like to see the old man try." He laughs, making me shake my head at him. Beck's only like three years older than us. Certainly not *old* by any definition.

"So you're game?" I ask, delight threading my voice at the promise of violence.

"Little Warrior, I'd agree just to watch you throat-punch Hawk again. That was fucking priceless."

A grin lights up my face as I laugh. *Yeah, that was pretty fucking epic.*

"Speaking of the asshole, where is he?"

"Ah, we usually have lunch at our place, away from prying eyes, so I figured I'd come to get you."

When my food arrives, I get a to-go box for it, and the two of us leave the inquisitive eyes of the dining hall behind us as we head for a quiet lunch with the others.

CHAPTER 7

Hadley

There's a buzzing under my skin, and I'm on edge, bouncing on the balls of my feet as we make our way toward the clearing in the forest. Blood and violence are exactly what I need after the last few days of being gawked at like a fucking zoo animal. I miss being a fucking nobody. I've been feeling stifled, suffocated under everyone's attention and this newfound fame. But it's nothing a sweaty brawl can't rectify.

"You have the same excited look on your face that other girls get when they find the perfect pair of shoes." Cam laughs.

"It's been far too long since I've been in a fight, and beating on a bag hasn't done anything to shake off the annoyance from the last few days."

"You just killed a mercenary the other week," Hawk argues.

"YEAH, BUT I'VE HAD TO PUT UP WITH YOUR SHITTY ATTITUDE," I quip. "It would make any sane person crave an outlet for all their pent-up aggression." He snorts like I'm being melodramatic, but it's not like he's had a personality transplant. He might not hate me anymore, but he's as cranky and dickish as ever. "Just be thankful I haven't taken it out on you yet," I say sweetly, fully intending to change all of that tonight.

He grumbles something under his breath that I'm sure would only piss me off, but I get distracted as we enter the clearing. West gets to work setting up flashlights, spacing them out so they form a large circle while Hawk and Mason stretch.

"How did all of this start?" I ask, looking around the ring. The glow from the flashlights makes it look eerie and ominous, and a shiver of anticipation rolls down my spine. "Is it another tradition?"

"When we started at Pac, our parents made it clear we had to prove we could control the other students. Some sort of bullshit about proving ourselves capable of taking over for them when we graduate," Cam begins. "Technically, *that* is the tradition. Our forefathers started the girl of the month tradition to control the girls and keep them in line, and there have been various methods used on the guys."

West takes over as he walks back toward us, having placed all of the flashlights around the clearing. "We decided scheduling regular fight nights where the guys worked out their issues with one another would fit best for us."

"What if someone breaks the rules?"

There's a malicious grin on Hawk's face. "They fight us." The dark thrill of excitement in his voice tells me he gets off on inflicting pain just as much as I do. I wonder if that's a Davenport thing or a 'kids with fucked up lives' thing.

"Like with Deke? When he called you out at that party, then Mason fought him in the ring."

"How did you know about that?" Hawk questions, looking up

at me from where he's bent over at the waist, stretching out his hamstrings and lower back.

"It was the first fight I snuck out to watch. It was hot as hell."

Mason grins darkly, throwing me a dirty wink that immediately drenches my panties.

"Exactly," West nods, getting us back on topic. "It only took a few fights back in freshman year before the rest of the guys realized they didn't want to be on the other end of Hawk or Mason's fists."

"Smart," I praise. "And the girls would do whatever you wanted, because they thought they might get a chance of being a girl of the month when senior year rolled around," I say thoughtfully, voicing my thoughts aloud.

"Yup." Popping the p, Cam confirms my line of thought.

"What are you going to do about them now, then? The girls weren't too happy after your little speech yesterday. It won't be long before you have an uprising on your hands. And I'm guessing any grievances amongst the students will get back to your parents."

"Us?" Hawk laughs darkly. "Oh no. *We*"—using his finger, he points at himself and the others—"are in charge of the guys. *You* are now in charge of corralling the girls."

"Me?" I gape. "You must be fucking crazy. I have no idea how to keep those pretentious bitches under control."

Hawk—the infuriating fucking dickhead—shrugs, evidently not giving a shit.

"Seems only fair," he says. "Everyone's gotta prove themselves. And if our parents think you can be useful, they're less likely to retaliate to our little rebellion."

Fuck, he has a point there.

"Fine, the girls can have a fight night too. I'm more than happy to beat the shit out of Bianca and her princess posse."

"Fuck yeah," Cam hoots. "Everyone has to wear bikinis and we'll get a mud pool."

"Unless you're also wearing a bikini and rolling around in the mud, then that's a hard no," I snark, rolling my eyes.

"I mean, if that's what you're into." He gives me a playful wink. It's the most banter I've gotten out of him in a long time, and it's great to see him acting like his old self. He's still awkward when it's just the two of us, but around the others, I can almost pretend that there isn't so much tension between us.

"There's no way that will work with the girls," Hawk argues, tearing apart my fantasy of pummeling the ever-loving shit out of Bianca. *Spoilsport.*

A less exciting yet just as satisfying idea comes to mind. "Do you guys keep dirt on the other students?" I ask.

"Of course we do." Hawk's 'duh' tone grates on my nerves, making me scowl at him. "Why?"

"I have an idea. I need to see what you have, though."

"Yeah, okay. I'll get them for you later," West promises as the noise of students approaching permeates the otherwise quiet evening.

It's not long before a crowd has formed around the makeshift ring. It looks like every boy in the school is here, and I don't miss the confused glances my way. I don't think they're used to seeing a girl present at these things. The clearing is silent as everyone looks at the five of us—well, the four guys—waiting expectantly for…something. Do they ring a bell or beat on a drum or something as some sort of commencement signal?

"This is supposed to be guys only," Deke calls out, glutton for punishment.

"She's one of us," Hawk states in a non-negotiable tone. "She has as much right to be here as we do."

"If we're done with the stupid questions," West drawls, "we're here to fight. So someone get in the ring."

Everyone hesitates for a moment before a freshman steps forward. He calls out another freshman and explains his issue with him—apparently, the other guy slept with his girlfriend.

Personally, I'd be taking issue with the girlfriend, but whatever. Then the fight begins. It's all rather…civilized.

They're stick-thin freshmen with no meat on their bones or muscles to pack a punch, so the fight is pathetic. I know ten-year-olds who could have them unconscious in seconds. Still, as the other guys egg them on, the atmosphere is enough to ease some of the buzzing under my skin.

The fight doesn't last long before another one begins, and on and on it goes. I lose myself in the thrill of it. In watching blood spill as lips are split, the redness that rises to the skin's surface as any accessible body part is bruised. It's nothing like the fast-paced, athletic, deadly fights I'm used to watching, but it's sufficient to quell some of the bloodlust I've been craving.

I'm so lost in watching some guy grab another in a headlock that could easily be broken that I nearly miss a flash of movement in the trees opposite me. My body stiffens, immediately suspecting that it could be another mercenary lurking in the dark, but I relax when I catch sight of Beck, hidden just behind the tree line. He's engrossed in the scene of violence playing out in front of us, watching it with hawk-like eyes.

He needs tonight as much as I do—possibly more. Everything he's had to manage by himself for the last few months has taken its toll on him, but tonight, he can let all of it go. He can exorcise his demons and expel all of his rage on Mason and Hawk. Tonight should help him clear his head and stabilize him a bit, so we can work out our next move. Because there is no fucking way I am letting any of our parents continue to use and abuse us like this.

I've fallen so deep into my own thoughts, sucked in by the idea of bloodshed and retribution, that I don't even realize the fights have ended and the boys are all breaking apart, some of them starting to make their way toward the tree line.

The five of us stand and watch as the other students disappear into the trees one by one or in small groups. As the sound of their voices fades into the distance, everyone else making their way back to the dorms, Beck steps out of the trees.

Out of the corner of my eye, I notice West tense, and I make a point of walking past him on my way to greet Beck. The two of them—well, West in particular—need to sort out their shit.

"Behave," I growl in his ear, not giving him a chance to respond as I close the gap between Beck and us. I meet him on the far side of the ring with a smile on my face as I wrap my arms around his neck and kiss him.

"Right, let's get this show on the road," Hawk calls out, making me smile against Beck's lips.

"Yeah, let's see what you've got, old man," Mason taunts.

Beck gasps in outrage. "What did he just call me?" he murmurs, in a low voice that only I can hear.

I chuckle, turning back toward the guys. Mason is now standing in the center of the ring, staring brazenly at Beck, while the other three are still lined up along one edge.

"No, me first," I call out across the open space, walking back toward them, sensing Beck following behind me. "Then you can let Beck kick your ass."

I smile sweetly as I meet Mason in the middle of the ring, and he scoffs, looking affronted at my suggestion. *I guess we'll soon find out.*

"Alright, Little Warrior, whose balls are you planning on busting tonight?"

I smile wickedly at Hawk. *Obviously, it was going to be him.* I definitely want to try my skills out against Mason someday, but I need him good and fresh for his fight with Beck.

Hawk smirks confidently as he steps forward. "No problem, baby Davenport. Let me prove to you that last time was just a fluke."

Beck snorts behind me before he and Mason both move to stand with West and Cam at the edge of the makeshift ring. "Five bucks she beats him," I hear Beck say.

"Pfft, there's no way I'm taking that action," Mason retorts, shaking his head. "We all saw her last time. There's no way he's beating her."

My smile only grows more prominent at their friendly ribbing, although Hawk doesn't look impressed as he throws them a dirty look over his shoulder before pulling off his top and throwing it toward the outskirts of the ring.

I do the same with my hoodie, leaving me in my sports bra and lycra leggings. In this outfit, I've got plenty of flexibility to move, and with my hair pulled back, nothing can get in my way. Tonight, Hawk's all mine.

"No dick blows," Hawk announces, making me roll my eyes.

"Fine, but no titty shots then. That shit hurts."

"No hitting each other's faces either," West calls out. "We don't need the whole school speculating about what you two have been up to."

Dammit. He's got a point, but still, he's totally killing my fun. Nothing is more satisfying than seeing your opponent walking around with a shiner you delivered.

When Cam calls the fight, we circle each other, both of us testing the waters with glancing blows. We spar back and forth. Occasionally, one of us lands a solid hit to the other's chest or abdomen, but it's not enough to have any lasting impact.

I can tell Hawk is much more focused this time. Although he walked into the ring with a confident attitude, there's not the same cockiness in his movements, making it much harder for me to find an opening to take him down.

It takes a while, but as he goes in to deliver a punch to my kidneys, I get the shot I've been waiting for. Hawk drops his arm just a little, but it's enough for me to knock him round the head, quickly following it with a kick to his leg. He moves to try and grab ahold of my calf, in an attempt to take me to the ground, leaving his head and chest completely exposed. Side-stepping him, I knock him around the head twice more, disorientating him.

On reflex, his arms come up to cover his face, giving me an opening. I rush in, delivering two lightning-quick jabs to his kidney and stomach that have the wind knocked out of him as he doubles over.

"Fucking hell," he wheezes.

Swiping his legs out from underneath him, he crashes to the ground, and I'm left victorious, standing over him with a satisfied grin on my face.

As easy as that.

"I win," I sing-song as Hawk coughs and splutters in the dirt.

"Fuck me, next time you can beat on Mason," he rasps, making me laugh. Stretching out my arm, he slaps his hand into mine, and I help him up off the ground.

"You did well. Much more focused and less cocky than last time."

"Remind me again where you learned to fight like that?" he questions, still sounding pained.

"Just something I picked up along the way." I shrug casually before shouting, "Mason and Beck next," in a feeble attempt to change the subject and distract him as the two of us make our way toward the others.

Beck is dressed more informally than the guys have probably ever seen him. He's wearing a pair of dark-colored basketball shorts and a matching muscle shirt that shows off his large, well-defined biceps and toned arms, giving me a nice view of his tattoo sleeve. His usually styled hair is messier, giving him a more rugged appearance, especially with the short stubble he's rocking. All in all, it's a pretty irresistible picture.

Oops, was that a bit of drool? Subtly swiping at the corner of my mouth, I watch as the show gets even better when both Mason and Beck take off their shirts. *Oh, yes, please.* Both men are built to perfection. While Mason is broader than Beck, and packing more muscle, Beck is leaner and defined but no less powerful looking as he stalks into the middle of the ring with Mason following closely behind.

"Same rules as last time," West calls out.

"Yeah, man, don't hit my titties," Mason jokes, making the corner of Beck's lip tilt up as I belt out a laugh.

The two of them face-off against each other in what is my

favorite wet dream come to life, and when Cam calls the start of the match, there is no slow build-up like there was with Hawk and me.

The two men launch themselves at one another, going straight in for brutal attacks as they pummel any part of their opponent they can reach. It's violent and ferocious—and so fucking hot. My panties are a wet mess. Other girls might get off on their guys being sweet and caring, but this right here—this battle of power and brutality—*this* is what gets me revved up.

It's a fast-paced fight, and for the most part, it's impossible to tell who has the upper hand. The two are evenly matched as they block each other's hits and deliver merciless punches of their own, neither of them holding anything back.

Just when I'm beginning to think there won't be a winner—unless we spend all night standing out here, which doesn't sound all that appealing now that the cold air is blowing against my sweat-coated skin, and my stomach is starting to grumble—Beck delivers some fancy maneuver so quickly that I hardly see it. The next thing I know, he's got Mason in a headlock, his arm squeezing his neck.

Mason fights him like a rabid animal, twisting and turning his torso and punching at any part of Beck he can get at. However, Beck holds firm around his neck until I'm concerned that Mason is going to pass out—he's too much of a heavy fucker to carry all the way back to the dorms.

I don't even realize I've taken a step forward into the ring, until I notice Mason smacking his hand against Beck's arm, the signal that he's tapping out.

"Woohoo!" I cry out, racing toward the two as Beck lets go of his hold around Mason's neck. Mason bends over, placing his hands on his knees as he coughs and splutters. After giving Mason a slap on the back, Beck shifts to face me with a grin. "Underdogs for the win," I shout out, laughing as I launch myself into his open arms, and he spins me around.

It's a rare carefree moment, and I soak up every second of it because you never know when things can take a turn for the worst. One second you can be loving life; the next, everything around you has crashed and burned. So yeah, I take in every aspect of this moment—Beck's white teeth as he laughs and how his arms tighten around my waist. How Mason has a small, rare smile playing at the corner of his lips and the feel of the other guys' eyes as they watch us. In this peaceful moment, Lawrence doesn't exist. I didn't grow up isolated in a compound where I was beaten and tortured into becoming a killing machine. I wasn't robbed of getting to know my brother.

Nope. Instead, I'm a normal teenage girl, feeling content in the arms of the boy she's falling for, while she senses the heated stares of her three other crushes warming her up from the inside out. Like I said—normal.

Setting me back on the ground, Beck keeps an arm around my waist as he turns to Mason, holding out his hand. "Good fight, man," he praises in an act of sportsmanship.

Mason shakes his head with a defeated chuckle, slapping his hand into Beck's. "Yeah, you too, old man. Didn't know you had it in you."

Cam comes strolling over. "Well, well, I never thought I'd see the day Mason got his ass kicked," he exclaims. "Man, you'll be getting beat by baby Davenport next if you aren't careful."

He laughs, and Mason clocks him around the head. "Shut up, asshole."

"You are not calling me that!" I argue.

"Why not?" Cam pouts. "Hawk did."

"He's not calling me that, either. I'm several seconds younger than that dickhead, and I'm not a baby anything. I'm a strong, fierce warrior."

"Yeah, you are, baby." Mason swoops in, draping his arm over my shoulder and tugging me in against him, planting a kiss on my temple. Of course, Beck refuses to move his arm, so I end up wedged between their sweaty chests. Their sweaty, naked chests that look so hot and lickable.

"I think this calls for a celebration," Cam hollers. "Drinks at ours!"

"Sounds good," Hawk shouts back before saying something to West that's too quiet for us to hear. West doesn't look pleased, though he doesn't argue either, so I guess that's progress.

"Dude, I lost," Mason says, looking at Cam in bafflement.

"Exactly." Cam gives him a shit-eating grin. "We're celebrating your first-ever loss. It's the end of an era, man."

I laugh at their antics as Hawk and West start collecting the flashlights and meet us in the middle of the ring. Handing a flashlight each to Cam and Mason, the six of us make our way back through the dark, quiet forest toward the dorms so we can start the celebrations.

CHAPTER 8

West

ALL SIX OF US PILE INTO THE APARTMENT, SPREADING OUT ON THE couches and chairs. I get comfortable on the sofa, leaning back and resting my arm on the armrest while Mason unglues himself from Hadley's side to grab beers from the fridge and hand them out to everyone.

Grabbing Beck's hand, Hadley walks my way, giving me a soft smile before sitting beside me. Her thigh presses against mine, and I have to resist the urge to wrap my arms around her and drag her into my lap. That urge only increases when Beck sits on her other side, and I have to push it down, taking a gulp of beer to distract me from her tantalizing scent. The usual subtle vanilla and honey tones of her shampoo are wrapped up in the muskiness from her fight, and the heady aroma has gone straight to my dick as it presses uncomfortably against the zipper of my jeans. I have to shift awkwardly in my seat, trying not to draw attention to myself.

After our parents insinuated that Beck was working for them, and his outburst the other night about how he'd lost the closest thing he'd ever had to a sister, I did some digging. Not that I found much beyond the usual college and school records.

No evidence of an actual sister, or any other siblings, but I wasn't expecting there to be. When I investigated more into the possible deaths in the Black Creek area to see if I could find this 'sister' he was talking about, it was like looking for a needle in a haystack. The number of people every year who are run down, outright shot, or killed assassination-style, is shocking. Even when I searched for teenage girls—guessing that that's probably the age Beck and his friends were when whatever happened, happened— I still came up with too many potential cases.

Honestly, it sickened me to see so many kids pointlessly killed, all in the name of gang wars. Kids hit by stray bullets while they were out playing or gunned down on their way home from school. Even if they were lucky enough to make it past their child- hood, from what I could tell, they wound up dying for whatever gang they'd pledged their allegiance to. All of it seems like such a senseless waste of life. Yet it looks like the police have all but given up on the town, pulling their men and resources from it and leaving its citizens to fend for themselves.

Is that how Beck grew up? With death and danger on every corner? There was no faking the raw emotion pouring off him the other night when I accused him of not knowing the significance of family. I've never experienced actual loss, but I only had to look into his eyes to see that he had. Whoever his self-made family was, they were everything to him. Is that why he kept seeking me out when he first showed up? Did he see me as some sort of emotional Band-aid that could curtail his grief? I just don't under- stand why he would come here, if not for money. He claims it was to get to know me, but I don't understand how that could be the case. I'm nobody special or important. So why would he sucker himself into becoming a pawn for our father just to be near me? It makes no sense.

Yet, watching him now as he tilts his head back and laughs at something Mason says before glancing down at Hadley with what looks a lot like love in his eyes, he seems relaxed. More himself than I've ever seen him. Out of his stuffy suits and away from the fake persona he wears on campus, he seems so much more like one of us.

He must sense me staring at him as he glimpses over. Our gazes catch for a second before I break away, taking another swig of my beer, but I could have sworn I saw something in that split second—a rare moment of vulnerability or openness. I'm not sure whether he meant to show me so much; even so it was the most open with me he's ever been. Usually, he keeps himself guarded and closed off, rarely allowing anyone to see behind the mask he carefully dons. Hadley seems to be the only one who has seen the real him.

"West." Cam calling my name breaks me out of my thoughts, steering my focus back to the room and whatever they're talking about. "Tell them how much you love to go swimming in the lake at the cabin."

I groan, giving a fake shiver of horror as everyone else laughs. "You couldn't pay me to get back in that lake."

I always hated the lake. I hated the fact that you had no idea what was swimming around in the murky water beneath you. There could be dead bodies or anything just sitting decaying down there. Why would anyone be okay with swimming in that?

The last straw was Cam sneaking up on me and pulling me under the surface. I swear to god I thought an eel or something had gotten ahold of me, and I was going to drown and be forever lost to the muddy lakebed. I've never been more terrified in my life. Strangely, I never set foot in the lake again after that day, and now I get ribbed mercilessly for it.

"What about the time in freshman year when you thought you had herpes." I smirk, causing Cam's face to redden with embarrassment as he glowers at me.

"I thought we agreed to never talk about that again," he hisses.

I shrug, all the while laughing. It was fucking hilarious. He was convinced his dick was going to drop off at any second. Considering the fact it was freshmen year and girls had only just started showing an interest in all of us—well, mostly them—he was freaking the fuck out.

Hadley gasps, her face scrunching in disgust. "You got an STD? Eww, Cam, that's gross!"

"No, he didn't," I admit, coming to his rescue. "Turns out he had poison ivy all over his junk from fucking some girl in the bushes by the admin building."

Everyone bursts out laughing. It doesn't matter how many times we bring this story up, it's still fucking hilarious.

"Oh, dude, that must have been painful." Beck laughs. "You sure everything still works alright?"

"Don't you worry, old man, it's all good as new," Cam volleys, adopting Mason's nickname for him. He gets to his feet and strides toward us. Lifting his hands, he pops the top button on his jeans. "Wanna see for yourself?"

Beck throws his hands out to try and stop him from coming any closer. "God, no, I'll take your word for it."

Cam's gaze falls on Hadley, the cocky swagger falling out of his shoulders as heat blooms in his eyes. I can feel Hadley's entire body tense beside me, reacting to whatever moment they are sharing. It doesn't last longer than a few seconds before Cam coughs and drops his gaze, breaking whatever connection between them. There's no way we all didn't feel the sexual tension heating the room, though. It's only a matter of time until they fuck and make up. And surprisingly, I'm okay with that.

"You got any funny childhood memories, Beck?" Hawk asks as Cam saunters back to his chair and collapses into it, suddenly appearing more withdrawn than he did a minute ago.

"Umm." Beck picks at the label on his beer as he ponders over Hawk's question. After a few seconds, a fond smile grows on his face, and he chuckles.

"There was this one night my friends and I managed to get our hands on one of our parents' liquor stash. We were only eleven or twelve, so we were fucked up from like half a can of beer."

The guys all laugh—we've all been there.

"Cain, he was always doing reckless shit. I'm pretty sure he thought he'd be dead before he was twenty-five." There's a sadness in his tone, but he quickly shakes it off. "Anyway, we were just walking around the neighborhood, thinking we were cool as shit, when Cain spotted an old merc parked at the curb. His dad had just taught him that week how to disable the alarm on one and hot-wire the engine so he could steal it, so he wanted to try it out for himself. Of course, none of us had a fucking clue how to drive. A problem we didn't consider until we'd already broken in and messed with the wires.

"All four of us were sitting in the car, arguing over what to do, when a light switched on inside the house beside us. Well, I'm pretty sure I shit my pants." Everyone laughs again, and I have to admit, I'm pretty caught up in the story. It's a million miles away from the life we had growing up. Sure, the guys and I all had each other and got into some shit, but never anything illegal. It was the one thing drilled into us from a young age—not getting the police involved in our lives. We thought our parents just didn't want the bad publicity, but obviously it was more than just their social standing they were concerned about.

"So I dove into the front seat, practically sitting on Cain's damn lap, as I tried to work out which pedals did what and quickly tore off down the street. Thank fuck it was an automatic, or I wouldn't have had a clue. Not that it was much help when I could hardly see over the dash. I hadn't had much of a growth spurt yet, and once Cain wriggled out from underneath me, I was doing well to see over the wheel. We were veering all over the place, all of us freaking out that whoever was in the house was coming after us.

"We made it a few streets before I accidentally side-swiped a bike. Then we were really fucked. Less than five minutes later, there was this deafening roar behind us as a dozen bikes chased us down the road, shooting at us. Fuck, we were shitting our pants by then. I didn't know what the fuck to do. Stop? Keep driving? I'm pretty sure I was crying like a baby." He chuckles. "They eventually hit one of our tires, and the car spun out, losing control. We were still dazed when they tore the car door off and shoved their guns in our faces, but, fuck, the look of surprise when they realized it was a bunch of kids in the car. I think they thought it was a rival gang trying to piss them off."

Hadley gasps as the rest of us laugh. "What happened?"

Beck shrugs. "They made us promise that if we were ever looking to get into the life, we'd go with them. I think they were impressed with our recklessness."

"Holy shit, that's insane." Cam laughs, watching Beck with what looks like respect, or at the very least, a modicum of admiration. It doesn't sit well with me how easily the guys seem to be letting him into our circle. What happened to not trusting him? Are we seriously done with that because he *claims* whatever he's doing is to protect me?

The six of us chat for a while longer, before tiredness starts to kick in. Leaning in, my shoulder brushes against Hadley's as I whisper in her ear, "Stay with me tonight?"

I've never asked a girl to spend the night with me. Except things have been chaotic lately, and now that she's so close, sitting right beside me, I can't stand the thought of her leaving to go sleep alone in her own bed.

Her eyes roam over my face, and a small, shy smile crosses her features as she nods. "Course I will."

Damn, well, now that I've gone and asked her, I'm done with the rest of this night. I don't think I've ever been more ready to call it a day and go to bed, although the thought of having her soft curves pressed against me all night has my thoughts heading down a filthy track. Thankfully, it's not much later when Beck gets up to leave.

"I'm gonna stay here tonight," Hadley explains when he looks at her.

I expect to see some jealousy or anger at that. Most people wouldn't be okay with their girlfriend sleeping at another guy's house. Especially when he knows damn well she will be sleeping in either mine or Mason's bed. Instead, he almost looks relieved to hear that.

"Okay. I'll see you on Thursday."

He leans down to give her a quick kiss before waving goodnight to the rest of us and heading out.

The other guys begin to tidy up, placing the empty bottles over by the sink.

"Right, well, I'm going to bed," Hawk says. "I don't wear headphones or listen to music while I sleep, and I'm not about to start." He gives each of us the stink eye before sauntering down the hallway toward the bedrooms. Cam lingers in the space between the living room, where Hadley and I are still sitting, and the hallway. He's glancing back and forth, looking unsure about what to do as Mason joins us on the sofa, sitting in Beck's vacated spot. After a tense moment of awkward silence as Cam debates what to do, he makes up his mind and mumbles out a hasty goodnight before he saunters down the hall after Hawk.

Hadley worries her bottom lip as she watches him disappear into his room. "Is he doing okay?" she asks softly after we've heard the click of his bedroom door shutting behind him.

"He's actually been doing a lot better," I reassure her. "He's stopped drinking, and has been going to class more."

Some of the tension drops out of her shoulders. "He doesn't know how to act around me anymore."

"He seemed to be doing pretty well tonight," Mason supplies.

"When we're all together, he isn't so bad. When it's just the two of us, it's...awkward." She sighs heavily. "Talking to Cam used to be so easy. I miss it."

I lace my fingers through hers as Mason drapes his arm over her shoulder, tugging her in against him.

"You'll get back to that," I promise her.

The way she looks into my eyes, I can tell she wants to believe me.

"You will," Mason agrees. "It's in the way he looks at you. He's fighting with himself because he doesn't know how to handle his feelings, but it's a losing battle. Just give him some time."

Hadley leans her head on his shoulder, and the three of us sit in comfortable silence for a bit, with each of us lost in our own thoughts until Mason yawns. That starts us all off as Hadley and I yawn in reflex.

"Well, I'm heading to bed," Mason announces, gazing at Hadley. "Which one of us do you want to sleep with?"

"I was going to sleep with West, if that's okay?" She suddenly looks nervous and I don't like seeing that expression on her. She's got no reason to be nervous. Not that Mason or I have really talked about it, but our dynamic with Hadley feels right. Like this is how it was always meant to be.

Mason tucks his finger under her chin, lifting it so she's looking into his eyes. "Of course that's alright, Little Warrior. You never have to be embarrassed about spending time with one of us or Beck." He presses a kiss to her lips and her hands come up to slide through his hair, holding him to her as she deepens it.

It's probably creepy as hell that I'm just sitting here watching my best friend and my girlfriend suck each other's faces, but it's too fucking hot to look away from. Watching them get lost in one another is captivating.

They're both breathless when they break apart, their lips swollen.

"Night, Little Warrior," Mason murmurs before getting to his feet and smirking at me before leaving the room.

"Ready for bed?" I ask, unable to tear my eyes away as Hadley's tongue sweeps out to lick her lower lip, likely tasting the last remnants of Mason on her skin.

Fucking hell, that should not be hot. I'm curious to know what he tastes like, mixed with her, and before I can second guess myself, I lean forward and capture her lower lip with my teeth, sucking it into my mouth. "Mmm." I release her lip with a pop, watching her pupils dilate and her eyes widen as her cheeks and chest flush with need.

"Come on, Firefly, bedtime." Taking her hand in mine, I lead her to the bedroom. I hesitate outside the door, the thought of bringing her into my personal space weighing on me more than I thought it would. It's stupid. I know she's been in here before when she snuck into our apartment, yet somehow, this feels different.

I've never brought another girl back to my room. Never invited anyone other than the guys in here. Not that it's anything unique or particularly personal, but it's *my* space. Where I come to get away from the world. Once upon a time, my bedroom was the one place I could come and be comfortable in my own skin. Where my father wasn't judging me for not being strong enough, man enough, buff enough. Despite knowing I can be whoever I want to be at this school, and no one would dare say anything, my room is still that safe space for me. So, letting someone new into that is unnerving.

She gently squeezes my hand in hers in a comforting gesture, and I take some strength from that as I turn the handle, pushing open the door to my sanctuary.

Flicking on the light, it illuminates a forest-green room. I have a large desk lining one wall, with several computer screens covering it, along with various pieces of hardware and other technical items. A large king-size bed is in the middle of the room, taking up most of the space, and I have a bookcase, a reading chair, and another desk with all my school stuff scattered across it on the other side of the room.

A large window opposite the bed overlooks the woods that run along the back of the dormitories and dining hall. Moving over to it, I pull the blinds, tidying up the desk and whatever other clutter I can shove in the drawers—I probably should have tidied up before asking her to stay the night—until I feel a warm palm on my back.

Clutching the book in my hand, I turn to face Hadley. She looks so beautiful, standing there in only her sports bra and tight leggings.

"Can I have a top or something to sleep in?" she asks.

"Right. Yeah, of course." I drop the book in my hand and cross the room to my chest of drawers, lifting out a t-shirt and handing it to her. I don't know why I feel so awkward. It's not like we haven't been alone before. I've seen her naked and coming all over mine and Mason's dicks, for Christ's sake. Yet I can't handle her being in my bedroom? What the hell is wrong with me?

She smiles softly as she takes the t-shirt from my outstretched hand before moving to the bed. With her back to me, she peels off her skin-tight bra while I stand there starstruck like a total fucking idiot until she slips the t-shirt over her head, cutting off my view.

Hitching her thumbs under the top, she wiggles her ass in an inviting manner that has my dick hardening until her leggings peel down her legs. Kicking off her battered trainers, she steps out of them and looks back at me over her shoulder. "Are we getting into bed or what?"

When I don't respond, unable to do anything more than stare at her standing there in only my t-shirt that just about hits the top of her thighs and gives me a front-row view of her long, toned legs, a small smile graces her lips.

"West," she coaxes gently, "which side of the bed do you sleep on?"

"Oh." I tear my eyes away from her legs, slowly lifting my gaze to her face. "The right side."

She peels back the covers on the left side and slips between the sheets, appearing like every wet dream I've had about her in my bed.

"Well, are you going to join me or just stand and stare at me all night?" Her words and inviting smile jolt me into action as I quickly strip off my top and jeans and climb in beside her, wearing only my boxers.

"Why are you so nervous?" she asks, scooching closer to me until the bare skin of her arms and legs are pressed up against mine. Heat radiates out from where our bodies touch, making goosebumps pebble along my skin. How does she have such an effect on me? I've never been this nervous or awkward around a girl before. I like to be the one in charge. If I sleep with a girl, I'm the one making the rules and telling her what to do. Only I don't feel any of my usual confidence right now.

"I don't know," I admit. "I've never had a girl in here before."

Shifting onto her knees, she lifts her leg over mine until she's seated in my lap and, *holy fuck*, does she feel fantastic with her warm, wet pussy pressing against my straining cock. Nothing but the thin fabric of her panties and my boxers separating us.

"I like that," she murmurs, trailing her fingers over my pec. I don't have any of the muscles that Mason or Beck, or even Cam, have. I'm much leaner—skinnier looking—and I can only imagine what she thinks when she looks at me.

Lifting her gaze, she looks into my eyes. "I like you, just the way you are."

"You don't wish I was more of a fighter like Mason?" I half-joke, suddenly feeling self-conscious. Not only am I built entirely differently to Mason, but I also think and behave differently from him too. We probably couldn't be more opposite.

"You're more like Mason than you think." Her words catch me by surprise, and she must see it on my face as she explains. "Where Mason uses his fists, you use your words to eviscerate your opponent. I see the same darkness in you as Mason; it just manifests differently. That's good, though. It means people under-estimate you. They think you're incapable of destroying them, but they don't realize that your sharp tongue can do more damage than a roundhouse kick ever could."

My hand slides into her hair as I lean forward, pressing my lips to hers. I can feel her fingernails digging into the soft flesh of my chest as I tug on her hair tie until her hair falls down around her shoulders in long, wavy strands.

My other hand slides under her t-shirt, gliding across the smooth, warm skin of her back and pressing her more firmly against me. She grinds against my cock, our tongues sliding over one another while I groan into her mouth and she sighs. She tastes like everything I never knew I needed, and I can't get enough of her.

Eventually, I push her back, breaking our kiss even though my dick starts up a protest, and Hadley regards me in confusion.

"I didn't ask you to stay over so we could have sex. I just wanted to spend the night with you."

She smiles seductively. "I kicked Hawk's ass tonight, for the second time," she says, confusing me as to why she's bringing up her brother right now.

"Do you know what I like to do after a fight?" She bites her lip seductively, trailing her fingers down my chest. "I like to fuck."

CHAPTER 9

Hadley

THE SECOND THE WORDS ARE OUT OF MY MOUTH, MY VISION TILTS. The next thing I know, I'm on my back with West's lean body wedged between my thighs and his hard-on pressed perfectly against my wet panties as he hovers over me.

"You asked for it, Firefly," he growls in a dark, seductive tone that has me grinding shamelessly against him. "You're going to have to be quiet, though, unless you want your brother to come in here before I can make you see stars. Can you do that?"

He pins me in place with a serious look. *This* is the West who likes to be in control. The one who is in charge behind closed doors. Seeing him go all alpha and taking control only makes me wetter as I nod my head, biting down on my lower lip. I'm already suppressing a whimper and he's barely even touched me.

He gets a feral look in his eye at my obedience before slowly roaming his gaze over my body as though trying to decide where he should start. Tugging on my top, I sit up slightly so he can remove it, and he does the same with my panties until I'm lying naked on the bed for him to feast his eyes on.

His tongue runs along his lower lip as his pupils dilate, and his hands trail over my hips and up my stomach before he grabs my tits, pushing them together and squeezing them.

My head falls back and a small moan escapes me, having already forgotten about my promise to keep quiet.

A sharp slap across my nipple has me gasping, and I snap my gaze to West's. He gives me an admonishing look as he massages the spot he just slapped, and even though it was supposed to be a punishment, I can't help the way my eyes roll back in my head as the bite of pain goes straight to my clit.

"I'll have to stop if you can't keep quiet," he growls in warning.

Fuck no. He can't stop.

I bite into my lower lip, more than willing to make myself bleed if it means he'll continue to make my body come alive under his touch. His hands glide down my torso and over my thighs before he pushes them further apart.

"Fuck, you're already dripping all over my sheets, Firefly."

As soon as his fingers touch my clit, I jump off the bed, already so sensitive and eager for him.

He chuckles darkly, pleased with my reaction. With a hand pressed against my lower abdomen to pin me in place, his other hand trails through my wetness before he inserts two fingers into me, making my back arch as I fist the bed sheets and bite my lip harder.

I'm practically vibrating with the need to come as he slowly slides his fingers in and out of me, driving me wild as I buck against him. It takes everything in me to stay quiet, which is only heightening my desire.

When he presses his thumb against my clit, I go off like a bomb. Blood floods my mouth as I pierce the skin with my teeth, barely feeling the sting as pleasure flashes through my body, my legs trembling.

West doesn't give me a chance to recover, and I'm still experiencing the aftershocks of my orgasm when he pushes his boxers down his legs and, in one swift move, slams all the way into me.

I can feel myself spasming around him and my mouth drops open as he bottoms out, the tip of his cock hitting my cervix. "Ohh," I moan, losing any control I had over my ability to stay quiet. My brain is hazy with the surge of hormones from my climax, and all rational thought has left the building.

Unfortunately, West hasn't forgotten the rules, and just as quickly as his fucking amazing dick sunk into me, he pulls out, leaving me feeling empty. I whimper at the sudden loss, searing him with a pleading look.

"If you can't keep quiet, Firefly, I'll have to stop," he threatens, all the while running the head of his cock up and down my pussy lips, smearing my juices and teasing me. "Do you want me to stop?" He presses the tip of his dick against my already highly sensitive clit, and I can't do anything but shake my head. "Are you going to keep quiet?"

I nod my head this time, silently begging him with my eyes to shove his dick back inside me and make me fall apart.

"Good girl," he purrs, slightly rocking his hips to tease me before pushing his way back in. He never breaks eye contact with me, his intense gaze holding me hostage as he picks up the pace, chasing his release. I wrap my legs around his narrow waist, my heel digging into his ass, urging him on as I race toward the light.

My pussy constricts and my back arches as I fist the bedsheets. I can feel it, that intense tightening in my lower belly, and I know, regardless of my promise to keep quiet, I'm not going to be able to.

West must sense it too, as his hand clamps down over my

mouth, silencing my scream as a blast wave explodes outward from my core, racing through my nerves all the way to my toes.

Panting heavily, I can hardly move when I'm suddenly tossed onto my stomach, his nails digging into the soft skin of my hips as he hauls them up off the bed, lining me up before slamming into me. I bury my face in the pillow, silencing my whimpers as he hammers into me relentlessly, quickly sending me crashing toward my third fucking orgasm of the night.

This time, he dives off the cliff with me, grunting out his release as his cum hits my inner walls, before pulling me down onto the bed beside him.

"Fuck," he pants breathlessly as he tugs me into his arms. He plants a fierce kiss on my lips, his tongue pushing its way past my teeth, and I suck him greedily into my mouth as our tongues clash together.

Despite how wrung out I am, I can feel my body gearing up for round two when he breaks away, climbing off the bed to get some tissues and wet wipes so we can clean ourselves up. Throwing the used tissues in the trash, he climbs back into bed, placing his glasses on the bedside table before once again wrapping his arms around me so I can rest my head on his shoulder, our legs intertwined. A tired, sex-hazed bliss surrounds us as sleep pulls me under, dragging me into oblivion.

I'M AWAKE EARLY THE NEXT MORNING IN EXACTLY THE SAME POSITION I fell asleep—both of us must have slept like the dead.

Peeking up at West through my eyelashes, I see he's still out for the count. His face is relaxed, with none of the usual hardness scoring his features. He looks so peaceful, like he doesn't have a worry in the world. I wish that were the case.

Carefully, I untangle myself from him and slip out from between the sheets, pulling on the discarded t-shirt he gave me last night and slipping out of the room.

The fantastic thing about sleeping over here—and the same at Beck's—is that I don't have to make myself look semi-human before caffeinating my system. So it doesn't matter that my hair resembles medusa's or that I have a terrifying resting-bitch face first thing in the morning.

If anything, Mason seems to find it amusing, as he chuckles when I enter the kitchen, not at all deterred by the dark scowl I throw his way.

"Aren't you a sight for sore eyes in the morning." He laughs.

He's sitting at the barstools, drinking his own freshly made cup of coffee, but before I can throw something at his head, he gets up and grabs me a mug, filling it as I take a seat next to him.

"Mmm," I groan as I wrap my hands around the hot mug and take a sip of the hot life force within it.

"You have fun last night?" he asks with a knowing smirk, throwing me a dirty wink as I roll my eyes at him.

"I don't kiss and tell."

He scoffs. "I'm pretty sure you were doing much more than just kissing last night."

Tossing him a dirty look, I snark back, "What were you doing, standing at the door listening to us?"

He throws his head back and laughs. "I wish, babe. If I'd heard those sweet moans coming from your lips, I wouldn't have been able to stop myself from turning your two-way into a three-way."

Well, damn. I totally would have been okay with that.

"Instead, I settled for jerking myself off to the thought of your hot mouth bobbing up and down on my dick."

Fucking hell, he's going to have me wet and needy before I've even had breakfast.

His gaze zones in on my lips as my tongue inadvertently flicks out, making him groan.

"Head out of the gutter, Little Warrior," he murmurs, like I'm the only one whose thoughts have strayed to a dirty place. "Your brother will be in here any minute. We're going to the gym. Do you wanna come?"

I take another sip of my coffee as I think over his offer. Last night satisfied my urges for now, and honestly, I'm still a little sore from the fight. Not to mention the delicious ache between my thighs from West last night. "Nah, I'm good. I think I'll just stay here, if that's okay?"

"Of course it is. You can come here any time. I'd give you a key, but it would seem you can just let yourself in."

Hawk saunters into the kitchen, still looking bleary-eyed in his gym gear. "Morning," he grumbles as he pours himself a coffee and sits down on the opposite side of the island.

"Good to see you look as shitty in the morning as I do." I smile sweetly, feeling more alive now that I've finished my first cup of the day.

Mason laughs. "Ha, you think Hawk is a grouchy shithead during the day? You should get on his bad side first thing in the morning."

"Shut up, asshole," Hawk snarls, taking a large gulp of his coffee. "It's a fucking ungodly hour of the day to be awake. Why do you go to the gym this early?"

"Why did you agree to come then?" Mason retorts, unfazed by what I'm guessing is Hawk's typical early-morning cantankerous nature. "You could have said no."

"I must have been drunk. It's still fucking dark out. No human should be up before the sun."

Someone's clearly not a morning person. I might look like death warmed over first thing in the morning, but I'm definitely an early bird like Mason. I love being up before everyone else and watching the world come to life around me. Maybe it's because I spent so many years locked away in the compound, barely allowed to experience much of the outside world, but now that I'm free to do whatever the fuck I please, I want to soak up every second of it.

I share a look with Mason as he rolls his eyes at Hawk's pissy attitude.

"Make sure you get whatever information you need from West today," Hawk reminds me. "Now that we've announced the second month of not picking girls, they're going to be out for blood."

"Great," I snark sarcastically.

I guess I'll just have to show the pampered girls of Pacific Prep exactly how things will roll under my reign.

There's bound to be dirt on every girl here. It's just a matter of finding it. I'm hoping whoever the guys are getting their intel from has enough for me to pull this off. Otherwise, I'm out of ideas. I haven't the first idea how to befriend these girls or get them to do as I say, so there's no chance I can endear them into accepting that the girl-of-the-month tradition is finished.

I huff out a frustrated breath when Hawk stares pointedly at me. "I'll get it done," I assure him.

It might be a job I couldn't give less of a shit about, but I'll do whatever I have to to make myself seem useful to our parents and avoid any backlash on any of the guys.

Seemingly satisfied, he nods, downing the last of his coffee before getting to his feet.

"Right, we going?" he asks Mason.

"Sure thing."

As Hawk walks toward the door, Mason swoops in to plant a quick, searing kiss on my lips, leaving them tingling as the two of them leave the apartment.

Once I'm alone, I swivel slowly on my stool, taking in my view of the kitchen and living space from here while I ponder what to do with myself. We still have several hours before we have to head down for breakfast. I don't know what time West or Cam get up, but I'd guess Cam is a last-minute kind of guy. I'd imagine West likes to take his time, so he'll probably be awake in another hour or so.

Getting up, I refresh my coffee from the pot and saunter over to the living room to curl up on one end of the sofa and face the

TV. Grabbing the remote, I surf through a few channels before finding something that looks half-decent to watch.

I couldn't even tell you the last time I just sat and scrolled through various television channels. Watching TV wasn't something we ever had the opportunity to do at the compound. Occasionally they would put on a movie as a reward, but it was once a year at best. After I managed to escape, I mostly lived on the streets for the few weeks before starting here. There were a couple of nights when I sprung for a motel that sometimes came with a TV, yet for the most part, I had to conserve every penny I had. It took me over a year to save that money and get everything in place for my big escape. I couldn't just throw it away for the sake of a hard, lumpy bed for a night.

Leaning back against the cushions, my whole body relaxes as I get engrossed in a crime show where some woman has been murdered, and the detectives are running around in circles as they try to uncover her murderer. It's painfully apparent the guy killed his wife; how the police can't see that is beyond me.

Although, whoever the show's producer is, clearly didn't know anything about what happens when you slit someone's throat. The best way is to stand behind the person so that way, you have the necessary force to pull your knife through their throat. It's no easy job cutting through all that skin, muscle, and cartilage, especially if you want to be sure they'll bleed out quickly and not gain a second lease on life for long enough to call the police after you've gone. Plus, it stops you from getting completely saturated in the blood, which is always a win.

Only by the looks of things, the guy on this TV show had barely more than grazed the dead woman, and the angle of the wound was all wrong for someone of his height. It's laughable how inaccurate it all is.

My stomach grumbles as the show ends a half hour later— they caught the guy eventually, but what took me two minutes to piece together took them the whole forty-five-minute episode to figure out.

When my stomach grumbles again, I realize I won't be able to wait until breakfast, and decide a raid of the guys' pantry is in order. It's already bad enough that I have to sit and be gawked at every morning while I eat. If I go in there hungry and someone pisses me off, it will only cause more problems that none of us need.

CHAPTER 10

Cam

Maybe it's knowing that Hadley is currently asleep mere feet away from me, that only a thin wall separates me from her. Whatever it is, I'm awake at the ass-crack of fucking dawn. I toss and turn for a while before eventually giving up and deciding I may as well get up, throwing on a pair of sweats and a t-shirt before leaving my room.

As I walk into the kitchen, I come to a stop, watching Hadley as she bends down to reach into a cupboard. Her firm ass in the air acts like a red flag to a bull as my dick hardens in my sweats.

I stand and watch her—something that has become my norm—unable to keep my eyes off her. It doesn't matter if she's just sitting and studying, interacting with the guys, or full-on fucking them. Apparently, I've turned into a complete fucking pervert and will watch her do just about anything.

I'VE LOST COUNT OF THE NUMBER OF TIMES I'VE JERKED MYSELF OFF TO the image of her fucking Mason while West stood behind her, pulling on her hair. It's the hottest thing I've seen since I watched her come all over my dick—the second most commonly played video in my spank bank.

She doesn't notice me as she lifts a bowl from the cupboard, standing upright. The only thing she's wearing is an oversized t-shirt that barely covers her ass—most likely West's if the banging of his headboard against our adjoining wall is any indication of who she spent the night with.

I'm happy for him. I know West has had issues in the past when it comes to girls and sex, so if he can find someone he can be himself with in the bedroom, then that's great, but that doesn't mean I'm not jealous as fuck.

The way the top clings to the curves of her ass makes her look absolutely fuckable, and despite me mentally berating my dick to calm the fuck down, it's as hard as a fucking rock in my pants. Not an uncommon occurrence when Hadley's around. Though it's sure as fuck not comfortable, and jerking off to the image of her is a shitty substitute for the real thing.

I don't even remember moving, but the next thing I know, I'm standing beside the island in the kitchen, close enough that the overwhelming scent of her washes over me, flooding my senses. The combination of vanilla, honey, and sex is intoxicating. My mouth waters at the thought of tasting her again, my dick twitching to remind me of his presence and ensure I haven't forgotten about him and his needs.

As if I could forget how fucking much I want to be buried balls-deep in that tight pussy, having her scream my name as her juices drip down my dick.

Sensing someone behind her, she spins to face me. Her fists are clenched tightly as though she's about to hit me. *Why does that only make my dick strain harder to get to her?* I'm on the verge of coming in my pants like a fucking virgin.

Her eyes widen in surprise, and she drops her fists.

"What are you doing creeping up on me?" she snaps, although there's no real heat behind her words.

"Sorry," I mumble distractedly, my attention caught on where her nipples are peaking through her shirt. *Is she as turned-on as I am right now?*

I don't know if she can read something in my expression or see the obvious fucking hard-on in my pants, but her pupils dilate.

"Cam?" Her voice is breathy. That one word has so much confusion, hesitation, and heat. I can't blame her for being confused and unsure. Ever since I opened my fat mouth and said her name in the dining hall, everything's been so fucked-up. I can't believe I was so stupid as to think that wouldn't change things. How did I not see that that's the last thing she would have wanted? I was so busy thinking about claiming her publicly and showing her off so every other asshole in this place would know to keep their hands off her, that I didn't think about what *she* wanted.

Her tongue flicks out to run along her lower lip. There's no way she doesn't feel whatever the fuck this is between us, right? Even when I was furious with her, wanting to bury her ten-feet under, thinking she was fucking my father, I still couldn't ignore how much I fucking wanted her.

Despite how intense this chemistry is between us, she still shouldn't want anything to do with me. After what I did to her... What my father has done to her. The same blood runs through my veins as is in his. It's no longer bright red and flowing but black and sluggish, like tar. It's sick and tainted, poisoned by generations of malicious hate and greed. The Rutherford blood is infected. *I'm* infected. Diseased to the fucking core. I should come with a fucking hazard sign.

"Stop it," she seethes, somehow able to tell my thoughts are spiraling out of control. "I'm sick of watching you drown yourself in self-hatred."

"You would too, if your family was as heinous as mine."

She steps toward me, closing the distance between us.

"You can't be held responsible for anyone's actions but your own." Her tone is soft yet insistent, and I can see the truth of her words in her eyes. "As for your own actions...you have to learn to live with them. I've already forgiven you, but you have to forgive yourself."

"I don't..." I trail off, sighing while I shake my head. "How?" I don't know how to move on from what I did. I don't understand how *she* can forgive me. As far as I can tell, there's nothing within me worthy of forgiveness.

"I have done far worse shit than you can ever imagine," she murmurs. "The reasons behind your actions are what matter. Yours came from a place of pain; mine were for survival. We do what we must, to scratch out some sort of existence for ourselves and hope we can live with the consequences of our decisions. You need to learn to accept everything that's happened and move forward with your life. It doesn't do you, or anyone else, any good to drown in it all."

While there's sorrow in her eyes, it's clear, whatever she's done, she doesn't regret her actions. I find it impossible to believe her, in any case. Sure, she's probably had to do some fucked-up shit to get by, and who can blame her? But there's no way it can be as bad as what our parents are involved in. Or what my father has done to her. Just like I don't fully believe she came here to kill me. They're just words she's said to try and make me feel better, to try and ease my guilt, and while I appreciate her effort, it's not necessary.

She reaches out, linking our fingers together, her palm resting on the back of mine. "I can think of much better things we could be doing with our time instead of hating on one another," she whispers in a low, seductive purr, peering up at me through her eyelashes, a coy smile dancing along her luscious lips.

She slowly directs our hands toward the hem of her shirt, using her hold to place my hand over her pussy so I'm cupping it.

I groan at finding her naked and my fingertips instinctively curl, sliding through her wetness, eliciting a moan from the back of my throat. She's fucking soaked already, and I can't remember ever needing someone the way I ache for her. My balls are blue and ready to fall off, not the slightest bit impressed at having been denied her sweetness for so long.

She pushes against my hand as her fingers and mine slide into her tight channel. Her lips part on a breathy gasp, and I stare transfixed at the glisten of moisture on her lower lip as I slide deeper into her, feeling her walls spasm around us.

I want this—her—so badly, but disbelief that she could want me after everything stills my fingers inside of her, even as my dick practically screams my ear off for putting a stop to this when he was so close to getting where he's been dying to be for months.

"You already have the others. Why would you need me?"

Her eyes dart back and forth between mine, a rare vulnerability taking over her features. She walks around with walls so high and thick that nothing can break through them. Except, right now, she's letting me see a part of herself she doesn't show many people. In fact, when I think back to her wary, barbed-wire attitude when she first arrived at Pac, I'm not sure she let anyone get close to her before she showed up here.

"None of them are you," she says in a quiet whisper, looking deep into my eyes and letting me see just how much she means what she says. "You constantly remind me of what I've been fighting for. When I found the strength to escape Lawrence, my entire focus was on survival, but you've shown me what it's like to live. The nights we spent in the dining hall, when you told me about everything you and the guys used to get up to when you were kids, made me realize what I'd been missing my whole life. I craved that sense of belonging, of having friendships, and feeling that deep-seated loyalty the four of you share.

"You were the first one to *see* me. To make me laugh and forget about the dark past I was running from and the uncertain future I was heading toward. With you, I was able to live in the moment and enjoy it.

"I miss that. I miss *you*. I miss how your touch burns my skin and ignites a fire in my soul. I want to feel that again. I don't want to go another day without you."

Well, fuck me raw and piss on my grave. What the hell am I supposed to say to that?

There's nothing I can say. Nothing I can do except give her exactly what she wants. With my fingers still deep in her pussy, I flex them, pressing against her sensitive bundle of nerves. Removing the last bit of distance between us, my chest pushes against hers as I wrap my hand around the back of her neck, drawing her toward me.

I slant my lips over hers, swallowing her moan of pleasure when I press my thumb against her clit. Her small hands fist the front of my t-shirt as I pump my fingers in and out of her, repeatedly gliding over her G-spot until I feel her clenching around me, her soft cries driving me on.

"Cam," she pants in a half plea-half moan just before she finds her release, her juices running down my hand while I continue to finger-fuck her through her orgasm.

As her scent permeates the air around her, I lose myself to my basic needs. Carnal hunger takes control as I wrap my hands around her thighs, lifting her up onto the island.

She gasps as her bare ass hits the cold marble, and I fist the bottom of her t-shirt, tearing it over her head and exposing her to me. Her nipples harden in the room's cool air, and I dip my head, licking her areola before sucking her nipple into my mouth, biting teasingly on the sensitive skin.

I push against her chest until she's lying flat on the island, staring up at me with half-lidded eyes, her pupils blown with desire. Her breaths come in rapid pants that make her tits bounce up and down in the most inviting way.

Fuck, I want to stick my dick between them and come all over her chest.

But I want to taste her more. I've been fucking dreaming about eating her out again. I swear, some mornings, I've woken up with the lingering taste of her on my tongue.

Pushing her thighs apart, I lick my lips as I devour her glistening pink pussy with my eyes. She's so fucking wet, the evidence from her last orgasm still coating her folds.

Lifting her legs so they rest on my shoulders, I lower my head between her milky thighs, nibbling on the soft skin until she's a writhing mess beneath me.

Only when she's practically begging for it, do I push my tongue between her drenched pussy lips, moaning against her skin as I lap up her juices. When I place my lips over her clit to suck it into my mouth, her hands thread through my hair, smooshing my face against her pussy, and I inhale her scent. She smells like the best wet dream: all dirty sex and carnal desire.

"Fuck, Cam," she moans, grinding against me as I slide my tongue down her slit until I push it inside her.

With one hand wrapped around her thigh, I use my other one to undo the drawstring of my sweats, shoving them and my boxers down my thighs until I can free my cock. Gripping my length, I give it a few quick pumps, groaning in pleasure and causing her to moan at the vibration.

Her hands tighten in my hair, and she tugs on the strands, pulling my head back.

"You're fucking amazing at that," she pants, "but I need your dick in me. Now."

Yes, ma'am.

I don't waste a second shucking out of my sweats and boxers as I pull my top over my head.

The height of the island has her swollen pussy lined up perfectly with my throbbing dick, and I don't give a single fuck about how unhygienic all of this is as I push inside of her.

The feel of her wrapped around me has my balls tingling, and I'm close to spilling my load already, but there's no fucking way I'm coming so soon. I focus on reciting the months of the year backward until the feeling subsides and only then do I dare pull back until only the tip of my dick is left inside her.

I can feel her clenching, as if trying to stop me from pulling out, and I smirk down at her as she gazes up at me in a blissed-out haze before I slam all the way in.

Her mouth drops open on a silent gasp as I repeatedly hit that magical spot inside her until I feel her spasm around me, and her head tilts back, eliciting a scream from her.

I hope Hawk isn't around to hear that, or I'll be getting an earful later — totally worth it, though!

I continue to pound into her as she gushes all over my dick until my balls draw up and I find my own release, grunting as I come.

"Fuck, that was way better than I remember," I groan, leaning down and kissing her as she chuckles breathily against my lips.

"Let's not wait so long to do it again." Her voice is raspy, her cheeks flushed, and she looks royally fucked. Just looking at her has my dick twitching within her, and we both groan before I reluctantly pull out. I doubt we'd get a second round uninterrupted. I'm surprised no one has disturbed us already, and I don't really want Hawk to tear my balls off for fucking his sister on the kitchen counter.

I'm handing Hadley her top and pulling up my sweats when West's voice takes us by surprise.

"About time," he quips, leaning against the kitchen doorway in his perfectly pressed uniform. *How long was that asshole watching us?* I can't get a read on his expression as he pushes off the doorframe, clapping me on the shoulder as he walks past. Moving in front of Hadley, he plants a heated kiss on her lips. He doesn't appear to be the slightest bit bothered by the fact I just fucked his girlfriend.

Hadley smiles into their kiss.

"Morning," he murmurs against her lips, sounding like a sappy idiot. *What the fuck has this girl done to all of us?*

"Morning." She smiles at him before jumping down from the counter. "I'm going to go shower." With a final, lingering look my way, she walks out of the room, leaving me feeling awkward as fuck as I blatantly ignore West's gaze drilling into the side of my head.

"So, that happened."

"Yup," I respond dismissively, grabbing food out of the fridge to make omelets for breakfast and putting on a fresh pot of coffee for everyone. I'm the only one who knows how to cook. Growing up, there wasn't much to do, and when I wasn't with the guys, I'd be bored out of my mind. One day, I accidentally flicked onto the cooking channel and thought it would be a laugh to give it a go. After setting off the smoke alarm and somehow managing to start a small fire in the pan, our housekeeper agreed to help me, so long as I promised to never attempt anything when she wasn't around.

After that rocky start, I quickly discovered an enjoyment in the process. It was a great distraction when my dad was even more of a prick than usual or when none of the guys were free.

I don't cook often—there's not much of a need when the dining hall is right beside us and you can order food to go from it —but every now and again, I like to immerse myself in it and forget about whatever problems we're facing—or distract myself from awkward questions and unwanted opinions from West.

"I'm glad, man. It's about time you stopped moping around."

My eyebrows pull together. "I haven't been *moping*," I argue.

"Well, whatever you wanna call it, it will be good to have the old Cam back."

He squeezes my shoulder before lifting down two mugs and filling them with coffee while I chop the vegetables and make us breakfast with a bit more pep in my step than I've had recently. *Nothing like morning sex with the girl you can't stop thinking about to put you in a great mood.*

"Mmm, something smells good," Hadley states as she walks into the room, wearing her hoodie and leggings from last night, her damp hair framing her face.

Grabbing a mug she must have been drinking out of earlier, she refills it before sitting at the island.

"Where's Hawk? He not up yet?" I ask, lifting out plates and cutlery for us.

"He went to the gym with Mason," Hadley informs us.

"More for us then," I grin at her before dishing up the food and setting all three plates down on the island and putting out plates for Mason and Hawk in the oven for when they get back.

"Mmm, this is delicious," Hadley blurts out around a mouthful of food. She eats like a half-starved savage, shoveling her food into her mouth as quickly as possible. It's as if she's afraid that someone will take it away from her if she doesn't eat it quickly enough. What sort of childhood do you have to endure to grow up with such a mentality?

"I wouldn't have pegged you as knowing how to cook," she says as she finishes off the last remnants and pushes her plate away. West and I are barely halfway through our meals, and I notice him watching her closely out of the corner of his eye, likely picking up on the same behavior I am.

"I'm just full of surprises." I give her a dirty wink across the island, making her laugh.

"Oh, can I get whatever information you have on the other students?" she asks, turning to West.

"Sure, I'll get it all together and give it to you tonight."

"Thanks." She smiles at him like he hung the moon for her instead of just grabbing a bunch of folders from his room. "Well, that was delish, but I'd better get back to my dorm before anyone thinks I'm doing the walk of shame." She laughs at her own joke as she slips off her stool. "See you at breakfast," she calls over her shoulder before heading out the door.

CHAPTER 11

Hadley

I'VE SPENT THE LAST FEW EVENINGS GOING THROUGH THE FILES WEST gave me, completely sucked in by all the drama going on here over the past four years. Girls cheating on guys; guys cheating on girls. Friends sabotaging friends. It's downright vicious. And that's before you even start in on the blackmailing of teachers to improve grades and the threatening of other students to do people's bidding.

Then there's the out-and-out illegal shit. This is where things get seriously fucked up. Apparently, our fifty-five-year-old chemistry teacher moonlights as the school's drug dealer. The great thing is that he offers flexible payment plans to his clients. Can't front the cash for your coke or Ritalin? No worries, he's happy to accept payment in the form of underage sex. The best part is, he's not fussy as to whether it's dick or pussy. You won't get any sexism from this guy.

THE DOWNSIDE IS THAT MOST OF THESE KIDS DON'T REALIZE THEY'RE being recorded as they perform these sexual acts, and based on the videos on the teacher's OnlyPorn account, he's uploading them and selling them as soft porn. *Fucking gross.*

It actually pisses me off that none of the guys have put a stop to this. Are they seriously okay with this dude getting away with that? I fucking hope not; I had higher expectations of them. All of us have been flat out with schoolwork and ensuring the Princes still have control of the school, so I haven't had a chance to call them out on any of it yet, but you can be sure that talk will be coming real soon.

For now, my focus is on the material I can use against the girls. Whispers and rumors have been spreading all week as girls speculate about the reason behind the Princes' change in behavior. I've heard everything from the plausible to the hilarious, to the downright absurd. I swear I overheard some guy telling his buddies he was certain the guys were all in one big gay relationship together —I laughed my head off at that.

Of course, the rumors mainly revolve around me. It's far too coincidental that I show up this year, and the guys suddenly change things up. Thankfully, no one seems to have worked out the truth. I don't know if it's because Hawk's my brother and the guys very much give off the impression that they do everything together, that has people not immediately jumping to the fact I'm sleeping with two—well, now three—of them, but whatever the reason, I'm glad. The last thing I need is the girls breathing down my neck or our parents finding out about us. The most popular theory seems to be that our parents have demanded the change due to my sudden reappearance—a theory we are all happy to go along with.

Regardless of the reason, though, the girls aren't happy. None of them have acted on it yet, but it's only a matter of time. The discontent is heavy in the air. It's in every conspiratorial look they share. It's in the hurt, angry, confused glares they throw at the guys and the sneers and dismissive looks at me. None of them are pleased, and it won't be long before they make their objection known.

Bianca has kept her distance since the party, but I've noticed her watching me, as though she's measuring me up and trying to decide if I'm a threat. If she hasn't figured out by now that I am, there's no hope for her. She should know by now I'm the big bad wolf. I may look innocent, but my claws are sharp, and I like to bite. If she pisses me off any further, I'm going to tear her to pieces, and I'll fucking enjoy it.

But then, because I'm a sick bitch, I actually *want* her to come at me. We've been butting heads since day one, and the tension is only rising. I'm just waiting for her to present me with the perfect opportunity to bring her down and then show the whole school what happens if they mess with me.

I've spent the last few nights familiarizing myself with all the possible blackmail information I have, trying to work out who people are and remember their names in case I need to recall any of this shit on the fly. It's been the perfect distraction from the nauseating butterflies doing somersaults in my stomach. Cam asked if I wanted to meet him in the dining hall tonight, just like old times. Ever since I agreed, my stomach's been in knots. I don't know what the hell has come over me. This is *Cam*. There's nothing for me to be anxious about. We've done this a dozen times before.

A giddiness takes over me as I gather up the folders and pull the bookcase away from the wall so I can drop the folders into the hole I made. It feels like it's been forever since Cam and I had one of our late-night chats, and I'm pleased to see him reaching out. I was worried he'd be awkward after what happened the other day. It was unexpected, but honestly, I think it's what we needed to move forward.

Throwing a hoodie over my head, I shove my feet into my boots and grab my key as I head out the door, trying to ignore the fact I feel like someone who's going on their first-ever date—at least, that's how I imagine it feels like.

With sweaty hands, I pull open the door to the dining hall, but the high-pitched whine of fucking Bianca has me hesitating in the doorway. Shifting my body so I'm hidden behind the door, I hold it ajar to eavesdrop on them. I know, I shouldn't be listening, but I'm curious as to what they're talking about and, well, I guess I wanna hear what Cam has to say. After his back and forth with her all year, who can blame me?

"I don't understand what's going on," I hear Bianca grate. "Why have things suddenly changed?"

"Bianca." Cam sounds tired, making me wonder how long she's been bothering him for. "Things change. Just accept it."

"But why?"

God, she sounds like a stropping two-year-old.

"Because of *her*?" she sneers, the venom clear to hear in her tone.

"It's got nothing to do with *her*," Cam seethes, making me wince. I know he's only trying to get rid of her, and he can't let her think there's anything between us, but damn, that hurts.

"But we used to be so good together." I can picture the pout on her face as she changes tactics, trying to suck up to him instead. Peeking my head around the door, I see she has stepped closer to him. So close her breast grazes against his arm, momentarily making me see red. A little voice in my head snarls, *Mine*, and even though that's not technically true, it *feels* fucking right.

"I even got these for you," she goes on to say, lifting her tits. It would be fucking impossible to miss her double D's that are so out of proportion to the rest of her slim body. "Because I know how much you liked to fuck them."

Eww! Yup, that lasagna I had for dinner does not taste so nice on its way back up.

Cam grimaces. "You shouldn't have done that, B. It was just sex. Nothing more."

"So what, you're fucking celibate now?" she gripes, instantly dropping the 'woe is me' act as her temper flares. "Don't bullshit me, Cam. If you're not getting it from me, you're getting it from someone else. What makes *her* so fucking special, huh? You know when the school finds out—and they will find out—they'll crucify her."

Cam's hands dart out and grab onto her upper arms, shaking her roughly. The expression on his face is like nothing I've seen on him before. Even when he wanted to murder me, there was always this spark in his eyes that told me he would never take things too far. Only today, that spark is gone. His gaze is ice-fucking-cold, his eyes nothing but a blank void as he towers over her.

"You better be careful, Bianca," he snarls menacingly. "Threats like that will get you in real trouble one day."

In the next second, he shoves her away from him, shrugging his shoulders indifferently and tucking his fingers into the front pockets of his jeans. A complete one-eighty from the gargoyle he resembled a second ago.

"Anyway, you're wrong. There's no girl. We're graduating soon—moving on to bigger, better things. The four of us are just over the whole skanky, desperate thing. We want someone with more…substance. With a bit of a backbone. Not a whiny bitch."

Having heard enough—and admittedly feeling a tad smug after Cam's little speech—I push open the door, announcing my entrance before Bianca can start on another unwanted tirade.

Bianca's back is mostly turned toward me, so Cam notices me first. A wicked glint enters his eye.

"I wondered what that smell was." My voice echoes around the otherwise empty hall as I wrinkle my nose in disgust and grimace.

Bianca turns in her obscenely tall high heels, giving me the stink eye. "What smell?" she says irritably.

"The stench of desperation that's coming off of you. I could smell it all the way from the dorms."

Cam barks out an arctic laugh as Bianca's eyes narrow and her lips purse.

"Get out of here, trash. Cam and I are busy."

I scoff. "Yeah, I don't think so."

"Fuck off, Bianca. And stop sending me twat shots. I don't wanna see that shit," Cam sneers, going into full-asshole Prince mode.

Her cheeks tint in embarrassment, or rage—probably both—and she throws each of us a scathing look, but I don't miss the hurt in her eyes.

"Word of advice, girl. If you don't want to be treated like a walking, talking cumbucket, don't act like one." It might sound harsh, but it's a life lesson she evidently needs to learn. Although if the murderous look she tosses my way is anything to go by, she doesn't appreciate the advice.

Oh well, you can't help people who refuse to help themselves.

With a venomous snarl, unable to form any real comeback, she stamps her feet and storms out in typical Bianca fashion.

"Twat shot?" I chuckle after she's gone.

Cam shrugs. "Like a female dick pic. I'm going to need therapy if I have to look at them anymore."

"Just stop looking at them," I retort, rolling my eyes.

"You think I look at that shit?!" He fake gags. "Hell no. The image automatically appears at the top of my screen when I get a notification. That's enough to have me wanting to pluck out my eyeballs, never mind looking at it on the full screen." He shudders, looking thoroughly sickened.

I can't help but laugh at his dramatics, although, yeah, I'd probably feel the need to scrub the image out of my eyes, too, if I had to see that shit.

"Anyway, enough about her. I, uh, wasn't sure if you'd want coffee or ice cream, so I grabbed us a coffee-flavored ice cream to share, if that's okay?"

His demeanor has wholly changed from the asshole he acted like in front of Bianca. Now he seems nervous as he rubs awkwardly at the back of his neck, seeming unsure.

I smile reassuringly at him. "Coffee ice cream sounds awesome." The tension drains out of his posture immediately, and he smiles back as I close the distance between us to sit down in a chair facing him. Neither of us talks as he pops the lid off the tub and hands me a spoon, the two of us digging in.

The tub is nearly empty by the time my stomach screams in protest, and I lean back in my chair, watching as Cam finishes it off.

"I missed this," I say quietly, as though the truth of the words would be too much to handle if I spoke them any louder.

Cam glances up at me, setting the empty tub on the table along with his spoon. A softness enters his eyes, and a sad smile dances along his lips.

"Yeah, me too."

Awkward tension burns up the air between us until Cam laughs sheepishly. "I don't know how to act around you now. I have no idea what we're doing. Do we go back to the way things used to be? Is that even possible?"

"I don't know," I admit, chewing anxiously on my bottom lip. "What do you want to happen?"

He takes a second to think over his answer, but a heated resolve enters his eyes.

"I want all the things with you." His voice has taken on a deeper tone. A hungry rasp that has my vagina waking up and suddenly paying attention. "I want what we had before, and so much more."

My eyes bulge at his admission. *Well, damn.* I'd kind of hoped that's what he'd want. I can't explain it, but this pull between us is irresistible. Fighting it is exhausting. I was fully expecting him to go back to trying to put distance between us, and while I'd respect that if it's what he wanted, I'm honestly tired of all the hate and anger. If he's willing, I want to see how amazing things could be between us.

Slipping out of my chair, I round the table and slide onto his lap. His hands instantly come to rest on my hips, as though he couldn't bear to go another second without touching me.

"I want all that too," I murmur, looking into his eyes, right before he crushes his lips to mine and the two of us lose ourselves in one another. My fingers tangle with the still-damp strands of hair at the nape of his neck, Cam having most likely come straight from a training session at the pool. We shouldn't be doing this here, where anyone could walk in and see us, but the heat between us is an unstoppable force. We're like two magnets being pulled toward one another, and there's no stopping the inevitable collision.

All too soon, we pull apart.

"Come with me." He hurriedly gets to his feet, pulling me up with him.

"What…Why? Where are we going?"

He steps into me, his nearness ratcheting up that magnetic pull between us. "If we stay here, I'm not going to be able to hold you. I won't be able to kiss you or do any of the things I want to do to you."

Well, when he puts it like that. "Lead the way."

A bright grin lights up his face, reminiscent of the old Cam that I've missed so much. I love seeing that smile on his face, and I'd do pretty much anything to ensure he never loses that happiness.

Leaving the dining hall, we step into the gloomy night. It's nearly midnight, so not many people are about, but we still need to be careful.

"Are we not going to your dorm?" I ask when he starts to walk in the opposite direction. I'd just assumed that's where we were going.

"If I take you there, I'll have to share you with West and Mason." Leaning down, he whispers in my ear, "I want you all to myself for a little while." The tickle of his breath against my ear and the sexual husk in his voice have me suppressing a shiver as my pussy clenches, already hungry for him.

He's all but sprinting as he pulls me after him, and I giggle as we quickly make our way through the forest toward the lake. We continue at a hurried pace, skipping past the boat house until we reach the tree line on the opposite side of the lake. I've never been to this part of campus before. It's so far away from everything that I just assumed there was nothing out here. Hidden amongst the trees is a small hut and a short boardwalk that goes out into the water.

We walk to the end of the boardwalk, and Cam shrugs out of his jacket, setting it down on the wooden boards. He sits down, patting the space beside him. Doing as he commands, my thigh presses against his, our legs dangling above the dark water.

Neither of us speaks. Instead, we sit and listen to the slight breeze whistle through the trees overhead as we look out over the cavernous lake.

"So," Cam begins, back to his initial awkwardness, "my dad's trying to trap you into being his bitch bride."

I snort. Of course, Cam has to turn the whole fucked-up situation into a joke.

"I guess that makes me almost your bitch mommy."

His face scrunches in disgust before he bursts out laughing. "Fuck, that would have been super weird."

"You're telling me," I agree.

The two of us chuckle before Cam's features grow serious. "So, how did you get away from him?"

I glance away and peer out over the lake as I contemplate the answer to his question. "I ran away." It's difficult. I can't give him many more details without coming right out and telling him about the rest of my fucked-up past. I'm not entirely sure why I'm still keeping it from the guys. I told Beck, after all. But out of all of them, he was the easiest one to open up to. And not because the others have made me feel like I can't be honest with them. I guess it's since they're closer to their parents, and they're the direct heirs of the company. It makes it that much harder to be entirely open with them.

"Why now? Why didn't you run away years ago?"

I sigh. It's a good question. "Have you ever been so consumed by your fears that they've immobilized you?"

"Like night terrors?"

"Yeah, but when you're awake. That's how I felt every time your dad was around me. I wanted to fight back, yet I was frozen with fear. He was the scariest thing in my universe—and that's saying something. Over the years, he convinced me I could never get away from him. He swore he'd never let me go. Hearing that over and over messes with you. The words get into your head and make you believe they're real. It took me a long time to realize his words were just that—words.

"One day, when he was with me, he received a call from the school...about you. You'd done something that had obviously warranted a call to him. Before then, I knew nothing about this man who visited me once a month and brought me unwanted gifts. I felt powerless, which further reinforced his influence over me.

"However, that day, he said your name and the name of your school. I know it wasn't much, but it was enough for me to work with. Enough for me to feel like I had some control. Something I could use to fight back with."

"So you made a plan to escape?"

I nod my head. "More or less."

"And came to Pac?"

I nod again.

"To kill me."

It's not a question, and I can tell by the tone of his voice that he doesn't believe me or believe I'm capable of doing something like that. He's seen me fight twice now, so he knows I have the skills to do it, but there's a massive difference between physically being able to overpower someone and being mentally strong enough to take someone's life. If only he knew I could do both. Despite the darkness that lives inside him and likes to rear its ugly head now and again, Cam is all light and happiness. Honestly, he's the one I worry about the most when it comes to telling them my truth. I don't think Mason will be all that shocked, and I believe West will be able to rationalize it. Hawk, I'm not sure about yet, but Cam...I worry it will be too much for him.

"Yeah. I know it sounds far-fetched—"

"Not really," he admits, shaking his head. He's deep in thought, lines furrowed across his forehead. "You're physically capable, and you've proven you can get in and out of our apartment without us noticing. If you'd wanted to, you probably could have done it ten times over by now."

More like fifty, but who's keeping count?

"So why didn't you?"

He looks genuinely confused, and it breaks my heart a little. I've seen true evil. I've stared it in the face every day for years, so I *know* Cam is anything but evil. Yeah, he's got demons within him, but who doesn't? This world tries to beat you down every damn day. It's only a matter of time until all that locked-up anger and resentment takes on its own form. We all like to think we're not capable of horrible things, but in the right circumstances, with the right incentive, we're capable of anything. We all have demons inside of us; some people's are just more vile and barbaric than others.

I shift onto my knees and move to straddle him, needing him to see the honest truth in my eyes. I've told him this before, but I get the impression that he wasn't really listening, or he didn't believe what I had to say, so I want him to genuinely hear me now.

With my face taking up his whole field of vision, I press my palms flush against his cheeks, so he has no option but to look at me. "Because you are nothing like your father." I see the protest forming on his lips, and I quickly lean in, pressing a chaste kiss to shut him up.

"You are the sunlight on a dark day, the rainbow when it pours, the lighthouse in a storm. You're *my* sunlight. *My* rainbow. *My* lighthouse. I was barely alive when I turned up here, but *you* helped me learn to breathe. You made me see there's more to life than just surviving. I *need* you in my life, making me laugh and reminding me of the good times when things go wrong. So please, *please* don't let all this self-hatred and guilt you're carrying around swallow you up, because I don't know what any of us would do without you."

A tear leaks out of the corner of his eye and runs down his cheek, catching on the edge of my thumb before I swipe it away. The way he looks at me...I don't know how to describe it. It's almost like reverence. No one has ever looked at me like that, like I'm some sort of angel sent to guide them.

His hand wraps around the back of my head, his fingers tangling in my hair as he draws me in. His lips collide with mine, hungry and eager. It's more than just carnal need, however. The way he kisses me, it's like I'm his lifeline. The only thing keeping him alive right now.

I kiss him back with as much fervor, needing him just as badly as he needs me. Our hands are everywhere as our bodies burn up. Tearing our clothes off, Cam wastes no time sinking into me in the most delicious way possible. It doesn't take long before we're both cresting that peak, and I cry out my release into the night sky.

"I hope you know I'm never letting you go," he pants in my ear.

That suits me perfectly fine. I have no intention of going anywhere.

CHAPTER 12

Hadley

I STORM INTO THE COMPUTER SUITE, SENDING THE DOOR BANGING OFF the wall as I sear anyone who so much as dares glance in my direction with a heart-stopping death glare.

We knew the girls would do something, but this has Bianca's dirty fingerprints written all over it. I'm going to tear out her fucking ovaries and force-feed them to her.

"Wow, why do you look like you want to murder someone?" West asks, cocking a brow as I dump myself in the seat beside him.

"Have you seen this?" I snarl, opening my tablet for him to see. Navigating to the page, I thrust it under his nose and watch as his eyes widen and his features tighten, a scowl forming across his face.

That dead fucking bitch set up a website where any Tom, Dick, and Harry can watch that stupid fucking video Cam and Hawk released last semester. I make a mental note to tear them new assholes when this class is over.

"Look at the number of views." I'm practically vibrating with anger in my chair. "And do you see what it says about me? That *bitch* even got her hands on fake medical records that say I've been in a fucking psychiatric unit all this time. She's got the whole school thinking I'm fucking unstable. No one will even look at me today. One kid nearly peed himself when he accidentally walked in front of me."

He quirks an eyebrow. "Thought you hated everyone trying to get your attention."

"Doesn't mean I want them thinking I'm about to go apeshit on their asses."

I know he's about to come back with another stupid retort, but he sees my deadpan stare and thinks better of it—smart boy. He focuses back on the tablet for another few seconds before setting it down, pulling the same screen up on his computer, and split-screening it along with one of his gibberish code programs.

"What are you doing?" I ask curiously. "Can you take it down?"

"Better," he assures me with a smug smirk, his fingers flying furiously over the keyboard.

I want to know what he means by that, but I don't want to distract him when he's busy, so instead I sit and watch, not having the faintest idea what he's doing.

After about fifteen minutes, he hands the tablet back to me. "Okay, refresh the page and play the video."

"What? West, I really don't need to see that thing again. I know what my body looks like, thanks."

He rolls his eyes at me like I'm being deliberately obtuse. "Just play the damn video, Firefly."

"Fine," I sigh dramatically, doing as he asks.

I'm only half-watching as the video begins to play, but the second I realize I'm not looking at myself but at Bianca's head on a blob of a body, jiggling as it does some sort of weird naked dance, I throw my head back and burst out laughing. *Holy shit, that's fucking amazing.*

"How did you do that?" I exclaim, a massive grin on my face. Damn, I want to kiss him so badly right now. "And what about the other stuff?"

He's got a wicked glint in his eye as he smirks back before concentrating on the screen, hopefully getting rid of the fucking article that claims my scars are all self-inflicted and the reason why I was locked away in a psych unit all these years. It's the fake medical records that infuriate me. They look fucking real, and they bluntly state that I'm a danger to myself and others and that I was removed from the facility against medical advice. Fucking bitch is going to pay for this.

"I've erased everything else on the website," West confirms. The tension immediately drops out of my shoulders as I collapse back in my chair. "As for the video, it's pretty easy, really. I've done it before, so it took no time at all to recreate it."

"You've done this before? To who?"

"You read through all the files I gave you, right?"

"Of course." I made sure to read through them all the night he handed them over to me, and I've been keeping them safe since then, scouring through them at every available opportunity.

He nods his head, having expected that answer. "So, you know about our chemistry teacher."

"Yeah, I've been meaning to talk to you guys about that."

Again, he nods his head, pulling up the chemistry teacher's OnlyPorn account on the computer. I'm guessing he was able to bypass whatever website restrictions the school has in place. Somehow, I doubt they would be okay with their students having easy access to such sites during class.

"Did you play the videos he's uploaded?"

"What?! No. Why would I do that? Why the hell haven't *you* taken them down yet if you're so damn talented?" I argue.

The smug look he throws me lets me know I've underestimated him. He passes me an earphone so I can hear the sound as he clicks on the video. Instead of the underage porn I was expecting to find, I have the horrific pleasure of watching Mr. Dillman, our chemistry teacher, trussed up like a thanksgiving turkey as some dominatrix woman spanks his ass, and he screams like a little girl. West pauses it just as the woman produces a monster dildo—there's no other word to describe the ten-inch black dick that's lined up with his asshole, sans lube.

"What," I stutter, flapping my hand at the screen in protest. "It was just getting good."

West laughs as he exits the site.

"How did you manage to do that?"

"It took a lot of work, and required Cam to scare the crap out of him so I could record that girly scream you heard."

I laugh. "Damn, that's amazing. I need a copy of that."

"You seriously thought we just left those videos up there for anyone to see?" he asks, looking hurt. His expression makes me wince.

"Why haven't you gotten rid of him, though? That's all well and good," I say, pointing toward the monitor, "but he's still preying on vulnerable students."

West grits his teeth. "I know," he spits out. "We haven't been able to get rid of him. He's in our parents' pockets, along with several other staff members. We have a mountain of evidence against him, but if we take it to the police now, our parents will just get him off and the school will sweep it under the rug. We're waiting until graduation to release it. We figure by then our parents won't care as much about who in the school is on their payroll."

Well, that makes sense, and now I feel bad for thinking the worst of the guys.

"I'm sorry," I grimace.

West sighs, moving his chair so our knees are pressed together. His fingers come up to press firmly on either side of my chin in a dominating hold that ensures I can't look anywhere but at him.

"It's okay. I know you have difficulties trusting people, and I know you don't fully trust us yet. We might be assholes, but we don't condone what he or our parents are doing." He releases his hold on my chin, clasping my hand between his large palms. "Hawk told us what you said to him, about taking down our parents and the company."

I nod my head.

"We're all in. We're sick of them controlling us. I'm sick of them holding me as leverage over everyone's heads."

I stare at him slack-jawed. "You want to help take them down?"

"Yeah, Firefly. We're going to destroy them, once and for all."

WEST'S LITTLE COMPUTER TRICK WITH BIANCA WAS PRETTY AWESOME, and it's certainly become the gossip of the school. The video spread like wildfire until Bianca locked herself away in her room, refusing to come out. That was over a week ago, and no one has seen hide nor hair of her since. But, it's not enough. People are still whispering about me. Don't get me wrong, I kinda love the way the color drains out of their faces when I enter a room, but *I* want to instill that fear in them, because they know what I'm capable of, not because some fake document states that I'm mentally unstable. It's crucial that I exert my control over the girls, and the only way to do that is to make it perfectly clear that *I'm* the one with all the power around here.

So that's why I've gathered all the girls in the dining hall this afternoon. Okay, so I had to get the guys to spread the word that *they* were the ones that wanted to speak to the girls, to clear the air with the whole girl of the month thing—I'm pretty sure no one would have shown up if they thought it was me asking for the meeting—but either way, the method worked. Casting my eyes over the crowd as I step into the hall, I see it looks like every senior girl is here. *Excellent.*

With my head held high, my school skirt swishes around my thighs as my combat boots smack against the wooden floor, effectively silencing the crowd as I stride to the front of the room. The guys wanted to join me, but it would make a much more powerful statement if I did this on my own.

When I reach the Princes' table, I pull out a chair, lifting my foot onto it before I step up onto the table so I'm standing above the crowd.

"Where are the Princes?" someone shouts out.

"Are they reinstating the tradition?"

Jesus, is sex with the Princes all these girls think about?!

"No, the tradition is *not* being reinstated," I bark out more harshly than is necessary.

"Then why are we here?"

Oh, look who climbed out of their hidey-hole to join us today.

"Ah, Bianca. It's so great you could be here," I say in a sugary sweet voice, topping it off with a cherry smile.

Breaking eye contact with her, I look out over the assembled girls.

"As you are all aware, a website was set up this week containing slanderous allegations and a compromising video. A video that I did not consent to. Now, if the person who did it will step forward and own up to what they did, this can be sorted out quietly." Whispers erupt in the crowd. I know Bianca did it, and Bianca knows she did it, but I'm guessing most others don't know who the primary suspect could be.

"*If* the offending party does *not* own up to their actions, then everyone will suffer," I declare threateningly. Honestly, I don't expect Bianca to ever own up, but putting the fear of God in the rest of the girls will ensure they think twice before stepping out of line.

"What does that mean?" a nervous voice near the back of the room asks.

"Excellent question. What does that mean? Well, I guess it means that the secrets all of you have that you don't want everyone to know about will start coming to light."

Another round of whispers as girls gasp and frantically consort with the person beside them.

I don't miss Bianca's scoff, though, or how she rolls her eyes. "Do you have something to say, Bianca?" I smile politely at her, like I've all the time in the world.

Huffing, she crosses her arms across her ample chest, cocking her hip. "Please, you've only just started here, and you've been a pariah all year. You don't know anything about any of us."

A few head nods and murmured agreements are scattered throughout the crowd, and my polite smile turns positively vicious as I drop the act and let them see every part of the predator I am.

"Is that so? Let's see." I tap my finger against my lip in time to the tapping of my boot against the tabletop. "I know Tiffany has chlamydia that's gone untreated for over a year." A gasp comes from somewhere on the left side of the room.

"How dare you," Tiffany yells, sounding offended.

"Am I wrong?" I question her with a raised eyebrow. "Would you like me to show you the proof?"

Lifting my phone out of my blazer pocket, I shrug my shoulders like it's no big deal, because *it is no big deal*. With a press of a few buttons the swoosh of an email being sent echoes around the room—okay, so West spent over an hour teaching me how to attach a document to an email and mass send it, but that's so not the point right now—and a few seconds later, everyone's tablets and phones go off.

There is another round of gasps and whispers as everyone reads my email. Attached is the latest letter sent by Tiffany's gynecologist, urging her to contact him immediately regarding her positive chlamydia result from over a year ago. It also lists the long-term consequences of the disease, and trust me, that shit is nasty. Why the fuck she doesn't just get it treated is beyond me.

Tiffany starts screaming a litany of abuse my way, but I just give her a megawatt smile in return, feeling fully in my element right now as I bring all these bitches to heel.

I notice a movement in the far back corner of the room, and my attention flicks to the doorway leading into the kitchen, noticing it's slightly ajar. I have to restrain my eye roll when I spot Mason and Cam squinting through the crack. *Idiots.* They just had to check out what I was doing, didn't they! Noticing me looking at them, Cam gives me a thumbs-up in encouragement, and Mason winks. Ignoring them, I focus back on the girls before me. They are much more subdued than when I first entered the hall.

"Alright," I yell over Tiffany, who's still screaming like a banshee. "Who's next?"

"We don't know who leaked that video," one girl near the front cries out.

"No?" I swivel my gaze around the room before landing on Bianca. She looks paler than before, but she holds her ground—gotta give her credit for that. "None of you have a clue?"

Everyone shakes their heads adamantly.

"Bianca?" I question. "You have no idea who did it?"

"No," she bites out, but I don't miss the quiver in her voice.

I sigh in disappointment, shaking my head as I press another button on my phone. Once again, the flurry of notifications goes off across the room a few seconds later.

After my initial excitement, I was particularly shocked at this revelation, and I didn't even get it from West's blackmail pile. Nope, I found this little beauty all by myself, when I had to pee in the middle of history class. It's amazing…The gossip you over-hear while sitting in a bathroom stall.

My eyes stay pinned on Bianca as whispers crescendo around us. For a long moment, she stares back at me, refusing to lower her gaze. Eventually, though, the need to know exactly what bomb I've dropped that will destroy her life gets the better of her, and she glances down at her phone. The color leeches out of her face as her hands start to tremble. She peeks nervously at the girls around her, all gaping with open mouths in her direction.

"Is it true?" I hear someone ask her.

With tears shining in her eyes, she spins on her heels and rushes out of the room, the door closing echoing behind her.

"Take this as a warning," I shout out, making sure everyone can hear me loud and clear. Now that I've dropped the giant bomb, I'm keen to get this shit show over with. "Do not cross me. Do not cross the Princes. Do. Not. Step. Out. Of. Line. I am watching you and will gladly reveal your deepest, darkest secrets to the rest of the school. There's a queen on the throne now, and she won't be taking any prisoners." I pin every single girl with a fierce look that shows them how fucking serious I am. "Now get the fuck out of here," I bark in my best impression of Hawk and Mason.

Everyone jumps into motion, eager to get away from me as quickly as possible. As the girls push and shove their way out the door, I hop down off the table, landing solidly on my feet.

"Holy shit, babe, that was amazing," Mason praises, once we're alone in the hall, pushing his way through the kitchen door with Cam hot on his heels. Gathering me in his arms, he swings me around, making me laugh.

"Seeing you go all demonic on their asses was hot as fuck." Cam is bouncing on the balls of his feet as he waits impatiently for Mason to let go of me, pulling me in for a heated kiss as soon as he does.

"Yeah? You think I made my point?"

"I think you made them piss their pants, Little Warrior." Mason laughs, looking weirdly proud. His praise makes me grin, even if it's a little sick and twisted. "But you have to tell us, what dirt did you have on Bianca?"

I smirk. "She has a secret baby."

Cam gapes at me with wide eyes, and I can see the wheels churning in his head.

"She, what?" Mason exclaims. "How did you find that out?"

"I overheard her arguing with her mom about it one day in the bathroom. I got West to do a little digging, and we uncovered the birth certificate."

"It's not mine, is it?" Cam asks in a strangled voice, sweat forming along his brow.

"No," I assure him, reaching out to squeeze his hand. "It's not."

"Thank fuck," he breathes out, relieved.

Fuck, that would have been a catastrophe. There's no way Bianca would have kept that a secret, however. She's been trying to hook Cam all year—and now I think I know why—but if he was the baby's father, she would have made sure to use it to lock him down tight. Thank fuck for condoms, right?

Word spreads through the campus like wildfire, and by the end of the day, everyone knows about Bianca's not-so-secret baby and Tiffany's untreated chlamydia. The latter quickly packed her bags and escaped campus amidst a bunch of enraged boys.

"Holy shit, girl. Do you have any idea of the mayhem you have unleashed?" Emilia giggles that evening. "Everyone is terrified of you now."

"They should be." I laugh.

"I don't get why you had to do it," Michael chimes in, bewildered. "Or why the guys are no longer picking girls?"

"I had to exert my dominance," I explain casually. "When the guys arrived freshman year, they had to prove they were the top dogs or no one would take them seriously, so now I have to do the same. Stopping the tradition they had with the girls, means I'm the only one in control of them. It makes me look more powerful if I'm doing it on my own instead of riding their coattails."

I didn't really understand why I had to do it, either. Still, now that I've done it, and seen for myself how effective it was at getting everyone to fall in line and see me as the new queen of Pac, I can admit that rush of adrenaline you get from knowing you're the biggest, baddest bitch around is intoxicating. I think I'm a little high off of the power.

"What now?" Emilia asks.

"I'm not sure. I guess I don't need to do anything unless someone steps out of line."

"So." Emilia gets an excited glint in her eye. "Bianca's baby..."

We spend the rest of the day speculating about who the baby

daddy is. There was no name on the birth certificate, and apparently Bianca disappeared all of last summer. She told everyone it was because she was getting her boobs done—which it seems she also did—but the main reason she wasn't at any of the summer parties was that she was having a friggin' baby.

Of course, when I first overheard Bianca in that bathroom, my initial concern had been that Cam was the dad—what a fucking disaster that would have been—but West and I were able to work back from the date on the birth certificate. We calculated that she must have gotten pregnant in October or November, and West assured me Cam only started sleeping with her last spring after she was already pregnant. The lucky bitch must have had one teeny-tiny baby bump to pull that one off.

I don't really give a damn who her baby daddy is. Although I'm guessing he's not rich or of the 'right breeding' since she's not shoving a diamond engagement ring in everyone's faces and is instead chasing after *my* filthy rich boyfriend.

CHAPTER 13

Hadley

Everything falls into place after my little show in the dining hall. The girls rightfully look at me with fear as I walk past, always either saying nothing or stuttering out a polite hello before scurrying off.

The boys are still annoying as hell, trying to flirt with me at every opportunity. The fact none of them knew my name before all this Davenport crap came to light shows they're just after me because of my supposed money and status. It's repulsive, and I don't have the time of day for them. Yet, they have the audacity to think *I'm* the rude one when I tell them to fuck off. The arrogance of some people!

Over the next week, I try to stay on top of my homework—and fail miserably—and I get to spend time with my friends and the guys, both as a group and some one-on-one time. Life actually feels good right now, except for the dark cloud that is our parents constantly hanging over our heads.

I'M SITTING IN MY ROOM, TRYING TO BLAST THROUGH SOME OF THE backlogs of schoolwork I have, when my phone ringing interrupts my concentration.

No one ever calls, so I'm surprised when I see Hawk's name flash on the screen.

"Hey, is West with you?" he blurts out before I can say anything. The unusual strain in his tone has me instantly on alert as I drop my pen and focus on the call.

"Uh, no. Why?"

"Fuck," he curses. "None of us have been able to find him."

"What do you mean?" I rush out, frantically trying to remember when I last saw him. He was at breakfast this morning, but we didn't have any classes together, and I grabbed lunch with Emilia and Michael today, so I haven't seen him since then. "You checked the library and computer lab?"

"Yeah." I can hear the worry in his voice, and it only makes me panic more.

"Have you talked to Beck? Maybe he's with him?" It's a long shot, but it's the only idea I have right now.

"No, I haven't."

"I'll phone him now."

Not waiting for his response, I hang up and dial Beck. He picks up on the second ring.

"Hey, sweetheart, what's up?"

"Have you seen West?" I rush out, sounding panicked as I get straight to the point, a sick feeling settling in my stomach.

"Uh, no, why, what's going on?"

"No one has seen him all day. We were hoping he might have been with you."

I can hear rustling in the background and the flurry of movement before the sound of a door slams shut.

"He's not. I'm coming over now."

"Okay, meet you at the guys' room."

Hanging up, I jam my feet into my boots and rush out the door while my brain frantically tries to think of where he could be. I'm desperately making excuses to myself that he's gotten caught up in his computer stuff or something and lost track of time—anything to stop me from thinking of the alternative—that something has happened to him.

I take the stairs to the guys' floor two at a time, banging my fist on the door.

"Anything?" I ask hopefully, when Hawk answers.

"In the last two minutes? No."

Ignoring his pissy attitude, I stride past him, saying, "He's not with Beck. He's coming over now to help."

Cam and Mason are sitting at the island. Cam's typing on his tablet, and Mason sighs as he hangs up his phone. "His cell just goes straight to voicemail."

"He's not answering any of my messages either," Cam tacks on.

"Has he ever done this before? Is it possible he's just working on a project and lost track of time?" My voice is tinged with optimism, even though I know it's futile.

"Nah. He wouldn't not answer his phone," Cam insists. "He must have about twenty missed calls from us by now."

I absently nod my head as I contemplate where else he could be. "Is there anywhere he likes to go on campus that you haven't checked yet?"

"No. We've already looked everywhere he usually hangs out."

I've only been in the apartment for a few minutes when there's another knock at the door.

"What's going on?" Beck demands, sounding slightly breathless from his rush to get over here as he strides into the apartment in his workout gear, a serious expression on his face and a tightness around his eyes.

"We don't know yet," Hawk responds. "The last we saw West was at lunch. He had physics and biology this afternoon, but none of us are in those classes with him."

"It's seven o'clock. How are you only realizing now that he's missing?" Beck growls angrily, causing Hawk to glare in his direction.

"Not that you would know, because you don't know anything about him," Hawk snarls, digging the knife into Beck's chest, "but he usually goes to the library or computer lab after class. It was only when he didn't show up at dinner and none of us had heard back from him that we suspected something wasn't right."

"Guys," I bark. "This isn't helping. We need to work together."

"We should split up and scour the campus," Beck insists.

Hawk scowls at him but nods his head. "I agree. Between us, we should be able to cover most of it pretty quickly. Mason, check the rec and sports center. Cam and Beck, both of you check the main school buildings, then when you're done, meet Mason and spread out to search the forest at that end of the campus. Hadley and I will search the forest behind the dorms and work our way toward the lake."

Everyone nods and quickly gets to their feet.

"Here, take these." Mason hands each of us flashlights. "In case it gets dark before we find him."

His voice is tight, and his words leave an ominous chill in the atmosphere that none of us want to acknowledge.

"Everyone keep their phones handy, check in every half hour and let the rest of us know if you find anything," Hawk directs before we all set off out the door.

<hr>

"I'M REALLY BEGINNING TO WORRY," I RELUCTANTLY ADMIT AN HOUR later. We've searched most of the forest, and there has been no sign of him. Although, honestly, I'm not sure if that's a good thing or not. I mean, what the fuck would he be doing all the way out here? *This is where you'd take a dead body to dump it.* That's the thought that keeps playing on repeat in my head. As the sun starts to set, making the shadows grow longer, every fallen log and pile of leaves that looks like it could be a dead body makes me shiver in fear as nausea churns my stomach, freezing me in place for a second before I can gather my wits and convince myself it's nothing more than foliage.

"He's stronger than he looks," Hawk assures, sounding like he's trying to convince himself as much as me. The two of us are about six feet apart, scouring the ground and surrounding forest to our left and right with every step we take.

"I know, but I keep thinking about what if our parents got to him. If they sent someone after him, he wouldn't stand a chance against them."

"He's fine," Hawk growls, refusing to believe anything else.

We walk on in silence for another beat until the crack of something hidden in the leaves underneath my boot has both of us freezing and staring down at the ground.

Hawk rushes over to me as I lift my boot, revealing a now cracked phone. He bends down to lift it, but all I can do is stare at it. This has got to be a bad omen, right?

"Is it his?" I croak out.

He looks it over before attempting to turn it on, but the thing is nothing more than a black brick.

"I don't know." He blows out a breath in frustration.

I mean, it *has* to be his. Only a few people come this deep into the forest, and anyone who dropped their phone would search for it. They wouldn't just walk off and leave it.

He tucks the phone away in his pocket. "Come on, let's keep searching." His eyes roam over the area, looking for any other clues before he fixes his stern gaze on me. "This doesn't tell us anything, and it might mean nothing. We have to keep looking."

The sharpness of his words is what gets through to me and locks down the out-of-control swarm of emotions I'm feeling right now, forcing myself into the headspace I've had to engage so many times when I was out on a job. Emotions have no place when you need to keep your head and think rationally, so all this fear and worry won't do me—and it certainly won't do West—any good. Shoving all those useless feelings into a box, I nod my head, ready to keep going.

After another fifteen minutes of searching, we reach the edge of the forest by the lake. By now, the sun has set, and the dark sky makes the deep water look more sinister than I ever remember it being. A deep-seated sickness flows through me as I look out over the water, and I feel Hawk tense beside me as he does the same. Both of us know the best place on campus to get rid of a dead body is in that lake.

We shine our torches over the pebbled shore as we walk along it toward the boathouse.

"Over there!" I point toward where something glints in the glow of my flashlight slightly further down the beach. "What is that?"

The two of us rush toward it, hoping it's a clue and fearing it's something bad.

I gasp as I skid to a stop on the stones. "They're his." My voice is strained, emotion choking me as I bend down to lift the broken pair of glasses. The lens in one eye is missing, and I can see small fragments of glass on the ground. "He must have gotten into a fight."

Frantically, I shine the light around us, desperately wanting it to show us another clue. Something. Anything. He must be nearby. He wouldn't have been able to get far without these.

Not seeing anything, I squint into the darkness, barely making out the outline at the far end of the beach.

"Hawk," I gasp. "The boathouse."

We share a glance before we take off, running full-force toward the small shack, no longer taking our time to search as we go. He *has* to be there.

I beat Hawk there by mere seconds and take a steadying breath, mentally trying to prepare myself for whatever we might find on the other side. Alert for any sound that could indicate an ambush, I push the door open, and we peer into the dark interior. There's nothing but silence which only makes me feel more on edge as we step inside, our flashlights sweeping over the weathered floorboards.

"Oh my god," I breathe, when Hawk's flashlight washes over a pair of legs—a pair of very still, unmoving legs. I scramble forward, Hawk right behind me as he moves his light to show us West's body and battered face.

His uniform is torn and bloodied, and his face looks like it was used as a punching bag.

"West," I cry out, dropping to my knees beside him. My hands hover over him, unsure of what to do or how I can help without causing him further pain.

When he doesn't respond, I shout again, "West!"

Hawk crouches down on his other side. "West, man," he calls out, shaking his shoulder. "It's me. Come on, we gotta get you out of here."

West groans, and I release a sigh of relief. *Thank fuck he's alive!* The stress from the last few hours vanishes, quickly being replaced with concern as I try to assess how bad his injuries are.

"West," Hawk yells, shaking him roughly again.

Another groan and a feeble swipe of his hand as he tries to dislodge Hawk's hand from his shoulder.

"That's it, man. You're gonna be fine," Hawk assures him before looking at me. "Stay with him, and I'll phone the others. Then we've gotta try and lift him out of here."

I absently nod my head, not once removing my gaze from West's face while Hawk gets to his feet and heads outside. He leaves the door open though, so we can still see each other.

I lean down so our faces are inches apart. "West?" I murmur softly, running my fingers through his hair, ignoring how the strands feel wet and sticky.

"Firefly," he whispers so quietly I barely hear him. "Not safe."

"It's okay," I reassure him. "Hawk and I are here. Whoever did this to you is gone."

He tries to nod his head, groaning at the pain that little movement causes him. I press my forehead to his, not giving a shit that he's sweaty and bloody.

"I'm so sorry," I murmur. "This is all my fault." My voice breaks and tears fall onto his closed lids, making them flutter.

"Shhh," he soothes, wincing as he lifts his arm, cupping the back of my neck. He manages to peel his eyes open, and it takes a second for him to focus his gaze on me. The pain I see in them only heightens my guilt. "This was *not* your fault," he insists in a tight voice, sounding hoarse from lack of use.

"It was. I was the one that said we should go against them. Look what they did to you," I croak. "They beat the shit out of you. They broke your glasses." A broken sob escapes me, and he lets out a pained chuckle, which quickly morphs into a groan as he winces. "I have a spare pair, don't worry about them. Just kiss me."

I press my lips to his, needing to be as close to him as possible to reassure myself he's actually alive. Intending to keep it quick, knowing he's not exactly in the right condition for a prolonged, dirty kiss, I go to pull back, but his hand on the back of my neck holds me in place as he deepens the kiss.

A snort behind me has us breaking apart, and I peer back over my shoulder.

"He can't be that bad if he's able to kiss you like that." Hawk scoffs, looking disgusted as he comes toward us. "Right, man, let's get you up. The others are on their way."

West gives a slight nod of agreement, and between Hawk and I, we manage to get him on his feet.

"Fuck, everything hurts," West groans. "Why the hell you and Mason do this to yourselves for fun is beyond me."

Hawk gives a small laugh. "Well, we don't usually go so hard."

West grunts, and we start moving. All conversation ceases as we focus on taking one step at a time. The sweat is dripping off West's forehead by the time we've reached the far end of the boathouse. Before we've even reached the edge of the forest,

Hawk and I are pretty much supporting all of his weight, and it's making my thighs burn.

Rustling and the sound of footsteps has my body tensing while Hawk awkwardly tries to shield a more or less passed-out West with his broad frame. The two of us share a quick glance as we wait to see who's out here with us.

When Mason, Cam, and Beck come bursting out of the trees, I let out a breath of relief. I don't know what we would have done if the mercenaries who beat up West were still around. I'm not sure how many I could take at once, and with West's condition, we need to get him back and check him over for any internal injuries.

Spotting us, all three of their eyes widen as they see the state of West.

"Fuck, are you okay?" Cam asks, looking him over.

"He'll live," Hawk answers brusquely. "But we need to get him back to the dorm."

Mason steps up in front of me, obviously intending to relieve me of West's weight that I'm supporting, but I hesitate and glance at Beck. The same concern is in his eyes as is in the others. I can see he wants to help, but he's holding himself back, unsure of what West would want.

Stepping out from under West's arm, Mason takes up my position, and he and Hawk manage to carry West through the forest with the three of us silently trailing along behind them. Sensing what a nervous mess I am as I worry about the extent of West's injuries, Cam reaches out and wraps his hand around mine, giving it a reassuring squeeze. Holding on to him, I link our fingers together and hang on to his small act of comfort as we slowly walk back to the guys' apartment.

It takes forever for Hawk and Mason to navigate up the stairs while carrying a nearly passed-out West between them. Although, we all eventually make it and the two of them get West settled on the sofa.

Cam rushes off to get his spare pair of glasses while I sit down beside him. Sliding my palm into his, I take comfort from the warmth of our touch—a solid reminder that the blood is still flowing through his veins, telling me he's alive.

"Should we call a doctor?" Hawk asks Mason, the two of them eyeing West critically. He's sitting with his head resting on the back of the sofa, his eyes shut, only cracking open a lid when Cam returns and hands over his glasses. Putting them on, his eyes drift shut again, his face scrunching at a flare-up of pain.

"I dunno." Mason purses his lips.

"Of course, we should," I argue. How could they think otherwise?!

"It would be our parents' doctor," Hawk explains, making me realize their indecision.

"No doctor," West groans, peeling his eyes half open. "I'll be fine."

"You're clearly not fine," Beck snaps. His expression is dark and angry, yet I can feel the concern coming off him in waves as he hovers uncertainly behind Hawk and Mason, watching West like…well, like a hawk.

He thinks on something for a second before stepping up beside Mason. "I'm by no means medically trained, but I've seen and patched up my fair share of battle wounds. I can take a look…if you want." He tacks on the last few words, indicating his hesitation.

Usually, he acts all tough and confident around the guys, but right now, he wants to be here for his brother, to help in some way, but he's got no idea how or if West would even want his help. The rocky state of their relationship breaks my heart. The two of them need each other more than they realize. West needs to wise up soon before Beck gives up trying altogether, and he misses out on what could be a pretty incredible relationship.

West dawdles, and I give his hand a squeeze, silently asking him to try. For his sake and Beck's.

"Yeah, okay," he relents with a sigh, sounding too tired to argue.

Giving Beck a small, reassuring smile, I help West remove the tattered remains of his shirt while Beck asks one of the guys if they have a first-aid kit and to get it for him.

I gasp as West's body is revealed. Bruises are beginning to form over his ribs and abdomen, and there are a few shallow cuts scored along his chest, the straight lines giving away the fact that a blade carved them. *I'm going to murder whichever fucker thought they could get away with that.*

The wounds are superficial. Intended to make a statement rather than do any actual harm and, honestly, I've seen far worse damage on some of the kids after they came out of the ring at the compound. The difference is that I didn't give a shit about any of those kids. Sure, I empathized with them. I felt awful for them, but I didn't have a smidgeon of the feelings I have for West.

Other than Meena, I've never had to see someone I care about get hurt. As I watch West wince, his breathing shallow, as he tries not to inhale too deeply and spark a flare-up of pain, the blood-thirsty assassin within me screams out for retribution. It's a debased part of myself I usually keep locked-up tight, only letting her out to play when I'm on a job or my life is on the line. Since leaving the compound, I haven't had to become that person— other than when I finished off those two mercenaries. However, right now, I welcome the coldness that seeps into my veins as my baser instincts rise to the surface, dulling and heightening my emotions as I burn the fuckers' unknown names into the muscle around my heart. Promising myself their death will be at my hands.

I move out of the way, giving Beck space to assess his brother as he approaches with the first-aid kit. His gaze roams over West, assessing the damage, his face pinching when he spots a particu-larly nasty-looking discolored patch over his left kidney.

We all watch as Beck pokes and prods West, inspecting his cuts to make sure they're as superficial as they look.

"Are you sure you know what you're doing?" West growls when he flinches for the fifth time under Beck's touch, grunting as the move causes him pain.

"Yes, I'm sure." Beck groans frustratedly, getting irritated at West's lack of trust in him, and fixing him with a look that says, 'stop being a baby'. "My friends and I were constantly patching each other up when we were kids. It's not like we could go to a hospital with every possible broken bone or deep cut. No one in Black Creek could afford healthcare, and gang life isn't a career path that comes with health insurance, so you quickly learned the basics of examining, disinfecting, and stitching up any sort of injury."

Despite his obvious pain, West watches Beck closely, scrutinizing his every move. "What if it was life-threatening?"

Beck shrugs indifferently. "Then you'd probably die before anyone could do anything. *Maybe* a buddy or someone would have driven you to the hospital, but if you were lucky enough to live after that, you'd be saddled with a hefty bill that would only push you into taking greater risks for whatever gang you were working for. Risks that would ultimately get you killed later on down the line anyway." Beck paints such a hardened, bleak picture of Black Creek, it has me feeling sorry for any kids who have to grow up in such an environment.

I was sent quite a few times myself when I was out on the job, and I have made a couple of contacts there, but it's not a place I'd rush to visit any time soon. The people there are all hardened by the things they've had to see and do. Their souls are black, or various shades of gray at best. I've always gotten the heebie-jeebies when I was there. That ick feeling when far too many unwanted eyes are watching your every move. Even with my blatant 'leave me the fuck alone' face on, it never stopped cocky shitheads who thought they were all that because they carried a weapon and wore special gang tats from approaching me. Assholes who thought I'd happily fall all over their dick just because they thought it was cool to be in a gang. Honestly, for the most part, everyone there are a bunch of children, playing at being tough and fighting over territory like it's their favorite toy. The whole lot of them need to grow the fuck up.

"Some of the bigger crews, like The Feral Beasts or the Antonellis, would have had a doctor or medical person under their thumb who could sort out any gnarly wounds. On the other hand, anyone who wasn't a part of their crew, or any gang at all, just had to pray no injury was too serious."

It's the way Beck says all of this so nonchalantly, like that's just how things were. Like it's normal, that is the most devastating. It's all incredibly fucked up, is what it is. I don't know what happened that resulted in his mom finally dragging them out of there, but I'm glad she did. Based on the worry lines on his forehead and the way he glances down at his Reaper Rejects tattoo on his forearm with a dejected look, I know whatever happened was something terrible. Something that he's carried with him, alone, for far too long.

As Beck says all of this, he continues his careful prodding of West, all the while ignoring him as West scans over his face. The way West is looking at him, with a sad and thoughtful look in his eyes that I noticed last time Beck opened up and shared some of his childhood with us, has a spark of hope igniting within me. Hope that one day these two can get past their differences.

"Well, what's the verdict?" Hawk asks as Beck gets to his feet, finished with his assessment.

"The cuts are all superficial. They just need to be cleaned and bandaged to ensure they don't get infected. His ribs and kidney are bruised, but I don't think anything is broken. He'll be stiff and sore for a few weeks, but he'll be fine."

"Good." Hawk's voice is gruff, and if I wasn't getting to know him better or seeing for myself how much he cares about these guys, I'd think he didn't give a shit. Even as his gruffness is chock-full of emotion that he doesn't know any other way to express.

Taking the kit from Beck, I slip back into my seat beside West and begin cleaning him up as the guys talk around me.

"So, are we all thinking this was our parents?" Mason begins, taking the chair opposite me as Cam brings over beers for everyone before sitting on my other side.

A resounding "yes" comes from everyone except West, who hisses when the antiseptic I'm using touches his cut.

"It definitely was," he assures us, looking a bit more alert than earlier. "There were three guys. They wore masks so I couldn't see their faces, but the way they moved was similar to the guys who attacked us at Christmas. They were so coordinated, and the level of precision…" He trails off, shaking his head, sounding both impressed by their skills and aggravated that he got jumped. "It was obvious they were highly trained and used to working as a team."

I grit my teeth and focus on stopping my hand from shaking with anger as I move on to clean another cut just beneath his pec. I'm going to gut every single fucker who touched him, and then I'm coming for the conniving sickos who call themselves our parents.

The roaring in my ears as I try to control the rage consuming me drowns out the continuing conversation around me, and I'm only pulled out of it when the loud ringtone of a phone going off penetrates through the red haze coating my mind.

Everyone looks at Hawk, whose lips are pressed tightly together as he stares at the phone before answering. Immediately putting it on speaker for the rest of us to hear, he tosses each of us a look to be quiet.

"I'm disappointed, son." Barton's voice comes out clearly across the speakerphone as he sighs. "I thought we told you to resume the tradition with the girls, yet we had to find out through another source that our own sons were defying us?" He snarls out the last few words. It's the first time I've heard him sound anything other than indifferent, and it's the first hint at the darkness within him—the same controlling darkness in all of our parents.

"We wanted—" Hawk begins.

"I don't care what you wanted," Barton yells down the phone. "You will do as we say. You will *all* go back to the old tradition with the girls."

He waits silently for Hawk to agree, but Hawk hesitates, staring at each of the guys for confirmation.

"Tonight was only a warning," Barton threatens when Hawk takes too long to respond. "We can do far worse. And not just to Westley."

Sighing silently, Hawk agrees—it's not like he has a choice.

"Okay. We'll start up the tradition again."

"Good. And Elizabeth is to join in as well, for now. We'll let you know when that changes."

What the fuck is that supposed to mean? The five of us share confused, worried, and angry glances. No one is entirely sure what exactly Barton means by those cryptic words.

Hawk looks at me, as if waiting for my confirmation that I'm okay with that, but, just like him, I have no other choice, so I reluctantly nod my head in agreement.

"Okay," Hawk responds to his dad.

"Good. Pick someone for her. You know who's suitable. Take this as the warning it was intended, son. Next time, do better."

With that, Barton hangs up, leaving us all staring dejectedly at one another and working out what the fuck we're supposed to do now.

CHAPTER 14

Hadley

I spend the night with West, the two of us sleeping fitfully. He tosses and turns all night, struggling to get comfy with his injuries, and his restlessness keeps me awake.

At five a.m., I give up and slip out of bed, grabbing a pair of sweats to pull on underneath the oversized t-shirt I borrowed last night before sneaking out the door. I creep down the hall, not wanting to disturb the others so early. It was after two before we all went to bed, exhaustion getting the better of us after the day's events. It felt like we got nothing sorted last night, the conversation going round in circles as we discussed what we were going to do about this stupid tradition and, ultimately, what our plan was to get rid of our parents, because it's become abundantly clear we can't continue to live under their rules and restrictions. I refuse to let anyone else dictate my life for me ever again, and I won't let them drag the guys deeper into their shit or tarnish Beck's soul further with the horrendous job they've asked him to do.

I PAUSE IN THE THRESHOLD OF THE OPEN PLAN KITCHEN AND LIVING space, studying Beck as he sleeps on the couch wearing only his boxers. His blanket is on the floor, having kicked it off at some point during the night. He refused to leave last night, and thankfully, no one argued with him, the others understanding his need to be close to his brother after everything that had gone down. Even if they had taken issue with it, I wouldn't have let him walk out of here. I needed to know all of us were safe last night, and the only way to be sure of that was if we were all together.

Instead of heading toward the kitchen for coffee, I veer off course, moving on silent feet toward a softly snoring Beck. Careful not to disturb him, I ease my knees onto the cushions on either side of his hips and hover over him. My eyes drift to his Reaper Rejects tattoo as I again wonder what happened in his childhood. He's alluded to the loss of someone close to him, but he's never volunteered more information, and I've never asked. He doesn't push me to tell him anything I'm uncomfortable with, so I won't do that to him. I trust that when he's ready to share, he'll let me in —and, hopefully, the others too.

Twirling around the tattoo are various black tribal designs, extending down to his wrist and shoulder. There's also a smattering of color intertwined with the other, smaller designs, making them stand out. From this angle, I can make out a compass with the words 'stay true' scrawled underneath, an image of a tree bare of leaves, and another one of an hourglass with the sand mostly run through.

Following the designs until my gaze lands on his face again, I can't help but stare at him. He's stunning when he's awake—all rugged handsomeness and wicked intent—but he's beautiful when he's asleep. The tight lines that far too frequently mar his face have faded away, letting his true age show through. He's so much younger than you'd think when you initially look at him. His past and life experiences have hardened him, both on the outside and inside, but he's not much older than the rest of us. Yet, he's trying to take the weight of all of this on his shoulders so the guys and I don't have to. I know that's why he's never mentioned what our parents are making him do. He's willing to risk the guys not trusting him if it means he can let all of us be kids a bit longer. It's selfless, really, but how much is bearing that burden alone going to cost him? I'm thankful that he opened up to me the other week. Hopefully, now, he knows he's not as alone as he thought he was.

"Morning, creeper." His deep voice is thick with sleep and he still doesn't open his eyes, but his hands slide up my thighs, resting on my hips and pulling me down so I'm sprawled across him.

"I didn't mean to wake you," I murmur against the soft skin of his neck.

"Then you probably shouldn't have been climbing all over me."

Okay, fair point, but he just looked so peaceful I had to get a closer look.

"How's West?"

"He's doing okay. He didn't sleep well, so I'm letting him rest a bit longer."

He nods his head, his eyes still closed as his fingers trace lazy circles on my back.

"How are you?" I know last night got to him, regardless of how well he tried to hide it.

He sighs, finally peeling his eyes open to look at me with a soft smile. He kisses the crown of my head before resting his head back on the pillow and staring at the ceiling above us.

"I was so worried about him," he admits. "I only just found him, and he still fucking hates me. The thought of something bad happening to him before we have a chance to get to know one another..." He trails off, but he doesn't need to finish that sentence. I know what he means. Hawk drives me fucking insane, but we're only beginning to get to know each other, and the thought of losing him now, just when things are starting to go well for us? Well, I can't bear to think about it.

"I don't know how to make things better between us." The tightening of his fingers on my hip tells me how much the friction between him and West is getting to him. "I've tried opening up about my childhood, so he could get to know me, however he doesn't even want to spend time with me. I don't know what else I can do."

I run my fingers through his hair, hoping it will take away some of the tension that has his body wound so tight. He snorts at whatever he's thinking, shaking his head at his inner thoughts. "I stupidly thought admitting why I was doing what I was for our parents, and why I couldn't tell anyone about it, would help him warm up to me. I thought if he knew I was doing it all for him, to keep him alive, it would make a difference. Not because I want him to owe me or because I feel obligated to, but because I want to be in his life. I want us to have a future where we have the opportunity to get to know each other."

"So, you really are only doing it for me?"

Beck and I both jump. My eyes dart up to look at West standing in the doorway in his pajama bottoms, staring bleary-eyed at Beck. I carefully climb off Beck so that he can sit up.

His gaze never leaves West as he responds, "Yeah."

"What about the money? And the fancy job and better career prospects?"

"I don't care about any of that. Every cent our father has given me is sitting in a bank account. I've never touched it, and I don't plan on it. As for the job, I can't deny it's not an amazing opportunity that I'm hoping will benefit me someday, but I wouldn't have accepted his shady offer for that reason alone."

West's eyes dart between Beck's, trying to ascertain the truth in his words. "So why did you take it, then? You had to know it would come with strings you wouldn't want to pull on."

Beck nods his head slowly. "I did, but after losing touch with my brothers all those years ago, the opportunity to connect with you, my *real* brother, was more than I could pass up. It's not like I ever expected us to be friends or anything, but I wanted the chance to get to know you. To see that you were doing okay, and, yeah, I hoped we could maybe have some sort of relationship one day." He shrugs casually like it's no big deal, except this is a huge fucking deal, and I can practically feel the stress radiating off him as he waits to hear what his brother says next.

West's eyes bounce to me, and I silently implore him to give Beck a chance. He's got no idea how fucking worth it it will be.

Looking back at Beck, he takes another few seconds to mull it over before nodding his head.

"Okay," he agrees slowly. "I'll stop icing you out."

No longer able to hold back my grin, I squeeze Beck's arm in excitement.

"But if it turns out anything you're telling me, or any of us, is bullshit, you'll be out of here so fucking fast it will all feel like a distant memory. You won't see me, or Hadley again."

Okay, I don't appreciate him making decisions like that for me, and I make it clear with the scowl I aim his way. My glare is sharp enough it could pierce a hole in the front of his forehead, right between his eyes. But I let it slide because I know that won't happen. I understand he still doesn't trust him fully, and I—of all people—can appreciate that.

"Alright, now that we have all agreed we're on the same team, sit your ass down," I tell West in a no-nonsense tone, getting to my feet. "I'll get you some painkillers. You should still be in bed, resting."

"I'm fine," he assures me, ambling slowly over to one of the armchairs and carefully lowering himself into it so as not to jostle any of his many bruises. In the light of day, and now that the blood has had time to rise to the surface of his skin, he looks fucking awful. Still hot as sin, of course, but it's painfully obvious he was put through the wringer last night.

Despite his insistence that he's fine, he doesn't argue with me when I give him the meds and a glass of water, quickly downing them and relaxing back in his chair as I go to make us all some coffee. I have a feeling we're going to need it.

NONE OF US GO TO CLASS FOR THE REST OF THE WEEK. SINCE WEST isn't a fighter like Mason or Hawk, his sudden bruised appearance will only raise unwanted questions, and with the gauntlet hanging over our heads, the rest of us need to strategize about our next moves. So the five of us hole up in their apartment, relying on gossip from Emilia and Beck to keep us up to date on what's going on in the rest of the school.

The only time we leave is to go to Cam's swimming competition on Saturday. He's in the regional championships, which means nothing to me, but it's something he's proud of, and we all want to be there to support him. He's been in the pool every spare minute he's had—which admittedly is not as much as he probably would have liked considering all we've had going on. With a hoodie pulled up over his head, hiding the last of the bruising on his face, West is able to join us as we watch Cam once again kick ass—looking fucking panty-melting doing it.

Of course, Lawrence can't let the occasion go by without a visit. This time, he's standing poolside with his gaze fixated on me as I sit in the stands beside Hawk. I do my best to ignore it, but his eyes burn into me like a laser. I have to curtail my enthusiasm for Cam's win, not wanting to alert Lawrence to my intense feelings for his son. However, as Cam stalks into the locker room afterward and the guys get to their feet around me, I can't help glancing his way. I instantly regret it as the corner of his lip curls up in a confident sneer, momentarily immobilizing me.

"Ignore him," Hawk whispers in my ear, a scowl etched across his face as he gently nudges my shoulder, pushing me forward. Ripping my eyes away from Lawrence, I follow the guys out of the stands, but I swear, even after we're back in our dorm and Lawrence is long gone, I can still feel his eyes on me.

On Monday morning, our masks are firmly in place as we throw open the doors to the dining hall and make our way to the Princes' table amidst murmurs from the rest of the crowd. Taking our seats, I do my best to ignore the gawking and obvious whispers as breakfast is delivered. The five of us eat in silence—not that I manage to eat much with the lead lining my stomach—and once we're finished, Hawk gives us the signal and we all get to our feet.

"We understand there have been issues regarding recent changes to the girl of the month tradition." Hawk's voice echoes around the room, loud and clear for everyone to hear.

My hands clench tightly around the edge of the wooden table, hating that we have to do this, but we've discussed it in depth over the last few days, and none of us can see any way around it. Not yet, at least. Not without putting West, and all of us, at risk.

"When we first discovered Elizabeth was a Davenport, we stopped the tradition as she needed the opportunity to come into her own here in the school. Now that that has been achieved, she has agreed to join us with the monthly tradition."

I grit my teeth as excited whispers break out around the room from both guys and girls. It takes everything in me to hold back the truth I desperately want to let slip. It's all a bunch of bullshit, yet we can't afford for the school to think we're being forced into this. They need to believe *we* are in charge, and this was the best excuse we could come up with after a week of mulling it over.

"So," Hawk bellows, bringing everyone's attention back to us. "Starting today, all five of us will choose a girl, or guy, for the month. The same rules as before apply."

Without further ado, Hawk points out some girl, and the same song and dance as every other time ensues. The other guys do the same, and despite the fact they barely spare whatever random girl they choose a second glance, every time they pick someone, it makes my blood boil. Mental images of me stabbing our parents flitter across my mind as I make a silent promise that those thoughts will one day be a reality.

All too soon, it's my turn. When Hawk first mentioned me participating in this archaic tradition, I'd just assumed I'd pick

Michael. Except after Barton's little 'you know who's suitable speech,' we all agreed it couldn't be a scholarship student.

The guys gave me a few names of families our parents would deem 'suitable' who weren't total assholes, yet looking out over the eager crowd, I don't know who any of them are.

As I roam my eyes over the rest of the hall, I play 'eenie meenie miney mo' in my head with each of the names I was given —it seems like as good a way as any to pick one.

Hawk coughs, a wordless gesture telling me to hurry the fuck up and get this over with, and after mentally cursing him out in my head, I call out the last name I was thinking.

"Daniel Fairweather."

Roars erupt from a table in the middle of the room, and guys clap some nerdy-looking kid on the shoulder as his ears pinken. At least he looks more likely to keep his hands to himself. Meh, even if he doesn't, I can just break them. That will teach him not to touch without permission.

After breakfast, the chosen girls all crowd around the guys, and rather than have to watch that shit, I wander off to find Daniel. He approaches me through the crowd, looking both cocky and unsure at the same time.

"Alright, Daniel," I begin before he can say something that will only make me dislike him more, "this is how things are going to go. In public, we have to make it look like we're dating, but do *not* touch me. Do *not* kiss me. There will absolutely be no sex. Got it?" His face falls with every order I bark, and he nods his head dejectedly. "Oh, and you can't have sex with anyone else either for the month."

I know. I bet he's real happy about being the chosen one now, but I can't have word spreading that my fake date is fucking other girls while he's supposed to be with me. It would undermine everything I've spent the last few weeks achieving here.

"What—"

"Those are the rules," I state, cutting him off. "It's too late. You can't back out or change your mind. And if you break any of them, you'll have the distinct pleasure of meeting my bad side. Fair warning, she can be a downright bitch. Just ask Tiffany and Bianca."

He pinches his lips, looking annoyed—not that I can blame him—but he nonetheless agrees to my crappy terms.

"Great." I plaster a falsely bright smile on my face. "You can walk me to class then."

The rest of the day isn't too bad. I think I put the fear of God into Daniel as he does nothing more than graze my shoulder as he walks me to my first class, and I'm pretty sure it's by accident because every time he does, he jumps a mile and mumbles an apology. I don't see him for the rest of the day after that, and the guys manage to shake off their girls as well, so the six of us hide away in their dorm for lunch. Beck has started joining us for lunch most days, and it's been great having everyone together. I've even noticed him and West talking a bit. It's not much, but it's an awesome start.

On Tuesday, the good mood leftover from yesterday drops right out of me as we enter the hall and the girls practically throw themselves at *my* guys. None of them look happy about the physical assault and are quick to extricate themselves. Still, seeing it fucking pisses me off. It only gets worse when we all sit down, and I overhear Hawk's girl telling him the fucked up shit she can do with her mouth. Hawk's eyes fill with lust as he adjusts himself under the table, utterly oblivious to the dangerous churning in my stomach. On my other side, Mason's girl is pushing her tits against his arm, trying to gain his attention as he all but ignores her as he shovels his breakfast into his mouth like it's a race. It's a little funny but still annoying as hell.

"So," I snap, turning my attention to Daniel in a bid to distract myself from going apeshit in front of the whole room. "Tell me about yourself."

Daniel spends the rest of breakfast blathering on about his hopes and dreams. In fairness, he doesn't seem like a total asshole, and the tension drops out of his shoulders with every passing minute that I don't tear him a new one.

When the bell goes off for class, we all get to our feet, and I give the guys a wistful smile as I let Daniel lead me out of the hall. He's back to his nervous self as we walk toward the main building, and I can see his thoughts running rampant as he mulls something over. Not caring what's going on in his head, I let him stew as we walk on.

"Look," he eventually blurts out. "I don't know what your deal is." I'm about to tear into him when he rushes out, "And I don't care. You're hot, and if you were interested, that would be awesome, except you're not…right?"

"No," I state bluntly.

"Right." He nods like he expected that answer. "So if this is all for show, it needs to look legit." I ponder over what he's implying and, realizing I'm open to listening to what he has to say, he continues, "You saw the way the girls are with the guys."

I give him an unimpressed look, shooting him a snarky response. "I don't need you pawing all over me, thanks."

He laughs nervously. "That's not quite what I was thinking. Although people will expect me to have my arm around your shoulders or carry your stuff. Things like that."

I scrunch my nose. "I don't need you to carry my shit. I've two perfectly good arms to carry it myself."

He shrugs. "It's just what guys do for girls they're dating. I'm not talking making out in the hallway or anything like that, but there are a few small things we could do that would prevent people from asking questions that I'm guessing you don't want them to ask."

Huh, maybe he's not an asshole at all.

"And what do you get out of it?" I ask.

He shrugs. "I'm not looking for anything. Sure, if one day in the future you wanted to take pity on me and give me a job in your parents' company or something, I wouldn't say no, but just call it a gesture of goodwill."

"Don't you come from money? I'm sure you can find your own job or have your own company you'll run someday?"

"My parents have money, but it's my uncle who has made our family name popular. He's the one that paid for me to come here, but he runs a vineyard, and I'm really more of an indoor person. I prefer working with computers and gadgets rather than with people."

Huh. "Alright, Daniel. You have yourself a deal."

A huge grin lights up his face, and he cautiously throws his arm over my shoulder. I tense at the contact, not used to anyone other than my guys or Emilia touching me, but I slowly relax as he talks my ear off about his college and future plans, and we make our way to class.

CHAPTER 15

Beck

A week after West's run-in with our parents' mercenaries, I'm climbing into the backseat of a blacked-out SUV on my way to my first-ever visit to the compound. My first visit should have been weeks ago. But, for whatever reason my father neglected to share with me, it kept getting pushed back—not that I'm complaining. I'd secretly hoped he'd changed his mind. It's the last place on earth I want to be, especially knowing what I do about Hadley.

To say I'm nervous would be an understatement. I don't know what the fuck I am. I'm a whirling vortex of emotions. I'm apprehensive about what I'm going to see and find here, sick at the thought of what will be expected of me, and fueled by molten rage at knowing whatever I see today was Hadley's entire life until recently.

THE CAR JOURNEY TAKES TWO HOURS, BUT FINALLY, WE PULL UP TO A staffed gate. I've been looking out the window most of the way, mentally cataloging any useful signposts that could help guide us back here, should we need it. The last town we passed was nearly an hour ago, and really, calling it a town is a stretch. It was a rundown, one-street backwater place that looked like it barely had more than a gas-and-go.

Since then, it's been all open fields interspersed with little pockets of forestry, with barely a house in sight.

Turning off the main road, we veer onto a narrow dirt track that looks like it leads to nothing but more fields. I guess that's the point. After bumping along it for another five minutes, a long fence line appears out of nowhere, littered with warning signs indicating this is private property and trespassing is prohibited.

A wide gate with barbed-wire coiled around the top and yet more warning signs attached to it blocks the road forward in front of us, and two guards wearing black combat uniforms stand guard on either side of the road.

As the driver talks to the one closest to us, the other guard inspects the car, checks the trunk, and waves some device underneath the vehicle. Both guards are armed with guns strapped in their holsters, and their thorough professionalism and the way they carry themselves make it obvious they're no amateurs. These aren't the lazy wannabe cops who sit in guard houses outside rich people's properties, watching TV instead of doing their jobs. They come across as highly-trained, dedicated soldiers.

The driver says something that I can't make out through the divider, and a minute later, the gates roll back and we drive into the compound.

No turning back now, I guess.

We bump along the track for another few minutes until we come up over the hill, at the bottom of which is a large, low-lying building shaped like a hexagon. Several other large facilities are dotted around the place and, beyond that, fields as far as the eye can see. We really are in the backass of nowhere.

Making our way down to the main hexagonal building, the car comes to a stop outside the entrance where a broad-shouldered, muscular man, who looks more like he belongs in Black Creek with the thugs and gangbangers, is waiting. He taps his foot impatiently as I get out of the back of the car and head toward him. He's dressed in similar tactical gear as the guy at the gate, the guns on his belt immediately drawing my gaze.

"Beck?" he asks—well, it sounds more like a demand.

"That's right."

He gives a curt nod as he holds out his hand for me to shake, and I reluctantly slap my palm against his. "Welcome to Nocturnal Mercenaries. I'm Major Bowen. I'm in charge of this place when Mr. Rutherford isn't around."

In return, I give him a tight smile and a professional nod of my head.

"Follow me." He turns on his heel and heads into the building, leaving me no choice other than to follow him even as my stomach fills with lead, and I swallow roughly around my dry throat.

"I have to apologize. You should have been here weeks ago, but we had a security breach that needed to be resolved first."

"Of course, I understand," I pacify, keeping my questions about what happened to myself.

"I've set aside an interrogation room for you to use. I, uh, wasn't sure what all you would need, but you can just let one of my men know and we will do our best to accommodate you," he explains in a bland tone, not realizing his use of the words 'interrogation room' in reference to young children has bile crawling up the back of my throat.

Unable to speak, I give a sharp jerk of my head as he leads me down a brightly lit corridor.

"This building houses the gym, boxing rings, dining hall, and interrogation rooms. The recruits are split into teams based on their competence and age, and housed in the surrounding buildings you probably saw on your drive in."

"Teams?" I query, knowing I need to say something. I can't just continue to nod my head like a moron every time he opens his mouth and spews more words that make my skin itch to get out of here.

"Yes. We throw them all in together when they first arrive, but as they progress in their training, the weak are weeded out. We put them in teams, for which they remain in for when they go out on jobs, etcetera. They eat together, work together, sleep together. That way, they can learn to work cohesively as a team and get along with each other in confined spaces, should that be necessary for the job." He chuckles, even though I don't see what he finds so funny. "It's not always fancy kills and exciting getaways like in the movies. There are a lot of boring stakeouts and long hours spent following a target. It's important that each team can work through whatever challenges they may face in order to get the job done."

"Do the teams interact much during their training?"

"Not really. We hold a monthly challenge night where the teams face off against one another. We find it to be a healthy form of competition between them, enabling us to compare their skill sets and identify any issues. Other than that, they're kept pretty separate."

"Where, uh, are all the recruits?" I ask. We haven't passed a single person, child or otherwise.

He laughs before explaining, "This corridor loops round the whole building and is for staff only. There's a separate recruit entrance at the back, with a secure hallway leading into the middle of the building, where the main workout area is."

Coming to a thick, steel door, the guy swipes a card against a reader, the light turning green before he opens the door.

"Each section of the building is subdivided for security reasons," he explains.

Security reasons, my ass. More like safety measures to ensure no one escapes. How Hadley managed to break out of this place is a miracle in itself.

Entering another similar hallway, we continue walking. "So, from what Mr. Rutherford explained, you're going to assess which kids are the best candidates for training and which are duds." The guy says it with such casual indifference, like we're talking about the fucking weather, further intensifying my disgust for him.

"That's right." That's the only response I can spit out, knowing if I say anything else, I won't be able to keep the edge of anger out of my voice.

"Cool. That would be helpful. We invest a lot of time and effort into finding suitable kids, but we don't always get it right. Currently, one in five of the kids we think could hack it, end up washing out."

Why do I get the impression that when he says 'washing out,' it's not like in college when kids drop out and decide to do something different with their lives? No, the way he says it makes it sound much more permanent, and I have to suppress my shiver of revulsion.

"How do you find these kids and determine which ones are worth your time?" Even though I am curious, I'm not convinced I want an answer to that question, although it's probably expected of me to have some questions, especially about the recruitment phase, since that's why I'm here.

"We have lookouts on the streets and contacts in the foster system and in children's homes that report back to us if they find someone they think would be fitting. Someone with no family, anger issues, prone to getting in fights, acts like a bully, that sort of stuff. Then we put surveillance on them and set up incidents where we can test them to see how they react. If they don't meet our expectations, we move on; if they do, we either approach them or take them.

"The younger we can get them, the easier it is. We can't test them the same way as the older kids, but they quickly learn here that it's a survive-or-die environment. We've discovered most kids, if they're younger, will adapt quicker and question us less."

What he means is that the younger kids are easier to condition.

Probably because they don't remember life outside these blood-stained walls. The older kids, even if they did come willingly at first, most likely come to regret that decision or at least go through a phase where they want their freedom back.

"Honestly, I think your help would be better suited during the surveillance stage before we bring them in, but Mr. Rutherford wants you to look at the last set of recruits we picked up a few weeks ago."

"How many kids do you have here?" I ask, changing the topic before he can dive too deep into what I'm going to do. Honestly, I have no idea what the fuck I'm going to do when I'm placed face to face with some tear-stained kid and asked to decide their future.

"Thirty." There's a proud lilt to his voice, like coaxing and kidnapping young children and forcing them into a life most people wouldn't willingly choose, is some sort of achievement. It takes everything in me not to lash out and throw him against the wall. "We have a lot of adults that we train too," he continues, unaware of the boiling rage inside me. "Guys that have been discharged from the army or from private security, who are looking for a new, lucrative gig. The board only started recruiting kids about twenty years ago. We now have three active teams, and the rest are still in training, but so far, they've proven to be much more effective than those that come to us as adults."

We stop at another door, and after yet another swipe of the keycard, we step into a different sector.

"Alright, these are the interrogation rooms," he says, taking me to a door on the right. Scanning his keycard, the door beeps and unlocks to allow us entry into yet another hallway. This one is a complete juxtaposition to the one we left behind. It's dark, lit by dim, intermittent overhead lighting, and I'm not sure if it's my imagination or not, but I swear I can smell piss and fear all around me. It's potent, activating my gag reflex, and I struggle to lock that shit down.

Thick steel doors are placed at intervals down both sides of the wall, and I don't miss the hatches in each of them—one at eye level and a larger one closer to the floor. The whole area resembles what I imagine the confinement section of a prison looks like.

Bowen stops outside one of the doors, where a guard stands to attention. "We've set you up in here," he states as I follow him into the windowless room. A single bulb hangs from the ceiling, providing an eerie glow that only adds to the foreboding pit in my stomach. Maybe it's for the best that I can't make out any more of the room. The smell of piss is more pungent in here, combined with a tangy rust smell that I know all too well. Blood. I knew, based on the little Hadley has shared with me, that I'd see some shit here. And I thought I'd prepared myself, but every instinct in me is screaming for me to run, to get the fuck out of here and never come back.

There's a small table in the middle with two chairs on either side. Other than that, the space is empty.

"I wasn't sure what all you would need to do for your assessment, but Officer Gordo will be in the hall. If you need anything, ask him."

I nod my head. I'm not physically capable of doing anything more than that right now.

"We have five kids for you today. We've already vetted them from a physical aspect, so I guess you're here to see if they can withstand the psychological aspects of training. Honestly, I don't really understand what it is you'll be doing, but if you can stop us from wasting our time surveilling and training washouts, then I don't care." He laughs at his own joke. "Alright, I'll get someone to bring in the first kid. Hang tight."

He walks out, pulling the door closed behind him. A loud clatter rings out around the dark, depressing space as the door slams shut and a bolt is slid into place, locking it. The sound is so final, like the lid closing on a coffin, sending a shiver of fear skittering down my spine. If I'm afraid, I can only imagine the utter terror those poor kids feel when they're dragged in here unwillingly.

Just when I'm beginning to reach my limit of uncomfortableness, and I'm debating banging on the door and demanding they open it, I hear the grate of the bolt unlocking and the door is yanked open.

The guy guarding the door, Gordo, marches a young boy into the room. He gives me a brief nod and says, "Let me know when you're ready for the next one." The kid holds his head high, refusing to be cowered. There's a stern resolve in his eyes. He jumps, however, when the guard slams the door shut, leaving the two of us alone in the room. I also notice how his eyes are darting nervously around the darkened space.

Fuck, this is going to be a long day.

A headache is beating a drum against the inside of my skull, and I'm both physically and mentally drained by the time I finish up and Major Bowen comes to escort me out.

Instead of leading me back the way we came, though, he directs me deeper into the compound. We walk through room after room where kids are being put through grueling exercises as trainers yell and threaten them, even when the kids shudder in terror and cry out with exhaustion.

I hate to admit it, but it gets to the point where I try not to look, instead attempting to block it all out until I'm finally directed back to the initial corridor and can let out a silent breath of relief. There's a tightness in my chest, and the adrenaline in my body is pushing me to go back and help them. Witnessing that and not being able to do anything about it, not even *trying* to stop it, goes against my very nature. Only there's nothing I can do right now to help any of them. Every time I saw a guard hitting or screaming at a young kid, all I could picture was Hadley. How the hell she endured this place and didn't turn into something cold and detached is beyond me. It's a true testament to her strength. Most people would break eventually. You can only hold on to hope for so long; once that flame goes out, all that surrounds you is darkness.

When we're finally back outside the building, I bid a hasty

farewell to the sick fuck masquerading as a Major, greedily gulping down the fresh air. I already know I'll be burning these clothes and jumping in the shower as soon as I get home. I can feel the fear and hopelessness that cloaks this place clinging to me like an unwanted second skin. One that's not going to be so easily washed away.

STEAM BILLOWS OUT OF THE BATHROOM BEHIND ME AS I STEP BACK into my room, wearing nothing but a towel wrapped around my waist after a long, hot shower that did nothing to remove the grime adhering to my skin from today. I pause, finding Hadley lounging on my bed, a sight for sore eyes in her shorts and t-shirt. I smile softly when she catches my gaze.

"What are you doing here?"

"I wanted to check on you after today." Her eyes probe against my skin, and I know she's trying to read me, to gauge the lasting impact of the horror I had to witness. She slides across the bed as I sit down on the end and leans her head on my shoulder.

"I don't know how you survived it all those years. I could hardly stand being there for an afternoon."

I feel her shrug, feigning nonchalance. "I think you become indifferent to it all. It's the only life I know."

I let out a long breath, closing my eyes as I soak in the feel of her pressed against me. "I couldn't stop picturing you there, imagining what it must have been like for you—"

"You can't think like that," she chastises, reaching out and wrapping her hand around mine. "I'm here now, with you, and that's all that matters."

ON FRIDAY, I KNOCK ON THE GUYS' APARTMENT DOOR AT LUNCH. Ever since West got attacked, and they all had to resume the stupid tradition, it's become the norm for all of us to hang out here at lunch. I have to admit, it beats eating alone in my office or making stifled conversation with the other faculty members in the staff room, plus it's given me more of an opportunity to hang out with West.

I'm pleased to say he looks a bit better every day, and the bruises have faded considerably. True to his word, he's stopped icing me out, yet things are still awkward as fuck between us.

The door swings open, and the man himself stands in the doorway.

"Hey," I greet, striding past him into the apartment. Glancing around, I don't see anyone else.

"Hey, everyone else should be here in a few minutes. The guys are just grabbing food."

"Sounds good." Sitting down on one of the bar stools, I scan my eyes over him. "How are you doing?"

"Much better. Still sore over my ribs, but nothing like what it was." He takes a seat on the opposite side of the island, and we stare awkwardly at one another, neither of us sure what to say.

"This thing you have with Hadley," he begins. "It's serious?"

"As serious as it is between you and her." I know, just from the way he looks at her, how much she means to him—to all of us.

"And you don't care that she's dating three other guys?"

"It's not quite what I'd pictured for myself," I admit. I don't think many people plan to end up in a poly relationship. Certainly, any pre-Hadley fantasies I would have had about the idea included more women than men in the relationship, but Hadley is more than enough woman for all of us. "But she deserves to be happy. If you guys make her happy, then I'm not about to stand in the way of that." I hesitate before continuing, "I've spent most of my teen and adult life feeling like I don't fit in anywhere, yet with Hadley, I feel like I'm exactly where I'm supposed to be."

He stares at me for a long moment. "You love her."

It's not a question, but I answer anyway. "I do."

We don't break eye contact, and I tap my finger thoughtfully against the countertop as I mull over my question before finally just blurting it out, "How do you feel about sharing?"

"It feels natural with Mason and Cam. We've never shared a girl before, but with Hadley, it just feels right."

A lump forms in the back of my throat. I'm painfully aware he didn't comment on sharing Hadley with me and, good or bad, I need to know his thoughts about it. I'm not going anywhere, regardless of what he says, but I still need to know. "And with me?"

He doesn't say anything for a moment, nerves making my palms sweat. It's ridiculous that, as a fucking adult, I want to be accepted—by him, by the others, but dammit, I feel like I'm so close to finding somewhere I might actually belong.

"I thought it would be weird…seeing you with her. But I see the way she is with you. Because of you, she dropped her barriers and let us in after everything we did to her." He hesitates. "I should probably be thanking you, old man." One side of his lips quirks up in an easy smirk, the tension dropping out of his shoulders when I bark out a laugh. *Damn, I'm never getting rid of that stupid nickname, am I?*

The jingle of the keys in the lock alerts us of the others' arrival and cuts off whatever else West might have said. Hadley strides in, a large grin on her face when she finds us both sitting here, with all of our limbs still attached, and not—for once—yelling at one another.

"Hey," she purrs, wrapping her arms around my neck as I draw her into me.

"Hey, sweetheart." I plant a quick kiss on her lips before she extricates herself to go say hi to West. I watch as he winds his arms around her waist, recognizing the look in his eye as he smiles at her. He loves her too.

"LOOK AT THAT SMUG FUCK," MASON SNARLS, GLARING DAGGERS AT Daniel. I'm surprised he can't feel our angry stares drilling into the side of his head as he laughs at something Hadley says.

I was heading to my office when I came across Mason leaning casually against a bank of lockers in the corridor, staring at a classroom door further down the hall. It all made sense when he said he was waiting on Hadley's class to finish.

"Thinks he can just walk around with his arm around our girl."

Of course, when the door opened and Hadley walked out, Daniel was right by her side, his arm draped over her shoulder. She's grown more comfortable with his nearness as the week's drawn on, and even though I trust her, it doesn't stop me from wanting to rip the asshole's head off any time I see him touching her. I rarely come into the main school building, choosing to stay away from the majority of the student body so I just have to deal with whatever students are sent my way. Then again, all week, I haven't been able to stop myself from wandering through the halls just so I can check up on her and make sure the little fuck, Daniel, isn't overstepping his mark. Hadley is like a breath of fresh air in this place, so I don't trust that he won't get as infatuated with her as we are.

I can feel the rage coming off Mason, his jealousy fueling my own.

"Miss Davenport," I bark out in a menacing growl that makes several students stop and stare in my direction. Freezing, Hadley turns to face me, Daniel's arm dropping from her shoulder. "A word."

She glances wide-eyed at the other students, an impassive expression on her face. She gives a tight nod of her head, whispering something to Daniel before coming toward us.

"Yes?" Although that one word sounds polite and patient, the fire burning in her eyes tells me she's not happy about being called out in front of everyone. But I don't care. I'm sick of seeing that shithead glued to her side every time I walk through here.

"In private. My office. Now."

Her lips flatten as she presses them together.

"You coming?" I ask, turning to Mason. He's staring at Hadley with a mixture of carnal need and jealous rage, but he grits his teeth and shakes his head at my question.

"Can't. I have class."

With one final, longing glance at Hadley, he takes off. I turn on my heel and stride through the emptying hallways with Hadley trailing behind me, until we reach my office.

"What the hell—" she begins as soon as the office door closes behind her, but I cut off her words, slamming my lips against hers and sucking her tongue into my mouth.

"Do you have any idea how difficult it is to watch him with you all day, every day?" I growl, my body pressed flush against hers, pinning her to the door.

Some of the anger melts out of her expression.

"That still doesn't mean you can act like a caveman and boss me around."

I tilt my head a fraction, staring into her mesmerizing gray-blue eyes that suck me in like a vortex. "You like when West does it." My voice is a low husk as I grind my erection against her core, loving the way she sighs, her hands squeezing my shoulders as lust overtakes her body.

"That's different." The breathy quality of her tone gives away how much I'm affecting her. *Good.* I hope I affect her even half as much as she consumes me. She's infiltrated my every thought, my every action. Thoughts of her dominate every spare minute in my day, and it's still not enough. I just can't get enough of her.

My lips hungrily meet hers, our tongues clashing as we give into our need for one another, neither of us coming up for air until we've sated our urges.

"I'm sorry you have to see me with him," she says twenty minutes later, when we're re-dressed and in our usual position on the couch. "I feel the same way when I see the girls all over the guys."

Well, now I feel like an asshole. Of course, this is as difficult for her as it is for me. We're all struggling.

Leaning up on her elbows, she stares into my eyes. "It's not fair to you, though. You're not even part of the stupid tradition, and you still have to see all that." A soft smile graces her lips. "One day, it's going to be your arm around me in public while we walk down the street, or go to the theater, or out for a meal. Everyone will know you're mine."

"Is that so, sweetheart?" I grab her ass cheeks firmly with both hands, dragging her on top of me. "And are you mine?"

She leans down, her wavy hair falling around us, hiding us from the world. With her lips a hair's breadth from mine, she whispers, "Always." After a second of hesitation, she adds, "I love you."

I didn't need to hear the words to know she felt that way about me. I can see it every time she looks at me. It's in her every action, but the fact she now knows how she feels, and has the courage to say the words aloud, shows how far she's come since she first arrived here. My heart swells with pride as I close the distance between us, both of us getting lost in one another for the rest of the period.

CHAPTER 16

Hadley

It's Friday, which means there's a party. One that we all have to attend with our stupid tradition dates. I hate parties as it is, so I'm already not looking forward to this one as I bang on the guys' door.

Mason's eyes instantly fill with heat when he answers. His gaze roams over my skin-tight black vest top and black skinny jeans with rips along the thighs. Paired with my black combat boots, and my blonde hair flying loose around my shoulders, I look like one sexy badass bitch.

"Damn, Little Warrior, you sure know how to dress up for your fake boyfriend," he teases, a hint of jealousy underlying his humorous tone.

"Shut up, asshole." I roll my eyes as I try to push him aside to let me in, but the immovable bastard just stands there.

"Don't you know you've gotta pay the doorman before you can get in," he jokes, a dirty glint in his eye.

"Is that so?" I purr, playing along as I run my finger down his navy shirt until I reach the belt buckle on his dark jeans. He looks hot as fuck, all dressed up for tonight. "And what's the price of entry?"

"Hmm, I'm not sure yet. It might be more than you can afford. I think you'll have to tempt me into letting you in."

With a playful smirk, I step in toward him, my body pressing up to his and ensuring my breasts graze against his chest. Wrapping one arm around his neck, I trail my other down his pec and over each ridge of his six-pack.

With my lips inches from his, I breathe out, "Is that so?" before rubbing my hand over his growing erection.

He groans when I squeeze his shaft. Diving in to close the distance, his lips crash against mine in a wet, heated, sloppy kiss that instantly has me skyrocketing to dizzying heights. His hands grab large fistfuls of my ass, holding me in place as he grinds his now hard cock against my jean-clad pussy.

"You may be going to the party with that asshole," he grunts, "but you'll be coming all over one of our dicks before the end of the night."

Fuck, the way he says that is so hot, and I'm so here for coming over *all* of their dicks tonight. I mean, why choose, right?

With another dirty kiss and enough grinding to have my panties soaked and my pussy clenching around air, he lets me go, and with my cheeks flushed, I step into their apartment.

Daniel is meeting me here, and the six of us are heading over to the party together. The guys never arrive with their dates, but apparently, it's expected of me to arrive with mine. It's fucking sexist, is what it is. This whole thing is ridiculous. The guys get away with treating their girls like crap, and it's presumed that the entire tradition is nothing more than fucking for the month. Although, as a girl, I'm held to a higher standard. I can't just pretend to use Daniel as a fuck toy like they can. No, I have to act like I'm fucking dating him. As I said, it's ludicrous, sexist bullshit.

Before I get too caught up in my anger over the whole thing, Mason drags me over to the sofa, pulling me down so I straddle his waist. His lips descend on mine and his hands go back to squeezing my ass, as the two of us kiss like the horny teenagers we are. I soon forget where I am and my anger is snuffed out as I grind shamelessly against him.

I'm completely lost in the feel of him, more than ready to strip him naked and climb aboard his dick, when there's a tug on my hair. Breaking our kiss as my head is pulled backward, I find myself staring up at West upside down.

Smirking, he leans in to kiss me, his pillowy lips soft against mine. His kiss is no less possessive than Mason's as he pillages my mouth with his tongue. I'm faintly aware of Mason's hands skirting up underneath my top, hitching it up.

I gasp into West's mouth when Mason pulls down the cup of my bra, exposing my nipple to the cool air in the room. While I grind harder against him, he brushes his thumb over the peak before running his tongue around it. Flashbacks of the last time we were in this position drive me wild, and my eyes drift shut until West pulls on my hair again, forcing my head to tilt so I'm looking at Cam. He's standing in the doorway, watching us with a prominent bulge pressing against his pants. I lick my lips invitingly, and he moves closer, quickly closing the distance as he comes to join us.

West steps to the side, maintaining his firm grip on my hair as Cam's lips replace the ache West left behind. Cam's kiss is more hesitant at first. Nevertheless, the moment I bite down on his lower lip, causing him to groan, he stops holding back and gives me everything he's got as he fucks my mouth with wild abandon. Mason stops with the ministrations on my tits and instead moves to undo the button on my jeans, shoving his hand inside until his fingers are pressing against the sopping wet fabric of my panties.

"Jesus," he groans. "She's fucking drenched. You love having all of us worshipping you, don't you, baby."

I can't do anything but moan into Cam's mouth as West pulls

down the thin strap of my top, exposing my shoulder so he can lick, suck, and nip his way along it. Fuck, having all three of them touching me is like nothing I've ever experienced before. It's too much and not enough all at once.

"Better hurry up and make her come, man, before Hawk shows his face," West growls to Mason.

"She's fucking ready to explode," he assures him, pushing his fingers inside me.

He's not wrong. I can already feel the telltale tingling in my fingers and toes. Mason sets a fast, rough rhythm, his other hand pushing its way beneath my jeans to play with my clit. It takes mere seconds before I'm rushing toward the cliff, crying out into Cam's mouth when West bites my shoulder.

Cam doesn't stop kissing me right away. Rather, he slowly eases the pace before breaking away.

"That was the hottest thing I've ever seen," he says, staring at me with blown pupils and lust-filled eyes.

Mason fixes my panties back in place and rebuttons my jeans, and I climb off him so he can go wash his hands while I fix my bra and shirt. By the time Hawk makes an appearance, we're all sitting casually on the sofas like nothing ever happened.

A knock on the door signifies Daniel's arrival, and I get up to answer it. Only Mason, with his stupidly long legs, manages to get there before me, blocking the doorway with his large frame as he glowers at the poor guy. He's a good head taller than Daniel, painting an intimidating picture as he looms over him.

To say it's been difficult, balancing the stupid tradition with our relationship, would be an understatement. There's been jealousy on both sides, and I've lost count of the number of times one of the guys has pulled me into a dark corner of the school and kissed me stupid, reminding me that no matter what it might seem to everyone else, I'm theirs. As if I could forget, especially when they drop to their knees and make me see stars. But we all agreed the only way to get through this was if we trusted one another and talked it out if any of us were unhappy at any point.

Not that there's much we can do, but open and honest communication can resolve many problems.

"Let him in, asshole," I huff, shoving Mason in a futile attempt to get him to step aside.

With one last threatening glower, he steps aside, letting a slightly terrified-looking Daniel into the apartment.

"Ignore him," I placate, trying to put him at ease with a smile. It doesn't work though, because as soon as Mason closes the door, Hawk appears along with West and Cam. All four assholes form a brick wall of muscle behind me.

"You keep an eye on her all night," Hawk begins threateningly, making me roll my eyes as I throw my hands up in exasperation. I just can't with these boys sometimes. "Do not give her alcohol or let her out of your sight. If she comes back here with so much as a scratch on her, you're a dead man, got it?"

"Y-Yes."

"No touching and sure as fuck no kissing," Cam growls out.

"No p-problem." By this point, Daniel's head is bobbing up and down like a bobblehead. I'm pretty sure he'd agree to a blood sacrifice if it meant they would leave him alone.

"Guys, stop being assholes," I seethe. "I plan to sit by the fire all night with you guys, so I don't know what you think is going to happen."

Tonight will be the first true test of whether or not we can all survive this. It's one thing watching each other with another person at breakfast. However, at a party where there's alcohol and dancing, as well as the girls having certain expectations, it's going to be exponentially more challenging.

Not long after, when the apartment is so thick with tension you can hardly move, we all pile out into the fresh air of the evening.

"Fuck," Daniel breathes out from beside me. "I thought they were scary from a distance, but they're so much worse up close."

I can't help but laugh.

"I'm sorry. They're not usually that bad. This is all a bit of a fucked-up situation," I explain vaguely, unable to tell him anything more.

He snorts. "I'll say. I'm surprised my balls are still attached to my body. You're dating all three of them, right?"

I give myself whiplash with how quickly my head snaps to look in his direction, my eyes wide as I gape at him. He laughs at my shocked expression. "It was obvious as soon as I arrived tonight."

He must see the fear in my eyes as he quickly tacks on. "Don't worry. I don't think anyone else will realize. I didn't even suspect it until tonight. I figured you were maybe dating someone, but I had no idea who. Nonetheless, the whole alpha dominant thing they were doing, yeah, that was a dead giveaway."

"You can't tell anyone," I implore him, still fretting over the fact someone else now knows about us.

"Hey," he soothes. "I won't. Promise. It's none of my business. And after what I saw tonight, there's no way in hell I'd willingly cross those guys." When I scowl at him, he rightfully adds, "Or you. You're pretty scary too."

"I'll have you know I can make whatever they do to you look like child's play." There's a pressing note in my tone and a menacing smile on my face, and I can tell he doesn't know whether or not to take me seriously.

"So, Daniel." Cam throws his arm over his shoulder in some weird bro thing that I'm pretty sure he isn't doing out of friendliness, pulling him slightly to the side as he whispers something in his ear that I'm not able to hear. West slips in between us, the back of his hand occasionally grazing the back of mine as we follow the rest of the crowd toward the increasing noises of the party at the lake.

For the most part, the party isn't too bad. Michael and Emilia arrive shortly after we do and join us around the fire. If I ignore the half-naked girls rubbing themselves against *my* guys and constantly trying to gain their attention, it's a pretty decent night.

We all sit in a circle around the pit, talking, and the rest of the school avoids us as usual.

Halfway through the night, Daniel goes off to join his friends. Unfortunately, the girls refuse to leave the guys' sides, and as the alcohol starts to course through their systems, they become bolder about their intentions.

When one of the sluts tells Cam how she can't wait for him to feed her his giant cock, and places her hand over his crotch, I've reached my limit of what I can handle. I jump to my feet as Cam brushes her hand off, failing at masking his disgust.

"I'm going for a walk," I snap out, not waiting to hear their protests as I stalk off through the crowd. I don't even know where I'm going, but I need to get the fuck away from here before I break that bitch's arm.

As I reach the tree line, I hear footsteps chasing after me, and Cam catches up just as I slip into the forest. Out of view of the partygoers, he pulls on my arm, spinning me to face him and wrapping his arms around me. "I'm sorry," he murmurs against my ear, even though he didn't do anything wrong. He's just playing his part—a hell of a lot better than I am.

"This is so difficult," I mumble into his t-shirt, resting my head on his shoulder as I breathe in his apple and water lotus after-shave, trying to draw some comfort from it.

"I know, but none of it's real. I wanted to cut her hand off every time she touched me, and I know the others feel the same."

I sigh wearily. "I know, but it doesn't stop it from hurting." I lick my lips nervously, drawing back to look into his eyes. "I've never felt this way before."

A tender smile graces his lips as he peers down at me. "Neither have I," he admits. With his palm on my cheek, he leans down to kiss my lips softly. It's slow and steady but no less passionate than his other kisses as he conveys just how little that slut by the fire means to him.

"Come on." He tugs on my arm, pulling me deeper into the forest.

"Where are we going?"

"My girl's not happy, so I've gotta find a way to put a smile on her face." He tosses me a dirty wink that has my panties melting.

Hmm, I can think of a few ways he can improve my night.

Half an hour later, we're both fixing our clothes back in place before we reluctantly return to the party, when I hear a rustle in the trees.

"Did you hear that?" I whisper, snapping my head in the direction where I swear I just heard a twig snap.

"Probably just an animal." He shrugs, unperturbed.

I squint into the darkness between the trees for another minute, but I don't see or hear anything else. *Yeah, he's probably right. I'm just being paranoid.*

Shaking it off, the two of us return to the party, and I ignore the scowl on Hawk's face as I reclaim my seat.

"Where are Emilia and Michael?" I ask no one in particular.

"Emilia's over there." West points toward where she's grinding on some dude, both of them looking drunk enough that they'll likely regret their decisions in the morning. "Michael went to get a drink. Are you okay?"

"All good." I plaster on an over-the-top cheery smile. The girls are so drunk by now I could probably fuck West in front of them and they wouldn't even remember it.

Thankfully, everyone calls it a night not much later, and the guys drop off their mostly passed-out dates back in their dorms while Daniel walks me to the guys' apartment. I can see the questions in his eyes, except he wisely keeps them to himself, dropping me off and saying goodnight before disappearing back down the stairwell.

West is the first to return, and I can sense how close he is to losing it the second he enters the apartment. Tonight was hard on all of us, and I get the impression he's feeling particularly out of control at the minute—a feeling I know he hates.

His alpha persona is in full control right now as he storms toward me, grabbing me firmly by the wrist and tugging me behind him as he strides toward his bedroom. I have to jog to keep up with his long legs—damn tall man.

The second the door slams shut behind him, I know I'm in for a fun night of blissful orgasms and watching West in his element.

He makes me see stars three times before pressing a final searing kiss to my lips. "I love you," he murmurs. The second the words spill out, his body stiffens. I keep running my fingers through his hair as I kiss him, pulling him back into that noxious cloud of passion until he's once again relaxed.

"I love you too."

Collapsing onto the bed beside me, he sets his glasses on the bedside table and wraps his arms around me, and the two of us fall into a peaceful sleep.

The first time I said those words aloud to Beck, my heart was slamming against my ribs. Before then, I'd never spoken the words aloud to another living soul, but since he said them to me several weeks ago, I've been thinking about it a lot, trying to put a name to this feeling I have for each of the guys. Now I've come to the conclusion it has to be love. There's nothing else it can be. No other word feels big enough to encompass all of these complicated feelings I have for each of them.

"Ahhh, look! Look!" Emilia screams, waving a page in my face as she bounces into my room. She didn't even knock before barging in, making me jump out of bed, thinking some madman was chasing her.

"What is it?"

I snatch the page from her outstretched hand as my heart rate settles back to normal.

"Oh my god, Emilia, this is amazing!" I exclaim. "Congratulations!"

She beams at me with an authentic, brilliant smile showing how thrilled she is at this moment. And so she should be. She just got a full-ride scholarship to one of the most competitive colleges in the state.

She bounces into my arms, and I happily return her hug, letting her squeeze me half to death in her excitement.

"I can't believe it. I mean, I know that's what the last four years have been for. Why I've been working my ass off, but I can't believe it's real. That it's really happening."

"Believe it, girl. You're amazing. Of course you deserve this."

Taking the letter back, she falls onto my bed with a dreamy sigh, staring at the page like it's a love letter. I guess to her, it is.

"What are your plans after school?" she asks, looking up at me.

I move to sit opposite her on the bed. "Eh, I'm not sure. I haven't given it much thought."

"What? How? It's your future!" She gapes. Neither of us has really talked about the future in much depth—well, *I've* never talked about the future. I know all about Emilia's prospective plans. They mean everything to her, but as much as having a feasible plan in place is vital to her, not having any idea what's in store and just seeing what happens along the way is important to me. At least it means I have a future that's all mine. Other people have mapped out my whole life, but now *I* get to decide what I want to do with it. I haven't quite worked out the 'what' yet, but the fact that I have options is everything.

"I know. I just haven't decided what to do with it yet." I shrug as she keeps staring wide-eyed at me.

"I'd just assumed you'd applied somewhere and were keeping it on the DL until you heard from them."

"Nope." I shake my head, but all this talk has me wondering, do I want to go to college? I'm not exactly academic. If it weren't for my fake transcripts, I wouldn't be here at all. I'm barely scraping by this year. Even so, isn't college like one of those things you have to experience? It's not like I have any ideas of what I want to do with my life, so college could be the perfect place to figure out who I am and what I like.

Equally, I've probably missed all the application deadlines. I don't know if I can even afford to go, and I can't see my parents being accepting of me just going off and deciding my own life. I feel like I'm forgetting another reason...Oh yeah, the fact Lawrence is trying to drag my ass back to the compound and we're in the middle of trying to figure out how to take down all of our parents and their fucked-up company.

Yeah, college plans might have to wait.

CHAPTER 17

Hadley

Emilia, Michael, and I are ordering lunch at the kiosk when Daniel and his friends walk in. He smiles when he sees us. "Hey."

"Hey," I greet awkwardly. Other than breakfast and parties, we don't interact much and are rarely around other people where we have to pretend to be something we aren't.

"Dude," his buddy hisses, jamming his elbow in his ribs. "Ask her to sit with us."

"Oh, right, do you, uh, wanna sit with us?" He rubs the back of his neck in obvious embarrassment.

"Sounds great," Emilia answers for me, earning herself a 'what the fuck' look. She knows this is all for show.

When her eyebrows waggle up and down a couple of times, I catch on to what she's silently trying to say. Basically, the guys are hot, and I'd be a horrible friend to rob her of this opportunity.

"Sure." I sigh, giving Daniel a tight smile.

He quickly puts in his order, and we follow him over to his table as his friends put in their lunch requests.

"SORRY," HE WHISPERS IN MY EAR AS WE TAKE OUR SEATS.

"It's fine." I smile so he knows I'm serious. It's actually hasn't been too bad spending time with him. It would be fun if we weren't busy pretending we're in a fake relationship. He's a genuinely nice guy and easy to get along with.

His friends all join us, and Daniel introduces them. Their eyes all bounce inquisitively between Emilia, Michael, and me.

"Oh, this is Emilia and Michael."

"Aren't you guys scholarship students?" one asshole asks.

"So?" I snap, glowering menacingly at him, daring him to say one bad word.

He holds up his hands in surrender. "Didn't mean anything by it. It's just that the Princes don't hang around with the scholarship kids."

"Do I look like I have a dick swinging between my thighs? I'm not a Prince, and I'll be friends with whomever I want to be friends with."

"That's cool. Like I said, I meant nothing by it," the guy persists, nodding his head frantically.

The rest of lunch goes by without any issues, but I catch Michael looking quizzically at me several times over the hour. Especially when Daniel nudges my shoulder and whispers in my ear, making me laugh.

"Are you actually dating him, or is it just for show?" Michael asks later that afternoon as we head to the library.

"Why?"

He shrugs. "You just looked comfortable today at lunch. You're rarely like that."

I guess I had fun. I am learning to let down my walls a bit, and all the frequent touches from the guys have helped me feel more at ease around others.

"It was fun, but no. I barely know the guy."

"Are you dating anybody?"

I hesitate, wondering how much to tell him and why he's even asking. I know he had a crush on me when I first arrived, but I thought that was long over. I mean, we're friends, right?

"Eh, no. Things have been a little hectic, what with the whole Davenport bomb drop and adjusting to that, never mind throwing a boyfriend in the mix." I laugh tensely.

Whatever weird tension was in his shoulders drops out. "Cool." Before I can ask him why he's suddenly interested in my love life, he continues, "We should hang out and do something fun sometime soon. It's been ages since we caught up."

"Yeah, we should," I agree, feeling bad. Sure, the three of us hang out together a lot, but I haven't spent much one-on-one time with Michael, and like Emilia, he gave up the only other friends he had when he agreed to be friends with me. So I do really need to make more of an effort.

"We could book a theater room for tonight. I'll grab us some ice cream and coffee."

I hesitate for only a second, thinking of the guys, but I'm not that needy girlfriend who has to be with them every spare minute of the day, so I quickly chastise myself and agree to tonight.

We spend the rest of the afternoon in the library getting some work done, and that night I stop by Emilia's room, wanting to get her two cents on the conversation I had with Michael earlier, before I head out to meet with him. I still struggle with navigating these newfound friendships, and I can't figure out if Michael was off earlier or if I'm reading too much into it.

"Hmm, sounds like he still has a thing for you," Emilia unhelpfully tells me, making me groan.

"What am I supposed to do about that?" Now I feel super awkward and don't even know if I should meet up with him tonight.

"Nothing. You're not leading him on. He's a teenage boy, he'll get over it."

"So you think I should still hang out with him tonight?"

"Absolutely." She nods her head. "You're still his friend, and he's probably confused about everything going on with you lately.

What with you spending a lot of time with the guys, and now with Daniel. He could be feeling insecure that you don't have time for him anymore. Tonight will hopefully put him at ease."

Feeling reassured, I head to the rec center to meet him. The night turns out to be good fun, and I remind myself to make more of an effort to spend time with him. As the movie credits roll across the screen, Michael turns to face me.

"How are you coping with everything that's happened recently?" he asks.

Sighing, I rest my head back against the seat. "It's been a lot to take in, but I'm doing okay."

"And you're getting along with Hawk and the guys alright? You've been spending a lot of time with them."

"Yeah, they've been great, actually." I have to suppress my smile as I think about them. "There's been a lot to work through with Hawk, but we're turning a corner now, and the others have been accepting me into their fold."

A look I can't place crosses Michael's features, but I blink, and it's gone. Studying him for a second longer, he looks like his old self, so I brush it off. Probably just the way the dim lights in here glance across his face.

"So you're like friends with them all now? Even though they bullied you throughout the first semester."

There's a harshness in his voice, and I don't appreciate the accusatory tone he's using as I turn to look directly at him.

"Things are different now," I snap. Yeah, it sounds weak to my ears, and I can't blame him for thinking I'm insane, but he doesn't know everything that's going on or what we've had to deal with.

I sigh, trying my best to let go of my anger. "It's complicated. Nevertheless, they've apologized, and we're working through it," I tell him.

Gathering our stuff, we start to head back toward the dorms.

"We should do this again," he says. "Sunday night?"

"Ehh, let me get back to you. Things have been hectic recently, and I just want to make sure there's no Davenport nonsense I need to deal with." I know I'm being a bitch by blowing him off, but I do have a lot on my plate right now, and Sunday is only a few days away. Plus, we still have our standard Saturday night movie night with Emilia, so I don't really see a need to do two.

"Oh, yeah, sure."

I'M SITTING IN THE LIBRARY, WITH DANIEL BESIDE ME AND HIS FRIENDS taking up the rest of the seats at the table. When Mason comes in, his slut of the month is draped all over him. It's been three weeks since we started up this stupid tradition again, and I still can't get used to seeing any of the guys with one of them. Uncontrollable rage overtakes me every time I have to watch them with one of their sluts. It's a miracle no one has gotten a knife in the eye or a fork to the hand yet.

He's clearly not having a good day—if the furious look on his face is any indicator—but if he looked pissed off when he entered, it's nothing compared to the look on his face when he notices me sitting with Daniel and his friends. His head looks like it's about to pop off his shoulders, and I can't do anything except silently apologize with my eyes as he stomps over to a nearby table and bangs his bag onto the surface, not giving a shit that he's disturbing everyone around him.

It's not my fault. I was just sitting here minding my own business when Daniel and his friends walked in. I saw him try to convince them to go to another table, but they weren't having any of it and practically dragged him over here to sit with me. So now we're stuck playing pretend while we do our best to focus on our schoolwork.

Of course, now that Mason is here, zero work will get done. I watch as his little slut follows him to the table, oblivious to his rage as she tries to sit in his lap, laughing like it's some game when he shoves her off him.

I try to ignore him, focusing back on my workbook and tablet, but I can feel his furious stare like laser beams burning into the side of my head. Giving up on trying to ignore him, I decide the best thing to do is give him an outlet for all that rage. Biting on my lower lip in thought, I decide to play a dangerous game with the fuming beast glaring at me.

Leaning in, I whisper in Daniel's ear, "Play a game with me?" I flick a glance in Mason's direction, and he hesitantly agrees. "Put your arm around me," I whisper, squashing my smirk.

Doing as I tell him, he leans in and drapes his arm across the back of my chair, his fingers dangling over my shoulder. Pretending to focus on my work, I peer up at him through my eyelashes, watching Mason's features narrow, his jaw clenching as he strangles his stylus, oblivious to the girl who may as well be doing naked star jumps beside him.

Daniel bends down to whisper in my ear, and to anyone else, it would look like two lovers sharing a secret. "You're going to get me killed," he says, half joking. I let out a girly giggle, batting my eyelashes at him like he just said the sweetest thing.

"He's going to bury my body out in the forest. Tell my family that I love them. Make sure my brother gets my baseball card collection." He sighs dramatically. "I never got the chance to tell Wendi how amazing I thought her tits were." My laugh is real this time as he continues with the theatrics.

"Jeez, will you two get a room already," one of his friends hollers, his words loud enough to carry across to Mason's nearby table.

It's the last straw for Mason as he jumps to his feet, sending his chair crashing to the floor as the bimbo gasps in shock, and he stomps toward us to haul me out of my seat.

Glancing back over my shoulder, I ignore the shocked looks from the other guys at the table as I give Daniel a conspiratorial wink, and he shakes his head while rolling his eyes at me.

Mason yanks me behind him until we reach the back of the library, where the private study rooms are. Barging into one with people in it, he barks, "Out," glowering at everyone as they hastily gather their stuff and run out of the room like their asses are on fire.

He slams the door shut behind them, pushing me against the door with his large body.

Fire glows in his bright blue eyes, mixed with carnal need and desire. Shoving his hand between my thighs, he cups my pussy and curls his fingers beneath the fabric of my panties before tearing them clean off in a move that leaves me panting.

Clamping my dripping wet pussy in his hand, he growls, "This cunt is mine." He slides his fingers through my slick wetness, coating them before sliding further back, pressing the tip of his finger against the tight ring of muscle. "This ass is mine." His eyes flick down to my lips, the thumb of his other hand pushing its way past my teeth. I suck him into my mouth, licking his thumb with my tongue. "That dirty mouth of yours is mine."

He watches, enraptured, as I suck on his thumb before slowly removing it with a pop. His hand moves to take mine, placing it over his rock-hard erection. "Just like this dick is yours." I squeeze his shaft, and he groans, his hips involuntarily thrusting into my grip.

Using his grip on my hand, he pulls it away and slowly slides my palm up his shirt until it's resting over his heart, as the look in his eyes softens. I can feel the steady beat of it beneath my hand, and I can't look away from the unusual vulnerability I see in his eyes. "This heart is yours. *I* am yours."

I swallow around the lump of emotion in my throat.

"You're perfect for me, Little Warrior. We were always meant to be together. You're mine—not because you belong to me, but because you own every part of me."

Well, fuck me. Give this man a standing ovation, because that was one hell of a declaration.

My voice is hoarse as I lick my dry lips. "You own all of me, too," I admit, clenching my hand into his shirt and using it to yank him toward me.

Our kiss is brutal. All teeth and violent possession as we

assault one another. My hands roam frantically over his chest, pulling and tugging on his clothes until they come apart. In no time, he's throwing me back against the door and driving into me, making my eyes roll back in my head.

His hand clamps down over my mouth, silencing my cries. The sex is rough and intense, but with our faces inches apart, our eyes never straying from one another, it's intimate and over-flowing with raw emotion. All too soon, I feel him swelling within me, and as his cum hits my inner walls, I fall apart, my ecstasy muffled behind his hand.

When we're done, he removes his hand from my mouth, resting his forehead against mine.

"I love you," I pant, loving how his eyes soften and a boyish grin graces his lips.

"I love you, baby. You're mine, and I'm yours. That's the way it's always going to be." He kisses my forehead, and the two of us share a moment of blissful contentedness before he speaks again. "I actually came here to get you. West found something."

"He did? What?"

"I dunno yet. He wanted to wait until all of us were together."

Satisfied and with a renewed purpose, we quickly redress and leave the study room. I quickly gather my belongings, blurting out an excuse to Daniel and his friends before rushing out of the library with Mason.

By the time we make it to the guys' dorm, everyone else is there, waiting impatiently.

"About time," Cam grouses. "What took you so long? This asshole won't tell us anything."

"Sorry. We're here now. What's going on?" I ask, skipping over the reason for our tardiness and wedging myself into the space on the sofa between him and Hawk.

When we all are seated, we stare impatiently at West, waiting for him to share his findings. He's sitting opposite us, with a laptop open in front of him on the coffee table.

"So, I've been monitoring the security cameras at both our

parents' offices and their homes. It's all been pretty boring stuff, but today I was reviewing the footage from last week when I came across this from a few days ago." He turns the laptop around, and we all huddle together to see the screen as he presses play.

The footage is of the kitchen in one of our parents' houses. At first, it's just an empty room, but after a second, a woman in a revealing dress and sky-high heels enters the frame. We can't hear what's being said, but based on her frantic hand gestures, she's upset. I don't recognize her, but I do recognize the man who enters the room next—Frank Hayes. His face is thunderous, and it looks like he's yelling at the woman. An argument ensues, and I gasp when he slaps her across the face hard enough to have her stumbling sideways into the kitchen counter.

She stares at him in shock, cradling her stinging cheek in her hand, but Frank is on a roll now. He stalks toward her, his cheeks reddening as he yells in her face. I can see the terror in her eyes as she tries to backtrack, cowering and most likely apologizing to him. The asshole isn't hearing any of it though, too lost in his rage as his hand grips tightly around her upper arm, easily throwing her across the room.

The woman goes flying, crashing onto the tiled floor. She curls in on herself, but Frank still manages to get his foot in as he kicks her relentlessly. Not caring what body part he connects with.

It feels like it goes on for ages, and based on how the woman's muscles slacken, she must pass out at some point. Nonetheless, it's not enough to stop the sick bastard from beating on her. I have to look away, unable to watch anymore. My hands begin to tremble as I struggle to force back long-buried memories. My gaze lands on Mason's hard one. His body is wound tight, his fists clenched as he watches his father beat the ever-loving shit out of an innocent woman. I can only imagine the extent of the beating he took as a kid. For that reason alone, the fucker in the video needs to pay.

When the woman is bloody and lifeless on the ground, Frank finally stops his assault. Panting heavily, he stands and stares at her with a vacant stare. There's no remorse over the fact he's just killed someone. No guilt. Nothing.

As he storms out of the frame, leaving the woman lying on the cold floor, West pauses the recording. "This was three days ago."

"He killed her?" It certainly looks like she's dead, but I need to know for sure.

"Yeah, he did. He got some guys from their organization to come clean up his mess."

"Who was she?"

"Lacee Hamilton," Mason supplies, staring off into space. "Her family owns a chain of high-end jewelry stores." He grits his teeth, looking ready to explode as he pushes himself out of his seat, pacing back and forth across the living room.

"How do you have this?" Hawk asks. "Surely he would have wiped the tapes?"

"I've been downloading all of the security footage onto my own secure drives, so we'll still have a copy of it even if they delete anything."

"So what do we do with this?" Cam questions, watching Mason out of the corner of his eye.

Mason turns on his heel to face us. His features are dark and terrifying as he struggles to deal with what he just witnessed. "We use this to put that sick fuck away for good."

CHAPTER 18

Hadley

HAWK: *WE'VE BEEN SUMMONED FOR DINNER TONIGHT. 7 PM.*

I GROAN, ALREADY PREDICTING HOW BAD TONIGHT WILL BE. IF THE last two times I've met my parents are any indicator, it's going to be pretty grim. I haven't seen either of them since the night of the party, nor have I spoken to them. Which is totally fine with me. I've decided it's much better to skirt by, lurking on the periphery of their awareness. I'm not sure they know what to do with me yet, but I have no doubt they're contemplating how they can get the best use out of my unexpected arrival.

The problem with maintaining as much distance as possible from them is that I'm no closer to finding out what happened to me or if they are involved. I mean, they have to be on some level, right? Even if they aren't, they're shitty parents for not funneling all of their resources into finding me and instead putting the priorities of their company first.

SIGHING, I FIRE OFF A LESS-THAN-ENTHUSIASTIC RESPONSE TO HAWK as I lean back against my headboard, trying to think of a way to get the information I need from my parents. They aren't just going to come out and tell me the truth about what happened.

I spend the rest of the day going back and forth between homework and thinking about all of our parents and what the hell we're going to do. West finding that footage of Frank enables us to finally fight back. It's a small step, but a step forward nonetheless. West sent a copy to the local police, the state police, and another one to the family. He's also kept a secure copy for us, which could come in handy. Now, all we have to do is wait and let the chips fall where they may.

As for the other parents, the six of us have thrown around a few ideas, but we need to sit down and come up with a real strategy for tackling them, and the company. The end of the school year is quickly approaching, and things will only get worse once the guys graduate and work full-time for them. I don't even know—or want to know—their plans for me after graduation. I can hazard a guess that the future they've mapped out for me is not the one of freedom I envisioned when I escaped the compound.

By the time Hawk knocks on my door that evening, I'm dressed in a pair of jeans and a t-shirt. I've done my best to flatten my hair, and I even borrowed another pair of flats from Emilia— look at me making an effort!

"Ready?" he asks when I open the door.

"No," I grumble. "What do they want this time?"

"No idea, guess we'll find out soon."

We make our way out of the dorm and along the path to the parking lot, before I speak up again. "West told me you all want out from under your parents' thumbs."

"Yeah," he agrees. "Obviously, we've never wanted to head up the company. Initially, we'd hoped we could at least talk them into letting us go to college first, so we could buy ourselves a few more years of freedom and enough time to come up with a better exit strategy, but now..." He shakes his head. "None of us want anything to do with what they're involved in. They want us to spend some time shadowing them over Easter break at the company, but honestly, I can't imagine anything worse.

"After the way the guys were treated growing up, and the threats our parents have been shoving down our throats this year, I can't stand to be in the same room as any of them."

"Even your own parents?" I ask cautiously, knowing his relationship with his parents was nothing like what the other guys had to endure.

"Them most of all," he growls out. "Yeah, the other guys had a harder time growing up, but at least they *knew* their parents were shitty. I thought mine were okay. Not overly affectionate or around much, but they never harmed me or made me feel like a failure. But this past year, they've been completely different. Nothing like the parents I had when I was a kid. It's making me doubt everything I thought I knew growing up, and I hate that. I hate how I can't trust any of my memories and that I'm second-guessing every second I have spent with them," he growls in frustration. "I probably sound like an asshole. Compared to Mason or West, or fuck, you, I have nothing to complain about. At least I had those years where things were good with my parents, right?"

I bump my shoulder against his. This is the most he's opened up to me, and while it's a complicated, convoluted subject, I'm silently squealing like a girl on the inside at the new level we've reached in our relationship.

"You're entitled to feel whatever you're feeling," I assure him. "It doesn't matter what anyone else's past is. That doesn't negate what you have experienced or how you feel with all these new developments.

"I can understand where you're coming from. You felt more blindsided than the others because you didn't think your parents were as bad as theirs. The others had time to prepare, so while the whole mercenary discovery might have been a shock, the fact their parents were caught up in that shit wasn't a complete surprise."

"Exactly." He sighs, lapsing into silence as we reach the car, and he starts the engine, driving us out the campus gates.

As we enter the house, Maria saunters toward us. "There you are," she scolds, like we're late, but I know for a fact we're exactly on time. The clock in the car read seven on the dot as we got out of it. "Hair and makeup are waiting for you, Elizabeth."

Uh, what now? Why the fuck do I need my hair and makeup done?

"What's going on, Mom?" Hawk asks.

"We're having a couple of guests this evening. It's important everyone looks their best," she answers vaguely, looping her arm through mine as she drags me away from Hawk.

I glance over my shoulder, begging him with my eyes to get me out of this, but he shrugs his shoulders, not showing any signs of coming to my rescue. *Fucking asshole.*

Sighing in defeat, I accept my fate as we climb the stairs. All the while, Maria rambles on about some shit or other. The woman honestly baffles me. Right now, she's almost acting as though we're friends, except she's barely said more than a handful of words to me before now. Most of them have been snapped out in irritation—guess I know where Hawk gets his shitty personality from.

Directing me to a bedroom where two women are waiting, Maria lifts a garment bag off the bed. "Put this on," she orders, shoving the bag against my chest and leaving me with no choice but to catch it before it drops to the floor.

She doesn't bother to turn around as I strip out of my clothes, opting to avert her eyes instead, like that's going to do any good. I don't give a fuck what this bitch thinks of me and my scars, so if she wants to watch, then fine. I shimmy into the skin-tight dress that I have to stretch over my breasts. It clings to my hips, the sheer black material barely covering my ass.

Maria gives up all pretense of pretending not to watch, staring openly at me with her lips pinched as she assesses me.

"Not bad." She taps her index finger against her lip in thought. "We might have to do something about that tattoo, though. It's unseemly. Thank goodness the dress covers it all for tonight." Before I can tell her she's not doing shit with my tattoo, she twirls her finger in the air. "Turn around."

Not seeing that I have a choice, I bite my tongue and do as she says, hearing her gasp when she notices the scars covering my shoulders and back. If you look at me from the front, you can hardly notice them. There are only a few faint, white lines along the tops of my shoulders and my collarbone, but when you look at my back, it would be impossible to miss the prominent white lines marring the skin.

"Oh my," she breathes.

You'd think this might be the moment she softens toward me, now that she realizes what hardships her daughter has had to face. However no such kindness or compassion exists in this hard shell of a woman.

"We can't have that. I'll make an appointment with my plastic surgeon."

"No," I bark out sharply as I spin around to glare at her. There is absolutely no fucking way I am letting anyone come near me with a scalpel. My scars are a part of who I am. Yeah, they might be an eyesore, but anyone who can't bear to see them can just look the fuck away.

Her lips purse and her eyes narrow in warning at my outburst, but she doesn't push the matter, for now.

"Stella, make sure her hair covers that...atrocity on her back."

I grit my teeth, biting my tongue against the nasty words that I want to pour out, knowing it will do nothing but rile her up more.

"Yes, ma'am," a demure woman responds, nodding her head.

Happy with that acknowledgment, Maria exits the room, leaving me alone with the women who usher me into a chair in front of a floor-to-ceiling mirror. I can't do anything but let them fuss over me like mother hens, too overwhelmed with everything to tell them to stop.

"You have such thick curls," the one sorting out my hair coos as she runs her fingers through my thick locks before attacking it with a brush, while another woman wipes my face and starts to apply gunk to it. Between them, they tug on my hair, and direct me to close my eyes and push out my lips until they're satisfied with my appearance.

"Much better," Maria praises when she enters the room nearly an hour later. Her gaze roams over my too-short dress, primped hair, and over-the-top makeup. I've never been so dolled up in all my life, and I don't mean that in a good way. I look like some sort of expensive, high-end prostitute.

"Put these on." Her words are a sharp order as she hands me a pair of black peep-toe high heels. I sway dangerously as I struggle to get my feet into them, not seeing the point in arguing with her. God knows, my inability to wear heels will only give her another reason to dislike me. Before I even stand upright in my new shoes, she's already ushering me out of the room, looking impatient. "Come on. Our guests are waiting."

Cement forms in my stomach at her words as I try to figure out what the hell is going on. I'd naively thought tonight we were all going to sit down and discuss what would happen now that I was a Davenport. I'd hoped I would finally get some answers to what happened to me, but with each passing second, that is looking less and less likely.

When we enter the dining room, Hawk, Barton, and two men I don't recognize are sitting around the dining table. All four stop mid-conversation when we enter, their attention turning to us.

Hawk's eyes widen, and his lips press together as he struggles to hold back a laugh. *Yeah, I bet I look fucking ridiculous—like a five-year-old who got into her mom's makeup.*

I 'accidentally' knock my elbow against the back of his head when I walk past his seat. He glowers at me as I sit in the empty chair beside him to take in the guy opposite me. He looks around our age, with wavy, tousled chestnut brown hair. He's got a broad chin and dimples in his cheeks as he smiles at me. It's a dirty smirk that, combined with his honey-brown eyes that twinkle with mischief, lets me know his thoughts are in the gutter.

There's something wild about the look in his eye. It's not quite normal, yet I can't put my finger on what it is. Shrugging it off, I flick my gaze to a similarly built older man with tints of gray in his hair and lines around his eyes and lips sitting beside him, watching me intently. The way he looks at me makes my skin crawl, as though he's trying to determine my measure.

I quickly look away from him, but I continue to feel his eyes on me as Maria takes her seat at the end of the table, sitting opposite her husband.

"Benjamin, meet our daughter, Elizabeth," Barton introduces, barely sparing me a glance—as has become his usual. I don't know what it is about me that he can't bear to look at. Maybe it's guilt eating him alive?

"She's certainly something, isn't she?" the guy—Benjamin—says, only increasing the creep factor.

I sneak a glance at Hawk out of the corner of my eye. His face is its usual impassive mask, and I can't get a read on what he's thinking or what the hell is going on here.

"I understand she's been missing for quite some time," the guy continues, his beady eyes still watching me far too closely for my liking.

"Yes, that's right. She was kidnapped as a toddler and somehow ended up in the foster system under a new name, which is why we weren't able to find her all these years. It was a fortunate coincidence that she ended up at school with Hawk this year, and the connection was made as to who she really was."

Since my so-called father has never asked me about my past, I'm guessing he's gotten his hands on my fake records and put together his own theories, which he's now passing off as fact.

Servers bring out food for each of us, cutting off their weird conversation. A plate of something tiny and fancy is placed in front of me, and it's only then that I notice three different sets of knives and forks on either side of the plate. *What the fuck? What's wrong with using the same utensils for every course?*

Once everyone has been served, and we're once again alone, I subtly cast my gaze around the table, watching to see which set of cutlery everyone else starts with. I feel so far out of my depth right now, and while I mostly don't give a shit, a small part of me wants to fit in with these people. I don't understand it. Why do I care so much about what these people think when they clearly don't care about me?

I inadvertently catch the gaze of Benjamin's son—whose name I still don't know. He must have been watching me and picked up on the fact that I have no idea what I'm doing. He points to the smallest set of cutlery furthest away from the plate, silently letting me know that's what I should be using for this course.

"Wilder will be joining you at Pac for the rest of the year," Barton informs us—well, he's looking at Hawk, so his words are meant for him.

"It's a bit late in the year to transfer, is it not?" Hawk responds, looking between his father and Wilder.

Wilder has a wide grin on his face that makes him look every bit his namesake—wild.

"Yes, well, I think getting to know him and his family better will be very fortuitous for all of us," my father responds cryptically. Hawk's eyebrows pull together as he darts his gaze back and forth between the two men, as if he can somehow telepathically read their thoughts and figure out what's going on if he just stares hard enough at their heads.

The rest of the meal drones on. Barton and Benjamin talk about mundane work things that I struggle to follow, all the while ignoring Wilder's gaze boring into my head and the tension radiating off Hawk beside me. It's safe to say it was not the most fun meal I've had, even if the food was pretty decent.

"Why don't we leave the kids to get to know each other while we go over the finer details of the contract," Maria suggests after we've all finished eating.

"Yes, what an excellent idea, darling. Hawk, you'll see that Wilder follows you back to campus when you're done?"

Barton spears Hawk with a look that makes it clear his request isn't optional.

"Sure," Hawk reluctantly agrees. Benjamin and Maria stand from the table and leave the room without a backward glance. Barton hesitates, however, as if he has something else to say. His mouth opens and closes wordlessly before he decides against saying anything at all, and he silently follows after the others.

The minute we're alone, Hawk glowers at Wilder. I must admit, it's nice not being on the other end of that menacing look for once.

"What are you really doing here?" he demands.

Wilder leans back in his chair, casually placing his napkin on the table. His other hand plays with a knife left behind after dinner, and he absently runs his thumb over the pointed tip and down the sharp blade. There's a gleam in his eye as he smirks knowingly at Hawk, enjoying lording over the fact he knows something we don't.

"You mean you haven't figured it out yet?"

Hawk's eyes narrow to slits. "I can hazard a guess," he growls.

My eyes flick between the two of them, not having any idea what they're talking about.

"Uh, would one of you like to enlighten me then?!" I snark, getting annoyed at being left in the dark.

Wilder focuses his intense gaze on me as a crazy-looking grin splits his face. This guy is definitely off his rocker. There's no way he's right in the head. He looks like a deranged psycho right now.

"Sunshine, you and I are getting hitched."

A strangled laugh escapes me.

I mean, he's obviously joking. He has to be...right? He's so deep in crazyville that he's talking out of his ass.

An animal-like growl sounds in Hawk's chest, and he slams

his hand against the table, jumping to his feet. The chair squeaks against the wooden floor as it's pushed backward.

"No, you're not," he snarls.

"Well, no, not yet," Wilder says casually, not at all intimidated by the fact Hawk looks ready to gouge his eyes out. "I'm sure our parents will want to work out the fine print first."

I'm half expecting Hawk to launch himself across the table, so I'm surprised when he reaches out and all but yanks me to my feet.

I just about manage to pull my dress down, ensuring I don't give Wilder a free show as Hawk drags me out of the dining room. I have to run in my heels—which is fucking tricky—in order to keep up with his giant strides. He's grumbling under his breath, but I can't make out what he's saying.

"Hey," Wilder calls after us, and I hear his chair being pushed back before the sound of his shoes slapping against the floor chases us across the foyer. "You're supposed to show me the way back to campus."

Hawk ignores him, pulling open the front door with more force than necessary and, still with a tight grip on my arm, he tugs me out the door and down the steps. Doesn't he know I'm as keen as he is to escape the crazy madman following us?

Two cars are parked at the bottom of the steps. One is Hawk's black SUV, and another is a dark green classic Mustang convertible. It looks beautiful, and I can't help but admire it as we approach.

Hawk comes to a stop, fishing his keys out of his pocket, giving Wilder time to catch up to us.

"Get in the car, Hadley," Hawk growls.

"Wifey should probably come with me." Wilder throws his arm over my shoulder before I can move out of his way, acting as if we're best buds and he's not some weirdo I just met. "We need some 'getting to know you' time."

"I think I know all I need to know," I snark, jabbing him in the ribs with my elbow—hard.

The psycho just laughs as he doubles over in pain, and I shove him.

"Sunshine, you're going to give me an erection in front of my new bro-in-law. Not cool."

Hawk and I share similar 'what the fuck is this guy on' looks, ignoring him as I round the car, getting in, and Hawk climbs in behind the wheel to start the engine and take off down the drive.

CHAPTER 19

Hadley

"Who the hell was that guy?" I ask as Hawk hurtles down the road, driving recklessly in his attempt to get away from his parents' house and the deranged psycho stalking us.

"His dad is Benjamin Clearwater," Hawk states, as if that explains anything.

I get irritated when he doesn't elaborate, seething out, "Am I supposed to know who that is?"

"His company manufactures personal body armor, like Kevlar vests. He would provide the police and army with a ton of their gear." Hawk thinks for a moment before continuing, "It was recently announced that he was branching into weapons production. I'm guessing he and our parents are looking to get into business together." He turns his head to look at me. "And you're the bargaining chip."

My stomach churns violently. "What does that mean?" I ask, not truly wanting an answer. I can already guess for myself.

"IF WHAT WILDER SAID IS RIGHT, THEY'RE MARRYING YOU OFF TO HIM in exchange for whatever business Benjamin agreed to do with them."

"But, I don't understand." I'm ashamed to say my voice comes out more high-pitched than I'd like, although I think it's perfectly acceptable since I'm freaking the fuck out right now. "They wanted me to get involved in your whole stupid tradition, so why would they do that if they were just going to marry me off to some rando anyway?"

Hawk shrugs his shoulders, not having an answer for me. "No idea. Benjamin is a big fish, though. It would take the company to a whole new level if they got him on board. I know they had some business deal in the works with him years ago, but something happened and it fell through." He taps his finger rapidly against the steering wheel, still driving like a fucking maniac down the dark road. "They aren't going to let this deal fall through." His grim tone only exacerbates my unease as we drive on in silence, each of us lost in our own thoughts. What the fuck am I supposed to do now? I'm not about to marry that lunatic, or anyone else for that matter.

We're nearly back at campus when Hawk breaks the heavy silence in the car. "I don't know where the nearest strip club is, but I'm sure I can find one if you wanna earn a few dollars in that getup."

"Ha ha." I laugh sarcastically, slapping him playfully on the arm. "I look like a fucking hooker *and* I left all my clothes behind in our rush to get out of there."

Hawk laughs. "Oh yeah, they've probably been burned by now."

I groan. "Those weren't even my shoes."

"So just buy a new pair." Hawk shrugs, like it's no big deal.

"We're not all made of money, asshole. Some of us know the price of a dollar."

He glances away from the road, cocking an eyebrow at me. "You do realize being a Davenport comes with some benefits, right? Like a bank account with more money than you've probably ever seen."

"What? No."

He laughs, shaking his head. "I have one, so you should too. I'll talk to Dad this week and set it up for you."

"I don't need their dirty money," I grouse.

"No," he admits, "but you might as well get something out of this shitty situation."

Well, he has a point there.

Parking the car in the student lot, Hawk fires off a quick message to the group chat, telling everyone we need a meeting. *Great, this new, fucked-up development will be super fun to explain to the guys.*

Not hanging around for Wilder to find us, we quickly head back to the guys' apartment.

"What's going on?" West blurts out as soon as Hawk and I step into the apartment, finding all four of them already there. Beer bottles are sitting out on the table, someone having already figured it was going to be one of those kinds of talks. "And what the hell are you wearing?"

Oh, right, I forgot I look like a common prostitute.

I kick off my heels and walk over to the sink, splashing water on my face to wash off the gunk that feels like it's clogging my pores. I still look ridiculous in this dress, but at least my face doesn't scream 'street walker'.

Feeling slightly better, I sit in the free armchair. All eyes are on me as I sigh, suddenly exhausted after this evening's events. "Uh." I hesitate, unsure how to explain tonight's weirdness as I take in each of my guys. "I think I'm engaged?" If I sound confused, it's because I am.

"You're what?" Mason roars, jumping to his feet, his face like thunder.

"What the hell are you talking about?" Beck demands, anger lacing his words.

"You *think*?" West questions.

"It's pretty much a done deal." Hawk sighs, rubbing at his eyes before grabbing a beer, ignoring the murderous look Mason is giving him.

"Explain," Mason spits out between gritted teeth, slowly lowering himself back into his chair. I move to sit in his lap, sensing he needs some comfort, and he swiftly wraps his arms around me, pulling me in flush against him. I rest my head on his shoulder, my fingers tracing soothing circles along his forearm as Beck lifts my feet onto his lap and massages my arches.

Holy fuck does that feel good after having them crammed into heels for the last few hours.

"What the hell is she talking about?" Beck fires at Hawk.

Hawk explains what happened after we showed up at our parents' house tonight, and I can feel the tension rising in the room until it feels like lighting a match would be enough to set everything on fire.

"Absolutely not," Beck insists. "There is no fucking way she is marrying anyone other than one of us. Least of all him, he sounds fucking unstable."

My eyes widen. *What was that now? Marrying one of them?* Is that something he's given thought to? I have so many questions, but now isn't the time to ask any of them, and honestly, the thought of his answer makes me a little nervous.

The other guys nod their heads in agreement. None of them look like they're having the same internal freak-out over Beck's words that I'm currently experiencing.

Mason must sense the tension suddenly stiffening my muscles as he presses a kiss by my ear. "Don't overthink it," he whispers.

I glance up at him in confusion, seeing the laughter in his eyes. The asshole is enjoying watching me squirm and panic.

A loud knock at the door has all of us shifting our heads toward it before looking at each other and shrugging. Cam, being the closest, gets up to answer it.

"Bro, not cool," Wilder calls out, pushing past a stunned Cam. Hawk immediately jumps to his feet, and I'm unceremoniously dumped on the couch cushions as Mason and Beck jump up as well. "Insane driving, however. You'll have to teach me how to do that one day. I had no hope of keeping up with you."

"What the hell are you doing here?" Hawk growls as I scramble to my feet, pushing my way around Mason even as he tries to keep me out of sight behind his back. I don't know what he thinks Wilder will do; he's no immediate threat.

"I had to make sure Wifey got home safe and sound."

A chorus of growls erupts from each of my guys, making Wilder laugh. If I had any doubts about his sanity before, I know for sure now—he's certifiable. No sane person would laugh when they have five growling, beastly men glaring at them with murderous intent in their eyes.

"Oh, this just got more interesting." His wild gaze focuses on me, where I'm still partly sequestered behind Mason's brick of a body. "Good on you, Sunshine. I didn't know you had it in you." He winks. He fucking *winks*, like this is all some hilarious joke and he's not seconds away from being torn limb-from-limb and thrown into the lake.

Ignoring the death glares he's receiving, he saunters over to the armchair I vacated in favor of Mason's lap and sits down, grabbing a spare beer off the table.

He looks at each of the guys. "I'm guessing you four are the fearsome Princes I've heard all about," he says, pointing a finger each at Hawk, Cam, West, and Mason—what the fuck, he's been here for like five minutes—before his gaze lands on Beck. "And you are?"

"I think the better question is, who the hell are you?" Beck snarls.

Wilder gasps, clutching his heart with his hand. "Excuse my manners, so rude of me. My name's Wilder Clearwater, husband-to-be of Sunshine here." He gestures in my direction before holding his hand out to Beck as we all share 'what the fuck' glances. He doesn't seriously expect Beck to shake his hand, does he?

Beck sneers at his outstretched hand before smacking it away.

"Drop the act," Hawk snaps. "What do you want? 'Cause despite what our parents might think, you're not getting my sister."

Wilder shrugs, leaning back in his chair as he eyes me critically. I don't get the same itch under my skin that I did when his dad looked at me. Tilting my head, I stare at him curiously. He's impossible to get a read on, and his behavior too erratic to gain any sort of stable baseline. But despite the crazy glint in his eyes, I don't think he's any sort of a threat.

"Meh, blondes aren't my type, anyway. No offense, Wifey. I'm sure we could have had a blast."

Wriggling out from behind Mason, I stand in front of him, ignoring his huff of frustration.

"So why are you doing what your dad wants then? Why does your dad even want you to marry me?"

"He thinks a wife will help keep me in line." He snorts, but I don't miss the darkness that clouds his eyes. I'm not sure anyone else noticed it, and it's gone as quickly as it appeared, but it was definitely there. "As for why I'm going along with it...I have my reasons," he responds vaguely. "Just like I'm sure you have yours."

"What does your dad want out of this deal?" Hawk asks.

"No idea. He was on the fence until a week ago, then something changed." Before anyone can ask, he tacks on, "I don't know what. But all of a sudden, he was more than willing to sign the contract."

That has all of us exchanging uneasy glances.

MONDAY MORNING IS THE START OF A NEW MONTH, MEANING WE ALL have the joy of picking new people we're stuck with for the next four weeks. Hawk got a call from our father last night, informing him that I was to choose Wilder. It was obviously asking too much for him to phone and tell me himself—although I doubt he would have appreciated my colorful response.

Despite the guys making a fuss, I didn't argue about it too much. I had no idea who I was going to pick anyway, and at least Wilder has admitted he has no interest in being with me. Plus, he knows about me and the guys, so it's probably best that we keep a close eye on him until we can determine his motives.

After breakfast, the usual routine begins: each guy picks a girl. I notice Wilder slip into the hall as Cam takes his turn, propping himself up against the wall by the door and winking when he catches me staring. I have to admit, he looks good in his uniform —well, what he's wearing of his uniform. His tie is missing, his shirt is half unbuttoned and rolled up at the sleeves, and there's no blazer in sight. Looking down at his feet, I stifle my laugh. Instead of the standard black or brown loafers every other guy wears, he's got on multicolored Air Jordan's that look totally out of place with the school uniform.

When it's my turn, I quickly call out Wilder's name, ignoring the whispers and confused looks around the hall, everyone wondering who the hell Wilder is as the five of us get the fuck out of there.

"Wifey, I'm touched," Wilder says dramatically, swinging his arm over my shoulder. "You chose me out of all the reprobates in this place."

"Don't let it go to your head," Cam grumbles from Wilder's other side, looking decidedly pissed at the way his arm is slung around me. "She didn't have a choice."

"So what happens in this little tradition, then?" Wilder asks, ignoring Cam. "Do we get to make out in the hallway and grind on each other at school parties?" He waggles his eyebrows suggestively, making me laugh. I don't know what it is about him, but I can't take him seriously despite his constant flirtiness. The flirty banter doesn't meet his eyes, and I know it's all for show to wind up the guys, or maybe because he thinks that's what people expect from him. I'm not sure.

"Only if you want your teeth knocked out," Mason growls.

"Basically, you eat breakfast with me, escort me to class, and we go to parties together. That's pretty much it." I shrug. "People just need to think we're fake dating."

"Fake engaged," he corrects, earning another scowl from the guys.

"Not yet," I remind him.

"Sounds pretty boring. I thought it would be so much dirtier than that."

"I mean, it used to be." I shrug.

"Before you all started one big gangbang."

"Eww, gross." I jam him in the rib with my elbow. "Hawk's my brother."

"Right, that would be a bit awkward. Sorry, bro." He tosses Hawk a pronounced frown, and I can tell Hawk has no idea how to respond to that, choosing instead to ignore him.

"Well, I guess I should get the Wifey to class then." Wilder grins, well, wildly, earning more than one glare from the guys. "Don't want her to be late."

The rest of the week goes by in a blur. Between showing Wilder the ropes, catching up with Michael and Emilia, keeping on top of homework, and carving time out for each of my guys, it's hard to find a single moment of peace.

I have to admit, I actually quite like Wilder. He's definitely a weird one, and most of the school seems wary of him. Hard not to be when he spends most of breakfast with his feet kicked up on the table, twirling a knife in his hands like a certifiable lunatic. I dunno, he speaks to a deeper part of me that I've kept carefully buried since I escaped from the compound.

Of course, the guys all *hate* him with a passion. It doesn't help that Wilder makes a point of skipping so far over the line of what the guys will tolerate him doing with me, that it's nothing but a distant blur. Where Daniel only did the bare minimum of what was expected of him, Wilder has quickly weaved his way into my friendship group with Emilia and Michael, joining us for lunch most days and even inviting himself to our weekly movie night this weekend.

"Why does your father think a wife would keep you in line?" I ask Wilder. We're sitting in the theater room, waiting for Emilia and Michael to arrive. I've tried to broach the subject a couple of times this week, but whenever I mention his father or his past, he clams up. I can see him doing the same right now, closing himself off. It's a feeling I know all too well, when someone pries into shit you don't want them to see.

I expect him to shoot me down again, fobbing off my question with some fake-ass line, but he surprises me by actually opening up. "I got caught up in some shit last year; friends of mine died."

That's some heavy shit to deal with. The tight set of his jaw and the guilt in his eyes emphasize how much he's struggling to come to terms with whatever happened.

"My only friend died when we were kids," I share with him. "After she died, I gave up. I more or less wrote myself off as dead. It took a long time before I remembered I was still alive."

He stares at me thoughtfully. "Yeah, but I bet you didn't kill her."

As quick as it appeared, the vulnerability in his eyes disappears. Within a blink, he's pulled down his shutters and closed himself off. A maniacal grin splits his face. "So, tell me, Sunshine. Something I've always wondered… Are girls into period sex, or is that just a guy fetish?"

I'm looking at him with wide eyes, confused out of my everloving mind, when Emilia comes bouncing in with Michael following behind her.

"Hey, guys. What's going on?"

I break away from the intense stare-off with Wilder, ignoring his inappropriate question, as I smile at Emilia. "Hey. Nothing. What's up?"

Michael glances furtively back and forth between Wilder and me before slipping into the seat on my other side, narrowly missing being squashed by Emilia's ass as he sneaks in behind her to steal the seat.

She pouts before laughing it off, claiming the chair on his other side while Wilder starts up the movie he'd selected. It's technically my turn, but I never know what to choose, and if Emilia suckers me into picking one more romcom, I'm going to throw a bitch fit. Thankfully, Wilder had the good sense to go for an action movie.

"Hey," Michael whispers, smiling.

"Hey."

"We should grab a coffee this week, just the two of us."

"Sure, sounds good."

CHAPTER 20

Hadley

A WEEK AFTER WE SENT OFF THE FOOTAGE TO THE AUTHORITIES, WE get the news we've been waiting for.

"Dad's been arrested," Mason announces as he comes barging into the apartment. I'm kicking Hawk's ass in some shooting game, while Cam is showing Beck videos on his phone, and West is tinkering on his laptop.

We immediately stop what we're doing, sitting up and paying attention to Mason. "What? For real?" Cam exclaims.

"Yeah." Grabbing the remote, Mason switches over to the TV, flicking on a local news channel.

"—day's news, Frank Hayes, one of the founders of Nocturnal Enterprises, a high-profile private security company, was arrested today for the murder of Lacee Hamilton of Hamilton Jewelry. Police have not yet released any information regarding the case but they…"

"FUCK, THIS IS REALLY HAPPENING?" CAM GASPS AS WE ALL STARE wide-eyed at the TV. I mean, this is what we wanted, but I'm not sure any of us thought it would be that easy. Yeah, it's only one family of the four out of the equation, but it's a start.

Hawk's phone goes off, and I pull my attention from the image of Frank Hayes being escorted into the police station in handcuffs on the TV, to look at him as he fishes it out of his pocket, and Mason mutes the television.

"Son, I'm sure you've heard the news by now." Barton's voice comes out loud and clear over the speakerphone.

"Yeah, we just saw it on the TV."

He sighs wearily. "Yeah, it's a disaster. Not what we need right now. We have lawyers on it, though. Everything will be fine. We'll need all of you to step up in Frank's absence." There's no emotion in Barton's voice. Other than sounding stressed, he doesn't seem to be bothered by the fact that his friend and business partner is currently in jail for murder. "Especially Mason. He will have to start taking on some of his father's responsibilities. We will discuss it when you come to the office for Easter break."

He hangs up before Hawk can figure out how to respond to any of that.

"What does he mean, you'll all have to step up? What are you going to have to do?" I stare at Hawk before swiveling my gaze to the others, but none of them appear to have the answers to my questions.

"No idea. Guess we'll find out at Easter."

WEST TUGS ME DOWN THE HALLWAY AND INTO HIS BEDROOM, BACKING me up to his bed as his lips press against mine. His tongue sweeps in to claim my mouth as I moan. Stepping back, he pushes me down onto the mattress, and I bounce before he climbs on top of me, fusing his lips to mine again. His fingers trail over my clothes, slipping under my skirt until he's rubbing circles around my clit, making fireworks ignite behind my eyelids.

I honestly don't have time for this. I need to go and get ready for tonight, but I know the guys have been stressed out lately about this whole situation with Wilder, so if West needs this moment of comfort to remind him that I'm all his, then so be it. I'm sure as hell not about to say no when he's already got me soaring toward oblivion.

Pushing my panties to the side, he slides his fingers through my wetness, sinking deep inside me as he scissors his fingers, stretching me perfectly. "Always so fucking ready for me, aren't you, Firefly?"

I moan my agreement as I ride his fingers, cresting quickly toward the edge. Just when I feel my core tightening, he pulls out of me, and I whimper when he chuckles darkly, climbing off me to move to his bedside table.

His body blocks whatever he's doing, but a second later, I hear the drawer click shut and he comes back, pushing my thighs apart as he gets on his knees at the end of the bed, his mouth inches from where I need him.

Holding eye contact with me, he leans in and swipes his tongue from my slit to clit before pushing his fingers back inside me, once again starting the ascent toward heaven. I'm quickly losing myself in his touch when I feel him push something into my pussy.

"What the...Ho-oly fuck," I cry out when the thing starts vibrating. The extra stimulation has me hovering right on the precipice of an orgasm. Just when I expect West to send me soaring over the edge, he pulls back, tucks my panties back in place, and flips down my skirt, stopping the incredible vibrations.

I gape up at him with love-drunk eyes, trying to unscramble my thoughts so I can work out what's going on.

"What...why'd you stop?"

He smirks down at me, looking both deviant and wicked.

I press up onto my elbows, glowering at him as he leans down to hover over me, careful not to touch me.

"You didn't think you deserved a reward right before you're about to go off on a date with another man, did you?"

"So you're sending me out there turned on and needy?!"

"Exactly." His voice is a smug, seductive purr. He lifts a small black remote and presses a button. The vibrations start up again, making my body shiver as I moan. "And every time this goes off in your tight little pussy, you better think of me and remember exactly who owns you. Maybe I'll let you come when you get home if you're a good girl and don't touch yourself all night."

I whimper, so unbelievably turned on by his authoritative tone and the little vibrating device inside me that's doing crazy things to my pussy.

Pressing another button, the vibrations stop, and I can once again regulate my breathing as I clamber off the bed. "Now you better go get ready, wouldn't want to be late for your date." With a slap on the ass, he nudges me out the door with an evil chuckle, and I curse his name out in my head all the way back to my room.

An hour later, I'm showered, dressed, and sitting at a table in a fancy restaurant with Wilder and his father. The vibrator hasn't gone off since I left the guys' apartment, and I'm on tenterhooks with every passing second, waiting for it to start up. I have no idea how I'm going to keep from embarrassing myself when it does.

"So, you two have been getting to know one another?" his father inquires. I really don't like this man. The way he catalogs my every movement has the hairs standing to attention along the back of my neck, and every time I look at my steak knife, I imagine driving it into his neck.

"Yes. I'm her guy of the month," Wilder answers while I sip on my glass of water. *Ugh, I wish this evening would hurry up and be over already.* If I'd had any say, I wouldn't be here at all, but of course, I didn't, and, not wanting to piss off our parents any more than we already have, I have no option but to just grin and bear it.

"I didn't attend Pacific Prep," Benjamin explains, looking at me—his eyes have rarely left me all evening—"so I don't understand this tradition of theirs. Sounds emasculating to me." He grumbles the last bit under his breath, and somehow, I doubt he would say the same if I was Wilder's *girl* of the month.

Wilder just shrugs his shoulders, not giving a shit if it's emasculating or not. He's not one to follow the rules or give a shit about societal norms. He follows his own path in life, not caring if it pisses other people off.

I jump, gasping when the vibrator in my pussy comes to life, mumbling an apology as I take another sip of my water, ignoring both men's eyes as they observe me.

Thankfully our starters arrive then, and even though eating is the last thing on my mind, I'm grateful for the distraction as the two of them discuss something or other—I'm too busy clenching my thighs and wishing I could sneak off to the bathroom to rub one out to pay attention to what they're saying.

The meal goes on, and I slowly get more and more worked up every time the device starts up. Sweat coats my skin, and I've drunk about a gallon of water in an attempt to stave off the moans of pleasure that keep creeping up the back of my throat. My panties are soaked, and I've never been so grateful for a bra as my stiff nipples chafe against the fabric. I'm absolutely going to murder West once I get home—after he's made me come at least five times.

"Are you a virgin, Elizabeth?" Benjamin's question comes out of left field, making me choke on my drink.

"Excuse me? I don't think that's any of your business," I snap.

"Well, it is if I'm going to sign a contract that makes you a part of my family.

"Dad," Wilder hisses. "Everyone has sex before marriage these days."

His father's gross, beady eyes stay focused on me. "How many guys have you been with?"

I grit my teeth, refusing to answer as I glare daggers at him.

"Dad," Wilder hisses again, but his words fall on deaf ears.

"It's only a number. One, two, five? How many?"

"I dunno." I shrug casually. "I lost count."

A spark flashes through his eyes that makes goosebumps form along my skin, but it's gone so quickly I can't place what it was.

"I'll be asking for an STD screen and pregnancy test before the wedding then," his father responds blandly all business. I can't shake off whatever I saw in his eyes, though.

With the exception of that weird blip, the rest of dinner is uneventful. Benjamin hardly spares me anything more than a passing glance, talking with his son for most of the meal.

"Excuse me, I'm just going to freshen up," I say after dessert, smiling politely even as the vibrating demon in my pussy starts up again. Fuck, I've never been so desperate to come in all my life. I swear to God, I'm not going to let West come ever again without edging him for a good fucking hour beforehand.

Slipping into the bathroom stall, my hand snakes under the waistband of my jeans, hovering above my throbbing clit. I debate back and forth between touching myself or not, finally groaning when I decide West would probably be able to tell and make me go all night without a proper orgasm.

Frustrated, horny, and so fucking done with this stupid dinner, I throw open the stall door causing it to bounce off the wall, but I barely hear it as I stand frozen.

What the fuck? Am I seriously so turned on that I missed hearing this asshole follow me in here?

"What are you doing in here?" I snap, immediately on the defense, as Benjamin Clearwater leans casually against the wall in front of the bathroom door. His arms are crossed over his chest as he blocks my exit with his body.

"You and I both know why I'm here." He disgustingly leers at me. "You've been gagging for it all night."

I open my mouth to protest, but he cuts me off, "Ah ha, no need to lie. You've been squirming in your seat all night, thinking about my cock."

I barely contain my snort, knowing that a knock to his ego will only make this situation ten times worse. *It's sure as fuck not his cock I've been thinking about all night.*

"You're a little old for my tastes, but I'm not one to disappoint someone as gorgeous as you."

I'm a little old for his tastes? What the fuck does that mean? *I'm* barely legal, and he looks like he's in his forties.

"Besides, you were meant to be mine all those years ago, so it's only fair I take that pussy for a test run. It's the least I deserve for how long I've had to wait.'

"What?" I croak out, my head spinning off its axis at all the confusing information he's throwing my way.

"Well, technically, you were always meant to end up with Wilder, but you should have been mine first."

As bile burns its way up the back of my throat, my head spins with everything he's saying, and I decide I'm now officially done with this sick conversation. I force myself to hold still as he prowls toward me. I know that look in his eye; I've seen it more times than I care to remember. He'll only restrain me if I resist or fight back, and I need my arms and legs free to escape him.

The stupid fucking demon in my pussy chooses that moment to start up again, and I swear it's more intense than it was before, making me whimper as the sick fuck in front of me grasps two fistfuls of my ass cheeks in his hands, using his hold to grind me against his pathetic half-dick.

"Yeah, I knew when I looked at you that you were a dirty slut," he growls in my ear, squeezing my ass to the point of pain.

Pushing past the confusing sensations between his grimy presence and the fucking vibrator, I hitch my leg over his hip. Unfortunately, it opens up my pelvis more, giving him ample room to rub himself against me. I have to push past the vomit in my mouth as I lean in, brushing my tits against his shirt so I can reach into my boots and lift out my pocketknife—see, *this* is why you should never go anywhere unarmed, not even to the bathroom.

He's groaning in my ear, but the gullible asshole is so far gone in thinking I'm as into this as he is that he doesn't expect my sudden movement. Quick as lightning, I grab his wrist and slap it against the bathroom wall. Not giving him a second to yank out of my tight grip, I slam my knife into his palm, driving it in all the way to the hilt, embedding it in the wall.

He starts screaming bloody murder, and I know I have to get out of here ASAP.

"You fucking, bitch. What did you do? My hand!" he wails.

"Don't touch what isn't yours, you sick fuck," I snarl, quickly running my hands under the tap to wash off the blood and wiping down my knife before tucking it back in my boot and making a hasty exit out of the bathroom.

Trying not to draw suspicion, I move as quickly as possible through the tables toward Wilder.

"We've gotta go," I rush out, a hint of urgency in my tone.

"Dad's just paying—"

"No, he's not—"

A high-pitched scream followed by a deep bellow that rings through the restaurant, and my eyes widen to saucers. "Let's go."

Not needing any more of an explanation, Wilder jumps out of his seat. Pulling out his wallet, he drops a bunch of hundred-dollar notes on the table—*way* more than what the meal cost—and the two of us scurry out the door.

"What do you know about the old deal that fell through between your dad and my parents?" I ask him as we climb into his gorgeous dark green mustang.

He looks at me like I'm fucking insane, which is an interesting role reversal. Backing out of the parking space, he guns it toward campus. "You gonna tell me what happened in there?"

"Only if you answer my question."

He laughs, shaking his head before getting serious.

"I don't know much about it. I know something happened on your parents' end that caused it to fall through."

"When was the deal?" I ask, a sick pit opening in my stomach.

"I dunno." He shrugs. "Like fifteen, sixteen years ago?"

"Right around the time I went missing," I mumble to myself.

"I guess so. Why?"

"Just something your dad said," I respond vaguely, knowing I'll have to give him more details soon, just not tonight. My head is a mess with everything, and as the stupid vibrations start up in my pussy again, the only thing I can think about is putting West's tongue to good use when I get home.

Sighing, I lean back against the headrest, closing my eyes until Wilder snorts.

"Let me guess, West?" He waggles his eyebrows, making it pretty obvious what he's referring to.

"What..." I splutter. "How?"

He scoffs. "That guy loves control too much. Of course, he wouldn't send you out tonight without making sure you thought about him all evening."

"That obvious?" I can feel my cheeks burning, and it's not from how turned on I am.

"Ooh, yeah. You couldn't sit still every time it started, and you barely ate a thing. I sit beside you at breakfast. I *know* how much you fucking love to eat."

Can't argue that.

He pulls into the student car park, and we get out of the car.

"Are you going to tell me what happened tonight?"

I sigh. "Can we do it tomorrow? It's nothing that can't wait."

His gaze roams over my face in a rare moment of seriousness. "Yeah, sure. You probably can't think with all those hormones floating about in your head anyway."

By the time I let myself into the guys' apartment, the need for release is all-consuming. I can't think about anything else, and when I spot West and Beck sitting and talking in the living room, desire so potent you can taste it in the air, courses through me.

If I wasn't so turned-on, I'd be ecstatic to see the two of them sitting and chatting to one another, but as it is, all I can think about is West's hot mouth on my body as Beck's dick drills into me.

West must know where my thoughts are as he gives me a dirty smirk. "Have fun tonight?" he teases, heat flaring in his eyes.

"I swear, West, if you don't make me come right fucking now, I'm going to do it myself."

He growls as Beck's head bounces back and forth between us, confusion and desire crossing his features.

"Bedroom, now," West barks, his dominant tone that he saves for the bedroom surprising Beck as his eyebrows climb up his head.

I hesitate, looking at Beck, wondering if he's going to join us. West must pick up on my hesitation or sees my need for both of them, as he turns to Beck.

"Do you wanna come see just how wet our girl is from thinking about us all night?"

Beck's eyes darken, and he smirks. "Lead the way, brother."

Oh, holy shit, I'm about to be the filling in a super fucking hot brother sandwich.

We all pile into West's bedroom, and I swear, my skin feels like it's about to melt off my bones with how they both look at me.

"Out of those clothes, Firefly. Show us how much you need us."

Well, you don't have to tell me twice. My movements are desperate as I kick off my boots and throw off my clothes, until I'm standing naked before them.

"Lie back on the bed. Spread your legs."

Doing as he says, I lie back, spreading my legs as wide as they can go so they can get a crystal clear look at my glistening wet pussy as I drip onto West's sheets.

"Fuck, she's drenched," Beck grunts in a gruff voice, adjusting himself in his jeans.

I'm already panting heavily, but my head falls back and I moan to the ceiling as West starts up the demon device again, setting it at a more intense speed than it was in the restaurant.

"Did you think about us every time you wanted to come?" West's silky voice flows over me, making my nipples pebble.

"Yes," I moan.

"Did you touch yourself?"

"No."

"Firefly," he growls in a warning tone, promising me retribution if I lie to him right now.

"I didn't," I groan. "I thought about it, but I didn't."

"Good girl." His praise makes me pant harder. I'm going to self-combust if I don't come right now. I feel a wet tongue sliding through my folds, making me nearly jump off the bed at the titillating sensation, and I tear my half-lidded gaze away from the ceiling to watch Beck as he licks and sucks his way to my clit. His stubble rubs against my inner thighs, only pushing me closer to the edge.

"Don't come yet," West growls from beside me, as if sensing how close I am.

"West," I plead.

Beck laps at my clit, and my legs quiver with the need to come. Just when I think I'm not going to be able to hold out anymore, West barks out, "Come, baby," and bright lights flash across my vision as I cry out, the buildup resulting in one of the most intense orgasms I've ever had.

I sag against the mattress as Beck continues to lick and suck at my juices, and West slowly rolls the vibrator down through the settings, easing me down from my release, until finally, he turns it off, and Beck retrieves it from my overly sensitive pussy.

"Firefly." West's husky voice has me leaning up on my elbows, ready for round two, even though I'm not sure my legs can hold me up.

Lifting his finger, he beckons me toward him. "Come here."

I stand and move toward him on shaky legs, and he pushes me onto my knees in front of him. Slowly, he unbuckles his jeans and pushes them and his boxers down low on his hips so his dick springs out, bobbing in front of my face. I lick my lips, holding back the urge to lick him until he tells me to.

Grabbing a hold of his long length, he pumps himself. Pre-cum beads on his tip, and he rubs it along my lips before pushing his way into my mouth. His eyes become hooded as he watches me take all of him until he hits the back of my throat. He holds himself there for a second before pulling back, repeating the movement over and over as he slowly picks up speed.

With each movement, I swivel my tongue along his head and down his shaft, causing him to groan as heat gathers between my thighs. I move to touch myself, but fingers wrap firmly around my wrist, yanking my hand away.

"Mine," Beck growls, moving in behind me. I can feel his skin against mine. He must have removed his clothes at some point. His fingers rub my clit, and I moan around West's shaft.

Beck lifts me slightly, lining his dick up with my entrance before pushing into me, and he and West quickly find a rhythm that has all three of us rushing toward the edge of the cliff.

Cleaning up, the three of us collapse onto the bed. I can feel my eyes dropping as tiredness takes over.

"Go to sleep, Firefly," West murmurs.

"You owe me at least three more orgasms," I grumble, half asleep.

I feel Beck chuckle behind me.

"Plenty of time for that in the morning, sweetheart."

Well, okay then.

CHAPTER 21

Hadley

A COMMOTION THE NEXT MORNING PULLS ME OUT OF MY DEEP SLEEP, and I'm instantly annoyed that whoever is talking so loudly is disturbing my quiet time with West and Beck. I've definitely decided my new happy place is being snuggled between these two.

"Where is she? Is she here?" I hear someone snapping from elsewhere in the apartment. "HADLEY!"

Oh, damn. That's Wilder.

"What's going on?" West mumbles as Beck yawns.

I quickly scurry out from between the two of them, grabbing the first items of clothes I find—Beck's t-shirt and West's sweats—before yanking the door open and rushing down the hallway. Only to find Wilder facing off against Hawk and Mason, all three of them looking downright furious.

"It's the crack ass of dawn," Cam grumbles, stumbling out of his room, still looking half asleep. "What are you two doing?"

"YOU PUT A *KNIFE* THROUGH MY FATHER'S HAND?" WILDER BARKS when he spots me, making everyone else stare in my direction as West and Beck come out of the room and join the party.

"In fairness, he put his hands on me first." I shrug.

"He what?" several voices bellow, furious tones flying all over the place.

"When were you going to tell us this?" Hawk snaps.

"This morning, after I'd had coffee."

"You should have said something last night," West argues, making me give him the stink eye. Maybe I would have, if I wasn't so crazed out of my mind with need—need that *he* caused.

"Let's all sit down, and we can talk about this," Beck rationalizes, stepping around me and moving between Wilder and Hawk, glaring at both Hawk and Mason until they take a step back. Cam stomps over to the coffee maker, filling it up as the others claim their seats. Mason makes a point of dragging me into his lap, scowling over my head at Wilder, who promptly ignores him.

"Did you finally get that release you needed last night, Sunshine?" Wilder winks, making Mason growl behind me.

"I'm still a few releases short," I admit. "Someone interrupted this morning." I scowl at him, and he gives me an oopsies face—it's literally the only way I can describe the look he's sporting.

Cam sets a tray of mugs on the coffee table for everyone to help themselves. Lifting two, he places a cup in my hands, kissing me on the forehead and mumbling a 'good morning' before sitting beside Mason and me.

"So, wanna explain what happened last night?" Hawk directs at me when we're all seated and adequately caffeinated.

I take them through the previous evening's events, only having to stop every few words when one of them curses up a storm. *Finally* we get through it, and everyone falls into silence, thinking through the various information drops.

"You keep a knife in your boot?" Cam asks, sounding shocked and having picked up on what I would have classified as one of the least significant things I said, but whatever.

"Yeah. Why, where do you keep yours?"

He just looks at me like he doesn't know whether to take me seriously or not, before mumbling something about not keeping a knife on his person.

Hmm, we'll have to sort that out. What idiot walks around unprotected?

"So I'm guessing you spoke to your dad today?" I ask, looking at Wilder.

"Yeah," he grumbles, looking unimpressed. "He phoned me when he was released from the hospital this morning—at four a.m." He glowers at me, likely not happy that the phone call disturbed his beauty sleep. *Oopsies.* "Going on about how he might need surgery."

I scoff. "Please, it was barely more than a flesh wound."

Wilder cocks an eyebrow. "You went right through his hand and out the other side." Despite the harsh tone in his words, he sounds hella impressed. At least, I think he does. I'm going to pretend he does, regardless.

"Is that why you always insist on wearing those boots?" Cam questions, clearly still stuck on the whole knife-in-the-boot thing.

"One of the reasons."

"What are the others?"

"They're comfy, and I know how to move silently in them."

"So it sounds like our parents agreed for you to be married off to Wilder when we were kids," Hawk theorizes, his brow furrowed in thought.

"Yeah, after he'd had his turn with me first." I shiver in disgust, burrowing deeper into Mason's chest as he tightens his hold around me. I take comfort from the soft vibrations in his chest as he growls deep in his throat.

"Did you know about that?" Hawk snaps, fixing Wilder with an intense, murderous look.

He holds his hands up in surrender. "All I knew was that a contract was drawn up, and then it fell through. I had no idea it included Hadley or I or anything else."

"So what, he's into little kids?" Cam scrunches his nose up, his face blanching at the thought.

All of us look at Wilder for confirmation.

"Honestly, it's news to me if he does."

"How do you not know?" Hawk snaps, making Wilder quirk an eyebrow at him.

"Do you know everything about *your* parents?"

Well, he's got a point there. Hawk seems to agree as he quickly shuts his mouth.

"So, what happened this morning?" I ask Wilder.

"Nothing, really. I don't think he'll be looking to spend much time with his new daughter-in-law."

Suits me just fine.

"He's not breaking off the agreement?" I ask.

"Nope. He didn't even mention it. Whatever he's getting out of it must be worth handing me over to a stabby psycho." He waggles his eyebrows. "By the way, I'm all for knife play in the bedroom, Wifey." He winks, even as the guys glower and curse him out, laughing like the crazy idiot he is before once again growing serious. "He's signing the contract today." His words settle in my stomach like lead as I glance nervously at the others. "Guess it's about to be official, Wifey. We're getting hitched."

THREE DAYS LATER—*THREE FUCKING DAYS*—AND I'M WEARING A stupid-ass gown—walking into the Davenport house for *my* engagement party. Okay, admittedly, it's another gorgeous piece selected by West.

My dress is a floor-length pale blue-gray that perfectly matches the color of my eyes and rises high on the back, once again ensuring my scars are covered from prying eyes.

My arm is linked with Wilder's, just as Hawk, Mason, Cam, and West form a protective circle around us, looking sharp as ever in their suits. Each one of them has something that matches my dress, be it their tie, handkerchief, cufflinks, or in Cam's case, his shoelaces. It's their silent way of letting me know they're here for me, and my heart just about stuttered to a stop when I saw all of them lined up. I know Beck is here somewhere, too, supporting me in his own inconspicuous way.

"Let's get this show on the road," Hawk huffs, straightening his suit jacket before moving away, weaving through the crowd as he makes his way to the bar.

The other guys break away, going to mingle while ensuring they keep me in their sights.

"Right," Wilder starts, his gaze sweeping around the room before focusing on me, "which set of shitty parents should we tick off the list first. Yours or mine?"

Ugh, what a crappy choice to choose between. "I'm sure my lovely mother will hunt us down fairly quickly."

"Bar it is then."

I laugh as he escorts me through the crowd. People constantly stop us, wishing us congratulations, starting up a conversation with Wilder, and complimenting me on my dress, which takes forever for us to reach our destination.

Eventually, we make it, and Wilder orders a scotch for himself and a water for me. I'm sipping on the drink, relishing the feeling of the cold liquid in my mouth, when I feel eyes on me. I knew it was only a matter of time until he sought me out. Making sure my mask of indifference is firmly in place when I turn my head, I search through the crowd for Lawrence, only it's not Lawrence that's watching me. It's Barton. *What the fuck?* He's barely spared me a glance or said a word to me since I returned, so what's with the creepy as fuck stalking now?

We've just finished our drinks when my mother spots us, piercing me with a stern glare like she knows I was deliberately avoiding her, as she marches toward us. "What are you doing? You should have found us as soon as you arrived," she seethes in my ear before standing to her full height and plastering on a sweet smile. "Wilder, dear, don't you look handsome as ever."

Wilder, the socialite suck-up that he is, laughs congenially. "Why thank you, Mrs. Davenport, but it's all your lovely daughter's doing. She makes me look good."

My mother's smile tightens, neither confirming nor denying his statement. "My husband would like to say a few words, if you'd both follow me," she says cordially, leading the way to the front of the room.

Seeing us approach, Barton gains the room's attention, beginning his speech.

"Ladies and gentlemen, I am honored to have you here this evening. We have some momentous news to share with you all. Not only are we lucky to have our blessed daughter back in our lives, but she has found true love in Wilder Clearwater."

I cough, hiding my snort as Wilder elbows me in the ribs, appearing equally amused. I'm sure the guys are somewhere nearby, grumbling under their breaths.

"The two met at a family gathering, and it was love at first sight." The audience coos and awes—are they seriously that fucking gullible?! "Tonight, I am so very pleased to introduce to you my soon-to-be son-in-law, my daughter's fiancé, Wilder Clearwater." The room erupts into claps and cheers as Wilder practically drags me up to stand beside my father.

"We haven't finalized a date for the wedding yet, but the two of them are excited for a short engagement"—*We're what now?!*— "so I'm sure we will have a date for you all very soon."

Somehow, amid all this mayhem, I forgot there would be an actual wedding. I'd kind of figured we'd be engaged for at least a year. I mean, that's what most people do, right? I definitely thought it would be enough time for us to wrangle our way out of it before it occurred, yet my father is making it sound like it's *weeks, months* at most, away.

I'm pretty sure I'm sporting a 'deer caught in the headlights' expression as Wilder maneuvers me back into the crowd, quickly fobbing everyone off as he ushers me out of the room.

"Wilder," I whisper-hiss, clinging onto his arm for dear life. "I am not marrying you."

"Oh, Sunshine, you wound me. There I thought we were in love." I try to scowl at him, but the whole panicked eye thing kind of ruins it, and he chuckles at my freak out. He directs me into a back kitchen, quickly kicking the few staff members out, and grabs me a glass of water while I collapse onto a stool.

I'm not someone who freaks out. Usually, I'm pretty calm in the face of challenging situations. Give me a surprise dead body any day, and I'll happily deal with it, but *this* is unchartered territory. I've never really given any thought to marriage. Growing up the way I did, it's not something I thought I'd have the luxury of experiencing—unless it was to Lawrence, in which case, fuck no— but now that it's a real-life possibility staring me right in the face, I'm kind of fucking panicking.

"What's wrong with her?" Mason snaps out, barging into the kitchen.

"She's fine. Chill your nuts." Wilder rolls his eyes. "She's just freaking out a little."

"What is she freaking out about? What did you do to her?"

"I don't think she was expecting an actual wedding," he says far too casually. How is he not freaking out as badly as I am?!

The next thing I know, Mason has bumped Wilder out of the way, taking the glass of water from my hands and setting it on the table. He cups my face in both hands and focuses my gaze on his eyes.

"Hey, Little Warrior." His soothing voice washes over me, and he smiles when he sees I'm looking at him.

"Mason, I can't marry him," I whisper.

"You're not going to, baby. It's all for show, remember?"

"But Barton made it sound like we'd be getting married in a few weeks or a few months." The pitch of my voice climbs with each word.

"These things take time to plan, and we're not going to let that happen, okay?"

I want to believe him, but I don't. He must see it in my eyes—

as his own harden—and he moves his hand to pinch my chin.

"If you're marrying anyone, it will be one of us. You got that?"

The steely resolve in his tone breaks through my panic, and I nod my head. Seeing that I trust in what he's saying, he dives in, sealing his words with a searing kiss that I can feel all the way to my toes.

"Good, now get back out there and put on a show so I can tear that dress off you later and make you forget about this whole night."

He goes to move away, but I wrap my hand around his blue-gray tie, pulling him back into me. He searches my eyes as I repeat the words he said to me in the library. "You're mine, and I'm yours."

His eyes soften, and he plants another kiss on my lips. "I'm yours, and you're mine, baby. To the end."

"Truly heartwarming," Wilder drawls when we break apart. "Armor back in place, Wifey?"

I give him a firm nod.

"Excellent." A bright grin spreads across his face, a wicked glint entering his eyes. "Let's go freak the fuck out of some conservative assholes."

Heading back to the party, we do a lap of the room. Wilder is undoubtedly the most fun person to be with at one of these stuck-up events. He turns everything into a game. We spend the next hour trying to figure out who is cheating on whom, while working to see how quickly we can make the women clutch their pearls with our outlandish stories.

"This was me in Italy last year," Wilder explains, showing some middle-aged lady his photos from Europe. "And this is me beside the Eiffel Tower." Swiping across the screen of his phone to the next image, the woman tilts her head at the phone in confusion, and Wilder feigns shock. "Oh, oops. My bad. I thought I felt something weird on my ballsack. Such a difficult angle to get a photo."

The woman gasps, taking a step back from us, while Wilder

continues muttering to himself. I can no longer contain my laughter as she rushes out with an excuse to leave. When a little bit of pee dribbles out from laughing so hard, I know I can't hold off my bathroom break any longer and excuse myself to search for one in this ridiculously massive house.

Refreshed and with a now empty bladder, I pull open the bathroom door, but before I can step out, I'm herded back in. Panic flares as I stare into Lawrence's cold, hard face as he slams the door shut behind him, flicking the lock. Somehow, in all the fun I was having with Wilder, I forgot this fuckface was lurking about. He never openly approaches me in front of any of our parents, showing nothing more than a passing interest in my arrival, but of course he would take the opportunity when out of sight of the other partygoers to corner me.

"You've been a hard woman to get a private moment with, Dove."

"Are you here to congratulate me?" I struggle to keep my voice from shaking, even as my hands tremble and my heart rate skyrockets.

His hand snaps out, wrapping tightly around my neck, and my mind goes blank as utter terror consumes me. If he were anyone else, I'd be cool and collected right now, strategizing and working out my best move to get out of this situation, but because it's *him*, I'm frozen in fear, unable to move as he towers over me.

It's fucking ridiculous. I was in a similar situation with Benjamin, and I was able to fight my way out of it without a second thought, but replace that person with Lawrence, and I'm reduced to that scared kid I used to be.

His face is the thing of nightmares, encompassing my entire field of vision. "You think I'm going to congratulate you," he sneers in disgust. "Have you forgotten who you belong to, Dove?"

His hand tightens around my throat, his other one pulling on my hair so I'm forced to stare up at him. I don't know how it's possible, but his features somehow darken. "Has he fucked you yet?"

His hand untangles itself from my hair as he roughly pulls up my skirt, not caring that he's tearing it in his haste.

"Has he?" he barks, roughly cupping my pussy and squeezing it. His loud voice echoes around the small bathroom, making me jump.

"N...No."

Curling his fingers under the fabric, he tears my panties clean off.

I should be fighting back, kicking out or hitting him—doing *something*, but my whole body feels numb as he shoves two fingers inside me.

"Who does this cunt belong to?" His words are a possessive snarl, leaving no questioning as to who he thinks it belongs to.

When I don't answer fast enough, he removes his grip on my throat, smacking me across the face.

"Answer me!" he bellows.

"Y...you."

"And has anyone else had a taste?"

"No," I respond immediately, making an evil smirk light up his face in the most menacing way. It's a look that will haunt my nightmares for years to come.

He curls his fingers roughly inside me, hurting me more, before finally pulling out and sniffing them.

"Good. It better stay that way. I'm getting impatient, Dove. You've made friends at that school, haven't you? The scholarship kids? If you don't fall in line soon, I might have to get one of my men to pay them a visit."

Tears are streaming down my face as I all but cower in front of him, my weak state only bolstering his confidence as he preens.

Wrapping his hand around my throat once more, he presses his lips roughly to mine, his fingers digging into my cheeks until I open for him, allowing him to shove his tongue into my mouth. He takes and takes until he's satisfied. Finally letting me go, he sneers down at me, "Clean yourself up. You're a state."

Turning, he lets himself out of the room, and I collapse to the floor, tears flowing freely as I beat myself up for being so weak around him.

I'm supposed to be a badass bitch. I can gut people without a second thought. Slit their throats, drive blades into their heads. You name it. Although I can't stand up to one measly cretin of a man? I'm pathetic. Completely fucking pathetic.

I don't know how long I sit there before finding the strength to get to my feet. Looking in the mirror at my tear-stained face and the pins that once held my hair in place, now hanging uselessly from the loose strands, I decide there's no fucking way I'm going back to that party.

With shaking hands, I lift my phone out from where I stored it between my boobs, texting Cam to meet me round the side of the house. I'm hoping he's the least likely to ask questions and just take me home.

Working my way outside, I notice Cam coming toward me.

"Hey," he says quietly, keeping his voice low. "What's going on? Is everything okay? Ooh, is this a booty call?" I can just about make out his eyebrows waggling in the darkness, and I release a teary chuckle that immediately has the coy smile falling off his face as he rushes to close the distance between us.

His hand cups my face gently, and his eyes darken as he takes in the red palm print smarting my cheek. "What happened?" he growls.

I extricate myself from his grip. "Can we just go to the car, please?" I plead.

He doesn't move. His body is practically vibrating with rage. "Did my father do that?"

I don't need to answer that question; he can see the truth in my eyes as he lets go of me, storming away before pacing back toward me, looking like a restrained beast as he fights to unleash all his pent-up anger.

"Cam," I plead. That one word is enough to snap him out of his murderous thoughts, and he freezes in front of me.

"Right, yeah, come on, baby." He drapes an arm over my shoulder, drawing me in against him as he leads me to the car.

He surprises me when he opens the back and slides in behind me instead of opening the front passenger door for me to climb in. Closing the door, he pulls me into his lap, and I burrow my head in the gap between his neck and shoulder, breathing him in. He rubs soothing circles along my back, neither of us saying anything for a long time.

"I need to know what happened, baby," he eventually murmurs.

"Can't we just go home?" I peer up at him through my eyelashes, imploring him with my eyes.

He grimaces. "We all came together, so we have to wait for the others."

"Oh." That's all I'm capable of saying. I don't even think I care. Other than wanting to get out of this ruined dress and into bed, I'm comfortable here with Cam, pretending the rest of the world outside our little car bubble doesn't exist.

"Tell me what happened," he repeats with more insistence.

Sighing, I rehash what happened with his dad in the bathroom, feeling the mounting rage within him with every word out of my mouth. By the time I'm finished, I'm sitting tensely on his lap, waiting for him to go absolutely apeshit, except he surprises me by burying his face in my hair.

"I'm so sorry," he murmurs in a broken voice. I can still feel all that rage pouring off him, but more than that, I can feel the devastation he feels for what I had to endure. For not being there for me, and most of all, for the part he feels he plays in all of this by being related to that monster. "I'm going to kill him someday. I won't let him get to you again."

I shush him, running my fingers through his golden hair. Not because I don't believe him, but because his father's death is mine. I don't know how since I'm not capable of even lifting a finger in his presence, but *somehow, someday*, he will die a slow, painful death at my hands.

CHAPTER 22

Hadley

I don't know how long Cam and I sit in the car, mostly in silence, occasionally exchanging the odd word, before the back door is wrenched open.

"Why are you two hiding out in here?" West asks. When he opened the car door, it activated the overhead light. So as he slides into the seat beside us, my swollen eyes and torn dress render him motionless as he frantically checks me over, his features hardening.

His gaze flicks to Cam's before landing back on me, and he quickly climbs into the backseat, closing the door behind him and bathing us in darkness once again. "What happened?" His voice is a low, menacing growl. I don't have it in me to go over it all again, so I let Cam explain the gist of it—no doubt it will all need to be brought up *again* with everyone back in the dorm.

Leaning in, West presses his forehead against mine. "You did so good, Firefly."

I scoff. "I was pathetic. I'm so weak around him. He just has to look at me, and I turn into a little girl again. What's the point in knowing how to fight when I'm frozen in place whenever he's nearby?"

"You're not weak," he assures me. The fire in his voice almost makes me believe him. "You've got so much power in you, you don't even realize how strong you are. He's been your monster under the bed for so long that you don't know how to overcome him, but you're not alone anymore. You've got us. We're just one more weapon in your arsenal against him."

When I look at him in confusion, he explains.

"He thinks you're all alone. He believes you're too brain-washed by him to let anyone else in, that you're too broken to love anyone. However, you've proven how wrong he is. He thinks he owns every part of you, but *you* are the one who decides who you give yourself to. No part of you is his."

"All of me is yours," I whisper, catching on to what he's saying.

He shakes his head no. "It's all *yours*, Firefly. Your heart, your body, your mind, your soul...every part of you is yours to give away to whoever you choose, *when* you choose."

"I gave all of it to you," I murmur, realizing that I've given each of these guys—my guys—small parts of myself at various intervals over the last few months. So much that, collectively, they now own enough that they could destroy me—yet I don't, for one second, believe they would. Glancing at Cam, I add, "All four of you. I'm all yours."

"And we're yours," they both echo.

"Lawrence doesn't know you've got an army of guys ready to dive into battle for you. You're no longer alone in this, Firefly. Whatever you decide to do, we'll be right beside you."

Cam nods his head in agreement with West's sentiment. "Every step of the way."

I smile softly, relaxing back into Cam's touch. When push

comes to shove, I don't know whether these guys will stay. Taking on our parents, the compound, and Lawrence is one hell of a battle. For now, though, I'll take comfort in their words and the fact that they're here with me.

West pulls out his phone and sends out a text, and then a few minutes later, he gets a reply.

"The guys are getting a lift home with Wilder." He turns to Cam. "Let's get our girl home to bed."

THE NEXT MORNING, I WAKE UP WEDGED BETWEEN TWO DELICIOUSLY hot bodies. I fell asleep between Cam and West last night. So when I peel my eyes open to find a very thick, muscular arm that definitely does not belong to either of my leaner guys, cupping my tit, I realize Mason must have climbed into bed with us when he got home—and mostly likely shoved Cam out of the way to steal his spot. A faint smile graces my lips at the thought. I didn't even hear any of them get back last night. After the adrenaline rush of the evening's events, I crashed as soon as my head hit the pillow.

Looking away from Mason's broad arm, my eyes roam over West's peaceful, sleeping face. He seems so different without his glasses on. He wears them all the time, even during sex, so I rarely get the opportunity to just look at him without them on.

Moving my gaze away from his face, I stifle a chuckle when I see a broad, tattooed arm draped over his hip.

Beck is snuggled up against West's back, his arm hanging over him, the back of his fingers brushing against my stomach.

"They make a cute couple, don't they?" Mason murmurs sleepily in my ear. His hand slowly massages my boob, making my back arch and pushing my ass against his morning wood.

"Mmm." It's the only response I can give, both in answer to his question and the way he's making my body slowly come alive.

He trails his fingers down my abdomen, slipping beneath my t-shirt, and he groans against the sensitive skin on my neck when he discovers I'm not wearing any panties. After Lawrence divested me of mine last night, I decided to go commando when I got home, not seeing a need to put on a fresh pair just to get into bed.

Hitching my thigh over his leg, he pushes down his boxers, sliding his thick length through my folds before slowly pushing his way inside me. He bites down on my earlobe, causing me to moan softly as I push back against him, the two of us thrusting in a slow, easy, early morning rhythm that is just as tantalizing as a good, hot fuck.

His hand is clamped over my thigh, holding it in place, and my eyes are shut as I get lost in the feel of him stretching me, so I'm startled when another hand starts rubbing my clit in time with Mason's lazy thrusts. Glancing down, Cam's hand slowly works me over, and as I pant and grind, chasing my release, I catch West watching me, a feral glint in his eyes.

He pushes my top up, exposing my tits. My already hardened nipples stiffen as he tweaks and pulls on them, driving me mad with all their teasing touches.

I'm approaching the edge, when I feel yet another hand slide down over my lower belly, and I know the last of my guys has joined in the fun, bringing a content smile to my face as Mason picks up his pace, finally giving me what I need.

Skimming over my clit, where Cam is rubbing me furiously now, Beck pushes two fingers inside me, along with Mason's dick, stretching me that extra little bit that sends me catapulting over the edge and into oblivion.

"Damn, we should wake up like this every morning," Cam states as Mason slows and pulls out. He's still rock-hard, letting me know he managed to hold off on reaching his own release. Keeping an iron-tight grip on my thigh, he returns to gliding his dick along my slit. Every time he thrusts forward, the head of his cock bumps against my sensitive clit, making me whimper.

West is watching me closely, and he must be able to see the need still burning through me, as he smirks wickedly.

"I believe I owe you a few more orgasms." There's a dark husk to his tone that has my pussy immediately weeping.

"I believe you do." My own voice is dripping in lust; the thought of having all my guys together makes me hot and needy.

In one swift move, Mason moves onto his back, taking me with him so I'm sprawled on top of him, my head resting on his shoulder. He drapes my thighs over him, spreading me wide for the others to see.

"So pretty and pink and swollen," Beck purrs as he moves between my thighs, flattening his tongue and giving me one long, languid lick that makes me moan and writhe against Mason's hard body.

Getting his hands beneath me, Mason spreads my ass cheeks, running his dick through my juices, ensuring it's slick before slowly pushing past the tight ring of muscle.

I gasp and tense at the slight burn, but then Beck goes back to creating magic with his tongue, and my whole body relaxes under his delicious touch.

Mason slides all the way in, filling me up, before giving a few shallow, testing thrusts.

"Fuck." I grind, pressing my head back against his shoulder.

"That feel good, Little Warrior?"

"So full," I groan.

"Just wait, sweetheart, you're about to feel so fucking stuffed," Beck growls possessively before slamming his dick all the way into me in one hard thrust.

I cry out, nearly coming there and then. "Oh, Jesus," I whimper. "I need to come so bad."

"Not yet, Firefly," West demands. "You still have two more dicks to take." His dirty words make me whimper again, my pussy clenching at the thought of having all of them at once. Both Mason and Beck curse when I strangle their dicks.

"Fuck, she's gushing all over me. She loves the idea of having all of us, don't you, baby?" Beck's voice gives away how much he's getting off on this too, as he struggles to hold himself back while thrusting impossibly deeper into me.

Glancing up at West, he jerks his head at Cam, who quickly comes to sit behind Mason and me. I adjust myself so my head is falling off Mason's shoulder, putting me at the perfect angle as I open my mouth and relax my jaw, enabling Cam to slide past my lips and down my throat.

Fuck, I've never been so full in all my life, and as all three of them start to move in a coordinated rhythm, I know I won't last long. Yet there's still one guy missing and, as Cam pulls back, I look at West out of the corner of my eye, holding my hand out for him in a silent gesture.

He smirks, coming toward me on his knees and lifting out his heavy dick, weighing it in his palm before letting me wrap my hand around him. I tug and pull on him as Cam repeatedly hits the back of my throat, spilling soft curses every time; all the while, Mason and Beck drill into me, the multitude of sensations driving me crazy with ecstasy. This is what being on drugs must be like. That heady, all-consuming feeling, like you can't take anymore but it's still not enough.

Cam comes first, spilling his cum down my throat before kissing my lips and moving to lie beside me. His fingers stroke my sweat-slicked skin, pinching and rolling my nipples as West takes his place. Unlike Cam, he doesn't wait for me to open. As soon as he's settled, he pushes the tip of his cock against my lips, smearing on the bead of pre-cum as he silently demands entry.

He shoves his way inside, groaning as my teeth graze along his skin until he hits the back of my throat, blocking my airway. He stops, holding himself there until my lungs feel like they're about to burst, before pulling back and letting me gulp down a large breath, only to do it again.

The lack of oxygen only heightens the sensations, and I quickly lose it. My moans vibrate over West's dick as he comes down my throat, and my pussy clenches, causing the other two to lose the last bit of control they had as they come inside me.

After getting dirty, passionate kisses from Beck and Mason, the five of us collapse into a sweaty pile on the bed. Mason removes himself from beneath me, and I flop onto Cam's chest, sated and content, not giving a shit that we're all lying in cum-filled bedsheets.

Just as I'm about to drift back to sleep, a loud knock on the door startles me awake.

"Get up, family meeting." Hawk barks.

"Ugh," I groan.

"Asshole seriously needs to get laid," Cam grumbles, unwrapping his arms from around me and climbing out of bed.

As the others grab clothes and towels to go shower, I lean into West. "Why do you normally wear your glasses during sex?"

His fingers trail tenderly over my face. "I want to see every bit of pleasure I make you feel."

He plants a quick kiss on my lips before getting up. *Damn, there's something so hot about his need for control.*

Half an hour later, we're all in the living room with cups of coffee. Hawk, Beck, and Mason are all staring at me expectantly, so I'm guessing this is where I have to once again go over what happened last night.

Sighing, I lean back in my seat and bring up my knees, wedging myself into the corner of the sofa before explaining what happened to them.

By the time I've finished, Hawk is stomping about the place like an angry bear, Mason looks like he's on the verge of hunting Lawrence down and killing him himself, and Beck is looking at me with a sad expression in his eyes, like this is somehow all his fault.

Grumbling under his breath, Hawk stalks over to where I'm sitting. Crouching down in front of me, he rests his hand on my knee. "Did he...?" He can't finish the sentence, his mouth clamping shut in refusal to even utter the words.

"Not as bad as last time," I whisper. However, West, astute as ever as he sits stoically beside me, overhears.

"What do you mean *last time*?" he growls, his pitch-black tone enough to draw the others' attention our way.

Hawk and I share a look, and he picks up on my silent plea for him to be the one to tell everyone else.

Sighing defeatedly, he nods, standing to his full height and looking at each of the guys.

"The day Lawrence came to campus, and I found Hadley alone with him in the headmaster's office—"

"You said she was fine," Mason barks, cutting across Hawk, already able to tell the end of this story isn't a good one. "That nothing happened."

"I know." Hawk sighs. "I lied." I can see it in his eyes. He's still beating himself up about not getting there sooner.

"I asked him to." I fix each of them with a look so they don't start shouting at Hawk for lying to them. He was only doing right by me. Glancing at me, I can tell he's surprised. We both know that's not what happened. He *offered* not to tell the guys. He put me first, above people he's been friends with his whole life. It's not something I'm going to forget any time soon.

Now that I've spoken up, all four of my guys look at me. "What did he do?" Mason's deep baritone and menacing growl send a shiver skittering up my spine. If I were Lawrence, I would run very far away, pretty fucking quickly, before Mason has a chance to gut him like a fish.

"He tried to get me to suck his dick," I blurt out, refusing to meet anyone's gaze. I don't want to see any the pity or disgust on their faces.

"How far?" Mason doesn't seem capable of saying anything more, but he doesn't need to. His meaning is clear enough.

Hawk sighs. "It was in her mouth when I walked in."

I close my eyes against the onslaught of tears threatening to leak out, burying my face in my hands. I jump when something goes crashing against the wall.

"Cam!" West calls before the front door slams shut. The sound of Cam leaving shatters the last of my restraint as tears drip from between my closed lids into my palms.

Broad arms wrap around me, and I breathe in Beck's cedarwood and eucalyptus scent. Usually it calms me, but today it just makes me feel more lost as I burrow deeper into his chest, internally freaking out about how this new development might change everything.

I just got Cam back. What if this breaks him? What if the others don't want to be with me anymore, knowing what I did? I mean, that's kind of cheating, right? Our already complicated relationship is still too new to survive this, and I'm too emotionally stunted to know how to save it.

I hear the others whispering nearby, but Beck holds me close, rocking back and forth while he strokes my hair. Not long later, I hear the front door open and close again. Someone probably went to check on Cam.

Silence envelops the apartment as I keep my head firmly pressed against Beck's chest.

"I'm sorry," I mumble into his t-shirt, when I finally find my voice again.

He stops rocking, and his fingers wipe away the tear tracks on my cheek, slipping under my chin and forcing me to look up at him.

The devastated look in his eyes nearly breaks me all over again.

"Don't be sorry." There's a husk in his voice, giving away the overwhelming emotions he's experiencing, yet the sternness in his tone is very real. "You didn't do anything. This is all on him. *I'm* sorry. *We're* sorry we didn't get to you on time." There are tears in his eyes, and I've never seen him look more emotional before. "We failed you."

"You're not angry I didn't tell you?"

He shakes his head. "Do I wish you'd felt like you could? Yeah, of course. But I understand why you didn't."

"I wanted to pretend it never happened."

He nods, understanding.

"He threatened West if…if I didn't."

He clenches his teeth, his nostrils flaring in anger, as he continues to stroke his thumbs over my cheeks reverently.

"We won't let him get away with this," he promises. There's so much hostility and determination in his words, I can't not believe him.

Glancing around the room, I realize we're alone.

"Did the others go after Cam?" I ask, worrying my bottom lip.

"Yeah, and to give us some time alone."

I nod my head absently, leaning in against him.

"Do you think he'll be okay?"

"He just needs some time. He'll be back."

I hope so. I can't do any of this without him.

We didn't stay on the sofa for long before Beck carried me back to West's room, lying down with me. After everything that happened in the last twenty-four hours, it didn't take long before I fell asleep.

When I come to, the sun is low in the sky, the bright red shining through the window. Beck is gone, and Cam is lying on his side, his head propped on his hand as he watches me with sad, broken eyes.

"Hi," I croak, my voice dry and thick with sleep and emotion. His fingers skim over mine and I interlink them. "Are you okay?"

His eyes lift to mine. "I should be asking you that."

Closing the distance between us, I wrap my arms around his waist and he falls onto his back, taking me with him.

"That was the first day Hawk stepped up and had my back," I tell him. "I hate that he had to see me like that"—Cam's fingertips dig into the skin on my hip—"but it strengthened our relationship tenfold. So rather than thinking about what happened that day in that room, I remember Hawk hugging me and how he looked at me—like he finally realized we were one and the same. Because of what happened, I now know what it's like to have a brother and, for the most part, it's been pretty awesome."

Cam pulls me up his body so my face is inches from his. "You're incredible," he murmurs, awestruck.

I shrug. "When you're used to awful things happening to you, you learn to focus on the positives."

CHAPTER 23

Hadley

WHEN CAM AND I EMERGED FROM WEST'S ROOM, MASON AND WEST scooped me into their arms with reassurances that they loved me. Even Hawk gave me one of his rare hugs, and we all finally sat down to discuss what Lawrence said at the engagement party. All of us agreed that the fact he threatened the scholarship students means he doesn't know how close I've gotten with the guys, which is good.

We also discussed the plan for Easter break. Mason, Hawk, Cam, and West will be at their parents' office building for the whole week. While we're all unsure of what new responsibilities they will have to take on, especially Mason, now that Frank is out of the picture, we've all decided it's the best opportunity we're going to get to dig up dirt on all of them. They'll have easy access to snoop around and, hopefully, find something we can use to not only take down our parents and destroy the company but free ourselves from the lives they have planned for each of us.

Beck relayed any details he could about his visits to the compound, without giving away the fact our parents are training kids. He and I have been talking a lot lately about what he's seen and had to do there. As we all get more entrenched in all of this, he's been encouraging me more and more to tell the guys the truth. I keep jumping back and forth on the matter. Part of me—okay, *most* of me—wants to be honest with them, but I'm scared. I don't think many relationships could survive when one finds out their significant other is a ruthless assassin who has killed, maimed, and tortured people. I think I'm getting there when it comes to telling them. The more time I spend with them and learn to trust them, the more I find myself wanting to. I'm just not quite there yet. The guys leave at the end of the week for Easter break, so I think I'll spill the beans when they get back—I know, I'm a total pussy. Beck mentioned that our parents might tell the guys what's really going on at the compound over Easter break—they have to eventually, right? But I think it might be better that they've had some time to stew in that little revelation before I add even more to their plates. *Yeah, basically, I'm making excuses.*

Unfortunately, none of us know what to do about Lawrence. He has been keeping his distance since it was announced to the world that I'm the long-lost Davenport daughter, but we're all a little worried the news of my sudden engagement will be enough to tip him over the edge. If last night is any indicator of what's to come, he will be gunning for me. Other than being on high alert and not going anywhere alone, I'm not sure what else I can do. If he sends any more mercenaries after me, it's not a problem, I can more than handle my own. Although if he comes for me himself, it's a totally different ballgame. I don't know how to get over my fear when it comes to him. It's utterly irrational, given that I could easily take him, but that doesn't make it any less real. It's like people being afraid of spiders. You know you're the predator in the room, that you can easily squash the spider beneath your boot, but it doesn't stop your body from locking up when the damn thing scurries across the floor.

I'm making my way down the corridor toward Beck's office when I hear the headmaster's door open further down the hall, and a girl in a school uniform steps out.

She's not looking my way as she flattens her hair and tugs down her skirt, but as my boot squeaks against the wooden floor, her head snaps up, looking in my direction, and I notice the girl is none other than Bianca.

She's got flushed cheeks and swollen lips, appearing freshly fucked.

My eyes dart back and forth between her and the headmaster's door, easily putting two and two together as my eyebrows rise up my forehead and a smirk crosses my lips.

"Well, well, what do we have here?" I sing cheerily, taking pleasure in her shocked, panicked expression.

I gasp, bringing my hand up to cover my mouth in fake dramatics. "Oh my, is he your baby daddy?"

Bianca has been staying out of my way since I announced her little secret to the whole school, but that doesn't mean I've stopped keeping an eye on her.

Instead of talking back to me like she usually does, she glances quickly at the door before rushing off. I quirk an eyebrow as I watch her disappear. *Weird.* I really thought it would have taken more than announcing one measly secret to put her in her place.

Shrugging it off, I quickly forget about her as I turn the handle and step into Beck's office.

"What has you looking so happy today?" Beck asks, getting out of his chair as I close the door behind myself and flick the lock. Striding around the table, he approaches me, planting a panty-melting kiss on my lips.

"Just caught someone doing something—well, someone—they shouldn't have been," I say cryptically.

As he pulls away, I reach out, placing my palm on his cheek and forcing him to stay as my eyes roam over his face, taking in the dark bags under his eyes. There's none of the usual light there, and his smile is tight.

Concerned creases furrow along my forehead as I run the pad of my thumb under his eye. "You got in late last night."

"Yeah, they had me going through all their surveillance tapes for their next targets. It took hours."

My lips pinch. He's going to end up in an early grave if he continues traveling to the compound and doing what he's doing.

"Come on, I just want to hold you."

He tugs me over to the sofa, and I curl up beside him, wrapping my arms around his waist.

"When do you have to go back?"

"Not for a few weeks."

Good. The guys will be back from Easter break by then. "Maybe we'll have something useful by then," I say hopefully.

"Yeah, maybe."

I hate the dejected tone in his voice. He's always really low after he comes back from visiting the compound. Not that I can blame him, but I hate seeing him like this. He always seems so strong, like nothing could get to him, but underneath his rough exterior, he's as vulnerable as the rest of us.

"You know what's weird?" he muses. "I thought I saw Wilder's dad there."

"At the compound?"

"Yeah. I remember him from the engagement party, and I'm sure it was him. But what would he be doing there?"

"How does he even know about the compound?"

We lapse into silence, and I can feel something tugging on my brain, a memory that I can't quite pull to the surface. Thinking back over my minimal contact with Benjamin Clearwater, I remember the night Wilder and I met him for dinner. Him blocking me in the bathroom. What he said.

I gasp as I lean up on Beck's chest. "What if the deal he made with my parents was so he could have access to the recruits?"

Beck looks at me, confused, not following. *Right, probably need to explain it better.*

"The night Wilder and I met him for dinner"—Beck's eyes

darken and his jaw clenches, remembering exactly what happened that night—"he said how I was older than his usual preferences."

Beck's face scrunches up in disgust but understanding dawns. "You think he demanded access to the underage recruits as part of the business contract?"

"Why else would he be there? I don't imagine it's easy to get your hands on underaged girls, but our parents have a bunch of them just sitting at the compound. Nobody cares about them. No one is going to save them. Hell, most of the guards have probably already taken their turn, so why not pass them around to one more person."

My stomach revolts even as I say it, and the dejected look in Beck's eyes confirms I'm right about the guards. "I've heard a few things on my visits," he verifies in a hollow voice. I'm pretty sure the only reason I wasn't violated in such a way was because of Lawrence. Not that I can be grateful to him for that small mercy, considering I'm pretty sure he's the one that stuck me in that godforsaken prison in the first place.

"Well, at least we understand his motives now." He sighs.

True. He's just another name to add to the list of fuckers I want to watch burn.

"So," Emilia asks, waggling her eyebrows. "What's it like to be an engaged woman?"

We're in the theater room, having our usual weekly movie night. Wilder decided to duck out of tonight. I think he realized I needed a bit of time with my friends, although I haven't told Michael the truth. Having discussed it with the guys, we agreed that the fewer people who know, the better. No one outside of Wilder, Emilia, and the six of us knows that the engagement is fake, and neither of us intends to go through with it. Unfortunately, that means I'm stuck pretending to be a happy bride-to-be tonight.

"Exactly the same as being *un-engaged*, except I have to cart this heavy rock around," I joke, flapping my hand in front of her face.

I nearly died when Wilder presented it to me this afternoon. It's legit worth more than anything I've ever owned, and it weighs a fucking ton. On the plus side, it would do a hell of a lot of damage if I decided to swing my left hand at some fucker's face. Small wins, I guess.

"You're seriously going to marry him?" Michael scoffs, looking disgusted. He and Wilder don't exactly see eye to eye, but I think Michael's just jealous. He's used to being the only guy in our group, and if he's still harboring a bit of a crush—which Emilia thinks he is—then he will be put out by Wilder's sudden appearance.

I shrug. "It's mostly a business arrangement, but I mean, I can think of worse people to marry."

"He's undeniably hot enough," Emilia agrees. "And rich. Other than being a little weird, he's the total package." She sighs. Clearly, she's given the idea of marrying him way too much thought.

"I thought you didn't care about money?"

I look at Michael in confusion. "I don't. I told you, it's mostly a business deal."

"Why do you care about agreeing to a business deal? You've hated the Princes and all the rich assholes in this place since day one. Now all of a sudden, you're fucking them and marrying someone just like them?"

You could hear a pin drop in the room as Emilia and I gape at Michael, shocked at his outburst.

"It's none of your business what I decide to do," I snap back.

He scoffs, looking repulsed. "Then don't have sex where anyone can see you."

I mentally wrack my brain, trying to figure out who he could have seen me with, but dammit, I've had sex in a public space with both Mason and Cam. It could be either or both of them.

Thinking back, I recall the night of the party when Cam and I snuck off into the forest. I was sure I heard someone in the trees that night, and when we came back, Michael was gone.

Gasping, I exclaim, "Was that you that night in the forest? Were you watching us?"

"What the hell, Michael?" Emilia gapes.

"You're just like everyone else here," Michael yells, "a two-faced bitch."

My jaw drops open in shock as I stare at him, flabbergasted, my fists clenched at my sides. "I'm not sure what I did to upset you," I start, trying very fucking hard to keep my temper under control. "And I'm sorry if I hurt you, but you have *no* right to talk to me that way."

Not waiting for him to dig himself any further into a hole, I stalk out of the room.

"I can't get over him," Emilia fumes when she catches up to me on the path back to the dorms. "And he saw you with one of them? Do you know who?"

"I think it was Cam." I sigh. "But that was *weeks* ago."

"And he never said anything?" she gasps.

"Nope." I pop the 'p', wholly baffled at what the fuck just happened in there.

"Damn."

Something in Emilia's tone has me looking over at her. "What?"

She grimaces. "Well, he must be hurt and confused. He's had a crush on you all year, then he catches you sleeping with someone you've spent half the year hating, and now you're 'happily engaged' to someone else."

Damn, the girl makes a lot of sense sometimes.

I sigh heavily, rubbing my eyes with my fingers.

"I fucked up, didn't I?"

"Maybe a little, but he also fucked up massively tonight. He should have just talked to you."

If the asshole wants to apologize and explain himself tomorrow, then fine, but otherwise, he can go fuck himself.

———

THE NEXT DAY, THE GUYS ALL LEAVE FOR EASTER BREAK. THEY'LL BE staying at their parents' houses for the next week since it's closer to the offices. None of us are happy about being separated, yet I'm hopeful this will be the perfect opportunity for us to gain some leverage. It *has* to be, otherwise I've no idea what we're going to do.

"Don't go anywhere alone," Hawk reiterates for like the ninetieth time. "And don't go out in the dark." I roll my eyes behind his back as he lifts his bag off his bed. "In fact, just spend all of your time with Beck. He won't have any sessions so he can entertain you."

"You realize I'm not a puppy or a child, right?"

"I'm being serious," he snaps, with a deathly scowl.

"So was I." When he continues to glower at me, I sigh. "Okay, I promise. I won't so much as insert a tampon without telling Beck."

His face blanches. "Gross," he grumbles.

I grin brightly, bouncing over to him and throwing my arms around him. "I'm gonna miss you, big bro."

He hesitates for a fraction of a second before returning my hug. "I'll miss you too, little sis," he mutters, sounding reluctant, even though I know it's all an act. We've made heaps of progress in the last few weeks and I really am going to miss the ornery fucker.

It takes forever to say goodbye to the other guys—mainly because Cam refuses to let me go. However, with one final kiss, they all head out, and my shoulders slump as the door closes behind them.

"None of that," Beck chastises, pulling me back against him.

"We have the whole apartment to ourselves. I bet you we can't have sex in every room before they come back."

Laughing, I turn around in his embrace. "Oh yeah? I'll take that bet."

I press up onto my toes, fusing my lips to his, wondering what room we should start this bet in. Hmm, the sofa's the closest, so the living room it is.

Despite my teasing of Hawk, I spend pretty much every moment of the next week with Beck. The guys check in frequently, and they send me plenty of sexts and dick pics which I use as fuel to win my bet with Beck. We don't talk much about whether or not they've managed to find anything useful, preferring to wait until we're all back together in person to discuss it.

Still, as the holidays draw to a close, my excitement at seeing them all again, and possibly taking some actual steps forward with the plan for our parents, has me bouncing around like a madwoman.

I'm in the guys' apartment—where I've basically sequestered myself for the last week, under the guys' orders—with Wilder. We're trying to watch a movie, but I just can't sit still.

"Sunshine," he gripes. "You're driving me crazy."

"Sorry. I'm just so sick of being in this apartment, and the guys are coming back tonight, and it just feels like it's been forever."

He chuckles, shaking his head at me. "Ah, to be in love."

"Shut up," I grouse, punching him hard enough to give him a dead arm.

Flicking off the TV, he turns to me. "Right, well, if you aren't going to let me watch my movie, you can at least teach me some of those knife-wielding skills of yours."

I cock a brow. "You wanna learn how to stab your daddy in the hand?"

"Or anyone else who crosses me." He gets that dark psychotic look in his eyes that should probably be a warning not to teach the guy to use sharp weapons, but I'm bored, and I haven't gotten to play with my knife in ages.

I spend the rest of the afternoon teaching him how to properly hold a knife and the best body parts to aim for if you want to do the most damage. The throat is a nice, bloody one, but it doesn't have to be messy. A well-aimed slice through the ribs is relatively blood free and will pierce a fucker's lungs. They'll be drowning in their blood in no time. Likewise, a nick to the spleen will have the blood pouring out into their abdomen so fast they won't even know what happened. The femoral artery is another good one, albeit the blood spray is just as impressive as the carotid.

It also doesn't have to be all about the deadly blows, however. A slice to your opponent's Achilles will have them crashing to the ground, unable to walk. Similarly, if you go through the back of their knee, you can tear through their ligaments and really fuck up their leg. If you're looking to do lasting damage to their upper arms, then going through their armpit and destroying their brachial plexus will have them losing all feeling and function in that arm. There are just so many ways to beat down and kill your opponent with a knife. That's why it's my favorite weapon.

We set up a target against one wall, and I get him to practice throwing. It's a lot harder than it looks, and the first few times—despite his cocky attitude—he throws it all wrong and the handle ends up tearing through the paper target.

I can see, with every new trick I teach him, questions linger in Wilder's eyes. He's most likely wondering how I know all of this. Yeah, some of it you can probably pick up, but as I get caught up in the comforting feel of palming my knife and twirling it in my hand, I think he picks up on the fact I'm more than just self-taught. Thankfully, he keeps his questions to himself. That's the great thing about Wilder. He never oversteps the mark. Even if he did ask a question, he'd just laugh and shrug it off if I told him to mind his own business.

I'm laughing my ass off as Wilder misses the target *again*, his inability to hit it getting to him as the color rises in his face, when my tablet pings.

Retrieving it from the kitchen, where I plugged it in to charge,

I notice a message from Michael. I haven't heard from him since he blew a gasket in the movie theater. He's been keeping his distance from me and vice versa. I figured I'd let him cool off and he'd come to me when he was ready to talk.

MICHAEL: CAN WE MEET? I THINK WE SHOULD TALK, AND I NEED TO apologize.

I GUESS HE'S READY TO TALK.

CHAPTER 24

Mason

This week has been the week from Hell. When our parents said we would be working for them over Easter, I thought it would be boring business meetings at the office and horrifying visits to wherever they keep and train their mercenaries, but nope. Since my dad is no longer around to do his part, I have to step up. Apparently, as part of his job, he would take quarterly trips to Black Creek. Without him around, no one else has been able or is willing to go in his place, so I was the lucky sod that was tasked with going.

I've spent most of the week here, meeting with shady fuckers. I was told to collect the packages, and that's it. I'm not allowed to open them or ask questions. Literally, just pick up the packages. So I'm basically a glorified delivery man. Yet every time one of the crazy-eyed druggies hands me the parcel, I'm torn between needing to know what's inside and feeling like I'd be better off if I never found out.

"THIS PLACE IS DISGUSTING," I GRUMBLE, SNEERING AT THE STICKY bar table that I'm fairly certain is going to give me hepatitis. I've never missed home more than I have in the past few days. The G&T is a rundown shack of a strip club, and even though it's barely midday, the place is packed with what looks like homeless vagrants. I'm pretty sure it's just how the people here look—gaunt and skeletal, like they're barely surviving. I naively assumed G&T stood for gin and tonic, but after making a passing remark about how it didn't make sense that they didn't stock any gin, the bartender informed me it stood for guns and titties. It makes much more sense, especially when I glanced around the bar and realized how many guys had a gun stuffed down the back of their jeans.

Some even have them sitting out in the open on their table while they lean back in their chairs, warily observing their surroundings. Obviously, carrying a firearm is a requirement in Black Creek.

The bodyguard I've been assigned chuckles. His eyes never leave the crowd, though, roaming over everyone and constantly assessing for possible threats. He looks far more at ease here than I do. Although being one of our parents' trained mercenaries, he's as broad as I am, so the two of us stick out like sore thumbs.

According to Barton, my dad never came here alone. A bodyguard was always assigned to him for personal protection, but I'm not sure if that's the truth or if it's just our parents' way of keeping an eye on me while I'm up here. Either way, I've been careful to watch what I say around him. For the most part, we've gotten along fine. He doesn't talk much, so getting a read on him is hard.

"Aye, it's a shithole, but it spits out the best recruits."

I have to squash my look of disbelief as I peer around at the people sipping their drinks and hollering at the half-naked women on stage. No one stands out as being mercenary material here. They're all druggies or alcoholics, skin and bone with zero muscle mass. No way is anyone here like the men they had attack us at Christmas.

"If you say so."

"Not people like this." The guy looks unimpressed at the riff-raff in the room. "But, yeah, there's a lot of untapped potential in Black Creek."

Cryptic. I don't dare ask him anything further, despite the number of questions dancing on my tongue. I can't be sure he won't report anything back to our parents, and I also don't know how much he thinks *I* know. He's more likely to let something slip if he thinks I already know everything our families are up to.

We sit in silence for a while longer, the guard constantly scanning the room. We're in this dingy bar to meet some guy who apparently has information for me that I need to take back to our parents, but I don't know who the fuck he is or what information he has, so I guess we're stuck here waiting until he shows up.

The crowd gets riled up, shouting and hollering when the music switches and a new dancer comes on stage. I'm guessing she's their favorite.

Following their gazes, I look up to the stage where a skinny girl, a few years older than me, with perky tits and a nice ass, sways her hips seductively. Her long coppery-red hair, I'm sure, has most guys here probably imagining twisting it around their fists as they fuck her. She doesn't do it for me personally, but I can see the appeal for why she would be a favorite among the men.

A greasy-haired man in a ratty trench coat approaches our table, gesturing with his head for us to follow him. Without question, the guard gets to his feet, indicating I should go in front of him as we trail the guy into a back room. It must be soundproofed since the noise from the bar dies as soon as he closes the door. I can only imagine what this room is used for, and I make sure not to touch any of the furniture or walls.

"You're not the usual guy." He eyes me warily.

"No. He couldn't make it. I'm here in his place."

Finishing his assessment of me, he moves on to the guard, giving him a once-over. He still doesn't relax his tense stance, and

I'm getting annoyed with every passing second I have to spend in this STD-infested room.

"Well?" I snap impatiently. "Have you got information for me or not?"

Focusing his gaze back on me, he hesitates before nodding his head.

"Everyone's been fightin' over Beast territory the last year," he begins. I've gleaned enough from the last few days to know the Beasts were a formidable gang that ran half the town until a few years ago when something happened. No one seems to know what exactly, just that they're dead and buried, and their territory is up for grabs. "But The Reaper Rejects have been makin' a name fer themselves recently. They've been claimin' the land fer themselves."

Reaper Rejects? The name sounds strangely familiar, though I can't place it. I can't think where the fuck I'd know a Black Creek gang name from. "Who are they?"

The guy shrugs. "No one knows. They're small, but they're gainin' territory fast enough to be noticed."

The guard lifts out a wad of bills and hands them over. "Keep an eye on them. We'll want to know more when we're back next time."

Snatching the money out of the guard's hands, the guy mumbles an agreement and scurries out of the room. I don't know what any of that meant, or why it matters to our parents.

I'VE SPENT THE PAST SEVERAL HOURS LYING ON TOP OF MY BED IN MY motel room—yes, that's right, a fucking *motel*, and a run-down ramshackle one at that. I'm fucking around on my phone, texting the guys to see how they're all getting on, which doesn't seem like they're fairing much better than I am, while also chatting with Hadley. Thankfully, we're heading home in the morning, and I'll be back in bed with her by tomorrow night. I've missed her more than I thought I would. It's weird, I've never felt this way before. Obviously, I care about the guys, but I've never felt this overpowering need to spend all my time with another living soul. Still, if the distance between us this week has taught me anything, it's that I can no longer live without Hadley in my life, in my arms, every fucking day.

She's started sending these teasing videos every day into the group chat with me, West, and Cam that West set up before we left for Easter break. As I respond to the guys' latest string of messages in our own private chat, a notification comes up from her, showing there's a video attached.

Clicking into the chat, an image comes up showing her very naked chest, with the triangle 'play' button in the middle of the picture.

Faster than lightning, I jump up from the bed and cross the small space to flick the lock between mine and the bodyguard's adjoining rooms, and I do the same with the door leading outside before collapsing back on the bed and getting comfy.

There's already a reply from Cam, but I ignore it as I press play, watching as she lifts the video, giving me an up-close view of her soft, puffy lips and hooded eyes before she slowly trails her fingers down the valley between her breasts, moving the phone to follow the movement.

She stops to massage her tit, pulling on her nipple as she moans softly, and I push my hand beneath my boxers, tugging on my growing erection. Moving back to the center of her body, she paints a line with her finger all the way to her clit as I pump myself.

Just as she sinks her fingers inside herself, she moans, ending on an evil-sounding giggle before the video comes to an end.

What the fuck?

After staring, bewildered, at the screen for a second, I start frantically typing a reply, ignoring Cam's grievances about leaving him hanging.

. . .

MASON: *TOUCH YOURSELF.*

HER REPLY IS INSTANTANEOUS.

LITTLE WARRIOR: *I AM.*

MASON: *SHOW US.*

AN IMAGE POPS UP OF HER FINGERS KNUCKLES-DEEP INSIDE HER dripping wet pussy. Only it's not enough. I need to hear her come.

Pressing the button for a video call, it rings once before she accepts, and I get to see her beautifully flushed cheeks.

"You wet for me, baby?" I smirk, running my thumb over my tip and wetting the head of my dick.

"So wet," she pants.

"Show me." The words are barely more than a growl as she lowers the phone to give me the perfect view of her pussy. She lazily pumps her fingers as I watch, jerking harder on my dick as I pretend I'm sinking into her hot center.

"Rub your clit, baby."

She moans as she does what I tell her.

"That's it, baby. Tell me what you're picturing."

"You," she pants.

"What am I doing?"

Another few breathless pants before she responds, "You're using your mouth on me."

"Yeah, I'm working you up real good."

"Uh-huh." They're the only words she seems capable of forming.

"Are the others there too?"

"Yeah."

"What are they doing?"

"West's—"

I pump faster on my dick as I add the guys to the video call. Cam's topless, and by the looks of things, he's halfway to getting himself off already, while West looks as stoic as always.

Before either of them can say anything, Hadley moans, and I focus back on her image, clicking on it so it fills the whole screen—I definitely don't need to see either of those guys' jizz faces.

"Fuck, baby, yeah. I'm fucking your ass so hard right now," Cam growls, making Hadley moan.

"Pinch your nipples, Firefly. Pretend it's my teeth," West commands. After another moment of breathy moans, West fires out his next order. "Reach into my bottom drawer. There's a rabbit and some lube. Lift it out."

Doing as he says, she lifts out the vibrator and lubes it up.

"That's it. Pretend it's Mason's dick filling you up."

I watch, enraptured, as the pink device sinks into her sweet cunt. I'm staving off my own release, not ready for this to be over with, but her moans are making it so goddamn difficult as I twist and pull on my cock. I imagine I'm actually sinking into her wet heat.

"Mason," she moans.

Hadley cries out our names as she comes, and a second later, I hear a door open. "Well, well, what do we have here? Looks like I'm missing out on all the fun," I hear Beck say.

In the next second, the phone is tossed onto the floor, and all I can hear is Hadley giggling before she starts to moan again, the unmistakable sounds of fucking coming down the line. *Lucky bastard.*

I quickly disconnect and clean myself up, deciding to go check with the bodyguard about what we're doing for dinner tonight. Maybe I can ply him with greasy food and a few beers and whittle some useful information out of him.

I knock lightly on the door between our adjoining rooms.

When he doesn't respond, I flick the lock, testing to see if his side is unlocked. It is, and the door swings open.

Before I can announce my presence, I hear him talking to someone. Peering my head through the doorway, I catch him looking at something on his laptop at the small two-person table.

"This kid, he's impressive," he says to whoever is on the other end of the line. Focusing on his laptop screen, there's a video playing and as I watch, a kid barely older than eight or nine tackles a kid who looks twice his age with all the ferocity of a grizzly bear. Taking him to the ground, the kid beats on his opponent until he's unmoving and bloody beneath him. "He'll make an excellent recruit. We should get someone out there to pick him up ASAP."

What the fuck? I stand frozen in the doorway, unable to comprehend what I'm seeing and hearing. The shitty tequila from earlier must have warped my brain. There's no way I fucking heard that right. Kids? They're recruiting kids? Surely not. I must have misunderstood.

"There's a couple of other potentials too." He laughs. "In the tape I watched yesterday, one kid lit another on fire over a loaf of bread. He's definitely worth bringing in."

Fucking hell. There goes the idea of misinterpreting him.

"Oh yeah?" Pausing the video, he exits the program while I stand there frozen. "Got it, one sec." Clicking on something, another recording pops up. This one is of a dark room and it's difficult to make out what's happening from this far away, but as a high-pitched scream blasts out from the speaker, I shudder. I've never heard anything like it. The loud cry is filled with unimaginable agony before it suddenly cuts off, making the room feel even quieter than before.

"Fuck, I love it when they scream." The bodyguard chuckles, staring riveted at the screen. Bile climbs up the back of my throat and I stumble back to my room in a daze, that scream playing on repeat in my head. I couldn't see what was happening on the screen, but I didn't need to. Whoever it was, was being fucking tortured.

My mind races as questions fly across it. What the hell was going on in that video? Why are our parents recruiting kids? I mean, *kids?!* I can't wrap my head around it. I always knew my dad was a sick man. The glee in his eye when he'd bring his belt down on me with all the force he could muster was enough of an indicator of the cruelty he hid inside him, but *this?* It's a whole other level of sick and twisted.

Ensuring the lock on the adjoining door is engaged, I collapse onto the bed. My hunger is long gone as I stare unseeingly at the damp ceiling. Kids. That's what all of this is about. And they're fucking torturing them. Why? As punishment? To keep them in line?

Sighing, I rub the heel of my hand against my eyelids as I try to erase the echo of that girl's pain-soaked screams from my brain. It's so much fucking worse than we ever imagined. Being involved in the black market assassins-for-hire services is one thing, but stealing kids off the street and forcing them to become monsters is just…fuck, I don't even know the word. Mind-blowing. Sick. Incomprehensible.

How did our parents ever expect us to be on board with this? Or is it their plan all along to get us so wrapped up in the illegal shit they're up to that when they do eventually tell us, we'll have no way out of it all.

I'm still in a daze the next day. Thankfully, my usual quiet demeanor and the hard, cold mask I wear around others come in handy, and the bodyguard doesn't pick up on the maelstrom inside my head. All the way home, I kept opening up the group chat with all six of us, desperately wanting to tell them what I found out, but we agreed to keep any information until we were all face to face, just to be safe.

After a final debrief in our parents' offices—one I don't pay any attention to—the four of us exit and quickly get in the car to head back to campus. The mood is subdued, and I have the feeling I'm not the only one with grim news to share. On the bright side, I get to spend all day tomorrow in bed with my girl. Nothing like a lazy Sunday with your best friends and your girl to reset your mood after a shitty week.

It's late by the time we arrive back on campus, and there's a cold chill in the air now the sun has set. Hawk's phone goes off as we're all grabbing our bags from the trunk. "Yeah?" he answers. I'm not paying him much attention as I reach for my own duffel, closing the trunk. "What the hell do you mean *you can't find her?*"

Those four words, combined with his snarling, venomous tone, have all of us focusing on him. *What the fuck has happened now?* His jaw is clenched so tight I'm surprised his teeth don't shatter as he listens to whatever is being said on the other end of the line.

"We're coming now. We'd better find her, or you're a dead man."

Hanging up the phone, he looks at each of us with unadulterated fury blooming in his eyes. The next words he bites out destroy any hope I had of curling up with my girl for the rest of the night.

"Hadley's missing."

CHAPTER 25

Hadley

My head feels like it's been stuffed with cotton wool. *Where the fuck am I? What the hell happened last night?* It's not like I drink or do drugs….drugs.

The flicker of an image skitters across my memory, but I lose it before I can catch a hold of it. I try to dig deeper into my forgotten memories, desperately trying to find something that could tell me what happened last night, but I only succeed in giving myself a headache.

Something doesn't feel right, though. The pounding in my skull as I try to turn my head only confirms that, and when I lift my arm, something cold presses painfully against the skin, a rattle echoing around the room as something pinches my wrist.

What the fuck?

I pry my eyes open and squint down at my hand. It takes me a second to focus, and I blink furiously. Even once my vision clears, I still can't process what I'm seeing. There's a metal cuff around my wrist, the other end attached to a ring on the wall, chaining me to it like I'm a fucking animal.

MY HEART RATE PICKS UP AS SWEAT BREAKS OUT ALONG MY FOREHEAD and down my back, and I force myself to think through the fog in my head. My eyes dart around the dimly lit room, nausea churning in my stomach, and I have to swallow it down before I throw up all over the floor.

This is my worst nightmare come to life. I slam my eyes shut, breathing past the nausea as I plead to whatever God is above that this is a dream. There's no way this is real. It can't be. I already escaped from here. I won't live to escape a second time.

Another memory flashes across the back of my eyes, and I manage to latch on to it before it disappears. Flashes of meeting Michael at the dining hall—he wanted to apologize—followed by flickers of the two of us walking toward the lake. I vaguely remember it was a lovely evening and he suggested going for a walk.

Everything after that is hazy. God, do they have Michael too? Is he okay? Another round of bile works its way up the back of my throat, and it takes everything in me to swallow it down. No way am I going to puke up my guts and let whoever comes in next realize how deathly terrified I am.

Time passes in a meaningless blur, and I'm still trying to come to terms with my new reality when the door unlocks and swings open, the light from beyond blinding me and painting the large man blocking the doorway in darkness, preventing me from seeing who it is as I squint up at him from my less-than-ideal position on the narrow bed.

"Ah, good, you're awake." Lawrence's cold voice runs over me like water, instantly chilling me to the bone. Being back here is one thing; being back here with *him* is something else entirely.

As he strides into the room, the door slams shut behind him. I hurriedly try to sit up, wanting to be in a better position to defend myself should I need to, but my muscles feel like jelly and I fall back down when I put my weight on my free arm.

The asshole laughs at my attempt. "It will be a while longer before you gain full control of your muscles, but that works in my favor for now." His smug tone and the way his lip curls maliciously have me swallowing around the lump in my throat.

He moves to stand in front of me, so I'm forced to tilt my head back and look up at him. He reaches his hand out to stroke my hair and the second his fingers wrap around the wavy strands, I jerk my head away. His other hand whips up to slap me across the face faster than I can blink, my head snapping to the side. The sudden movement only adds to the pounding headache I've got going, and I can feel the sting and flush of my cheek as blood rushes to the surface.

He goes back to stroking my hair reverently as though nothing happened. "Tut tut..." He laments disappointedly, sounding as though he's reprimanding a disobedient child. "I told you, Dove. I told you, you were mine. I wanted to give you everything."

"Yeah, everything but my freedom," I seethe. I have no idea where the sudden courage has come to talk to him like that. Maybe it's the drugs or knowing I'm probably going to die in this cell—or even worse, wishing I had.

He shrugs uncaringly. "Your mother had freedom, and she made the wrong choice. I couldn't have you do the same."

My mother? What the fuck does she have to do with any of this?

"Yet you still found a way to defy me. At first I kind of liked the challenge of chasing you." His fingers move to stroke over my cheek before running down my neck, the light touch making me shiver with revulsion.

In the next second, his hand is wrapped securely around my throat, squeezing until I can't inhale more than the slightest wisp of air. "But you just had to take it too far, didn't you? You just had to fuck him, you dirty slut."

I'm barely paying attention to his words as I focus on trying to push him away with my hands, but there's no energy in my movements.

He moves to straddle me, pinning me beneath him as panic courses through me. It's been a long time since I've felt this helpless, and my fear only escalates as dark spots bloom in my vision as he uses his weight to push me further into the thin mattress.

He lowers his face in front of me so it's all I can see, even as blackness creeps in at the edges of my vision. "You're exactly like your mother," he growls furiously. "Whores." Spittle hits my lips and cheeks as he sneers down at me. "But that's fine. You want to act like a slut, I'll treat you like one. I was going to give you everything. Now, I'm going to lock you away here and leave you to the mercy of the men who have been dying for a taste of you since the day you arrived." He laughs spitefully. "You thought this place was a nightmare you needed to escape before? You'll be wishing for death by the end of the week.

"I was too soft with you. I thought killing your little friend would be enough to break you." My eyes flare at that revelation, even as my vision blurs his devil-like features. "Clearly, I was wrong. Well, I won't make that mistake again. You'll be well and truly broken this time. Who knows, maybe then, when you're nothing more than an empty shell, begging for death to claim you, I'll take you back and save you from this hell." His fingers trail down over my abdomen and he pushes his way beneath my panties while his other hand tightens around my throat painfully, cutting off the last of my air. My energy quickly wanes as the black spots become large blobs. The last thing I'm aware of as everything goes black is the feel of his fingers shoving their way inside me.

The next thing I know, I'm jolted awake to the sting of freezing cold water being hosed over me. I gasp as the horrific realization that this was not some fucked-up nightmare settles in my bones, weighing me down.

"Wakey, wakey, rise and shine, Princess," a cold voice sings from somewhere in front of me. It takes a second for my brain to come back online after the ice shower, and I almost regret it when it does, because the sight that faces me is bleak and hopeless. I'm completely fucking screwed. I'm shackled to the stone wall behind me, splayed out like a starfish, butt fucking naked as

Bowen sprays me down with water so cold my body already feels frozen solid.

Another pass of the water has me crying out, and he laughs cruelly when my whole body wracks in shivers. Bowen is the worst guard here. I guess that's why he's in charge, but he's as coldhearted and morally rotten as our parents are. The glint in his eye as he comes closer tells me I'm about to experience first-hand just how sick he truly is.

Despite fear beating a quick rhythm through my cold veins, I glare at him as he approaches. He smirks, more than ready to rise to the challenge of breaking me as he unsheathes a knife from his waist, rolling it back and forth in his hand. All the while, his gaze is roaming over me.

"I always did like cutting you up." There's a sick reverence in his tone that has goosebumps rising to the surface of my skin. He lifts the blade and traces the scar along my collarbone. Every one of my scars occurred at his hands. The twisted fuck gets off on inflicting pain onto others and watching them bleed out in front of him. I know for a fact that begging and crying only spur him on, so I learned to hold my tongue a long time ago. He could literally stab me in the kidney, and I'd refuse to so much as whimper in front of him.

The thing is, I got so good at acting broken when I was here, at pretending they'd beaten me down and turned me into an obedient soldier ever-ready to do their bidding, that they've never seen my fire. All those years, they thought they crushed me, but they were only adding fuel to the building inferno of hatred inside me. I'm burning so fucking brightly, brimming with fire and hate and malice. So he can fucking bring it; I'm ready for him.

I let him see every ounce of contempt I feel for him, for this compound, for the fucking board that runs this hellhole. His eyes widen at the realization of just how alive and ready to fight I really am, before darkening. His lip curls up on one side, and his eyes sparkle with sick excitement.

"Oh D, I'm going to enjoy breaking you," he promises, dragging the blade down between my exposed breasts. He applies just enough pressure to bring blood to the surface, occasionally nicking the skin and causing tiny red droplets to form before they drip down over my white skin. His tongue flicks out to lick his bottom lip and he digs the blade in deeper. My body tenses, preparing for the slash of pain when he breaks the surface. Instead of pushing the knife all the way in, he loosens his hold to trail it further and further south until a red line runs from the base of my neck to my pubic bone.

"Nothing gets me harder than having my prey all trussed up and covered in blood." He smiles wickedly before pushing the blade through my folds, the cold steel making me gasp as my body freezes.

"I haven't been allowed to play with you the way I want," he pouts, pulling the blade away from my body. My muscles relax now that I don't need to worry about him nicking any of my sensitive bits right before a perverted grin crosses his face. "But my time is coming. Soon I'll have claimed every part of you."

FACING BOWEN HAS BECOME A DAILY PART OF MY ROUTINE. FOR several hours every day, I'm splayed out for him to slice and dice like a slab of meat. Of course, just to drive the knife in deeper, he opens up the gallery for any and every fucker to come and watch the 'Humiliating Hadley' show. It becomes the only way for me to tell the passing of each day. Based on my count, today is day number four. I've been here for *four* days.

It already feels like a lifetime.

The frozen water blasts over my skin—again—and I grit my teeth against the shivers wracking my body, blocking out the hoots and hollers from the guards. All of them are getting off on seeing me strung up and at Bowen's mercy. The tangy smell of blood in the air as Bowen trails the tip of his blade along my skin, decorating my body with brand-new scars, drives the men wild. They're like rabid dogs, biting on the bit and itching for a taste.

"Just like old times, D. I remember how much you and your little friend *loved* being chained to my wall." He leans in, whispering in my ear, "Keep fighting, D. Every day you hold out is another day Lawrence gets closer to caving and letting me do what I want with you." A wicked glint enters his eye as he presses the flat side of his knife against my nipple, getting distracted as he trails a circle around it. "In the meantime…" He nicks my skin, a bead of blood swelling before it spills over onto my milky skin. "Why don't we give the guys a show." The smirk that lifts his lips is positively vicious. "Let's see if I can make you scream."

Sweat beads my skin over the next hour as I strain and grunt, refusing to give these fuckers what they're craving—my pain. When Bowen is finally done making me bleed for the day, and I'm panting from the exertion, he steps away. One by one, the guards approach me with lecherous looks as they unzip their trousers, jerking themselves off until their cum hits my thighs, my abdomen, my hip—whatever body part they can reach.

"They're all going to get a piece of you one day, D," Bowen calls out. "You're only delaying the inevitable."

I don't have the energy to digest what he's saying. Instead, I let his words wash over me like rain, tuning him out, along with everyone else in the room. Disconnecting myself from my reality, I let my mind slip away to a better place. It's something I've become adept at doing, and it's only when my knees collide painfully with the stone floor that I abruptly crash land in the present again.

I'm a sticky mess on the floor, blood and cum combining and crusting on my skin. Without my restraints holding me upright, my body no longer has the energy to stand unaided. Instead, I'm a boneless heap sprawled out on the ground. I've had nothing to eat or drink since I arrived, so my muscles are running on nothing but grit and sheer determination at this point, except my adrenaline is quickly wearing off. I'm exhausted; beyond exhausted. Fucking numb.

The assholes don't even wash me down before dumping me, naked, back in my cell. I'm not sure how long I sit on the floor, staring absently at the stone slabs before I gather enough energy to drag myself onto the thin, lumpy mattress on my cot.

Just as my eyes droop, sleep threatening to drag me down, the screaming and banging start.

No. Please no. Not again.

It's the same death metal they blast every time exhaustion is about to pull me under. The lights start flashing next—a painfully bright strobing that has my retinas burning, even though I squeeze them shut and bury my head in the mattress.

Everything they're doing is intended to break me and, *fuck*, I think it might be working. I can feel myself slowly giving up the fight. The only thing that keeps me alive is the thought of my guys. Images of them all, of Emilia and Hawk, and even Wilder, flitter across my mind, providing me with the only source of energy to keep me going. I can't help but wonder if they're out there looking for me. Do they know where I am? The music, if you can even call it that, blares through the speakers into the cell, threatening to drive me mad as I clamp my hands over my ears. I need sleep. I need food. I *need* to get out of here.

I don't know how much more of this I can take.

Even if my guys do find me, will there be anything left to save?

CHAPTER 26

Hadley

TODAY'S THE DAY. THE DAY I FINALLY TAKE CONTROL OF MY FUTURE. I can practically feel the sun on my face, heating my skin; the light breeze whispering 'freedom' as it whips around me. By the time the sun sets today, I'll be standing on the other side of these tall, concrete walls, free to do whatever the fuck I want with the rest of my life.

That, or I'll be dead.

Lights out was hours ago, and I've been sitting impatiently in my small room ever since. Waiting. By the time I hear the lock disengaging, I'm a ball of nervous energy, no longer able to sit still. I've been pacing back and forth across the space for a while now, and the sound of the door opening freezes me in my tracks.

"Hurry up," a deep voice hisses. The guard is nothing but a dark silhouette in the narrow slit of my open door. Not wasting any more time, I close the distance and slip out the door without a backward glance, and he closes it soundlessly behind me.

*H*E DOESN'T SAY ANYTHING, BUT *I* CAN SEE THE TICK OF ANNOYANCE IN *his jaw as he strides down the corridor. Glancing nervously around at the other closed doors in the block, each one containing a sleeping soldier behind them, I scurry silently after him and catch up as he reaches the door leading outside.*

I suck down a deep breath of the cool night air, but I'm not free yet. Without a word, the guard takes off. He doesn't look over his shoulder even once to see if I'm following. He probably hopes I'll change my mind. That won't happen. Nothing will stand in my way tonight. The only way I'm going back into my room is if they drag me kicking and screaming.

I trail the guard in silence, the two of us stealthily making our way across the dark yard to a garage at the far side. I've never been to this part of the compound. Although I'd hazard a guess, there's a lot of this place I've never seen—not that I care to. The sleeping barracks and main building where we train, eat, and receive punishments are the only two buildings the recruits have any reason to be in. Whatever is in the other outbuildings I've seen is nothing more than an assumption to me—one I don't care to find an answer to.

"Get in and stay down," he orders in a low whisper, opening the back door of a compact sedan. There's junk strewn all over his backseat, and as I quickly wedge myself into the floorboard, squirming as far under the front seat as I can, he shoves some of it down on top of me to ensure I'm well hidden. I hate having to rely on him to get me out the gate, but what choice do I have? I've done all I can to guarantee he doesn't turn on me. I wiggle, arching my back so I can slip the knife I stole from a guard earlier out of my pocket. When he slips into the driver's seat, his weight further pinning me to the floor of the car, I poke my arm out from beneath the junk on top of me, sticking it through the small hole between his seat and the door of the car, and angle the blade at his kidney. I hear it—his gasp —when the sharp edge digs into his skin.

"Don't get any funny ideas," I bark out in a low, threatening growl.

I've been bribing Stevo, the guard so kindly helping me this evening, for the past year. Any time my team is sent on a job, he's ordered to come along to keep an eye on me. I'm precious cargo, after all—can't have Lawrence's plaything getting killed or disappearing. He's also up to his ears in gambling debts, so it wasn't difficult to coax him into taking a cut of the 'off book' jobs I accepted any time I was away from the compound.

It all started as sheer fucking luck. Right place, right time, sorta bullshit. We were on a job up in Black Creek, and I was running surveillance on our target. On my way to the rendezvous point, I came across some bikers harassing a curvy redhead. I wasn't about to let that fly, and I quickly pulled them off her. She offered to pay me if I taught her how to hold her own in a fight. It sounded like a bunch of bullshit to me, but she produced the cold hard cash there and then. I didn't ask why she wanted to know this stuff. That's her business. My guess would be, living in Black Creek, an attractive girl like her would stand out by a mile with her red hair, well-sized rack, and curvy ass. She probably just wanted some basic self-defense tactics to protect herself from sleazy scumbags. Whatever the reason, I accepted her offer.

With that first wad of cash, I bought myself a burner phone and rented out a locker at the rundown bus station in Black Creek. That way, I had somewhere to keep my money and a way to contact the redhead—Red—when I was next in town.

So, after that, any time we were sent up to Black Creek for a job, we'd meet up. I'd either make up some bullshit excuse for why I needed more time to do my job, or I'd bribe Stevo into letting me out for an hour. Red was a lifesaver. She was able to put me in touch with a guy who makes top-of-the-line fake IDs, and she even secured me a couple of quick and easy jobs, delivering cars to chop shops and running drugs, to help me get the money together.

Once I had papers sporting my brand new name, it was only a matter of waiting for Pacific Prep applications to open, and finally, last week, when I checked my PO Box, I had received my acceptance letter. With everything in place, there was no reason for me to stay here any longer. I lifted as much cash as I could from my locker and bribed a reluctant Stevo into helping me tonight. Of course, it's a big fucking difference between him letting me slip out for an hour and him actually helping me escape. It took a lot of haggling and threatening for him to finally cave, but that doesn't mean I'm about to trust him. Anyone who can be bought, can't be trusted.

I roll my eyes as he grunts and curses me out under his breath, the car slowly making its way through the compound. As we roll to a stop, I hiss out, "Remember, I can kill you faster than you can blink."

He ignores me, rolling down his window, and I pray the guards won't be able to make out the white skin of my arm wedged around the side of the seat or demand to rifle through the stuff in his backseat.

"Alright, Stevo," the guard greets. "Where are you off to tonight?"

"Off to drown my sorrows, man. The Cubs were supposed to be a sure thing." Stevo sighs, and his disappointment sounds too genuine to be fake. He probably had all of the bribe money I'm about to hand over to him riding on tonight's game.

"Ouch, man." I hear the guard chuckle sympathetically. "You won't be the only one drinking away the loss." There's a pause, and unable to see what's going on, I press the tip of the blade more firmly into Stevo's skin, only stopping when I hear him hiss. "You're all good, Stevo. Catch ya later, man."

There is another tense moment as Stevo waits for the gates to slide open before he rolls the car forward, and we drive through. Sweat coats my skin and my heart hammers against my chest. I keep expecting one of the guards to call out for him to stop, but no one does, and we drive down the dark road.

"Where am I going?" he growls, letting his anger show.

"Just keep going." I wiggle out from beneath the seat, shoving all of his shit off the backseat so I can sit on it. My eyes dart all around us, half expecting some sort of ambush, but there's only darkness.

We drive in silence for twenty minutes before I tell him to pull over. I've no idea where the fuck we are, but it doesn't matter.

The car idles at the side of the road, and I lean forward in my seat.

"Sorry about this," I apologize in a bland voice before jabbing the knife into his kidney.

He screams, "What the fuck?" as blood soaks through his shirt, and he scrambles for the door handle, getting out of the car. I follow quickly behind him, and the second he stumbles onto the road, clutching at his side, I launch myself at him. I slice the knife quickly through the soft skin of his neck, jumping off him as he collapses to the ground, gurgling and gasping.

I couldn't let him live. I couldn't run the risk that he would raise the alarm. It's why I chose to escape from the compound rather than when we were out on a job. It would have been so much easier to run then, but someone would have noticed me missing much sooner. I need every second I can get to grab the last of the cash and things from my locker at the bus station and disappear.

With Stevo dead, I know that no one will realize I'm missing until the morning. That gives me several hours to do everything I need to. Dragging his dead body into the undergrowth along the side of the road, I wipe off the few flecks of blood on my skin and climb in behind the wheel.

I flick through the radio channels until I find one I like, cranking it all the way up as I speed down the country lanes to freedom.

I'M IN AND OUT OF CONSCIOUSNESS, BARELY ALIVE, WHEN I HEAR THE steel door of my cell being pulled open. *No. Not yet. I'm not strong enough to survive another round already.*

"Up," a deep voice snaps.

When I don't move—because I'm not physically capable of it— he grabs onto my upper arms and yanks me up roughly. Once I'm in a sitting position, he shoves a tray of food in front of me.

"Eat."

Clearly, he's only capable of monosyllabic words.

I don't even have the energy to lift my spoon, and the smell of the soup has my stomach threatening to revolt.

When I make no effort to follow his instructions, he pinches my cheeks painfully, forcing my mouth open and starts shoveling the food into me. It's not long before I'm gagging and puking up what little he managed to get down my throat.

Vomit splashes over the front of his shirt, and he's quick to react, slapping me across the face as he curses me out. I don't know what he expected to happen when I haven't eaten anything in god knows how long.

Wiping himself down, he returns to his task of force-feeding me. I'm fairly certain most of it ends up on the ground or over both of us, but eventually the tray is empty.

When we're done, he hauls me out of the cell, dragging me into a large room with a drain in the middle of the floor. Grabbing a hose, he douses me in freezing cold water. The thing about being blasted daily with ice-cold water is that you never get used to it. You know it's going to be a shock to your system, but no matter how prepared you are, you still flinch away when it hits your skin. I can't do anything but lie there, shivering and naked on the floor as the water washes over me. I no longer even give a shit that I'm naked. That requires energy—energy I don't have.

I must pass out, as the next thing I know, I'm back in my cot. The same routine continues the next few times someone comes to my cell, and slowly I start to regain my strength, managing to keep the food down and feed myself. The question is why. Why are they feeding me? Why now? I highly doubt it's because they've taken a sudden interest in my well-being.

The next time the door clangs open, Bowen is standing there, looking as menacing as ever. I haven't seen him in several days, and while it's been a small reprieve, the panic of wondering when he'll come back and what fresh hell he'll have in store for me, has slowly worn me down.

"Put this on," he orders, throwing a pile of black tactical gear at me.

"Why?" My voice is hoarse from lack of use. *When was the last time I spoke?* Looking at the clothes, I do my best to keep the longing for actual clothes off my features. I've been naked since he first shackled me to the wall seven days ago, or was it eight? They are all starting to run together.

The wicked smile that brightens his heinous features has me forgetting all about the clothes.

"Tonight's challenge night."

On challenge nights, we usually work as a team, every team competing against one another to achieve a common goal, but I get the impression I'm not going to be working as part of a team tonight.

Standing on unsteady legs, I quickly pull on the black trousers and matching top, noticing the asshole didn't bring me shoes.

"What's the challenge?" I ask, making sure to sound uninterested.

"Why, D, I'm so glad you asked." He grins menacingly, his next words making me blanch. "You are. You're going to face off against all twenty recruits in your age bracket and see if you make it out alive."

Fuck.

"As an added incentive, if you lose, you'll get to find out what it feels like to have my blade shoved up your ass."

Fighting hard against the shivers threatening to overtake my body, I focus on trying to remain positive. Sure, I'm beyond exhausted, half-starved, and I haven't trained—or so much as stretched my legs—in far too long, but I used to be the best recruit here. That's got to count for something, right?

"And if I win?"

The maniacal look in his eye doesn't give me any reassurance.

"Then you'll only get to see what the handle feels like."

The sick fuck escorts me to the fight hall, and I'm unceremoniously shoved through the door. Based on the roar of the crowd, everyone is here, including the adult mercenaries who are here of their own free will; who *chose* this life.

Passing a few younger kids, their eyes are wide with terror, but as I meet the gaze of others my age, that terror is replaced with steely resolve. By the time you're our age, you've accepted your fate, if not grown to revel in the bloodshed.

Not about to let anyone think I'm weak, I throw my shoulders back and lift my head. Shaking off the sentinels tasked with ensuring I don't try to escape—where the fuck would I even go?— I make my way unaided into the ring. The ring itself is enclosed with a large wire fence that goes all the way to the roof, preventing the crowd from pushing against the ropes and stopping anyone from trying to flee if things don't go their way. As I step through the gateway, it's closed and locked behind me, locking me in with my opponent—a heavy-set beefy man I vaguely recognize. He wasn't one of my team members, so I only know him in passing. *Good*, that should make it easier. I didn't spend any time with my team members outside of training, and while there was a professional acceptance of one another, there was nothing more between us. Still, it's going to be awkward if I come face-to-face with one of them tonight.

The second the bell rings to start the fight, he charges at me, and despite his size and the fact I've been locked in a cell the last few days, I'm still agile and light on my feet, and I easily maneuver out of his reach, quickly coming up behind him. With a few well-placed kicks and an elbow to the head, he goes down.

Fight number one over. Only nineteen more to go.

I steadily make my way through opponent after opponent, bringing them to the ground or knocking them out. The room becomes blurred as I zone out, ignoring the roars and chaos around me. The only thing I focus on is the guys. They're all that matter. I know over the last few months I've grown softer. I've learned to relax into a hug and enjoy small touches. I'd deny it until I was blue in the face, but nothing beats a snuggle sandwich on a cold morning. Some might think that learning to rely on the guys has made me weak, but as I pull on the well of strength I can feel glowing within me, I know those people are wrong.

The guys are what I'm fighting for. Every time I punch, kick, and maim my opponent, it's because I'm fighting to get back to them. When I first found out about Cam and devised my plan to get out of here, it was because I wanted to survive. It was a novel goal, but now I want so much more. Now I want to live—for the guys. *With* the guys. The will to do whatever is necessary to get back to them is why I'm going to win every one of my fights tonight. It's why I'm going to survive this hellhole yet again.

Everyone here is fighting for survival, but I'm fighting for love, which is why I'll win every time.

Everything hurts. The cuts Bowen carved in my skin have torn open and are freely bleeding, and I have a fresh set of cuts and bruises to match. My legs are shaking uncontrollably, and I can tell I'm minutes from passing out as, with the last of my energy, I take my final opponent to the ground, pinning them to the mat until they tap out. When the whistle is blown, I roll off them onto my back, fighting to remain conscious. *I can't pass out yet. Not here, surrounded by enemies. I need to get back to my cell.*

All I can hear is the rushing of blood as it pounds through my ears, and I stare absently at the ceiling high above me until the face of a monster obstructs my vision.

"Looks like you've still got it, D." He pouts. "Guess my blade will just have to play with your asshole a different day."

On those lovely words, I promptly pass the fuck out.

CHAPTER 27

Mason

W HERE THE FUCK IS SHE?

I throw my mug at the wall as yet another lead turns out to be a dead end. Beck and Wilder filled us in on what had happened when we returned to campus—not that they seemed to know much. Hawk went absolutely apeshit on them, giving Wilder one hell of a shiner when he confessed he was the one that let her leave on her own. She was only going to the dining hall to meet Michael, so he thought it would be fine. Fuck, I wanted to hit him too, but honestly, I'm more pissed at myself for not drilling it into him that she wasn't to go *anywhere* alone. As much as I want to blame him, it's not like he knows the fucked up shit that's happening with our families or what a threat Lawrence is to her. Surprisingly, he hasn't tried to pry or ask questions about any of it, although, no doubt, he suspects *something*.

ONCE HAWK CHEWED THE TWO OF THEM OUT, WE SPENT THE REST OF the night scouring the campus for her. We tracked down Michael, who confirmed he had coffee with her that evening but claimed that after they were done, he went to the library, and Hadley was making her way back toward the guys' dorms. So what the fuck happened to her? She didn't just fall off the face of the earth.

Even weirder, we found her phone down by the lake, but after interrogating everyone in the school, no one was able to confirm if they remembered seeing her down there that night. It's fucking infuriating.

I hear them before they enter, Emilia's loud voice carrying as she demands answers and updates. That girl will not stop, and it's made me realize just how perfect her friendship with Hadley is. She's been on our asses since the minute she stepped back on campus after the break. Hadley hadn't been answering her calls or texts all day Sunday after she disappeared, and Emilia showed up breathing fire, demanding to know where she was.

It was a difficult one to explain. It's not like we could tell her anything about our parents or the compound. She also wasn't buying our bullshit about Hadley being in bed, sick, so that basically just left us telling her that something had happened, but we didn't know what, and that we were doing everything we could to bring Hadley home. I think it's fair to say she took that news about as well as Hawk did, and she's been demanding daily updates ever since.

Hawk sighs as the three of them come through the door. "I told you we'd let you know when we had something," he gripes.

Emilia spits fire at him with her eyes. "Right." She scoffs. "You wouldn't tell me anything if I didn't harass you daily."

Turning toward her, he pins her in place with a serious expression. "I promise we're doing everything we can to find her."

Emilia's brows are slightly furrowed as she studies him. I'm pretty sure she's trying to determine if she can trust him or not. Surprisingly, Hawk lets her look her fill. The two of them stare at one another for so long it grows uncomfortable to watch, but finally Emilia gives a tight nod of her head.

"Okay," she admits reluctantly. "I still want updates in any case."

Without waiting for a response, she turns on her heels and walks out. No one else would dare talk to Hawk—or any of us—like that and then turn their backs on us. They'd be asking to get their asses handed to them. But despite her meek appearance, there's a lot of defiance in that girl. She reminds me of Hadley. Thinking of my fierce Little Warrior has a now familiar ache forming in my chest, and I glance hopefully between Hawk and Cam, eager to see if they found anything. "Well?"

"Nothing," Hawk grits out.

"You?" There's a wistful look on Cam's face that only intensifies as I shake my head. He grimaces. "Maybe West has something."

Yeah, maybe. He's been glued to his computer screen, going through security footage on campus, verifying students' stories and trying to find glimpses of Hadley so we can see where she went after meeting with Michael.

It doesn't make any sense, though. She wouldn't just wander off on her own. She *knows* to stay with one of us when she's out. She spent all week with Beck and Wilder, so why, the night she knew we were due back, would she decide to go off alone?

The only thing we can think of is that Lawrence somehow got to her. Maybe he threatened her into meeting him or going with him somewhere. I don't know. I can't think of any other explanation. Of course, after we'd searched every inch of the school, we went home to make sure Lawrence didn't have her hog-tied to his bed or some sick shit like that, or her parents hadn't done something stupid, but there was no sign of her there.

West has been tracking Lawrence's phone and scouring the security footage for both our parents' homes and their office building, so we have eyes on him everywhere. The problem is, he hasn't gone anywhere suspicious—the office and home. That's literally all he does.

"We need to find out where she was before she came here. Maybe he's holding her there," Hawk growls in frustration.

I look between him and the others, clueless. She's never told me anything about her past. I know whatever happened was fucked up, but I don't know where she was.

Cam shrugs too, as unhelpful as I am.

"Seriously?" Hawk snaps. "She didn't tell you anything? You didn't think to ask?"

"Did *you* ask?" I argue, riling him up.

He snaps his arm out, shoving me. "*You're* supposed to be in love with her. *You're* supposed to get past her barriers and get her to open up to you."

"Yeah, and if you hadn't spent all of the first semester making her hate you, maybe she would have opened up to you!"

"Hey!" Cam yells, barging his way between us. "Stop it." The look he gives us is lethal, and it's enough to have us dropping our fists. "None of this is helpful. If we can't work together, then we don't deserve to get her back, so pull your heads out of your asses!"

Cam rarely raises his voice, and it's yet another reminder of how close we all are to losing it without her.

Cam flops down into one of the armchairs, scrubbing his hands over his face and groaning. "If he has her, I don't know where my dad would have taken her."

"He literally hasn't gone anywhere except home and the office all week," West updates us, strolling into the kitchen in a pair of sweats and a stained t-shirt. He goes straight to the coffee machine and fills his cup to the brim before joining us in the living room.

The door opens again, and Beck walks in, looking as bleary-eyed and exhausted as the rest of us. "Anything?"

The three of us shake our heads, and his shoulders slump in defeat.

"We're trying to work out where Lawrence could be hiding her," I explain as he collapses into a vacant chair.

Pursing his lips in thought, he asks, "What about the compound?"

West shakes his head. "Nope. Not since I hacked into his GPS, anyway."

"Still, he could be keeping her there," I argue.

"I just think it's too obvious, right under our parents' noses," Hawk dismisses.

"It might not be completely implausible…" There's an odd look on Beck's face as his eyes dart between each of us, making us sit up straighter in our seats.

"What the fuck does that mean?" Hawk snarls, sounding like a rabid dog.

Beck's lips flatten, and he looks reluctant to share whatever he knows. "She should really be the one to tell you this, but you need to know."

There's a sadness in his eyes when he looks back at Hawk, and I know whatever he has to tell us is something significant.

"Hadley grew up in the compound."

Hawk scoffs, waving away his words. "Yeah, right, like Lawrence could hide a kid in the compound all those years without any of our parents hearing about it."

I grimace. "Actually, that might be more plausible than you realize."

The attitude drops from Hawk's face as he stares at me, his gaze intense and slightly confused. I feel bad having kept this from them for so long, but with everything we've been dealing with since we got back from Easter break, there hasn't been the right moment to tell them all.

"When I was up in Black Creek, I, uh, uncovered something about Nocturnal Mercenaries."

I quickly rehash everything I overheard, and my words are met with stunned silence.

"Kids? What, like eighteen-year-olds?" Cam asks, confused,

while the other three sit quietly, mulling over what I've just said. It's not every day you're told your parents are grabbing kids off the street to turn them into weapons. So I fully understand the shock they're experiencing right now—hell, it's been nearly a week since I found out and I'm still in shock.

I shake my head. "The kid I saw on the video looked more like eight or nine."

Beck leans forward in his seat, resting his elbows on his knees. "So they're taking kids from Black Creek?" he questions. I get why that would bother him, having grown up there himself.

"Amongst other places, but Black Creek seems to be their main feeding ground. They have some sort of deal with the leading gangs there."

Beck purses his lips, but unlike the other three, he doesn't seem surprised at what I've said.

"Fucking kids?" Hawk snarls in disgust. "What the fuck is wrong with them? Is it not enough that they're already performing a black market service for god knows what sort of underground criminals?!"

My gaze is still focused on Beck's contemplative ones as Hawk goes off on a rant, cursing out all of our parents.

"Why are you not surprised?" I demand, watching him closely.

Beck looks up at me, sighing before leaning back in his chair and looking at the others. "I knew."

"You knew?!" West repeats, sounding outraged.

"And you never told us?" Hawk snaps, turning on him. He's been ready to beat the shit out of Beck every day since Hadley went missing, so this is probably only adding fuel to the fire.

"I couldn't," Beck responds, unfazed by Hawk's glower.

"That's the secret job they were getting you to do by threatening me," West states, successfully putting all the pieces together with his computer brain.

"Yeah." Beck sighs, rubbing at his eyes. He looks ten years older than he did before the guys and I left for Easter break.

Although, glancing at the others, we all have bags under our eyes. Without Hadley, we're struggling.

He spends the next ten minutes explaining precisely what they've had him doing, filling us in on all the details he'd previously left out when he discussed his visits to the compound.

Rage consumes me as he tells us all the fucked up shit he's been involved in. The haunted look in his eye is enough to see how much it's all been getting to him. Now that I see it, I don't know how I didn't pick up on it before. He's obviously expended a lot of energy trying to keep all of this from us. Simply keeping up the act of pretending he's not losing a part of himself every time he goes there must be exhausting. I get that he was protecting West, but we're a team. The guys and I always lean on each other when we need to. Beck needs to understand that he can do the same. He's one of us now.

"You could have told us, man."

He shakes his head. "Nah. This shit eats away at your soul. I didn't want that for you." He looks pointedly at West, before glancing at the rest of us. "For any of you."

Fuck, well, if that doesn't endear me to him, then nothing will. The fact he's been looking out for us all this time, even when West was pushing him away, makes me like the guy even more. I've never had any issue with him, other than doubting whether or not we could trust him in the beginning, but it's hard not to like the guy, especially when he looks at my girl the way he does. He solidified our friendship and his place in the group with me, when he kicked my ass in the ring. It's been a long time since anyone managed that, and I sure as shit didn't expect him, with his preppy waistcoats, to be able to best me, but he's clearly spent a fair bit of his youth at the gym, working out.

I know Hawk's pissed at him at the minute, but honestly, Hadley's disappearance could have happened under any of our watches. I'd be kicking myself if it happened to me, and I've seen the guilt in Beck's eyes every day since we got back. He's beating himself up enough for all of us. There's no need to lay it on any thicker.

Cam's laidback, so he's never been too bothered about having Beck join our group. After everything that happened between him and Hadley, I think he'd accept anything if it made her happy.

West has been the most stubborn, but it's been good to see him opening up to Beck over the last few weeks. A couple of times, I've come home and found them chatting in the kitchen over beers. I think it's been good for him to have another person in his life he can talk to. They're total opposites, apples and oranges, but they haven't let that get between them.

"So, it's actually possible that Lawrence could have taken her back there," Cam muses.

No one jumps to respond to him as we all contemplate the possibility. I mean, it's not *im*possible.

"I have to go back there in a couple of days," Beck eventually tells us. "I was planning on doing some snooping; try to find out if he was keeping her there."

"I still can't believe you've been doing all of this for me," West murmurs, still looking shell-shocked. "How have you coped, carrying that burden all by yourself?"

"Hadley figured it out—"

"Jesus Christ." Hawk throws his arms up in the air, stalking back and forth across the apartment as his anger consumes him. "It's like we don't even fucking know her. What other secrets is she keeping?"

Hawk grounds to a halt when he sees Beck's expression, and the look he pins him with is fucking lethal. "What?"

He hesitates before stating, "It wasn't luck that she was able to kill that mercenary. She had all of the skills to do much worse to him."

"There's no way." Cam scoffs, but I can tell he's not sure what to believe. "If that's the case, why didn't she kill my dad and run off years ago?"

"Lawrence is her Achilles heel. He's terrorized her since she was a little girl. All the attitude and combat skills in the world won't help her if she can't stand up to him psychologically."

———

THE SOUND OF THE DOOR CRASHING INWARD HAS ALL OF US SPINNING around as Beck comes rushing in, a grim yet hopeful expression on his face.

"I know where she is."

"What?"

"How?"

"Where?"

All three of us fire off questions, not giving him a chance to respond. He ignores all of us anyway.

"West!" Beck yells, waiting until he comes to join us in the kitchen. West's clothes are disheveled, and he smells musty, like he hasn't showered in a few days. I'm pretty sure he hasn't, and as I subtly sniff my armpit, trying to remember the last time I showered and took a nap. I reckon I probably look and smell as bad as he does.

"What?"

Beck's gaze bounces between each of us. He looks as haggard as we do, with bags under his eyes and his hair sticking up.

"She's at the compound."

"You have proof?" Hawk demands.

Beck grimaces. "Sort of."

"What the fuck does that mean?" I bite out.

"Last night, I heard the guards talking about a recent challenge night they did. One fighter bested twenty of their older recruits."

"So? That doesn't tell us anything?" I can hear the frustration in Hawk's voice as he clenches his fists.

There's a glint in Beck's eye, and fuck do I not want to hold on to that look of hope he's sporting. "The fighter was a girl."

No one says anything for a moment, and I can tell the others want to believe him too. I mean, our girl is one hell of a fighter, but to beat twenty trained professionals? Even I have a hard time believing that.

"That doesn't mean it's her," Cam says, albeit reluctantly.

"It's her," Beck continues to insist, making Hawk throw his hands in the air.

"You can't fucking know that," he snarls.

Beck gets to his feet, coming to stand chest-to-chest with him. "It's. Her."

"We need proof," Hawk snaps, not letting the hope of Beck's words get through his tough exterior. "We can't go off hearsay. We need to see her for ourselves."

"The open day," West reminds us. "It's next week. We can look for her then, see if she's there."

"She's there," Beck growls in frustration.

I guess we'll find out next week.

If you are there, baby, hold on, we're coming for you.

CHAPTER 28

West

"Do you really think she's going to be here?" Cam whispers. We're in the back of the car our parents sent to take us to the open day.

"I have no idea," I tell him. "I don't even know if I want her to be or not."

My words are met with silence. We've heard enough from Beck to know the compound is not somewhere you want to be kept against your will, and if what he's saying is true, that she grew up here, then it's a miracle that she not only made it out alive but with her humanity intact.

I can't wrap my head around the reality of that. If Beck is right, then our girl is a motherfucking mercenary. Bearing that in mind, some of the things we've seen her do, and the way she behaves, makes sense—like her blasé attitude after stabbing Benjamin in the hand, her ability to pick locks, and the fact she was able to kill that mercenary. She was the one that came up with the idea to dump the body in the lake—is that because she knew it was the best place? Had she done something like that before? My mind is a chaotic mess of questions as, with every passing minute, the car takes us closer to possibly finding her.

When we're officially far from civilization, we pull up at a manned gate. After the driver says a few words to the guard, the gate rolls open and we drive in, and a few minutes later, we crest a hill and see the compound laid out before us.

There are a lot of other cars on the road, heading in the same direction, and when we pull up out front of the main building, the small car park is already full.

We've already been warned to be on our best behavior today. None of our parents are here, preferring to leave the demonstrations to whoever is in charge of this hellhole, and they'll wine and dine whichever rich assholes are interested in investing or making use of their services, but apparently, being present today is part of our induction into the business. Just like Easter break, when I was forced to attend client meetings with my father. Some of them were for the legit aspect of our parent's company, providing private security to government officials, celebrities, and whoever else needs it. Still, for the most part, the meetings involved discussing targets, negotiating prices for hits, and setting realistic time frames—it was absurd. Like something you'd see in a movie.

"Ah, you must be the up-and-coming heirs of Nocturnal Enterprises," a slimy man greets, holding out his hand for each of us to shake. "I'm Major Bowen. Follow me. I'll show you to the hall where we'll be conducting today's demonstration, then I'll get someone to give you a tour of the facilities."

The four of us silently follow him through the bright corridors toward an auditorium.

"What will today's demonstration involve?" Hawk asks, miraculously managing to keep the contempt out of his voice.

"The whole point is to show off to potential clients and future investors why *we* are the best. Our men and women are ruthless because we push them to be. Today, we'll show everyone our best fighters, as well as demonstrate our recruits' abilities to handle various weapons. We'll also have several recruits competing in an obstacle course to show their agility, speed, and flexibility."

Major Bowen leads us into a large hall. An assault course has been set up around the perimeter of the room, with a boxing ring in the middle. Off to the side are various practice targets, along with a variety of guns, knives, and even a crossbow, all of which are being carefully guarded.

The room is nearly full as men in fancy suits consort with one another. There's a thread of excited energy humming in the air, everyone keen to get started with today's show.

"I have ringside seats for you," Major Bowen beams, directing us to four empty seats in the front row right by the fighting ring.

While we take our seats, Bowen disappears off to attend to whatever else he needs to do, and the four of us cast watchful eyes around the room. Everyone here is a criminal in one form or another. Whether they own their own criminal conglomerate, are a dirty politician, or someone from a rival company here to suss out the competition.

Not long later, the last of the audience filters in and Bowen comes to stand in the middle of the ring.

"Ladies and Gentlemen," he begins, his voice booming out through his microphone, ensuring everyone can hear him loud and clear. "We are honored to be able to host you today. We have some excellent talent for you, which we hope you will enjoy. If you have any questions or wish to discuss business further with our esteemed board members, come talk to me after the demonstrations."

With a brisk nod to a guy standing ringside, he makes his exit. Two prominent male fighters, who look to be in their late twenties, enter along with a referee. As the referee starts the fight and the two of them dive in, tearing into one another with their fists, it's clear how much they love the fight, the bloodshed. A gleam enters their eyes every time one of them lands a hit that makes the other bleed. It's the most vicious battle I've ever seen; both opponents are intent on killing the other to claim victory.

Both fighters give it everything they have, spraying the mat, and some of the audience, with blood as they land blow after blow, splitting lips and cutting open eyebrows. Neither of them wears mouthguards, and when the one facing me gives a toothy grin, blood stains his teeth red, only enhancing the maniacal vibe coming off him.

Eventually, the guy facing me manages to get the upper hand, taking his opponent to the ground and beating him repeatedly until I'm sure I hear his jaw snap. Only when the referee blows the whistle, calling the end of the fight, does the guy let up, glancing disinterestedly at his half-dead competitor before looking up at the crowd and grinning madly with his red teeth.

The audience claps and cheers as the guy heads off the mat, his unconscious opponent being dragged behind him.

"What the fuck?" Cam breathes. "That was insane."

A couple more fights take place, and in the last one, I noticed the fighters were more our age, if not younger.

"For this last fight, we have something special," the referee tells the crowd. "Our best fighter fought twenty of our own people and won, so we're going to give you a taste of just how capable she is."

She? I risk a glance at Cam beside me, taking in his tense posture as he leans forward in his seat.

Four people step onto the mat, and as the three large guys move to the edges of the ring, we all get a clear look at our girl. *Hadley.* I'm halfway out of my seat before catching myself and forcing my ass to sit down again. My fists are clenched tightly at my sides as I fight every instinct in me to get to her.

I hear Cam gasp beside me, and there's a small commotion on his other side as Mason most likely stops Hawk from doing something stupid. I can't tear my eyes away from her to look. She looks skinnier than she did before. Her face is sunken, and there's a hardness in her eyes I haven't seen in a long time. She's sporting the same armor she had when she showed up at Pac last September. I hadn't realized until now just how much she had opened up to us, but seeing her all closed off again makes me furious that these fuckers have destroyed all the progress she's made with us.

"What the fuck have they done to her?" Cam growls, likely seeing the same changes I am. She looks nothing like the Hadley we've all come to know and love.

"Are they going to make her fight all three of them at once?" I gasp, watching in horror as the three guys who've spread out around Hadley flex their muscles, stretching before lowering into a crouch.

In the middle of the ring, Hadley does a slow circle, assessing each of her adversaries before settling into her own fighting pose.

My hands firmly grip the sides of my chair as the referee blows his whistle and all three guys move in on her. Blood rushes into my mouth as I bite my tongue, preventing myself from screaming out to her when the guy behind her wraps his thick forearm around her neck.

She's fighting like a madwoman, trying to get out of his grip before he crushes her windpipe. Meanwhile, another asshole is slamming punch after punch into her gut. Somehow, she manages to get her legs up between her and the guy in front of her, kicking him away and using the resistance to push herself backward, knocking the guy choking her off balance.

Once she's free, she delivers several hard kicks to the guy before swiveling back around to deal with the two fuckers approaching her, clearly planning to tag-team her.

It's a tense few minutes that feel like they last a lifetime, all of us sitting on the edges of our seats, watching with a mix of awe and terror as our girl works her way through each of her opponents, systematically taking each of them to the ground and ensuring they won't be getting back up before moving on to tackle the next one.

Finally, she's the only one left standing in the ring, and we all breathe out a sigh of relief. Unlike with the previous matches we've seen today, she doesn't look victorious or satisfied with her win. She seems empty, like the Hadley I love is no longer in there, but she *has* to be. We haven't come this far to lose her now.

As she's swept out of the ring, Major Bowen announces the next demonstration. Still, I barely pay attention to the rest of the events as I stare at the spot Hadley disappeared from, my brain frantically trying to identify a feasible way of getting her out of here.

Time seems to go by in a blur while I'm lost in my thoughts, and it's only when Cam nudges me out of them that I realize everyone is getting to their feet.

"Come on," Cam urges. "We've got that tour now. It's our only shot to get a note to her."

We rise to our feet as a young guard comes over to us. "Hi, I'm Drew. Bowen asked me to take you on a tour of the facilities."

"That would be great," Hawk responds with a tight smile.

"Great. What did you think of today's demonstrations?" he asks as he leads us out the door where Hadley disappeared. This part of the compound is entirely different from where we entered. The halls are narrower and darker, making them appear more ominous, causing a shiver to make its way down my spine as Hawk blathers on with the guard.

"That female fighter was impressive," Hawk tells the guard, inflecting the right amount of interest in his tone.

The guard laughs. "She's something alright. Between you and I, though, she's got a real attitude problem."

"Oh yeah?" Hawk scoffs while I mentally praise Hadley for making these sick fucks' lives as difficult as possible.

"We're quickly bringing her to heel, though."

"How so?" There's a menacing growl in my voice—I'm clearly not as good as Hawk at hiding how disgusting I find this fucker—but the guy doesn't even notice as a dark and twisted grin crosses his face.

He shrugs indifferently, that small act enough to have me fighting back the urge to rip his fucking head off. "The usual methods. It took a few days to get a reaction out of her, but the Major is really good at his job." There's a sick gleam in his eyes. "Sometimes, he lets us watch. There's nothing quite like hearing a girl covered in blood screaming, to get your dick hard, right?" He laughs maliciously. "I just hope the rest of us get a turn soon." *Yup. This fucker's going to die, along with everyone else in this godforsaken hellhole.* I wouldn't consider myself a violent person—I don't relish in it the same way as the others—but right now, for Hadley, I'd happily embrace that darkness.

Glancing at Cam out of the corner of my eye, I can tell I'm not the only one holding myself back from going apeshit on this disgusting cretin. His body is thrumming as he struggles to restrain himself.

"We'd love to meet her," Hawk says casually.

"Ah, sorry, guys. No can do." The guard shakes his head. "She's a bit of a wild one, and we've had to feed her the last few days so she'd have enough energy to fight. She's probably overflowing with adrenaline right now. Wouldn't want her to lash out at any of you."

Fuck. There goes our only idea.

The guard shows us around the compound. With today being open day, most of the recruits are contained within their sleeping quarters. However, a few trustworthy ones are working out, bouting with one another, and generally milling around.

"What's in there?" I ask, pointing to a steel door. Beck was able to give us a brief rundown of the layout and having drawn-up a vague schematic based on what he could recall, I'm pretty sure that's the interrogation rooms.

"Interrogation rooms," the guard confirms. "Nothing exciting. That's where we're keeping D—the fighter from this morning."

"She's not out with the other recruits?" Hawk questions.

"No." The guard looks around before leaning in and whispering, "She actually managed to escape several months ago, and we only just got her back. So she's not allowed to interact with any of the others until we can get her back in line."

Hawk nods his head in understanding while Cam steps up beside the guard, throwing his arm around him. "You mentioned something about a fighting cage, Drew? I'd love to see that."

With a sleight of hand, he slips the guard's pass out of his pocket, holding it out to me behind his back. Quickly taking it, I bend down, pretending to tie my shoe while Mason and Cam distract the guard with various questions as he leads them to the fight cage. Hawk lingers back with me, neither of us daring to move until the three of them disappear out of sight.

When they're gone, I tap the card against the reader and slip into the interrogation block. It's even darker in here, and the stench of piss makes me gag as I look around. Along one wall are steel doors, marking out small cells, with the rest of the room broken up into what looks like several interrogation rooms, with large, darkened windows, showing brief glimpses into each one. In the center of the room is what looks like a small guard station, composed entirely of glass, providing the guards with a three-hundred-and-sixty-degree view of the room. Thankfully, it's empty, with all available guards pulled to accommodate the open day.

"Hadley," Hawk hisses. "Hadley!"

"Hawk?" Her surprised voice carries to us like a soft whisper from several doors down on the left. I'm itching to go to her, but I force myself to stay by the door, keeping an eye out as Hawk scurries toward her.

"Baby Davenport." I can hear the strain in Hawk's voice as he reaches the steel door separating her from us. A broken cry from behind it has my chest cracking open. *Fuck, I never want to hear that sound again.*

Hawk tries the security card on the keypad by the door, despite Beck already informing us only a few guards have access to these rooms, growling in frustration when the light flashes red. Even if we could get into her room, there's no way we'd be able to sneak her out of the compound unnoticed before someone sounded the alarm.

Closing his eyes, Hawk rests his forehead against the door, letting out a long exhale as he attempts to wrangle his emotions.

"Hawk." The relief in her tone crushes me. "What are you doing here?"

I can see Hawk gritting his teeth from here, struggling to contain his anger. "Beck said you were here, but we didn't believe him."

"He told you." I can't tell, through the thick door, how she feels about that.

We don't have time now to get into all that, something Hawk must realize. "We're going to get you out, little sis." His voice is a low growl, filled with dark promises of vengeance. He'll do whatever it takes to get his sister out of here, and we'll be right by his side. "Stay strong, okay? I have to go." His voice breaks and, *fuck*, if the moment doesn't have tears in my eyes. "But we're coming back for you…" He hesitates for a second. "I-I love you. We'll be back. I promise."

Another broken sob, followed by a quiet "I love you too," is the last thing we hear from behind the door as Hawk shoves a folded-up piece of paper through the narrow gap at the bottom of the door. It took a lot of arguing for us to decide who would seek out Hadley and who got to write the note.

Hawk pulled the brother card, and, well, what could we say to that? If it hadn't been for the overwhelming despair of the situation, it would have been a heartfelt moment. I'm so proud of him for opening up and accepting her, and I know this moment will have meant everything to her. As for who wrote the note, Cam won that one, claiming he wanted to be there for her the way she was there to pull him back from the ledge. Regardless of who got to speak to her, or write the letter, Hadley knows we're all with her in spirit and that we're all doing everything we can to free her.

Pausing, Hawk stares at the steel door for another moment, reaching out and pressing his fingers against the cold metal. His shoulders slump on a heavy sigh, and he closes his eyes for a second before standing up.

When he turns to face me, his expression is shuttered, but the fire burning in his eyes is something everyone in this place should be afraid of. He strides toward me, each step filled with purpose and determination. With one final glance at Hadley's door, we step back into the main corridor. It tears me apart to leave her behind, and I can see the same war waging in Hawk as he sears me with a haunted look, his jaw set in steely determination, ready to do anything to get his sister back.

We jog down the corridor in the direction the others disappeared, and thankfully Cam's loud laugh echoes further on up ahead, letting us know where they are. Slipping into a large room with a fighting cage built in the middle of it, I pretend to bend down and pick something up while Hawk strolls to the far side of the room, feigning interest in a collection of knives lining the wall. Actually, he's probably *very* interested in them—in jamming them into the guard's neck.

"Hey man," I call out, gaining the guard's attention. "Is this yours?" I hold up the security pass Cam swiped. "It was on the ground here."

With wide eyes, the guard pats his trousers. "Shit, yeah. Thanks, man."

"Don't sweat it," I assure him, smiling easily, all the while picturing smashing his head into the concrete wall.

We quickly finish up with the tour and get the fuck out of there, and I can feel the impatient atmosphere as the car drives us back toward campus.

I text Beck when we're nearly back at campus, and he steps up to greet us as the car makes its way out the school gates, having dropped us off.

"Well?" Cam snaps irritably when we're alone. "Did you find her?"

"Yeah. She was there."

"She got the note." Hawk looks determinedly at each of us. "Now we just need to come up with a way to get her out of there."

CHAPTER 29

Hadley

I'M ABRUPTLY WOKEN TO YET MORE NUMBINGLY COLD WATER BEING hosed over me. What day is it now? I'm losing count. My head constantly swims from lack of food, making it impossible to grasp onto a single thought long enough to figure anything out.

I've been so close to giving up, so close to losing myself. Every time I feel my will to fight slipping away, I pull out the note Hawk pushed under my door. It's the only reminder that it wasn't all a dream. That my guys were really here. They came to find me.

I'd forgotten it was that time of year—the yearly open day. After the challenge night, they left me alone. My world was nothing but deafening silence. The only noise was the sound of the hatch opening when food was delivered. It might seem better, but all that endless time left alone with my thoughts is just as damaging as what they were doing before.

Things went back to the way they were after the open day. The food stopped coming, my clothes were taken away, and I've spent most of the time living in a quiet corner of my mind where I pretend none of this is real.

THE HOSE PASSES OVER ME AGAIN, THE COLD WATER SEEPING INTO MY already numb bones. I swear, if I survive this, I'm never having a cold shower again, only steaming hot water for me. I want my skin to turn red from scorching hot water.

"Ah, good, you're awake. It's no fun if you're passed out." Bowen's deep, demonic voice pierces through the fog in my brain seconds before a blade digs into my thigh, making me grunt as it tears a path up to my hip. I can feel the blood dripping down my leg, pain flaring when I tense the muscle.

I'm yet again shackled to the fucking wall, wearing nothing and wondering what the fuck he did to me when I was passed out. The only difference this time is that my cheek is pressed against the cold stone, my backside exposed to the elements. Clenching, nothing feels overly painful, but that doesn't necessarily mean anything.

He trails his fingers through the blood dripping down my thigh before pressing down on the wound, the flare of pain making me hiss. I tense when his blood-coated fingers slip between my ass cheeks, the sick fuck chuckling in my ear.

"Not long now, D," he promises. "Lawrence will be back in a few days, and when he sees you're still fighting, he'll more than happily hand you over for me to break." Leaning in, his breath tickles my ear. "And trust me, when I'm done with you, you'll be shattered into so many pieces there won't be a hope of piecing you back together."

All I know for the next however long is the feel of his blade digging into my skin, tearing apart my flesh, and branding it. Although I'm acutely aware of what he's doing, I hardly feel the pain anymore. I don't know if I've just become so desensitized to it all or if it's because I am starting to break apart.

The only thing keeping me going is the note from Hawk and my guys. Every time I'm dumped back in my cell, I dig it out from where I hid it between my mattress and the bedframe. When I read it, that spark of fire I'm so used to holding close for warmth, sparks within me, reminding me I'm not ready to give up the fight.

My body may be weakening, but my mind is still strong. It screams at me to keep fighting, to not let *them* win. Smoothing out the crinkled piece of paper, I read the words scrawled in Cam's messy handwriting. I soak them up like they're a lifeline. They *are* my lifeline. They're the only thing keeping me going.

YOU'RE SO BRAVE, BABY DAVENPORT. WE'RE COMING FOR YOU. WE *love you.*

MY BOYS ARE COMING FOR ME. I HAVE TO MAKE SURE I'M STRONG enough to fight when that day arrives.

EPILOGUE

Hawk

I TORE THE DORM APART WHEN WE GOT HOME, BUT IT STILL WASN'T enough to squelch the insurmountable rage I'm feeling. The things I saw today, what I heard, the way she looked. It took everything in me not to go fucking apeshit right there and then in that vile compound, but that would have been a surefire way to have our parents getting suspicious and watching us more closely —the last thing we need right now.

"What's the game plan?" Cam asks, all business for once. We're all perched on stools around the kitchen island, and there's a fire in his eyes like nothing I've seen before. Cam is one of those people. When he sets his mind to something, he gives it a hundred and ten percent. He doesn't quit until he's the best. That's why he's done so well with swimming, and if he put his mind to it, he'd be challenging West for the top position in the year. Right now, though, all of his energy is focused on getting Hadley back and, looking at the others, they're just as determined.

"I'm just throwing this out there," Beck says, already raising his hands in a placating gesture as he looks at me, "but I take it there's no point in going to your parents?"

I shake my head. "I've thought about it, and I don't think so. I don't trust them to get her back. If they realize how instrumental she is, they may decide to keep her there indefinitely, and if they know that we knew she was there, they will make sure we never saw her again."

Beck grits his teeth, giving a tight nod in agreement, before he reaches out to grab a beer from the table. As his fingers wrap around the bottle, Mason's hand snaps out, holding onto his forearm.

He stares in confusion at one of the tattoos on Beck's forearm. "What's that?" The tattoo he points to is one of his more basic ones. It looks like it was inked on him by a child or a drunk person.

Beck's lips press tightly together as he pulls his arm out of Mason's grip, looking reluctant to share whatever the story is behind the tattoo.

"Seriously?" Cam snaps. "Now hardly seems like the time to reminisce and get to know each other better."

Scowling at Cam, Mason focuses his attention back on Beck. "There's a gang in Black Creek called the Reaper Rejects. Do you know them?"

Beck's brows furrow as he looks at Mason in confusion. "No. This"—he waves his hand at his forearm—"was just some stupid name a bunch of kids with nothing better to do came up with."

"Yeah, a bunch of kids that lived in Black Creek," Mason muses. "What happened to your friends?"

"I have no idea. We lost touch after I moved away."

Mason's fingers tap absently against the counter surface as he thinks. "What if they grew up and started a gang—one that's quickly taking over Feral Beast territory."

Beck's brows climb up his forehead at that revelation.

"So what?" Cam sighs, frustrated.

I see when Beck catches on to whatever Mason is getting at. They better start sharing with the class real fucking soon.

Mason turns his head to look at each of us.

"So, that could mean we might be able to level the playing field."

"I need to go to Black Creek to see for myself," Beck states, his mind running a million miles an hour as he thinks. "There would be no guarantee that they'd help. This isn't their war."

"But it is," Mason argues. "Our parents are lifting kids off *their* streets."

"If you're right, and it's my old friends running this gang, there's no way they'd be okay with that."

"Exactly." Mason nods his head. "What do you think they'd do if your friends got in their way?"

"He's right," I add, throwing in my two cents. "Our parents will soon become their problem. If you can convince them to help, we might actually have a chance of defeating our parents, for good."

We discuss it over some more, and Beck tells us more about the guys he used to run around with back in the day—Cain and Oliver—before he agrees to leave for Black Creek the next day.

That night, as I rest my head against the pillow and stare up at the ceiling, I think about Hadley and what she's had to endure; sick in the stomach at the fact we had to leave her behind today.

We've got a plan, little sis. We're going to get you out of there, and we're going to make every single one of them suffer.

ACKNOWLEDGMENTS

As always, there are so many people I need to thank. The biggest one goes to Nikki for all the hours she dedicates to putting up with my needy ass. She's as deep in these character's journey as I am, always on hand to help me when I'm stuck, suggest improvements and—most importantly—change my UK English to US English. Thank you so much for everything you do, and most importantly, for just being an amazing friend! I love you!

I owe another thanks to Nikki Number 2 AKA UK Nikki, who is always ready to dive into a beta document, even when it's still only half formed. Her keen eye and hilarious comments add the perfect finishing touches to this book, and I'd be lost without her.

A massive thanks to Shawna, Artemis and Jenni for beta reading and helping to make this book the best it can be, and to Angie for sprucing the whole thing up and making it readable.

A huge thanks to my street team and those who signed up with affinity to read and review this book. I appreciate all your hard work promoting every week and I've absolutely loved reading your reviews and seeing your edits.

Lastly, thank you to all of you, the readers, for picking up this book and reading it. Without you none of this would be possible!! If you loved this book, please help me spread the word by leaving a quick review.

ALSO BY R.A. SMYTH

Crescentwood Series

A dark, high school bully reverse harem with a stalker and gang element.

Pacific Prep Series

A dark, academy bully reverse harem with a taboo relationship.

Black Creek Series

A rival gang-mafia reverse harem with a vigilante FMC. Contains MM.

The Ruthless Boys of Ridgeway

A college, friends-enemies-lovers, second chance reverse harem with a stalker and secret society elements.

ABOUT THE AUTHOR

R.A. Smyth is best known for writing contemporary dark romance filled with unexpected twists, mystery, and plenty of steam. Rachel lives in the UK with her husband and two golden retrievers, and when she's not busy thinking up crazy cliffhangers to drive her readers insane, she enjoys inflicting the same torture on herself by reading incomplete series.

She has always been an avid reader, starting from the Harry Potter books as a kid. It's an interest that has grown into an obsession over the years and becoming an author has been a secret lifelong dream of hers.

www.ingramcontent.com/pod-product-compliance
Lightning Source LLC
Chambersburg PA
CBHW031005190726
48285CB00004BB/1476

9781915456106